Legacy of the Tropics

Legacy of the Tropics

Mary Deal

Books by Mary Deal at Amazon

FICTION
The Ka, a paranormal Egyptian suspense
River Bones, the original Sara Mason mystery
The Howling Cliffs, 1st sequel to River Bones
Down to the Needle, a thriller
Legacy of the Tropics, adventure/suspense

COLLECTIONS
Off Center In the Attic – Over the Top Stories

NONFICTION
Write It Right—Tips for Authors—The Big Book
Hypno-Scripts: Life-Changing Techniques
Using Self-Hypnosis and Meditation

CONTRIBUTED TO:
Killer Recipes (Susan Whitfield)
A Book and A Dish (Martha A. Cheves)
25 Years in the Rearview Mirror (Stacy Juba)

Books by Mary Deal at Amazon

Promises

Chapter One

The jagged scar on Pablo's belly protruded above his waistband and wriggled like a snake as he darted out of the yard to join his friends playing on the sidewalk. The mark started above his belly button and ran nearly to his pubic bone. Sweating in the tropical heat made it glisten, but the disfigurement never bothered him. Others were more conscious of it than he was. The erratic scar was the result of a surgeon who had been careless or, perhaps, in a great hurry to enter the child's abdomen. Back in Colorado, where Ciara Malloy was from, a laceration like that would be cause for a thorough malpractice investigation. But things were very different here. Moving to Puerto Rico was a first-hand lesson in culture shock.

San Juan's August humidity hung thick in the air. Even so, it was better to be out on the patio than sweltering indoors in front of the window air conditioner. Jalousies cranked tightly closed were neither capable of keeping out the humidity nor containing the cooled air.

The limp breeze finally picked up and carried with it spicy aromas of neighborhood cooking and the smell of fresh moisture. Moments later, the rain came. Huge drops made the fire in the barbecue spit and hiss.

Ciara ducked under the raised floral umbrella over the table. Rico dragged the hot barbecue across the concrete patio closer to the main house and under shelter of the eaves in order to finish cooking the game hens. His muscles flexed, and his torso glowed from standing too near the fire and from the late afternoon heat. Just like when she had seen him at a construction site. The sight of him reminded her of the first time she saw him at work. He wore only shorts and construction boots and with tousled wavy black hair, looked like a golden god in a hardhat as he tight-roped a two-story block wall supervising the construction crew.

Frequently in the Caribbean, rain showers passed over then ceased within minutes. This time, the rain continued. The air had been sultry and the breeze on the patio tempting. Maybe they would have to eat dinner indoors after all.

"It'll pass," he said, smiling in a way that said he would allow nothing to spoil this day. Being bilingual, his English retained a heavy Cuban Spanish accent. "Better today than tomorrow." They both loved being outdoors.

Rain hitting the large flat leaves of the nearby avocado tree played a constant rhythm in the background. Drops hitting the tin roof next door added accompaniment. Their eyes met.

"Nothing bad will happen today," Ciara said.

"You aren't going to leave me, are you?" he asked. His smile was facetious.

Leave Rico Rey? She loved him with all her heart. She loved Pablo, his little boy, as her own. She could not understand why she and Rico had not set a wedding date. After a freak storm last year that blew down her shack on the edge of the beach, she had moved into the cottage behind his house on Calle Delbrey. Not being married, they lived separately for Pablo's sake. That was the way Rico wanted things. They needed to maintain a level of dignity. Dictates of the Puerto Rican culture forced them to live in separate homes until they married. But to hear him occasionally allude to her leaving, if that's what he feared the most why, then, did he hesitate about finally tying the knot?

"Was this the kind of weather you had when your wife left?" Ciara asked. They had always talked openly about the past. Wounds healed more quickly when feelings were aired. Or was it because when she and Rico met the bonding energy between them had wiped out the pain of old hurts?

"About the same," he said. "Strange how bad things in my life happen on rainy days." He smiled and shook his head. "Like the day your shack went down."

"Sure, but we met the sunny day after," she said. She remembered the day she was picking through the rubble of the shack and looked up to find this gorgeous Latino watching her with a most tender expression. How the sparks shot between them that day. "The weather is only coincidental to events occurring, don't you think?" she asked.

"Wasn't raining when Pablo was born," he said. "But it stormed when his mother ran—"

Pablo came running around the side of the house. Rico looked down and tended the barbecue.

"Is dinner ready, Mama?" Pablo asked. His hazel eyes were large and round from the exertion of play. Then he saw his father at the barbecue near the back wall of the house. He smiled a silly precocious grin that clearly expressed the closeness that this father and son shared. "*Hola*, Papi," he said. "When do we eat?"

"About ten minutes," Rico said.

"I'm going back to the street then." Pablo started to run away. "I'm winning all the races."

"Hey-hey," Rico said. "Be on time for dinner."

"Si, Papi."

Too tall, but mentally advanced for just under eight years old, Pablo never let a little rain slow him down. He and some neighborhood children ran races up and down the block in front of the house. Long-legged Pablo usually won.

Rico watched his son scamper away. He had that deep pensive look that he got in his eyes every time he had a moment to study his son. Ciara thought of her own parenting abilities, something she had yet to fully experience. If she could be as attentive to her children as Rico was to Pablo, or, as her mother was to her, then she would have no worries about the type of mother she might be. Ciara thought of her mom, the only example she had available to emulate. She wished that someday soon she might have a chance to be the type of mother her mom was. In fact, she now longed for children of her own, lots of them. Rico's and hers would be sisters and brothers for Pablo, for whom she felt great adoration.

"You were saying?" Ciara asked.

"You know the details," he said. "Pablo was born on a bright sunny day in a hot spell. The day construction stopped early because of torrential rain was the day I found my wife's goodbye note."

Rico told her everything back when he first disclosed he had a son. While still living in Cuba, having to shut down the construction site due to a storm, he came home from work early and found his wife's hurriedly scribbled note saying that she had run off with their neighbor who had been, unbeknownst to Rico, her long-time lover. She told no one else and left the baby alone in his crib for Rico to find. Pablo was only two months old then. Rico's wife only stayed in the marriage for the duration of the pregnancy. Once the child was born and her body healed, she called it quits. Rico had evidently been too slow at making the decision to leave Cuba in the wake of the upheavals and change of government introduced by Fidel Castro. His wife chose to leave with the man who would take her to safety and a better life in America.

"Nothing's going to spoil our sail tomorrow," Ciara said. "The weather will clear."

"Besides, Pablo's looking forward to this vacation before school begins again."

"I hope you don't let the weather dictate—"

"I know what you're thinking," he said. "It rained a lot last year, too, when your shack on the beach went down." Then he added, "But it hasn't rained that much this year."

"Freak storms happen anytime," she said. "You really don't believe rain is some sort of omen, do you?"

"No...," he said, sounding more like he was trying to convince himself.

But that's all he said. As usual when conversation became too focused, he seemed distressed. Several times recently he had made an attempt at explanatory conversation. Something always got in the way. Some problem was eating at him and he needed to get it off his chest, but did not seem to know how to begin. The longer he waited the more desperation he seemed to harbor. Surely that was the reason he decided they take a week off, sail the ketch all the way to the Virgin Islands if time allowed. Get away from distraction.

Ciara was not too worried about anything. Rico had proposed. They were to be married. But then, that had been nearly nine months back. So, what he needed to say evidently had to be said before they could think about exchanging vows.

Certainly, he was not afraid Pablo would disapprove. His son already called her Mama, almost from the day they met when he was nearly four years old. She had been the only mother he knew. The way Ciara saw it, what woman would leave a devoted man like Rico, who so cherished his family? He had proven his love by refusing to participate in the double standard tolerated among the locals. Rico had no mistresses.

In the nearly four years she had known him, Rico had been every bit the man Ciara dreamed of spending her life with. Raising a son by himself was a monumental task, but an obligation he met head-on and at which he excelled. He was committed to the life he had been dealt, committed to making it all work for him and his boy, and committed to her. Though Ciara liked to go out Friday evenings, he soon taught her about *Viernes Social.*

Mistresses usually accompanied men on what was known in San Juan and all of Puerto Rico as *Social Friday.* To be seen in public with a man on Friday evenings usually got the woman labeled as the man's mistress. Rico would have no part of it. Friday evenings were usually spent barbecuing, sometimes with neighbors, or participating in not-so-quiet evenings at home with energetic Pablo. Once in a while Pablo accompanied them to the movies or when other social activities allowed. That was respectable. Rico had teased saying he loved having a blonde on his arm, but wasn't about to jeopardize her reputation just to show her off.

Rain pelted and poured off the eaves in torrents. Rico looked up from tending the hens. "Your house or mine?" he asked, smiling his silly smile as his eyebrows drew together.

He lived in the main house up front, with Ciara in the larger of the two rear cottages. "We're closer to my doorway," she said. "If you want to make a dash for it, I'll hold the screen open."

Once the hens were covered on a platter and safely indoors, they gathered up the eating utensils and some food out on the patio table and ran again for the doorway.

"You really loved your shack out at the beach," he said as he toweled off then slipped into his shirt again. "You've decorated this cottage in the same island motif."

"Your shack at the beach," she said, bringing glasses of cool tropical punch to the table. "I only rented."

"Even though you were warned it was about to fall down," he said.

"I needed the solitude to write," she said. "It was private. Plus, the rental agency said the owner would remodel." She teased, not having yet met Rico at that time.

"It's taken a lot to get around to doing that," he said. "I'll begin that job once we return from vacation. No freak storm will take the new structure down."

"What about that house you're building in the new Valle Arriba Heights? The one I helped you design." Ciara watched that house go from a spark in her mind to blueprints. The real thrill was watching the actual house being built, one Rico had given her full reign on designing just to show that he appreciated her creativity and input. She felt immense satisfaction seeing that project nearing completion. That must have been why Rico so loved his work.

He only smiled. "Got less than a month before it's finished," he said. Then there was that twinkle in his eyes again, like he relished some sweet harbored secret.

Rico had involved her in all aspects of the floor plan design, elevations and every last detail of that house. Since he loved what she designed and went ahead with the building of it, Ciara guessed he would invite her to be a partner in his business. With that house alone, she had learned what it took to build a house from the ground up. The idea of a partnership enticed her as she daydreamed, but she knew to direct her efforts to writing and publishing her children's books instead. Rico was of Latino origins and needed to feel in command of his life, his family. Ciara was not sure working together would be the best arrangement. But then, Rico did not exude a lot of machismo either. He had matured well beyond ego trips.

Finishing construction of the Valle Arriba Heights house could not be the reason he would delay their marrying. Too, he was remodeling the main house in which he and Pablo lived right there on Calle Delbrey in Santurce, walking distance to Condado Beach. When a freak storm had demolished the beach shack, Rico rushed to remodel the larger of the two cottages in which she lived now. He was just finishing the remodeling of the main house along with the studio cottage on the opposite side of the yard. But neither should those projects keep them from marrying. She had been happy living in the shack on the beach. Certainly, she could live amid remodeling debris, which was only temporary.

"Your construction activities must be the most excitement this old neighborhood's seen in decades," she said. Most of the homes on the block had been standing a while. In Puerto Rico, things moved slowly. No one was in a hurry to remodel if they did at all. Things were fine the way they were. Calle Delbrey was a quiet street with yards dotted with stately old mango, avocado and other fruit trees. With only occasional car traffic, the area was safe for Pablo. People living on the long block knew one another. A woman directly across the street took care of Pablo when she and Rico occasionally attended a social event or enjoyed an evening dinner and show at one of the resort hotels on the Condado Strip.

"I always meant to remodel this property," he said. "I've owned it since right after moving to this island." Then his expression saddened. "This was to be my mother's place."

"You told me," Ciara said sympathetically. "Your family sold everything before you left so you could sneak the money out of Cuba and all of you start over here in Puerto Rico. Your mom got sick before she could get permission to leave."

"Those were the bad years," he said. "Rained a lot." But his expression hinted at more. Time did not necessarily heal the wound of losing parents, but it should at least have helped him accept the tragic turn of events. Something was still fresh in his mind. Something haunted him. He reached over and nudged her by the chin, so he could look into her eyes. "You, Ciara; you gave my life new purpose."

"You're sure about that?" she asked, wanting to make him smile.

"All the work you put into that shack near the tide pool? I used to lie on the beach just to watch you making that place livable."

"You...!" she said with an angry smile. "You watched me and I never knew it."

"That's one thing I'll always remember you for, Ci-Ci," he said as he took her into his arms. "You gave me reason to go on. I lived for the next chance to lie on the beach and watch a very determined woman work on that shack."

"You... you voyeur! You didn't even offer to help." She laughed and playfully doubled up a fist. "I saw you out there two or three afternoons every week. I didn't know you were my landlord back then."

"The industrious little girl in the shack, who painted everything inside and out... including her nose and freckled cheeks."

"All the time you watched me," she said, "you were probably hoping I'd come over and paint your walls." He chuckled. "Go ahead, make fun," she said. "But I did it again decorating this cottage, didn't I?"

Rico raised an eyebrow, glanced around the room. "Quite nice," he said. "You have a way of making the best of everything." He held her at arm's length and looked into her eyes. "You have such determination, such dedication," he said, beginning to smile. "Evidently you didn't need all that seclusion to write your children's books. You've done just fine living in my yard."

"I manage," she said, sticking her nose into the air.

He drew her tighter to him. They did not have to kiss to share feelings. A loving bond was just there between them, like they were each a part of the other. She threw her arms around his neck and nuzzled her face against his cheek.

"You know the most important thing I like about you, Ci-Ci?" he asked softly.

Ciara pulled away to look into his eyes. "*The* most important?" she asked, half teasing. "What's that?"

His expression sobered. He tried to smile and then said, "How easily you're able to love a child who isn't yours." He pulled her close again before she could read his expression. "Nothing can change my love for that boy," he said.

They held together again, connected at the heart. The rain worsened. Droplets echoed through the glass blocks in the flat roof over the dining area. Ciara prayed that the rain would not rule the moment.

Pablo appeared outside the screen door. "Mama, Papi. Can I come in?"

Rico turned to face the doorway. "Go home and wash your hands and face…and change your shirt," he said quickly.

"I already did, Papi. Can I come in?"

"Okay, but remove your sandals."

Rico looked at his son's hands and face then motioned for Pablo to sit at the table. Young Pablo had even combed his hair. He was definitely the product of his father's loving and attentive upbringing. He knew what was expected of him and happily complied and got on with things. His puffy-cheek smile of expectation tugged at Clara's heart.

"I'm afraid if it's storming real hard," Rico said as he served red rice onto their plates, "we'll have to delay leaving till the rain lets up."

Ciara went into the tiny kitchen and returned to the table with a hot pot of *quingombos guisados*, an okra stew, and served it over chickpeas and the rice tinted red from *achiote*, an annatto seed powder.

"Oh, no, Papi," Pablo said. "We haven't taken the boat out since school finished in June."

Foil packages that had been kept warm on the side of the barbecue, contained *pasteles* made of pork and spices mixed with seasoned and grated green plantain bananas and steamed. On the side, she placed a small platter of Pablo's favorite *tostones de platano*, chips made from deep-frying boiled slices of green plantains.

"You know I've been busy with the houses, mi hi'jo," Rico said. "We have an agreement, you and me, you remember?"

9

"But we love to sail. Now Mama does too."

"Si, si," Rico said as he halved the game hens, serving each of them a side.

"Can we say grace?" Pablo asked.

They were both surprised. Pablo always said grace whether or not they did. Why would he make an issue of saying it now?

"Go ahead," Rico said. "You say grace."

Pablo clasped his hands, bowed his head and said the prayer. Just before finishing, he added, "…and protect us on our vacation from the rain because Papi says bad things happen when it storms."

Silence and the sound of rain above them filled the room as Rico glanced at her. A draft slammed the front door shut. Pablo looked up, startled, and then slowly picked up his fork.

"*Y que mas, Pablito?*" his father asked.

"Oh," Pablo said, laying the fork down as he remembered. He bowed his head again. "Amen," he added.

Rico spoke as they began to eat. "You think the rain's going to ruin our vacation, *Mi'jo?*" he asked.

"You don't like the rain so much," Pablo said. "You always tell people that bad things happen when it storms. So, I don't want any rain when we sail."

Chapter Two

"Why don't you sleep in our house, Mama," Pablo asked. "So we can be a family, like my friend Jose next door. His mama and papi live together. A renter lives in their cottage."

Rico smiled, raised his eyebrows to her, evidently pleased his son loved her as much.

"Mama and Papi will be married soon," Ciara said. "Then we'll be together forever."

"When?" Pablo asked, rubbing his sleepy eyes.

This time it was Ciara's turn to smugly glance over at Rico.

"Soon," he said, stroking his son's hair. "Soon now."

"Really?" Pablo asked. "And I'll have a mama for real?"

"Soon," Rico said. But Ciara realized that again he had not mentioned when. He bent over to kiss his son goodnight.

Pablo reached up and wrapped an arm around his father's neck, then raised his other arm to her. Ciara bent down too. "I want my mama to live with us. Promise me she'll be my mama. Promise?"

"Go to sleep, *Mi'jo*," Rico said, momentarily emotional. "Pray the storm goes away so we can sail. We'll talk tomorrow."

When they left the room, just before shutting off the light, Ciara watched Pablo bring up his hands and clasp them below his chin under the covers. He closed his eyes real tight. She smiled, imagining him praying for the storm to end. Or would he pray for a mother… or both?

Strange how Pablo looked nothing like his father. If anything, even with an absence of freckles, he looked more like her with those big hazel eyes and brown hair. His complexion was also fairer than Rico's. Even his bone structure was noticeably different.

Pablo had evidently taken after his mother's side of the family although his father's big green eyes could have influenced his eye color. Ciara had met quite a few Cubans since living in Puerto Rico. She learned just because Cubans were of Spanish descent did not mean they all had black hair and brown eyes.

A lot of lore she had learned in her small hometown in Colorado did not hold true in the world at large. During her late teens, she began to write stories for children because she felt they needed to know how the world really was. Her teachers said she was getting better and better at it. Yet, the expense of college was out of her family's reach and she wanted to work anyway. Earn money. Be independent. Then she found the workaday world boring in that all jobs she found, with her lack of higher education, were clerical. Then finally, she hit upon a part time job that allowed her to pursue classes in writing. Before starting that part-time job, she opted for a vacation in the Caribbean to clear her mind of past disappointments. It was during her visit to Puerto Rico that her mother had a massive heart attack and died. After returning home for the funeral, Ciara learned her mother's life insurance policy left her with enough money to last while she started over. Her father encouraged her to set a new course. She chose to do it in the little beach shack she had seen while on vacation in Puerto Rico.

Ciara wondered if the fact that Pablo looked more like his mother might play on Rico's mind, remind him of the woman who had walked out on him. Still, if Rico was troubled by the resemblance, he never showed it.

Later inside her cottage, Ciara peered out of the louvered bedroom window and through the rain and saw the light flick on in Rico's home office. Pablo's bedroom was in the center of the far side of the house. One rear bedroom across the yard from her own was Rico's office. His bedroom was across the yard from the living room of her cottage.

Inside the half-opened jalousies, Rico's shadowy form moved about. He would probably want to finish some last-minute paperwork before leaving for more than a week. She had seen him in there on many occasions working into the wee hours. Now he would also be listening to the weather reports to learn when the storm might blow over.

The smooth terrazzo floors under her bare feet felt cool. Ciara went to the refrigerator to double check that she had readied all the foodstuffs that would be packed into coolers in the morning. She went into the living room and looked at the opened suitcase on the sofa where all her shorts and tops, swimsuits and other necessities lay neatly in place. How many times would she inventory what she wanted to take on the trip? The rain and Rico's unfounded fear of something bad happening every time it stormed must have brought on the anxiety.

She would have to help him get over that one-and-only fear he seemed to harbor before it had an adverse affect on her too. Or was her apprehension due to the fact that they were secreted lovers? That had always weighed upon her conscience.

She walked to the TV and turned it on, checked the time and switched channels until she found the news. The hippies who had settled in California and all along the West Coast continued to be a problem. Scenes flashed showing longhaired young people glutting the streets of the Haight-Ashbury District of San Francisco, bedecked with flowers and carrying signs touting, "Make love, not war." The commentator said that more and more people were migrating west. Except for those who fled to Canada to protest or escape the draft. Those young people were from all walks of life, forsaking the lives well-intentioned parents had lovingly provided them, opting for drugs, free sex and acid rock.

Most likely, with the hippie movement happening at the end of the decade, that is what the sixties would be remembered for. Hippies and the Viet Nam war would overshadow memory of the President's assassination till some new horror claimed the limelight.

The storm would be lifting, winds dying, the weatherman was saying. Still, he warned, hurricane season was only half over. Boaters were cautioned to watch for squalls and put in at the nearest harbor should the weather become too disturbed.

The weather report predicted that after the storm passed, calm weather could be expected. That meant they would sail. Maybe she could get Rico to talk about wedding plans once they were on the boat and away from work.

She looked at the engagement ring on her finger, a huge round four carat diamond in a Tiffany setting on which he had been able to cut a deal. He knew everyone in the Cuban community on the island and knew where the deals were to be had. Not to mention everyone liked him for choosing to be the father he was and always tried to give him the best deals possible. Yet, Rico made lots of money in construction and always paid his own way. But she could not fault him for dickering for a discount on the expensive ring. She had not seen a diamond like that on anyone she knew on the island. Maybe only on the hands of snowbirds, wealthy winter visitors, who could afford to relocate to the warmer tropics for months at a time when home snow became too deep in which to live.

The incessant rain pelting the roof droned on. Ciara always thought of rain as being cleansing, restorative. She could not remember anything bad having happened to her during rainy weather. Rico's upbringing and hers were worlds apart. Maybe omens were something that had been ingrained in him from childhood. She would have to help him understand that his fears were unfounded. Even now, in whatever way she could, she would assure him that something as simple as sailing was joyful and fun, in spite of the unpredictable tropical climate.

Ciara turned off the TV and lights in her small living room and walked down the hallway past the tiny kitchen and bathroom. At the bedroom doorway, she looked at her empty bed and sighed heavily. The most disturbing aspect she learned to face when first moving to Puerto Rico was culture shock. In the local culture women remained subservient to their men. Ciara could allow only so much of that and Rico knew and accepted her American way. He teased saying she was a woman liberated and blossoming. Together they created their own culture, one in which they could lovingly express the individual people they were. That included Pablo. Or, perhaps Pablo's innocent precociousness is what promoted such liberal thinking.

Ciara was every bit a modern-day American woman. However did she learn to wait for a man to make all the moves? She wanted to see Rico in her bed when she looked at it, or wanted to share a bed they both called theirs. Why did they have to wait to be married? Certainly the living arrangement was for the sake of respectability in a Spanish culture, worlds apart from her own in Colorado and from the free sex of the hippie movement that swept the nation. Casual sex did not appeal to her anyway. But if she expected marriage any time soon, she was going to have to be the not-so-subtle American woman she could be and push for it. She did not like being kept dangling.

She loved Pablo as much as she loved Rico. For the time being, Pablo filled the empty spot in her life a child of her own would have occupied. Pablo was a bright and innocent boy. How could she not always love him? He would be a great role model for her children, hers and Rico's. She would be a real mother to Pablo and he would be a great older brother to his siblings.

Ciara hugged herself and remembered the feelings she and Rico shared as they held one another before dinner. She wanted him then and they would have made love on the spot had the opportunity presented itself. But there he was now, working in his office into the night as the *Coqui*, those itty-bitty island frogs, echoed their name in the dark.

She turned off the lamp and climbed into bed only to toss and turn, sleepless as the rain pelted harder than ever.

Sometime later a noise woke her. Everything was dark, except for the small night-light kept burning in the hallway socket. She rose up on an elbow and peeped through the jalousies again. No light shone from Rico's office or bedroom. The entire house was darkened. Then her front door closed. Rico had come in. Her heart quickened. She settled back against the pillows and suddenly he stood over her, unfastening his clothing. By the time he stripped, he was already excited. He slipped into bed and came to her with the same hunger she had stored up.

The storm raged into the night. Neither could sleep. Then, hours later, they noticed the wind had died down. Peeping through the jalousies, rain no longer pelted but came down in fine drizzle illuminated by the distant streetlight. Moonlight leaked through the slats and laid down stripes across the bed.

"Look," Rico said. "Pablo's prayers are being answered."

"So are mine," Ciara said as she pulled Rico to her again. The thought of Rico planting his seed and that they would eventually have children together, sent her passions soaring.

"Woman, you're gonna kill me," he said, nibbling her lips.

"We won't have a chance to do this on the boat."

"Yeah," Rico said, laughing easily. In the dim light, he lifted up to an elbow. "No spare room to hide away from Pablo."

Ciara's mood shifted. She felt guilty again. "Rico," she said softly. "I'm tired of hiding. I'm beginning to feel like a *Viernes Social mujer*."

"Sh-h!" he said. "You're not that kind of woman."

"I don't want to hide our love anymore. Pablo's suffering too."

"Yes, I know," he said with a sigh. "I see it every day." Then he smiled quickly. "I guess I can tell you now," he said.

"Tell me what?"

He traced the outline of her lips, and then kissed her gently. "While we're away on this trip, away from work and distractions, we should make our plans for marriage."

Ciara gasped. That was what she wanted to hear more than anything. She wrapped her arms around his neck and felt her body respond to the moment. He squeezed her to him as hard as he dared and she was again reminded of the desperation he, too, felt. "I want you, Rico...forever," she said, whispering.

"*Tu eres mi vida*, Ci-Ci," he said softly.

"Rico, I don't want to be your life. I want to share your life. There's a difference." She said it tenderly and finished with a kiss that turned fiery.

He pulled away, but not far. "If I last long enough," he said, because the comic in him could not resist. Even his Spanish accent enticed. His expression showed he was determined to respond to the suggestions her body offered. "Tonight is going to have to last us a long time," he said.

"A whole week," she said. She could barely speak as Rico worshipped her body.

His heavy warm breath was all over her. "I want to give you my child," he said in a desperate whisper.

She could no longer respond with words.

Chapter Three

Singers, Rafael from Spain, and Puerto Rican born Marisol, dominated the air-waves. Wearing only his bathing suit and a thick slathering of Sea & Ski suntan lotion, Pablo played his little transistor radio constantly. Each time Rafael aired, Pablo sang along pretending to be Rafael delighting an ocean of fans. When Marisol or any other female voice aired, Pablo would harmonize with them, sometimes sounding just like them with his pre-pubescent boy's voice. Rico's smug expression said he was pleased his son was growing up so self-assured. To think his son could sing too!

The next time Ciara noticed Pablo, she found him gleefully swinging upside-down from the bowsprit. Below him, dolphins effortlessly surfed in the pressure wave in front of the boat. Timbers of the old vessel creaked and groaned in compliance with demands of the sea and wind.

She joined Rico at the wheel. "You'd better get your son back on deck," she said, directing Rico's attention forward to the bow.

"Here, take over a moment," Rico said as he stood on the stern shelf and peered forward over the roof of the cabin. "Luckily, there's a net hanging under him." He smiled mischievously. "I'll snap a couple of pictures of my little monkey first."

Ciara took the wheel located in front of the shelf astern and ahead of the rudder post. The floral print cotton shirt she wore over her shiny green bathing suit trailed in the breeze behind her. The wind roamed freely through her curly hair. She had never been on a ketch until meeting Rico and had never sailed before for that matter. Now she loved it.

Just after leaving Cuba, Rico located a boat sunk off Key West. During a leisurely dive, he found a sixty-four foot gem of the sea. Once an owner abandoned a sunken vessel, anyone wishing to bring the boat to the surface to re-furbish had the right to claim ownership.

Refurbishing included downsizing both the mainsail and mizzen from more than five hundred to four hundred square feet. Smaller sail sizes provided greater manageability for one person at the helm of the gaff-rigged ketch. The engine was replaced with a newer one, as was anything else that could not be salvaged. Surprisingly, the older ketch remained in remarkably good shape in spite of having been submerged.

Once completed, Rico christened her Mercy after his mother, Mercedes. Then he single-handedly sailed the ketch from dry dock in Miami to Puerto Rico without the aid of a compass, which the boat never had. More recently, he toyed with the idea of installing a compass and trading the ketch for a newer model. He did not know too many people who could sail as he did by following the sun or stars. A compass would be necessary to clinch a deal.

Mindful to always keep one hand on the wheel, Ciara stretched and filled her lungs with salty sea air and unhurriedly yawned. She learned a lot from Rico, and about him and what made him tick and was awed by it all. She breathed deeply again. Today the sea was friendly, the trade winds refreshing. Under motor power half a sunny morning out of Fajardo on the northeast corner of Puerto Rico, they had already passed Vieques less than twenty nautical miles south on the horizon. To the north loomed Cabo Icacos. Cabo Lobos was farther northeast. A string of tiny islands and the larger island of Culebra began to appear on the eastern horizon. Wispy clouds drifted far off to the southeast.

Another song played on the transistor radio, a song about Cuba that Rico had not yet translated for her. Rico took a turn dancing a Latin beat as he sung, "Coo-ba, Coo-ba, Coo-ba, Co-o-o-BA!" She even liked the way he prop-erly pronounced Cuba. "Coo-ba, Coo-ba, Coo-ba, Co-o-o-BA!" he sang again. He always went barefoot on board. Though most of his body was tanned and bronze, his feet and ankles were white from wearing boots and socks at the construction sites. She had to smile as his pale feet nimbly paced the Latin rhythm over the wooden planking of the deck. Then he playfully threw a hip in her direction and asked, "What do you say we drop anchor and take a dip? The sun is good and strong today."

"And have some lunch too, Papi?" Pablo asked quickly.

Rico smiled at his growing son's insistent appetite. Nearing the shallows off Culebra, Rico sensed the air by standing in the open and feeling it with his body.

Ciara saw him do that many times. When he found a pocket where the trades were milder, they dropped anchor in the sparkling clear sea. Without the strong trades, the sun felt hotter. Ciara breathed in the dry hot smell of salty sunshine.

Today was not a bombing practice day on Vieques for the Marines and no bombing was known to have ever taken place on Culebra. Though Culebra's residents were quite incited about occupation by the Marines, so far uprisings remained small. With no bombings being carried out, all the waters of the twenty nautical miles between Vieques and Culebra were presently safe.

Pablo leaned over the side. "Papi," he said. "The water's so clear. I can see shells on the bottom. Can I go down, Papi, huh? Can I, please?"

Evidently, Pablo had forgotten that the crystal clear water distorted perception and made the sea floor seem within reach. It was not. Not even with a long practiced breath.

Pablo hurriedly pulled on his swim fins and adjusted his facemask and snorkel. A couple of quick inhalations through his nose to draw the mask tight to his face and he would have sprung over the side had Rico not grabbed his arm.

"What's the hurry?" Rico asked as he dragged Pablo away from the edge to calm him down. A child with too much eagerness was an accident waiting to happen.

"Papi, I'll bet I can name any shell I bring up," Pablo said. His eyes were large with excitement inside the mask. "I learned it in Senorita Avery's class." He pulled at his father's grip. Pablo had been hyperactive all morning; overjoyed that his prayers for fair weather had been answered. Being able to sail and swim one more time before school began had the same effect.

"At school?" Ciara asked.

"Not school. You know the tenant who moved out of the cottage next door? The cottage where Hurricane Ana took the roof off last year?" he asked. He pulled the mask loose and propped it on his forehead. "Senorita Avery took pictures and taught kids about the ocean."

"Ah, si," Rico said, easing his grip on Pablo's arm. "The lady who rented the neighbor's cottage. The lady who moved back to California."

"I remember," Ciara said. "I wish there had been time to know her better before she left. We might have collaborated. Her sea photography and my children's books." She shook her head about the missed opportunity.

"Papi-i!" Pablo said, his voice whining. "Put on your flippers."

"Pablito!" Rico said, capturing his son's undivided attention. "Even if you get down that far, you don't touch the shells. You hear? Those are live creatures down there. Many are poisonous. You hear me?"

"Si, Papi," Pablo said. "I know. Senorita Avery said it's okay to look but we have to let them live their lives too. But can we swim now?"

"Si, Chico!" Rico said, giving in with a wave of a hand.

Pablo eased himself over the lifeline about midship, adjusted the mask to his face once again, then jumped in flippers first. Rico lowered the rope ladder over the side and then stood at the lifeline with an *I told you so* smirk ready when Pablo would surface again.

Pablo came up, yanked the snorkel from his mouth and sucked in another breath. He grinned knowingly up to his father. "I'll bet you can't get down there either," he said. Before his father could call to him, he dived again.

"How deep is it exactly?" Ciara asked.

"This close to Culebra," Rico said as he looked around, "not deep at all...a hundred feet or so. We're on a shelf. But just a few miles northwest—"

"Oh, that's right," Ciara said. "The Puerto Rico Trench." She flinched.

"The Atlantic Ocean's deepest point," he said. "At minus twenty-seven thousand five hundred feet."

She shuddered again. "I'm glad you have a keen sense of direction," she said. "Even being safe on a boat, I don't think I'd like to sail over that and look down."

"You wouldn't see anything," he said, keeping sight of Pablo. "That deep, the water darkens." Then he wrapped his arms around her shoulders and smiled mischievously. "I could take you there," he said. "If you want to see firsthand."

"Thanks, but no thanks," she said, playfully waving him off. "I feel perfectly safe among these islands on the shelf." Not that the sea floor between the immediate islands was always shallow and, of course, they had sailed over deep water in the past. But with the unpredictable way the weather had been lately, the idea of being caught in a storm over water that deep made the thought of it much more sinister.

"C'mon," Rico said. "Let's get wet."

The sea was calm and currents gentle. After a good long swim, they rested and sunned on deck. They ate lunch under an awning that billowed with the continuing trades.

Pablo had worn himself out. He went below to take a nap. Ciara took over the wheel again. Rico gave her a lesson in how to manage the craft; how to read the wind, the skies, even feel the vessel's interaction with the elements through their bare feet resting on the deck and through their buttocks on the seat. "When you're really in touch with your body and the elements, you can feel the fetch," he said. "The direction of the clouds and wind pushing the ocean."

Within the hour, Pablo emerged from the cabin. "The fumes are making me sick," he said.

"Then stay topside," Rico said as he took over the wheel.

"Three's a crowd," he said, teasing.

"Come sit with me," Ciara said. She offered him a deck chair and pulled it close to hers. "Three isn't a crowd," she said, tousling his hair. "Three's a family." She turned to Rico. "Fumes from what?"

"From the motor," Rico said. "It's an old boat. Motor fumes build up in the cabin. I should improve the ventilation."

"If you're going to keep her," she said, gently reminding.

The wind came up. Rico trimmed the sails. Trade winds filled the canvasses. Ciara watched the hard muscles of a polished sailor flex and bulge as he worked the rigging.

Pablo had always been awed by the hoisting of those gigantic sheets of white, too captivated to be of much help. He was too young, with arms not quite strong enough. Still, he scrambled to grab hold of the rigging and emulate his father's movements.

They had traveled by motor power till that time but Rico wanted to practice catching the wind. The large old ketch was not the best vessel for leisure sailing. The Mercy had an aft mizzen mast and sail, which negated the power of the mainsail. Yet, Rico would see any difficulties as a lesson well learned toward sailing a newer more manageable craft with compliant rigging. He had talked about buying a sloop after the houses presently under construction were completed.

Rico spent a lot of time maneuvering the vessel under sail. According to the position of the sun, they went farther east. Then they headed west again, then south, finally turning north again. The grand old lady of the Caribbean Sea scudded across the waves as Rico gave himself a lesson in managing the craft. In complete rapport with the movement and following the direction of the sun, Rico enjoyed himself. She and Pablo enjoyed themselves, too, because sailing was what they liked to do the best.

Just as Ciara removed her sunglasses and lay back to sunbathe, a cold breeze raked across her body. She opened her eyes quickly to find the sky had darkened in only an instant. The wind increased with threatening velocity. Rico kept glancing toward the sky and horizon in all directions. Then she heard it, the rapidly approaching sizzle of rain pelting the ocean surface in the distance. Quickly, the sound became a deafening roar as opaque streaks of dark gray rain raced toward them. In the blink of an eye, the downpour drenched them. Wind yanked at her hair and snapped the beach towel from her hands and carried it away.

"Papi!" Pablo shrieked over the sound of the wind. "A freak storm!" That wise child had already scooped up the life vests and bravely groped his way toward them.

"Sea storm!" Rico called out as they struggled into the preservers. Rico secured the straps of his son's vest then yelled, "Get below, Pablo!"

The wind became frighteningly furious. Deck chairs, Pablo's radio and a few loose items flew overboard as if pushed by an invisible hand. The vessel lurched port to starboard again and again like a toy boat in a bathtub. Ciara clung to the wheel to hold the vessel steady so Rico could strike the sails. Just as he made his way forward, a fine bolt of lightning slithered and seared the entire length of the main mast. The excruciating sound of timber splitting filled the air. The mast held but the sails caught fire.

"Papi!" Pablo called out, looking for his father, as he crept up the ladder inside the cabin.

"Stay below, Pablo!" Rico yelled as he ducked a piece of burning canvas falling. He flung pieces of charred sail from the deck while grasping onto whatever might keep him steady. The wicked velocity of the wind intensified. Ciara felt her entire body lifted and dropped again and again on her perch behind the wheel. The rain pelted and stung her face and skin. She pushed matted hair off her forehead and sheltered her eyes with a hand. Her arms ached from trying to steer, which was mostly now out of her control. Through the churning wet air, she could barely make out Rico fighting the rigging. They were caught completely off guard, no time for them to steal safely around the storm as it approached.

The vessel pitched again and the mizzen boom broke loose. Seeing the mizzen sail and the boom caught by the wind, Ciara ducked barely in time and shrieked to warn Rico. The boom swung loose and in an effort to avoid being hit, Rico lost his balance. He must have hit his head somehow. He lay on the deck for what seemed an eternity. "Rico!" she screamed. "Rico!" She grabbed the boom as it listed toward her again. Now she had to hold the mizzen boom securely to keep it from striking her, all the while trying to steer. Each time the vessel pitched this way or that, it threatened to dump Rico's limp body into the ocean with the rest of their belongings. Ciara looked about hoping to spot a length of rope with which she might secure the mizzen and wheel so she could make her way to Rico to help him. Then, more splitting noises said the masts were breaking. "God, help us!" she said, crying out to the sky.

"Papi!" Pablo cried out. Just the top of his head stuck up out of the cabin. His eyes were wide with fright. "Papi," he cried when he could not see his father. He disappeared inside the cabin momentarily, the next moment creeping out on deck on hands and knees toward his father. Pablo had secured himself around the waist with a length of rope attached somewhere inside the cabin. Crawling on all fours, he struggled to drag his father away from where he lay precariously close to the edge of the deck.

Finally Rico struggled to right himself. He clutched the top of his head. Ciara strained to see through the dim light. Sheets of rain diluted what looked like blood pouring down Rico's forehead. Ciara felt helpless and near panic, but she was not about to give up now. To abandon control of the wheel at this most crucial time would be to subject them all to the ultimate disaster. She braced herself as the Mercy began to list again. Everything seemed to shift into slow motion. "You can do this!" Ciara said to herself. "Hold fast… hold fast!"

The heavy ice chest that held much of their food supplies glided across the deck like it had wings. When the vessel righted, the ice chest had disappeared into the sea.

Rico held to Pablo's rope and made his way like a drunken sailor toward a storage box. With one hand pressuring his wound, he struggled to bring out the ring of lifebelts he had fashioned for emergencies. He stuck flares under his vest and into the waistband of his swimming trunks and paused long enough to send one soaring. It raised high into the darkness and that's the last they saw of it.

In addition to the life-preserving vests they wore, Rico always kept three lifebelts securely strung on a yellow nylon rope about twelve feet long and tied end to end. Each standard lifebelt, made of circular rings of cork covered with canvas, was capable of supporting the weight of two people in water. In case they had to get into the water, they would not drift apart while strung on a rope.

The sky and atmosphere remained darkened. The wind continued its ominous howl. It may as well have been night. Rico's figure looked no more than a willowy shadow in the fading light. She barely made out Pablo huddled on his knees clinging to the storage box.

A rumbling and a vibration began. She felt it through her legs and buttocks as the hull scraped hard. The vessel lurched and dragged.

"Ay, coral!" Rico said, yelling over the fury of nature gone awry. "Coral!"

The rumbling and scraping came again, only this time accompanied by a wretched rending sound. The boat lurched then was suddenly still enough for them to feel the hull caught below the surface. Ciara strained to see in all directions. They had not been close enough to any landforms to come to grief on coral or rocks.

"Pablo!" Rico called as he reached for Pablo's hand. "*Ven aca!*" Rico clung to the roof of the cabin with one arm around Pablo's neck as lightning flashed perilously close again.

Ciara did not know what to do or how to help. She was unable to clearly hear instructions Rico barked as he untied the rope that tethered Pablo's to the inside of the cabin. She watched Pablo cling to one of the lifebelts and together he and his father crawled dragging the life ring. They reached her and clung to the wheel just as the ketch listed and a monstrous wave washed over the deck. The pull of the water stretched out their bodies. Pablo had twined both arms in one of the lifebelts dangling from Rico's bent elbow. Rico's grip on the wheel was their only hope. She, too, was being pulled by the flow of water and would have washed away had she not also held to the wheel. As the wave subsided and the Mercy righted, they choked and gasped for air. Pablo kept both arms wrapped around a lifebelt prepared for the next onslaught. A glimmer of fear flickered across Rico's face.

Then the Mercy began to list to port. Water again ran across the deck. Quickly, Rico put up another flare. Then rending sounds came again as the Mercy was slowly being ripped to shreds on the coral below.

Rico signaled to wait. Then he crept along the deck reaching and trying to free the dinghy. Something would not come loose. He yanked again. Then another rending sound vibrated from under the deck and made the whole vessel shimmy in the water. Rico abandoned his attempt to free the dinghy and returned as fast as he could. "We're sinking!" he yelled above the storm. "Hold tight to a lifebelt. Come!"

Even as Rico barked quick instructions, water filled the cabin where Pablo had clung to the ladder, then it backwashed out through the doorway in a furious rush. Another wave hit starboard and this time the sinking ketch tipped completely on her side. Rico kept an arm around Pablo's waist. As the wave rushed upon them and pushed them overboard, Ciara landed on top of Rico and Pablo. Their only recourse was to swim fiercely to get clear of the vessel. The sound of timber cracking made them look back. The main mast and what was left of the mainsail had dipped into the water. Then the mast snapped in two as it pulled up out of the waves when the Mercy tried to right herself.

They swam furiously until they finally had to rest. But even so, they kept kicking and pulling away, not knowing if the tide might push them again toward the Mercy if they stopped all together. As planned, they were able to stay together on the life ring. How insufferable it would have been had they not been attached somehow and each had swum in different directions. When they seemed clear of any possibility of being pulled down as the Mercy sank, they paused for one long last look. Strangely, the sun shone through a small break in the squall just as the Mercy began to submerge. Another smashing wave assaulted the vessel. The horrific sound of boards splitting said the sea was shredding the Mercy. She listed slowly then righted, then listed again as if waving one last farewell as the sea claimed her and she sunk midst a rush of white water.

Chapter Four

Ciara felt numb and could only stare through vague sunlight filtering through breaks in the storm clouds toward the area where the Mercy went down. Except for some floating debris, the sea quickly erased any trace of the sixty-four foot ketch among the churning swells. Yet, the sea could not be that deep. They had still been over the shelf that ringed the string of tiny islands. When the water calmed, they would be able to clearly see the Mercy lying on the bottom. Or what was left of her.

"Papi!" Pablo said, shrieking.

As Ciara turned to see what might be wrong, her shin jammed against something underwater. Her nerves electrified. She yelped then panted to quell the shock and pain.

Pablo had already made it to his father's side where Rico bobbed in the water. Rico's arm dangled tenuously over the lifebelt. When waves washed over his head, he made no effort to turn from the onslaught or protect his face. Pablo grabbed a handful of hair and held up his father's head. "Papi-i...!" he said, screaming.

Ciara worked her way along the life ring to Rico's side and she and Pablo managed to maneuver a float over Rico's head and bring his arms up through. Cradled by both the life preserving vest and the cork ring float seemed cumbersome but together they kept Rico's head well above water. He dangled lifeless as angry waves jostled his head back and forth and rain continued to pelt. Blood trickled down his forehead.

"Rico!" Ciara said as she firmly patted his cheek. "Rico, wake up!"

"Mama," Pablo cried. "What happened to Papi?"

Something had to be done to revive Rico immediately. Ciara could not evaluate the extent of Rico's injuries but suspected it had something to do with his earlier head injury. Maybe he had a concussion. Or, like her, maybe he had bumped something underwater that further weakened him. How long had he had his face in the water before they saw him in that position? "Help me, Pablo!" she screamed above the storm. "Hold him!" She managed to pinch Rico's nose and blow a breath into his mouth.

"Mama, did he drown?" Pablo asked, shrieking in fright. "Did my papi drown?"

"Not now, Pablo! Don't cry. Help me!"

Ciara forced another breath through Rico's mouth. Rico still hung limp. "Pablo!" she said, still screaming above the howling of the wind. Pablo hovered close, attentive and ready to try anything to revive his father. "When I tell you…." Pablo nodded eagerly. "Take a big breath…pinch his nose…put your mouth on his and blow hard as you can…okay?"

"Okay," Pablo said. He swallowed hard to make himself stop crying. His big dark eyes, full of readiness, stared into hers.

Ciara moved behind Rico and reached underneath his life vest and squeezed his stomach as sharply as she could in an attempt to remove any water he may have swallowed. "Now!" she said.

In one fluid movement, Pablo sucked air, pinched his father's nose, covered his mouth with his and blew all the air his little lungs held. Rico gave no response.

Then Ciara moved her clenched hands up under Rico's vest to put pressure on his lungs through his chest area. A fleeting memory came to her that she should not press on the end of the sternum because she could break off the *Xiphoid Process* bone at the lower end. Any pressure breaking it off could send the fragment into his heart. His hard body and the thickness of his and her life vests between them made getting a grip impossible. Her arms just were not long enough. "Again, Pablo!" she said. She could only pull against Rico's stomach area hoping the pressure would create an upward push on his lungs. "Again," she said.

Pablo blew hard again and again each time she called to him. Then finally he cried, "I'm dizzy, Mama."

Ciara moved in front of Rico and all she could do was breathe into his mouth at intervals and once or twice, pat his face firmly.

The wind began to die down. The rain hit without stinging. Ciara instructed Pablo to remain behind his father and to shelter his face with his hands as best he could. A swim fin sloshed nearby. Pablo reached to retrieve it. "Hey, it's mine," he said thankfully. Instead of putting it onto his foot, he used it to shelter his father's face from the rain.

After Ciara blew another forceful breath, Rico moaned and retched. They watched in the dim light as his eyes opened. He clutched his head. "*Ay, Dios mio!*" he said, moaning. He fought to swipe a wave that sloshed against him. He did not seem to know where he was.

"Rico?" Ciara said, nearly crying with relief. "Can you hear me? Rico?" Rico only rolled his eyes.

Though the sea was still angry, the wind and rain had lessened. Disappointingly, evening was upon them. Dusk in the western sky presented a blended palette of pinks, corals and salmon that would normally have been immensely joyful from a vantage point of safety. But safe they were not. The storm's expansive gray wall of rain obscured the horizon. Ciara had no idea where they were and Rico, who would know exactly, was totally incoherent.

A splintered board bobbed in the water nearby, then another and other bits and pieces of debris that once comprised the proud Mercy. Pablo quickly slipped the swim fin onto a foot and retrieved a splintered board, then reached for the other.

Pablo's actions made it seem like this was just another day of playful swimming. Saving the boards would not bring back the Mercy. "Let them go, Pablo," Ciara said, calling out sympathetically.

Pablo clung to them. "They'll keep us afloat when our vests get waterlogged," he said, yelling back. Again at her side, he said, "Senorita Avery taught us that. She said if you need help in the water, grab hold of anything that will help you float."

Truly Pablo was intelligent beyond his years. He could hold onto the boards. They would keep him occupied.

Rico sneezed, and then retched. Ciara fanned in the water to push the vomit away. He sneezed again and again, and then quieted. Finally, Rico mumbled again and this time sounded more like himself. Ciara tried to see the wound on his head but found no blood that would help locate the gash. The sloshing waves kept washing the blood away. How much blood had he lost? Was that why he was unconscious? Or had he also nearly drowned? He kept trying to clear his lungs. He turned his head away, made a sound from deep down inside his chest and spat again. Then he alternately pressed a finger against each nostril and blew his nose. He tried to clear his throat again. When he settled down, Ciara lovingly cupped her hand in the water and rinsed Rico's nose and mouth. "We're safe, Rico," she said. "Pablo's here. We're okay!"

Pablo came to his father's side. Rico reached up and weakly wrapped his hand around Pablo's neck. "Papi…you're okay!" Pablo said. "You're okay!"

"Ci-Ci?" Rico said, though it sounded more like a moan. He did not seem to understand why he was being jostled.

"I'm here, Rico," she said. "We're in the water. You remember? We abandoned the Mercy."

"The Mercy…."

"Rico, we're floating in the ocean."

It took another long while for Rico to regain some semblance of orientation. Finally, he was able to maneuver himself in the water and get a grip on what had happened. "Pablo…Ci-Ci…are you hurt?" he asked, gasping for air and coughing.

"I'm okay, Papi," Pablo said. "What about you?"

Ciara's attention was called to her shin that stung from the time she bumped something underwater. While the Caribbean Sea was usually comfortably warm, darkness and the storm had cooled the water temperature. She shivered. Unless warmer waters rolled in behind the exiting storm, they would find themselves wrestling with hypothermia.

"Ci-Ci?"

"Rico?" she asked. "What about you? Where do you hurt?"

He remembered his head wound and tried to find it but his arm dropped heavily back into the water. He seemed very weak. "My head," he said, "…will be okay."

"Your legs, Rico. What about your legs?"

"I-I can't feel them," he said. "I'm cold."

"Look!" Pablo said, pointing and shrieking.

As the storm pushed away, a large dark image broke through the sheets of rain. Like an artist's rendering of a muted landscape at dusk, fading sunlight minimally highlighted the white sand beach and barely perceptible lights and darks of the trees and rocks along the shore. "An island!" Ciara said. The long low mass jutted out of the sea a few hundred yards away and the diminishing outbound current would not be enough to keep them from reaching it. The tide would soon be fully in their favor.

Rico tried to reach over the lifebelt to his waistband but his arm was not long enough and he still had no energy "Ci-Ci," he said, then coughed hard. "The flares."

She felt under his life vest and around his waistband but found none. Then she remembered they had not been there when she tried to resuscitate him. "They're gone," she said.

No one had to verbalize the next thing to do. When a wave washed inward, she and Pablo, on opposite sides of the life ring, dragged Rico and swam fiercely with the current to close the distance between them and the island. At no other time had the value of swim fins been more evident. Ciara's bare feet felt useless but still she kicked and concentrated upon propelling herself with her legs. When the current washed out, they could only hope they were not dragged back as far as where they began. Rico kicked as best he could. He continued to cough and gag. Ciara kept an eye on him. He seemed much weaker than he let on.

After a long while the shoreline did not seem closer. Distance was difficult to gauge from water level. Still, they swam, resting only when it was evident they might waste energy fighting the outbound pull; pouring it on with each inbound surge that might grant them a few feet gained. Pablo never complained and occasionally drifted back to check on his father. They persisted, checking with each other occasionally by calling out and asking how the other was doing.

Ciara yelped as her knee again hit something hard and jagged underwater. Stunned, she drew her legs up and ceased all movement. "Coral!" she managed to call out. But Rico, weak and unable to stop himself from being dragged on the inbound surge, floated past her. He grunted painfully when he bumped something. It was nearly too dark to see below the surface.

Ciara could only guess it was coral below the surface as she gingerly extended a foot and rubbed her toe against something sharp. "Ay!" she yelled again, now afraid to move about. Rico made no other sound. He simply bobbed in the water and struggled pathetically to breathe.

Pablo had been swimming with the two splintered boards stacked and serving as water wings. Now he slipped off the boards. "I can feel it!" he said. "My flipper's rubbing something down there."

Ciara was not sure what to do or how to proceed. They certainly could not move about much for fear of being cut to shreds on the coral. They did not dare try to swim toward shore. If they found the coral reef to be expansive and without breaks, how would they get across it and get to safety in the dark? Surely if this was one of those deserted islands where few tourists frequented, then the coral reef would not have been worn smooth enough to cross and coral reefs were homes to many poisonous sea dwellers. Pablo would know that.

She strained in the fading light to see below the surface. Only a dark ridge presented, the image shifting and jostling with the waves. With the tide going out, they would certainly be pulled to deep sea again if they could not get into the safety of the tide pool on the other side of the reef.

Suddenly, Pablo asked, "Mama! Do you feel the water?"

"Yes," she said. "It's warmer."

"No," he said. "Feel it rubbing your legs?" Pablo reached down and scooped up a handful of water and rubbed both hands together, then another handful. "Sand!" he said. "The water's full of sand. It's shallow here."

Ciara immediately ducked below the surface and opened her eyes. If it meant saving their lives then she would suffer having burning bloodshot eyes caused by the salty water. She saw only a dark ridge underwater ahead of them, but in some places, the ridge was white. She came up again and pressed her fingertips against the burning in her eyes. "There's some sand," she said. "We have to move about twenty feet to the left."

With the aid of Pablo's swim fin as a probe, they finally found a sandy area. At last they could stand. The thought of earth under foot sent a shot of heat through her body. She felt both hot and cold. Sand had built up against the reef or perhaps filled a valley between the mounds. She felt the outgoing tide dragging loose sand over her feet as the tide swept out. The current was not strong anymore. They would be able to stand, maybe even sit if the outgoing tide dropped the water level and bared the reef. Ciara walked carefully and felt with her feet to make sure she followed the sandy bottom. She was able to elevate herself till she was only waist deep in water. She looked toward the island and in the dim light of sundown tried to see everything in between. Most of the area between the reef and the island was dark with only small occasional vague spots of white sandy bottom.

The sun had all but disappeared. Only the final glowing was left. The problem now was how to navigate the small bay in total darkness and get to shore without bumping into jagged coral. She was sure her legs and feet were slashed and certainly Rico's must be too. They could not stay on the coral till morning. They were already shivering and Rico needed tending to. He was too quiet and seemed to be slipping in and out of consciousness again.

Night fell at that very moment, even before she could decide what their options might be. Pablo hung close to his father and helped him stand. It was better to keep Rico in the water up to his neck so he would not become chilled in the night breeze. Deeper water also made it easier to help Rico keep his balance, or for them to keep theirs as they stood supporting him with only their heads sticking out of the water. Rico opened and closed his eyes and cleared his throat but said nothing. It was not like him to not participate in their safety. Surely his strength had been sapped.

Just as Ciara thought the shadowy gloom might win, Pablo became frantic and pointed upwards. "Look," he said, excited. "Look up."

She tilted her head in the direction he pointed and saw the moon. It was a first quarter waxing moon like a light being turned on dimly. She wanted to hug Pablo for being precocious and astute. She reached a hand toward him but something in the distance far beyond him caught her eye. Something twinkled in the night. "Pablo, look!" she said as she pointed. "It's a light… on the island!" Ciara screamed and screamed again. "Pablo," she said. "Scream! Scream for help!"

Pablo did not scream as he moved into the more shallow sandy area near the top of the reef. Instead he quickly examined both boards, and then flung one over the reef and into the tide pool. He tipped the remaining board upright and began to slam it down underwater till it hit the coral. Over and over he pounded. Then he brought the board up and checked the end. "Splinters!" he said.

"What are you doing, Pablo?" Ciara asked. "Yell for help!"

Pablo turned the other end of the board toward the coral and beat down hard again. "I'm breaking off the splinters!" he said.

Ciara managed to reach him and shook his arm. "Why are you doing that?" she asked.

"I'm going to use this like a surfboard," he said. "I'm going to get help."

"Pablo, the coral's too dangerous. Just scream," Ciara said as she yelled again and again.

"Mama," Pablo said. "I have to get help. Look at Papi. He's unconscious again."

Rico hung in the water with his head flopped over on one arm stiffly raised with the hand hanging limp. Ciara swam back to him. "Rico," she said. "Can you hear me? Rico?"

"Mama," Pablo said. "I have to go to the beach. There's someone there who can help."

She gave a quick yank on the life ring to get Pablo's attention. "It's too far to swim, Pablo," she said. "I can barely see the beach."

Pablo let the life ring jerk loose from his arm. "I have to, Mama," he yelled almost hysterically. "We have to save my papi!" Quickly, he slid the dulled board under his body, pushed off into the tide pool and began thrashing his arms in the water, pushing himself along on the board, with steady kicks and the aid of one swim fin.

In an instant, he was too far away to grab hold of to prevent him from risking his life. Ciara held her breath and worried about his lanky but light child's body being dashed against the coral. Holding tight to the rope of the life ring, she clasped her hands together. "Please, God," she said, whispering. "Please take care of our son."

Chapter Five

The moon had risen high. Clouds no longer obscured its First Quarter light. Stars twinkled brilliantly. The violent sea storm that ravaged them had either broken up or moved far out over the Atlantic. But the air remained cool. With nighttime upon them, the water temperature also dropped. Ciara shivered uncontrollably, maybe from fright since this was the warmest time of year in the Caribbean and the trade winds never before gave her a chill. She watched Pablo make his way toward the beach. Occasionally he swam to the left, then changed and headed toward the right. Her heart skipped a beat with the thought that he might have lost his sense of direction.

Ciara held to the life ring that allowed Rico to dangle in deeper water where he and his waterlogged life vest would be warmer instead of being exposed to the chill of the strengthening nighttime breeze.

Pablo all but drifted from sight and was now only a tiny speck from which she occasionally detected movement. Her attention went back to Rico who moaned again.

Then she noticed the water was now shallow enough to sit and that the little plot of sand where she stood continued over the reef and down into the tide pool on the other side. Shadowy coral abutments protruded out of the water all around. She pulled in the life ring and floated Rico to her. "Rico," she said. "Rico, don't sleep. Can you hear me?"

"Ci-Ci...." Rico said and moaned.

"Rico, I have to keep you awake," she said. "Can you hear me?"

"I'm here, Ci-Ci," he said weakly.

"Can you stand?" she asked, trying to help him up.

Rico flopped around and came to his knees with the little strength he could muster. He could not stand. "My head," he said. "I'm so dizzy."

"Crawl, Rico. Can you crawl?"

"Where?" he asked as he feebly reached forward. "Can't see. It's all blurry."

"Over the reef," she said. "It's sheltered on the other side."

"The reef?" he asked. "What... reef?"

Ciara could not stop the tears that came. The reason Rico had not complained was because he was incoherent and maybe not aware of the trouble they were in. She had to do something to help him gain back his strength. If she could get him into the sheltered area, a little rest from bobbing around would do him good. "Let me help," she said. She choked back panic. She crawled beside him watching his every move as he clung with one hand to a strap of her life vest. When they crested the sandy area, she made him sit again and she turned his legs around and slid him on his rear end down the other side of the sandy patch until their legs were in shallow water.

"Okay," he said flatly. His words sounded more like a need for him to stop all movement.

Ciara sat down behind Rico and wrapped her arms and legs around his sides. She pressed so closely against him that their life vests hissed and expelled water. Inadvertently, she had been told what to do. She continued to squeeze Rico's life vest until she could pressure no more water from it. She dared not take it off of him. Not out in the middle of the bay. When it seemed Rico was comfortable enough leaning back against her chest, she looked for Pablo again.

No perceptible movement shone in the expanse between the island and where they sat. She kept looking from left to right then back again along the beach hoping he had made it that far. The beach seemed so distant. The thought came to her that perhaps he had not made it. Then where might he be? She whimpered again as her chest wracked with emotion. The thought of her brilliant son—and Rico's—not being able to live out his life was unbearable. All three of them had so much to live for.

"Pablo?" Rico asked, mumbling.

"Sh-h-h," Ciara said lovingly. "He went to get help."

"Help...?"

"Yes, he's getting us some help."

"Good," Rico said. "He can run... faster than anyone."

Ciara's tears flowed silently, salty tears falling into salty water. She dabbed at her eyes. Rico truly had no concept of where he was and what had happened. He was not aware he was lying in the middle of a bay in a wet life vest with his body temperature probably dropping much too low to maintain consciousness. How long did it take hypothermia to set in? She tightened her limbs around him and squeezed gently hoping somehow to force his body warmth to circulate.

Ciara opened her eyes and immediately saw something move. Way down the beach at the end opposite the light, a dark speck moved. Then it stopped, and then it moved again. Then it stopped again. Ciara strained to see. Surely it was Pablo who had made it all the way to the beach. But why was he starting and stopping. Had he been hurt and needed to tend to himself? "Oh, Pablo!" she said. All the way across the expanse of beach, the dark speck started, then stopped, then continued again. It had to be Pablo. Then, before it was anywhere near the tiny speck of light at the other end of the beach, the dark spot disappeared. Maybe animals might live on that island too. What waited for Pablo?

She sighed heavily and could only stare at Rico's body, limp between her legs. His head rested back against her, cradled by her arm. He coughed a lot and probably still had water in his lungs. At least he was conscious, if barely. As far as she could tell, he was not cut or scraped except for an abrasion on a knee. She twisted and reached down to throw water across the scrape to wash out the sand. As she drew her own leg up and out of the way, she saw them. Three punctures that looked more like miniature volcanic eruptions spewed slow courses of blood down her shin.

The first thought that came to her was to question whether sharks were known to frequent these waters. Sharks lived in all seas and blood could draw them into a particular area from miles around. They had been bleeding in the water a long time, but no sharks had appeared. Maybe the storm had kept the predators in calmer seas. Still, she quickly dragged Rico and herself back to the top of the sandy mound to keep the fresh blood from further spilling into the water. More exposed to the wind, they would have to endure the breeze against their wet life vests until they dried out.

Ciara put her head down close to Rico's ear and spoke to him. "Rico," she said. "Can you hear me?" She wanted to make him think, get his mind working.

"Hm-m," he said.

"Your new sailboat, Rico. Have you found one you want to buy?"

"What?"

"Rico," Ciara said. "Rico, wake up!"

He coughed again and wheezed, then slowly reached for his head. "Ay-y," he said. "What…?"

"You got bumped on your head, Rico," she said. "Pablo's gone for help."

"Pablito. Where's my Pablito?"

"He'll be back soon," Ciara said as she looked toward the beach. Nothing stirred. "What about that new boat?" she asked.

"I like… the name… Ci-Ci," Rico said. Though his words faltered, he was definitely more coherent.

Ciara rejoiced. "What?" she asked, prompting him to remain alert. "Who is Ci-Ci?"

"Our new boat," Rico said. "Named… after you… my beloved."

She cuddled him and spoke to him and prompted his meager responses. His thinking seemed more and more clear. She had to keep him awake. Later she asked, "Do you know where you are, Rico?"

He wheezed heavily and did not answer right away, like he might be trying to remember. "No," he said finally. Then he began to pull at his life vest, trying to remove it.

"No, Rico," Ciara said. Though they were safe sitting in the sand in a hollow in the coral reef, they were still in the middle of deep water.

"This… is too cold," he said. He began to fight her.

"Rico, sit still," she said. "You've been hurt. Sit still." She pinned his weakened arms to his sides and he lay back against her again and coughed.

"Ay, Ci-Ci!" he said. "No strength. Forgive me."

"Sh-h," she said. "You've taken a nasty blow to your head. Just don't move around a lot, okay?"

"Whatever you say, doctor," he said. He took her hand and held it to his lips.

"Try to breathe slow and deep, okay?" she said. "The salt air is good for you."

Suddenly there was a muffled pop in the distance. Then a streak of light shot up into the night leaving a trail of moonlit smoke that burst high in the air. "A flare!" Ciara said, screaming. "Pablo made it! He made it!" Then she sobbed and hugged Rico. "Look, Rico," she said as she pointed. They watched light from the flare fade. Then another went up.

A moment later, the sound of a faltering outboard motor rattled in the distance and a steady light shone from the beach. Quickly, Ciara stacked the cork life rings and laid Rico back against them. Then she stood and yelled and waved her arms as a smaller additional light swept back and forth and back and forth in the water just off the beach. Then the light was shining directly upon her. She jumped and screamed and waved frantically. The boat turned and the light pointed in a different direction and for a moment her heart sank. Then the boat headed back in her direction and she realized why Pablo had swam first one direction and then another. He had been avoiding coral formations in the tide pool.

Finally, the boat drew near. Pablo and the man were nearly obscured behind the brilliant spotlight mounted on the bow.

"Papi! Mama!" Pablo said, screeching in his young boy's voice. "Papi... Mama!"

With the small boat no more than three feet from the reef, the man threw a weight overboard and Pablo dropped his flashlight and jumped into the water and swam to her. Ciara scooped him into her arms and cried. "I love you, Pablo," she said. "You are so brave."

While she cried and held to Pablo, the man rushed past them. He bent down and placed two fingers flat against the side of Rico's throat. "Humph," he said. Then he straightened long enough to send up another flare. He wore no shirt or shoes and his ragged jeans were torn off mid-thigh and threads dangled. Moonlight cast on the flexing muscles of his wet body told of a person fit and agile. Again he bent over Rico lying back against the stacked lifebelts. "Humph!" was all he uttered.

"He doesn't speak, Mama," Pablo said. "Look, he's got a scar too."

Not until the man scooped up Rico then turned to carry him to the boat did Ciara realize what a big hulk of a man he was, and how grotesque. Ciara was both shocked and fearful at the sight of his face. His weathered features were perhaps exaggerated by the shadows caused by moonlight. He had unkempt hair and a scraggly beard and moustache and a jagged scar over his left eye from his forehead to his lower jaw. The eye had healed closed in a lumpy lopsided manner that hid most of the eyeball. A speck of light was all that reflected back from between the folds. Hair at the sides of his face and bordering the scar into his scraggly beard shone white in the moonlight. Ciara stepped aside and let him pass. As he stood in chest high water, he carefully deposited Rico into the skiff and positioned him sitting in the bottom of the boat leaning back against a seat.

"C'mon, Mama," Pablo said. He was already treading water and making his way toward the boat.

The man retrieved the life ring and threw it into the bow then hoisted Pablo. Then his big roughened hand was on her arm and he hoisted her out of the water and into the safety of the boat without so much as a grunt.

Water was filling the bottom of the skiff. Ciara felt something underfoot. She picked up the object and examined it as best she could in the dim light.

"Flares? In waterproof jackets?" she asked. "These look like ours."

"They washed up on the beach. I picked up as many as I could find."

The man tried several times to start the old outboard motor. If it wouldn't start, Ciara would get out and swim and push the boat. They were going to get to shore if that's what it took to get there. After a couple more pulls on the rope to motor sputtered to life. As they zigzagged around coral abutments on the way toward the shore, Ciara looked down into the water. No wonder Pablo had known where to swim and what to avoid. Even though the moon was only in its First Quarter, the dim light was enough to reflect off the pure white sand at the bottom of the tide pool. Anything that did not reflect light was a dark mass of coral or rock outcropping. Ciara felt saved.

Pablo picked up two tin cans and offered one to Ciara. "Here, Mama. He showed me. Bail. We have to bail water."

They bailed frantically as the rag-tag skiff was guided around coral abutments by following white sand trails reflecting the moon's light from the sea bed.

More than once, Ciara noticed the big man staring at her. It made her feel uneasy. She wanted to cover herself because all she wore was a life vest and bathing suit that shimmered in the moonlight. She hugged close to Rico and could not decide if the man was leering. His expression was difficult to determine with the shadows exaggerating his ugly scar. She tried to put it out of her mind. This man had come to help.

A few yards from shore, the old outboard motor coughed and sputtered, then died. The man tried to get it going again with no success. The boat began to sink. Ciara and Pablo bailed like crazy. With a rope between his teeth, the big man jumped overboard, swimming and dragging the skiff. Ciara and Pablo abandoned the skiff to lighten the load. Rico had not moved.

Chapter Six

They arrived at a moonlit wreckage-strewn beach. The hulk still dragged the skiff higher up the white sand beach, but the rear was submerged. The motor was underwater. The man made noises that clearly said he was disappointed, but he lifted Rico to the sand and removed his life vest. Although conscious, Rico's knees buckled and it was plain to see that he had no strength left. Even though it was probably an embarrassing position for Rico to find himself, the man hoisted him over his shoulder. With a mighty one-arm tug, the man pulled the boat higher onto the sand. When it looked like the boat was high enough on the beach not to be washed away during high tide, he walked off with Rico like a sack of rice over his shoulder. Had he been able, Rico might have objected, but it was better not to allow Rico to exert himself.

Ciara and Pablo removed waterlogged vests and draped them on the bow to dry out. Pablo gathered up the flares. They walked up into the ribbon of dry white sand bordering the thicket, out of which rose majestic coconut trees silhouetted against a starry sky. Surprisingly, the higher dry strip of beach still held the warmth of the setting sun under foot. The sand slipped easily and molded to her feet and reminded Ciara how good it was to walk on land. The tiny Coqui frogs chirped from inside the thickets. While they were normally a nuisance to hear, now she relished the sound of them because it meant they were safely on shore.

Moonlight illuminated a small bay strewn with wreckage. How vicious and brutal the storm and sea had been. And having now coughed up much that had been claimed, how calm the ocean seemed as waves lapped lazily at the sand.

Pablo dashed ahead of them. "Look, Mama," he said, yelling as he dragged something. It was one of their ice chests. Pablo opened it as she arrived. She touched the food and found it still cool. She shut the lid quickly and she and Pablo dragged it as they followed the man toward his crude dwelling.

The man's house was no more than a piecemeal ramshackle shanty made from old slats of wood and palm fronds nailed together against live coconut tree trunks. Sun bleached and worn out fishing paraphernalia lay strewn about. Made from flat woven leaves and branches, the entry door was fastened in place with vines and hung lopsided. Another tree stood inside the middle of the room against which the pointed thatched roof had been affixed. It was strange to see a live tree jutting up through the middle of a room. The sandy floor was covered with a multitude of thick mats woven from long leaves. Ciara had seen such mats in the tourist shops. These were worn and looked as if an amateur, perhaps this man, had woven them. Many smaller mats lay strewn about. Two kerosene lanterns cast flickering light. Over the fumes of the lanterns, the odor of the place was that of a fisherman's shanty. Blocks of tree trunks were being used as chairs. In fact, his few handmade furnishings were fashioned out of materials most likely found on the island or washed up on the beach. Yet, the kerosene lamps, along with a few store bought items lying around, like the distilled water jugs and the sack of rice hanging on the wall in a piece of net, said he evidently had some contact with other people. Whoever was bringing this man his meager supplies would be their ticket home.

As carefully as if Rico had been a sleeping child, the man laid him onto a wide weathered mat-covered board stretched between two stumps and backed against the wall. Rico wheezed then relaxed as if someone had placed him into a luxurious bed.

"Oh, no you don't," Ciara said, going to his side. She sat him up but he slumped over. "You have to stay awake, Rico. Somehow, we're going to get help. But right now, you stay awake." Though it was old and dirty, she used the checkered blanket lying crumpled nearby to wrap around him and stave off the nighttime coolness and bring his body temperature up. The frayed fabric was worn and surprisingly soft in her hands and must have been, at one time, of very good quality.

In the dim light, as he sat slumped, she examined his head and found a doozy of a gash. The bleeding had stopped, though, and it seemed that there was not much swelling. His scalp did not feel soft when she palpated, but the pressure did make him moan sharply.

The big man went outside and carried in the ice chest. He sat down on a stump and placed the cooler at his feet seeming delighted as a child ready to open a toy chest full of surprises. He opened and rummaged through the cooler and retrieved a sandwich, one half of which Ciara and Pablo watched him devour with just two bites. At times it looked like he tried to smile while chewing. He seemed oblivious to their presence and plight.

Uncertain about the man's demeanor, Pablo crept to her side. "Ice, mama," he said. "We have to put ice on Papi's head."

In Spanish, Pablo asked the man for a clean cloth, which he could not produce. No way would Ciara use a filthy rag for an ice pack. Then she had an idea and retrieved the piece of Saran Wrap that had been used to store the sandwich. She wrapped ice cubes from the cooler in the dirty rag but placed the piece of Saran Wrap over Rico's wound before applying the cold compress.

That settled she turned her attention back to the man who polished off a can of soda. "Coffee?" Ciara asked mostly to hide her fright. "Do you have any coffee... for Rico?"

The man said nothing and gulped down the other half of the sandwich. When he stopped chewing, he grinned wide and groaned with pleasure. Some of his teeth were missing. The rest looked stained. As he leered again, her hair stood on end.

"*Por favor,*" Pablo said. "*Senor, tiene un café para mi papa?*"

Finally understanding, the man rose and went to the corner of the room. A two-burner propane cook top stood on a large metal washtub, which he had turned over and used for a low countertop. The cook top was not lit but he gingerly touched the side of an old dented saucepan sitting on one of the burners. Then he reached inside a small box nearby and surprisingly brought out a tiny demitasse cup into which he poured thick dark fluid from the pot.

Ciara bravely met him halfway across the small room and accepted the demitasse. "Thank you," she said as he stared at her.

The cup was made of bone china and elegantly decorated with delicate red and blue flowers. How would he, on a deserted island, have come up with a china demitasse?

She noticed no steam rising from the cup. She sipped the boiled brew and found it warm enough but not so hot that Rico would be scalded. It tasted as if coming from the bottom of the pan and so thick it might keep an army awake.

"Rico, drink," she said as she pressed the cup to his lips. He tasted then made a motion he wanted more. Pablo brought over a couple more sandwiches and they were able to get some nourishment into Rico's stomach and into theirs.

Then Rico had to go to the bathroom but it seemed there was none. That meant only one thing. After Pablo explained in Spanish, the big man helped Rico to go outside. Pablo went along and that was good. Later Ciara asked Pablo to show her as well where the outdoor facilities were to be found.

Finally, Ciara allowed Rico to recline and rest. She stood, walked closer to the big man and said, "My name is Ciara. This is Pablo." She offered her hand though she could barely stand to look at his disfigurement.

The big man's lips parted. He slowly reached out and took her hand. He shook it but he would not let go.

Ciara tried to withdraw her hand but still he would not let go. She tried again but he would not turn loose. He yanked a little, trying to draw her closer to him. The grip on her hand tightened. His strange behavior unnerved her. She forced herself to relax and asked, "What is your name?" Then she remembered he was unable to speak.

"*Cual es su nombre, Senor?*" Pablo asked, chiming in.

The man tipped his head and studied Pablo. Finally, he released her hand and disappeared through another flimsy door to what seemed to be a room at the back end of the dimly lit hut. As Ciara kneeled and bent over Rico, she could not help glancing nervously over her shoulder wondering where the big man was.

A few moments later, Pablo said, "Mama, look."

Ciara turned and found the big man standing right behind her. He grunted again as he dangled two pieces of tattered cloth for her to see. He dropped them to the floor near her feet. Then he moved his arms back and forth in front of himself in a motion Ciara interpreted as him telling her to wrap the cloth around herself.

"Why, thank you," she said, picking them up off the floor and standing. The cloths turned out to be two limp and faded bulk rice sacks. She handed one to Pablo and tore hers open down one side and across the bottom.

"What do we do with these?" Pablo asked.

Ciara had already wrapped hers around her torso and tied a knot in front over her chest. She smiled, pleased to finally having something more to wear than only a bathing suit. "How do I look?" she asked of Pablo.

"Well, that leaves me out," Pablo said, throwing the rag onto a stump. "I'm not wearing a dress."

Ciara could not help laughing. "Wait a second," she said as she retrieved the cloth. She draped it loosely around Pablo's shoulders leaving it hanging down his back. She tied a knot in front at the throat. At least it would protect his skin from the tropic sun during the day since they no longer had lotions to apply.

"Look, mama," Pablo said. "I'm Superman." He pranced around the small room making the cape billow behind him. Somehow a child's antics did not fit the tall Pablo, even if he wasn't yet eight years old.

She turned her attention back to Rico, who remained quiet. Ciara really did not know how to take care of someone who might have a concussion. She knew the person's head should not be jarred, nor should they be allowed to sleep a long time and that they had to be awakened at intervals. But perhaps Rico should be allowed to sleep since he could finally rest comfortably. She would wake him shortly and sit him up again. With fluids and a little food, then sleep, surely his energy would be restored.

Now she had to devise a way to get help. The two full water jugs she spotted under an old cloth in the corner said that perhaps the bringer of supplies would not arrive soon. They would be safe in this man's cabin for the night but something about him set her nerves on edge. When she turned to thank the man who had rescued them, he had already left the room. Ciara sank to the floor beside Rico and listened to his raspy breathing. Pablo came to sit beside her with an apple from the cooler and they shared bites.

The only things they had with which to send a message to anyone were the flares. "How many of those did you find?" she asked of him.

"Eight," he said. "Maybe I'll find more on the beach when daylight comes."

Pablo piled up two of the smaller mats, used his cape for a blanket and went to sleep. Ciara fell asleep sitting on the floor leaning sideways against the crude bed on which Rico lay. She woke with a start when a hand pulled at her ankle.

The kerosene lamps were still lit so she must not have slept very long. The big man knelt before her leering. In one hand he held a large green leaf used like a bowl on which was piled some sort of stiff whitish mixture. He sat the leaf on the mat beside her. Then he pointed to the leg she had so abruptly withdrawn. When she did not move, he grabbed the leg and pulled it straight before she could do anything. She would have screamed in fright but as he pressed on her swollen wounds, she yelped in pain instead.

Pablo woke and crawled to her side. "What are you doing?" he said angrily as he pushed the man's arm.

"Wait, Pablo," she said. Ciara looked at the three punctures on her shin. They had swollen a great deal since she last looked at them and even in the dim light the protruding volcanoes looked red and threatening like they were ready to erupt. The man smeared the mixture from the leaf thickly over the wounds. Then he wrapped the leaf around the area and secured the whole thing in place with a piece of long slender vine that he tied off. He had made a poultice for her. Ciara touched his arm. "Thank you," she said. "*Muchas gracias, Senor.*"

The man stayed in the same position on his knees in front of her. He leered again. Their eyes met and Ciara realized that the man smiled because he was proud of himself. He was not leering at all. He was simply smiling the only way his face would work with damaged features. But that still did not explain why he watched her every move.

The big man finally left the room and Ciara sat for a moment wondering about him. When she turned her attention back to Rico, she found that while she had slept, the man had also covered the wound on Rico's head with a poultice.

Ciara continued to wake Rico at intervals through the night. She sometimes woke with a start, not knowing how long she had allowed Rico to slumber. Each time he roused, he seemed more coherent. Pablo would wake, too, upon hearing his father's wheezing. They spoke in whispers and helped Rico understand what had happened to them and specifically what had happened to him.

As dawn illuminated their surroundings, Pablo and the big man entered from outside. Ciara rubbed her eyes and sat up on the woven mat.

"Mama, look what the man made for me," Pablo said. With both hands, he held up a large banana leaf that had pieces cut out. "It says Dom… Domin… Domingo."

Ciara smiled and reached for it. "Yes, Domingo," she said. "His name is Domingo." The man had cut out the letters of his name into the banana leaf. She stood and again offered her hand. "Thank you, Domingo," she said. "We owe you our lives."

Again, he would not let go of her hand. He tipped his head sideways and made strange noises and pulled her toward him. Ciara jerked her hand loose. He may know how to spell his name but that did not mean he was all there. Then he went out the front door and Ciara heard a sharp familiar chopping sound.

Domingo returned with an armful of fresh coconuts with the ends lopped off. Pablo followed, already drinking. Domingo handed one to her and she took it and tipped it to her lips and drank all the sweet translucent milk from inside.

As it boiled in the crusted saucepan, the smell of coffee woke Rico. The remaining three sandwiches in the cooler would have been waterlogged had Pablo not propped them up on cans of soda to keep them from floating in the melted ice overnight. Domingo reached in and took one, not mindful that they should divide them equally. Again, he ate as if he had never tasted a chicken sandwich in his life. Maybe he had not. Rico was able to eat only half a sandwich, but he was able to sit up and feed himself and drink. Ciara ate the rest of his sandwich and let Pablo have a whole one.

That morning, Pablo found only one more flare. He placed it in the box outside the doorway with the others. He also took Ciara to see Domingo's small, cultivated garden up the beach and into a clearing in the thicket where the soil seemed less sandy. All the plants looked healthy. The thriving jungle thicket surrounding the small cleared plot looked as if at any moment it might take over.

Ciara had no way of knowing on which island they might be, but, most likely they had washed up somewhere among the numerous unnamed islands and sandbars between Culebra and St. Thomas. Twin-engine planes shuttled tourists between the Isle Verde Airport on Puerto Rico and the Harry S. Truman Airport in Charlotte Amalie on St. Thomas, but not on a daily basis. They could wait to be rescued. Food was plentiful. Coconut, papaya, mango and breadfruit trees and other edibles grew all over the place. When they would hear the sound of those small planes, they would send up some flares.

When she next looked, Pablo was off and running before she could stop him. She followed him on a barely discernible trail, calling to him to return. Her bare feet suffered greatly in the brush and on the rocks. The forest, tall weeds, tree ferns and other tropical flora were dense. The island seemed small, the mountains not that high, but the jungle impenetrable.

Finally, Ciara managed to grab hold of Pablo's rice sack and halted him midmotion. "Where do you think you're going?" she asked sternly.

Pablo pointed to the low ridge of hills. "Maybe we could put an H-E-L-P sign up there."

"In that thick jungle? You need open space."

With Rico weakened, she was going to have to be fully responsible for the antics of this adventurous little dare devil. His playful smile begged to be understood instead of scolded.

"Let's go!" Pablo began to push his way through more bushes.

"Wait! There could be snakes, wild animals—" Pablo disappeared. "Pablo? Where are you?"

"I'm over here, Mama."

Ciara caught up. "Don't go running off like that again, you hear? Wild animals could be—"

"Well, Domingo lives here and nothing ate him yet." They heard the drone of a distant plane coming closer. "We have to get up there."

Again, Pablo was too fast as he ducked through a stand of trees. His cape trailed after him and disappeared as branches closed in behind him. The drone of the plane became louder as it neared the island. Then Ciara heard Pablo's scream cut short.

"Pablo, what happened? Where are you?" She listened but heard no reply. She cautiously moved forward, tried to follow the broken branches where he passed through. Then she heard him moaning. "I can hear you. Where are you?" she asked, frantically looking about.

"Careful, Mama. I fell over the edge."

"Keep talking so I can move toward your voice." She had to move swiftly. Pablo could be hurt.

"Stop, Mama. You're right near me."

Ciara looked around but did not see anything. She crept forward but unexpectedly slid over the edge of a huge embedded boulder. She grabbed at shrubbery and dangled until she was able enough to pull herself up.

Pablo was crouched on a ledge about six feet below. Had he gone over the far edge, he would have fallen to his death.

"Honey, are you hurt?" she asked.

"Get me out. We have to signal that plane."

But the noise of the plane had already diminished as it passed.

"Let's just get you out of there."

Ciara tried to ease around the edge of the boulder but it was too steep so she tried from the other side. She clung to dangling vines, allowing herself to slide down to the ledge. Pablo's knees and elbows were scraped. So were hers.

"You sure you're not hurt?"

Pablo was embarrassed. "I can walk okay."

Ciara tried to push Pablo up the area she had just slid down. Finding nothing to grip he slid backwards. Ciara braced herself into a crouch to catch his weight as he slid back, almost colliding into her. Ciara grasped frantically at the vines to keep Pablo's weight from throwing them both backward over the ledge. The vines were weak and the soil loose. The only thing she could do was dig her fingertips into the loose soil or try to grab at jagged rocks to cling to. Pablo grabbed at clumps of weeds that slowed his slide. Finally, they were able to scrape and pull themselves to the top where they sat down in a safe spot to rest.

"Tell me you won't ever pull a stunt like that again," she said through tightened lips.

"I fell. It was an accident."

"What did I just say?"

"Okay, I won't run away again." He knew he had been careless.

"I'm going to have to tell your Papi what happened."

Pablo looked down at his scraped knees. "No," he said, seeming apologetic. "I'll tell him." Then he whined, "But I want to go home."

Ciara stood. "I want to get us off this island too," she said. "Staying out on the beach is how help will find us."

"Nobody's coming," Pablo said as he stood. "Domingo's got lots of supplies."

Ciara immediately knelt down in front of him. "One thing we don't do in life is to give up. You understand that, Son? Never ever give up."

"I know," he said. "Papi says the same thing."

The rest of the morning she and Rico rested against one of the coconut trees that curved and leaned majestically out over the white sand beach toward the surf. They found some sticks and strung up the old blanket to shield them from direct sunlight.

Hues of sea and sky blended making the horizon line seem nonexistent. The trade winds had stilled. The strong morning heat permeated their skin and seeped into their bones. Domingo fished off the rocks at the far end of the cove. Sea birds screeched overhead and Pablo chased around and studied the habits of fleeing sand crabs. It felt good just being alive. Like the gentle wind, they moved slowly, if at all, due to Rico's inability to control his coughing and labored breathing. When they spoke, Ciara helped Rico understand how Pablo's intelligence and bravery had saved them.

The redness and swelling had gone down on Ciara's injured leg. The sun helped bake the crusty scabs. Rico still wore a small poultice on his head wound. He insisted they walk but struggled to do so. The effort made him gasp for breath and at times, he choked and spit, then kicked sand over the phlegm. His skin and lips had taken on a deep bluish cast. Surely, he still had water in his lungs and desperately needed attention, so they rested often.

Pablo found a sturdy stick and presented it to his father as a walking aid. Now Rico wanted to walk again. As he clutched the stick to pull himself up, Ciara noticed that his nails also had that same bluish cast. She was glad he felt up to walking a bit. The exercise would get his blood moving again.

She and Rico inched their way laboriously down the beach in the sparkling white sand. Pablo pranced, running back and forth with his cape flying, and talked about all the items he and Domingo had been able to salvage.

Domingo's old boat was turned upside-down away from the shoreline by the trees. The bottom showed old deep gashes and tears. Broken bits of debris were stacked near the skiff.

Farther down the beach it looked as if Pablo had laid a lot of items out across a lengthy span of sand. It was too far for Rico to walk this time so he asked, "What is that, Pablito?" Speaking made him gasp for breath. "Why have you laid everything in rows?"

"That's not in rows," Pablo said. "And it's not the stuff we found."

"What is it then, *Mi'jo*?"

"Mostly old coconuts and some rocks," Pablo said. "The beach is loaded with them."

"So is that the foundation for a new house," Rico asked, trying to smile.

"No, Papi," Pablo said as he jogged backwards in front of his father. The jagged appendectomy scar shifted with each step. Then he stopped jogging backward and turned halfway. "Can't you read it from here?" he asked. He waited but from that distance the beach was too flat for her or Rico to make out any pattern. "It says H-E-L-P," Pablo finally said.

Rico stopped walking. "Come here," he said softly. Pablo was not sure what to expect so he approached slowly. Rico put his arms around his son and held him to his chest so Pablo would not see the tears in his eyes.

Then coffee and something else that smelled utterly delicious called their attention back to the shanty.

Chapter Seven

Domingo stared at her constantly. She spent most of her time outside the shanty or on the beach, but when Domingo was in the area, he was always at an angle that allowed him to see her. He kept his distance and tended his chores, yet, sometimes cocked his head like he had something on his mind. His habits were peculiar. Judging by his actions, perhaps whatever accident had caused his scarring had also stolen some of his mental capacity. Ciara kept her distance, knowing she did not want to be alone with him. Possibly, something sinister lurked inside that mind of his.

Domingo's shanty was set back into the wooded area. Another large room at the rear could be his bedroom. The entire structure had no windows so she was unable to peek in to satisfy her curiosity and the door to that room was always closed. She was curious, not a snoop, but wondered why he would need such a large room to sleep in.

Living this detached from civilization, it would make sense to have some sort of radio to maintain contact with the rest of the world in times of emergencies. She tried to imagine what would make anyone want to live alone on a remote uninhabited island. Perhaps Domingo's appearance had something to do with his reclusiveness. The deforming scar running the length of his face and people's reactions to it might be why he chose seclusion. He lived off the land and sea and his enduring muscular physique was maintained by his outdoor lifestyle. He was definitely knowledgeable in survival techniques and seemed emotionally stable enough. But was he?

The second day, more of Rico's energy returned. His dizziness and blurred vision came only sporadically. When the men went to the toilet in the sandpit, Ciara could hear their voices. As much as she understood of Spanish, Rico had thanked Domingo for his hospitality. Domingo's guttural throat responses said he understood.

Rico insisted he was stronger and could finally walk unaided, but breathing difficulties lingered. He felt strong enough to try his hand at string fishing with Pablo, but weakened quickly and had to sit down. Pablo went to his knees in the sand to tend to his father. Ciara watched from a distance, allowing father and son to appreciate one another again.

She also watched the skies and listened but no planes approached. Then she sadly realized it was possible that the Mercy had sunk among a chain of tiny islands nowhere close to the flight path of any plane. Should she so much as hear the distant drone of one of those small excursion planes, it would be foolish to waste any of their precious flares from so far away on the horizon. Her best hope was that a sailing vessel might pass by. She wondered if Domingo had a pair of binoculars.

The next morning, Rico woke feeling dizzy and nauseous. "Just take it easy," Ciara said, reassuring, even though she worried. The blue tint in his fingernails seemed to have darkened. His breath was labored again as if he had just run a mile. "You're bound to have some good days and some bad ones till you're completely well." Still, he insisted on getting out into the fresh air and sunshine. After light morning showers subsided and he was comfortable at their favored spot against the leaning palm, he said, "Do something, Ci-Ci, please. Pablito has no little amigos to play with. He's getting bored. Help him occupy his time."

"You'll be okay by yourself for a while?"

"Of course," he said. "Unless a snake slithers out of the forest to keep me company."

"Ugh!"

"For that," he said with a crooked smile, "I think I can run away fast."

So Ciara and Pablo played hide and seek. Ciara hid first but Pablo found her easily. She had not gone far enough into the bush because of the snakes that were prevalent on all the Caribbean Islands. She would rather Pablo find her than a potentially poisonous slithering serpent. The fer-de-lance was the most venomous tropical snake that lived on some Caribbean islands. She hoped they would not have to meet any of those.

Then it was Pablo's turn to hide. Ciara closed her eyes and felt the spray of dry sand across her ankles as Pablo took off running. She heard him crashing through the brush. Then all was quiet. The sound of him running through the shrubs came from the direction of the shack. Pablo would be smart enough now not to go too far into the thicket. He was probably behind Domingo's shanty.

Ciara crept cautiously peering warily around the corners and irregular angles of the flimsy walls strung together with lengths of sturdy vines in various stages of drying and aging. Pablo had hidden well. Rounding the back corner of the shanty, she found him in plain view. He stood at an opened back door, the rear door to Domingo's secret room.

Pablo saw her arrive and seemed not the least concerned she had found him. "Mama, quick!" he said, as he beckoned frantically with a hand. "*Ven aca.*"

"Pablo," Ciara said, going to him. "You shouldn't be looking into Domingo's...." But all she could do as well was stand and stare.

Finally, Pablo slapped her playfully on the shoulder. "You're it," he said as he tripped, then took off running. "Bet you can't catch me."

Ciara took off after him. Pablo headed toward the beach. She caught up with him just as he plopped into the sand at his father's side.

"Some game of tag you play," Ciara said as she arrived.

Pablo smiled but turned to his father and took his hand wanting to help him up. "Papi, Papi! *Mira lo que—*"

"Ah-ah!" Rico said. "Speak English till Mama understands too."

"You've got to see Domingo's room," Pablo said.

Rico withdrew his hand sharply from Pablo's. Such a sudden effort made him gasp for breath. "Ay, *Mi'jo!*" he said. "You didn't go snooping, did you?"

"No, Papi. The back door was open," Pablo said. "His room is full of rusting boating equipment and stuff. They're all junky. And he's got...." Pablo hesitated and then looked up at her.

"Women's clothes," Ciara said. "Old faded and ragged things hanging on a small rack and around the walls."

"And women's shoes," Pablo said.

"Women's things?" Rico asked as his eyes hinted at adult questions. "The kinky old man must have salvaged them as they washed up."

"From what?" Ciara asked. "It's not every day a boat goes down. He's got shorts and blouses and sarongs—"

"Why does he have women's things?" Pablo asked.

Rico only shrugged. Ciara took it as a message that she should allow her two men a little time by themselves. She wandered off down the beach.

She caught sight of Domingo in the shrubs. He saw her looking and he ducked out of sight again. She thought she heard another plane approaching. She continued on, way past Pablo's H-E-L-P sign, and studied the tops of the rocky cliffs at the opposite end of the cove.

No entry into the jungle existed. She would have to break a new trail to the top. She saw a rocky ledge that might make the climbing easier.

She heard the rustling of bushes as if something or someone was in the thicket scrambling away from her, or finding a place to hide. Perhaps some small animal had been frightened by her approach. She called out, but nothing else moved or made noise so she continued down the beach.

At the end of the cove, she began to climb the rocks near the top. She suddenly sensed someone's presence and stopped to listen for whoever it might be. She called out again, and glancing back, saw Pablo climbing after her.

"I'm coming too," he said, finding a place to stand near her.

Her heart raced, but she was relieved to see him. "You should stay on the beach," she said finally.

"Maybe we could build a fire on top."

"That's too dangerous. We could set the whole island ablaze," she said. "We have no matches anyway." Pablo looked guilty. Ciara caught on and put out her hand. "Give 'em up," she said.

Pablo resisted. "It's not like I'm playing with matches."

"Give 'em," she said.

Pablo reluctantly produced several books of matches from his bathing suit pocket. "If people in planes always see smoke from Domingo's cooking pit on the beach," he said, "they won't think anything's wrong when they see our smoke down there." He pointed upward. "We have to light a fire up there."

Ciara stuffed the matchbooks down the front of her bathing suit. "Pablo—"

"I'm going with you."

"No, stay here."

"You shouldn't go alone, Mama."

"Was that you in the bushes?"

Pablo looked into the thickets and shrugged. "Maybe it's Domingo."

Ciara found a sturdy old stick in case she needed protection, but she did not want to alarm Pablo. "Maybe it's an animal or snake slithering around," she said. "If you're coming, take care so you don't fall again." They began to climb as the drone of the plane quickly faded into the distance.

As Ciara looked to the sky in the direction of the diminishing sound, she lost her balance. Her footing slipped. She screamed as she slid over rocks and grabbed at anything. She dangled from an exposed tree root jutting out of the cliff side, unable to pull herself up. She glanced at the pool below at the water's edge. The bottom was sandy and seemingly hid no boulders. The only way off her precarious perch would be to jump into the water.

Finally, she let go, pushing off to fall clear of the boulders that hugged the side of the steep hill. She splashed into the water in fright. That was soon replaced when she surfaced and realized how refreshing the water was. Her rice sack had come lose and floated. She grabbed it as it began to sink. Then she saw Pablo easing his way down the side of the rocks where she had clung!

"Pablo, wait. Stay there."

Too late. Pablo let out a long wail and hurled himself over the edge and into the pool, his rice sack flapping in the air. When he surfaced, they were face to face treading water.

"That was better than jumping off the Mercy," he said, jubilant.

"You could have been hurt," she said, spitting out water as waves bounced against boulders from one side of the pool to the other. "That wasn't very smart."

"It was fun." He began to swim toward some boulders.

When Ciara reached him and sat on a boulder beside him, she said, "Don't you come back here by yourself to try that again." She wrung water out of her sack and tied it around her throat to wear it cape fashion.

"Ah, Mama—"

"At low tide, that pool will be too shallow to jump into. You could be hurt. Or worse."

They stepped their way across the rocks to the sand again. Ciara pulled the soggy matchbooks from inside her bathing suit. Frustrated, she threw them to the ground.

"Won't these dry?" Pablo asked, as he picked them up.

"Listen, you and I are gonna have a talk about safety, okay?

Pablo flashed his little devilish grin again. "It's your turn to tell Papi that you fell." But his smile faded. He knew he had angered her. He glanced at his skinned knees and panted from the sting of the salt water. Then he asked, "You sure you wanna be my mama?"

Ciara softened when she saw the confused look on his face. "Of course. I already am your mama. Your papi and I are going to be married soon." She reached to comfort him. "Besides, I wouldn't give you up for all the world."

"You wouldn't?" he asked.

"But you and I are gonna have a talk real soon, aren't we?"

They made their way back down the beach to the leaning palm and helped Rico to stand. He was visibly weaker than when he had walked earlier. "I can't get my breath," he said. "I'm so sleepy." He had slept most of the morning under the palm.

Ciara felt helpless. She did not like seeing her Rock of Gibraltar so pathetically weak. But Rico could not help it. Certainly he must be suffering inside, not being able to contribute to their survival. Yet, Ciara would see him through this no matter what it took. He would be restored to the man she knew and they would be wiser for it.

It was nearly lunchtime. They made their way back to the cabin and saw Domingo cleaning fish out on the rocks on the other side.

Pablo scampered toward them again. "Mama, Papi," he said. "You should see what Domingo caught for lunch."

"More fresh fish?" Rico asked.

"Si, he caught *Capitan*."

Rico smiled sadly. "I was hoping to catch one for our dinner when we had our little talk, you and me, Ci-Ci. Remember my promise?"

Pablo seemed to sense the talk would be between his father and her. He frowned and looked at the ground. Ciara was sure Rico had intended to renew his proposal and finally set a wedding date. After that special moment, Pablo would then be included and told. "I've never tasted Capitan," she said.

Pablo perked up. He was not one to remain dejected for long. "Senorita Avery said this fish feeds on octopus and lobster. Capitan even tastes like lobster."

"Si, si. Food for the gods," Rico said as he gestured weakly, kissing his fingertips. "I can't wait."

Rico insisted on lying down inside to help himself feel better. After he was comfortable on the makeshift couch, Ciara went out to the small fire smoldering in the cooking pit. A couple of tuberous roots and wedges of breadfruit boiled in a large pot. An old metal pan set aside contained various small leaves that Domingo had gathered to flavor the food. Ciara decided she should be learning from Domingo which indigenous roots and herbs were safe to eat. Surely this man had knowledge most people lacked and she needed to stop letting his looks get in the way of her acceptance of him.

Domingo seemed overjoyed that she took an interest in what he was doing. With hand motions, he showed her how to shred some small round leaves and held them to her nose. The smell was pungent but once the leaves were stuffed inside the fish along with the heads of some green onions from his garden and placed over the fire, the odors that emitted were tantalizing.

While the food cooked, Domingo deftly fashioned plates from banana leaves and vines. They had been eating with their fingers but doing so seemed only to add to the flavor of the food and island life.

Ciara carried a serving into the shanty for Rico. He could barely sit up and complained about being sleepy. She worried that his concussion might not be healing and that, perhaps, the inside of his head had been jarred and the concussion might be bleeding again. Panic welled up. The only thing she knew was that she had to keep getting him to take nourishment to keep up his strength. Ciara picked all the bones from a piece of Capitan and balled up the meat just big enough to get it into Rico's mouth. He ate only a few bites but drank lots of coconut milk. Then he insisted on going back to sleep, looking almost asleep before having lain back down. His breathing was raspy.

Ciara went to look for Pablo and found him running toward her on the beach. When he arrived he was angry. "Someone threw all my rocks away!" he said. He was nearly crying but too mad to let the tears fall.

"What rocks?" Ciara asked, trying to comfort him.

"My sign," he said. "It doesn't say H-E-L-P anymore. Someone threw all my rocks and coconuts into the bushes."

Shock rippled through Ciara's nervous system. The only other person she knew of on the island was Domingo. Was he the only one? She and Pablo had not tried to find anyone else. Other than Domingo's dead end paths to some wild herbs, there were no trails to follow through the underbrush and no smoke from anyone else cooking meals. The beach dead-ended on both sides of the cove with steep rocky abutments pounded by waves, so it was unlikely anyone might come into the cove on foot.

"Pablo," she said. "You go back and make your sign again. This time, try to use only coconuts, lots and lots of them."

"Why only coconuts?"

"Because they're lighter to carry," she said. "If your sign gets torn up again, we'll just keep replacing it over and over until help comes."

"Did Domingo do it, Mama?"

"Let's not blame anyone," she said. "I'll try to find out, and why."

She watched Pablo run swiftly down the beach. His straight line directly to the area where he had first made the sign said he understood the urgency of what he needed to do.

Ciara went back into the house and listened to Rico's breathing, which was still labored. She felt his forehead but he had no fever that she could detect. She examined the wound on his scalp and it was healing as far as she could tell. The gash did not look infected. Without question, Domingo's poultices were working.

Why Domingo might do something to keep them from getting help was a mystery. If he did not wish them to be found, what else might he do? With that thought, Ciara jumped up immediately and went to the box outside the front door. Fearing what she suspected, she threw open the lid. The box was empty, the flares gone.

With ire triggered, she slammed the lid shut. She crossed through the small front room and entered Domingo's secret room but was stopped short inside the doorway. Again, the sight of a woman's decaying belongings seemed macabre. Once she recovered, she rummaged through the heaps of junk but found no flares. Of course, if Domingo had taken them, he could as easily have hidden them in the bush where they would not be found. If he had taken the flares and also destroyed Pablo's sign, what was the reason? What right did he have?

Ciara felt helpless as she paced the front room. She did not want to think that this man, this Domingo, held something sinister in his mind as she once suspected. If he was really deranged, maybe they were in danger somehow. But how? Surely if Domingo meant them harm, he had ample time to do something to any of them. She continued pacing and glancing at Rico. Each time she neared the doorway, she looked outside for Domingo.

Rico was restless. Ciara drew up some mats and kneeled on the floor next to him on the couch. She kissed him gently on the lips and on his cheek. "You're doing just fine, Rico," she said. "Rest when you need to. Someone will find us."

He opened his eyes, reached for her hand and clasped it, but had no strength. "*Yo te amo, Ci-Ci,*" he said, struggling to whisper. "*Tu eres mi vida…Pablito y tu.*"

"Yes, I love you too," she said, stroking his forehead. "This is our life. We're family."

Rico smiled weakly then drifted to sleep.

Chapter Eight

Sitting on the floor beside him, Ciara watched Rico sleeping. Her heart welled with great empathy. They were trapped in a horrible situation and somehow, she had to do more to make him better. She listened for noises outside and heard nothing. Domingo was probably off doing whatever it was he did when he disappeared each day. If she was going to do something to help get them back to civilization, there was no time like the present. She rose and headed for Domingo's back room. No person could live alone on this remote uninhabited island and not have a radio or some sort of communication. Someone supplied Domingo with his distilled water and other supplies. How would they know when he needed more and when to come?

Everything in the back room was covered with dust. She saw things she had not noticed before. Clothes and old blankets and lifebelts and boating equipment, everything, was covered with a layer of dust so thick it billowed into the air each time she moved something. The motor from the skiff was the only clean item in the room. It lay in a corner, torn apart, as if Domingo might have tried to fix it. One small box contained a couple pairs of shorts and several rumpled tee shirts. Evidently that comprised Domingo's entire wardrobe. She kept looking. Where might he hide a radio or some such equipment to contact someone? Still, if it were among all the trash that probably meant it would not work.

The only things Ciara found were some flares that must have been a decade old. They lay in a box, crumbling with age. Rico's flares were not among them. Nothing existed in that room that could be used to send a message in any form.

She paused wondering what to do. Domingo's life and they being caught up in it had her in a quandary. She sighed. She longed to wear something other than a bathing suit and a scratchy old rice sack for a sarong. Her attention went to the sarongs hanging limp and faded around the walls, then to the rest of the women's things, including sandals with decayed leather that curled up grotesquely. What woman could have lived here? Had she left Domingo? Why had she not taken her clothes? More than that, if anyone had died here, why had she or Pablo not found her gravesite during their wanderings. Covered with thick forest, not much of the island was clear enough to explore. Perhaps she was buried back in the forest and Domingo never went there again. Ciara reached up to feel one of the sarongs and it fell off the peg in flimsy pieces and into her hands. Dust billowed. She blew out a breath to clear the air and lifted a piece of the fabric gently with both hands and had to smile. The material and floral pattern had been a beautiful garment in its day.

When turning the fabric, she saw Domingo standing in the rear doorway! He had the strangest look on his face. His mouth smiled but the intensity of his glare said something was on his mind. Ciara's hair bristled. "Hello," she said nervously. "I'm sorry. I didn't mean to... I-I...."

Domingo crossed the room smiling and groping and making those strange noises in his throat. She screamed as he yanked the rice sack off of her and cast it aside. She fought to push him away but he pinned her to the floor as old metal clanked, rags fell and choking dust billowed. He stopped only long enough to hover over her and look at her again. Then he tried to kiss her.

Ciara screamed at the top of her lungs and pushed hard but he was too heavy. Domingo's wet lips were on her neck. His grip was relentless. She screamed again. He tried to force her legs apart with a knee. She fought and screamed again as he groped at her bathing suit.

Suddenly, she heard a crashing thump as something came down hard across Domingo's back. He flinched and drew in a sharp breath.

"*Deja a mi mama!*" Pablo said, screaming as he raised his father's walking stick into the air for another strike. "Leave my mother alone!" But with one mighty hand, Domingo rose up and shoved Pablo and sent him flying. "*Deja la sola!*" Pablo said, screaming again after landing on his bottom across the room.

The distraction was just what Ciara needed. Domingo had held her pinned to the floor with one hand. He had straightened up to swat at Pablo with the other. When he eagerly bent to come down on top of her again, Ciara swiftly brought up a knee.

Domingo recoiled, making pathetic sounds as he clutched at his groin. He tried to stand but fell to his knees moaning pathetically. Pablo came at him again with the stick and Domingo crawled away into the living room where he collapsed against the tree in the center. He curled up on the floor moaning with his hands between his legs.

Ciara had to act swiftly. She spotted a length of rope among the fishing gear in the corner of the living room near the doorway and managed to tie Domingo to the tree with his hands behind it. They would be safe for a while but how long could they keep him tied up? What would happen if he managed to get free? Would he understand that she was not to be taken for granted? She glanced at Rico whose head was turned toward the wall. He had not awakened and that was good. He did not need this situation to worry about. She and Pablo hurried outdoors. She needed fresh air to help her think.

After they had been outside a moment and talked but came up with no answers as to how to get off the island, they heard Domingo making sounds again. Only this time they were not the same. His moans sounded frantic, like he was horribly frightened. Ciara decided they had better check on him.

She stepped inside and strained to see as her sight adjusted to the dim light. Domingo's gaze was cast upward toward the ceiling. Then Ciara saw it and froze in her tracks. Pablo bumped into her from behind. A long snake with brown and grayish markings slithered downwards through the thatched roof of layered palm fronds. It made its way slowly as if it did not know where it was. It hesitated, turned upwards again, and then changed direction. Its forked tongue darted again and again sensing the surroundings.

Ciara crept farther into the room with Pablo behind. There was no time to get close enough to untie Domingo. Slowly, the snake eased its way down, twisting and turning and changing direction again and again. It was amazing how long the snake was as more and more of it slithered through the roof with its scales gleaming. Not a sound could be heard, not even Domingo's breathing, except the slow quiet drag of the snake's belly rubbing against the tree each time it advanced.

When Domingo saw the snake's tongue dart about eight inches from his cheek, he closed his good eye and froze. His chest no longer rose and fell. He had stopped breathing. Sweat poured down his face and neck. Then the snake wrapped itself around Domingo's throat as it coiled around the tree and came forward again and down over his chest.

Ciara had to do something. If this were not a poisonous snake, it would be easier to manage. Once it got to the floor, they might be able to shoo it outside or direct it with the stick. But could she wait to find out? People always teased about poisonous snakes in the Caribbean. Yet, she had never heard about anyone suffering from a bite, let alone having died. Supposedly, no poisonous snakes lived in Puerto Rico. But this was a remote island. After a bite from the most poisonous of Caribbean snakes, the fer-de-lance, the one bitten may begin to bleed from the eyes, gums, tongue, ears and even skin as blood vessels exploded. The venom was both hemotoxic and neurotoxic. She remembered the deadly serpent as having brown and grayish markings and that was exactly what this snake had! She had no idea what a fer-de-lance might look like. What if this snake got spooked and promptly sank its fangs into Domingo? This certainly was not the time to wait it out. Regardless of his bad deed, Domingo certainly did not deserve a prolonged fate worse than death. She had to act.

"Here, Mama," Pablo whispered from behind. Without looking away from the snake that took its time, she slowly extended her hand backwards expecting to receive the walking stick. Instead, Pablo placed the handle of a machete into her grip. She squeezed it firmly and a wave of thankfulness washed over her. Then Pablo eased to the side out of harm's way. With imperceptibly slow movements, Ciara positioned herself facing Domingo straight on. She lowered to a crouch and brought the machete up to striking posture.

The snake slithered over Domingo's shoulder and down his bare chest. How might it react if one of those droplets of Domingo's sweat fell in the wrong place? It slithered to the outside of his outstretched legs on the floor. Domingo fearfully opened his eye and watched the snake slide along the length of his leg as the rest of the body and tail slithered down his torso. The snake drew the rest of its body over Domingo's outstretched leg. Its probing tongue darted incessantly. The snake paused where it was. Domingo tried to move his other leg ever so slightly away and that set the snake in motion again.

Moving cautiously, the snake drew itself up over the leg and pulled the rest of its body between Domingo's flattened knees. It remained still momentarily, sensing and sensing, facing Domingo as droplets of sweat matted the hair on his chest. Then Ciara noticed it had pulled back on itself like a piece of ribbon Christmas candy. But there could be nothing sweet about that serpent. It looked ready to strike.

She would have only one chance to hit the snake behind its head as it swayed slightly, side to side. She hoped the long blade of the machete would not also cut into either of Domingo's legs. Ciara heard herself give out a blood-curdling scream as she lunged and brought the machete down.

The snake's head flipped up past her face and landed outside of Domingo's foot. The long body writhed underneath her as she held her bent-over position in front of Domingo. Then she straightened and yanked the blade up out of the floor where it had cut through the mats and sandy soil below. The snake's decapitated body writhed across her feet and between Domingo's legs as she stood trying to comprehend what she had just done. Domingo had not moved. Though numbed, she managed to step away.

"You did it!" Pablo said as he jumped up and down. "You did it!"

Ciara pointed to the snake's body. "Get it away from Domingo," she said.

Pablo grabbed the walking stick and pushed the head away. Then he was able to get the body draped onto the stick and carried it outside. He returned with a banana leaf onto which he coaxed the head and dragged it out the doorway.

She had to tend to Domingo. Surely, he would not try anything more with her now that she had saved his life. He could not be that ungrateful. His head hung to the side, his expression pleaded. Then, as she was deciding what to do, she heard Pablo talking excitedly out front in Spanish. Surprised, she looked to the couch where Rico still lay sound asleep.

Then Pablo burst into the room with both arms flailing. "*Mira, Mama!*" he said. "*Los hombres! Los hombres!*"

Chapter Nine

Ciara still stood with the machete poised in the air. She was astounded at having killed the snake and protected Domingo; numbed at the courage and tenacity that welled up from who knew where. The adrenaline rush that had helped her when she needed it most had filled her completely. As she glanced toward Pablo, she heard herself ask, "Men? What men?"

A tall dark figure of a man stepped into the doorway. From inside the shaded room, he looked to be nothing more than a silhouette against the bright sunlight outside. Ciara strained to focus. He eased a ten-pound bag of rice off his shoulder and dropped it to the floor in the corner. A second man carried a full jug of distilled water.

The men were American. The first extended his hand then withdrew it just as he saw the machete she still held rigidly in the air. As he carefully twisted the knife from her grip, he glanced down at Domingo, and then asked, "Why is this man tied up?"

Domingo wriggled and gurgled trying to free himself.

"He was hurting her," Pablo said. "He tried to hurt my mother."

"He tried to rape me," Ciara said quietly. She felt naked standing in her bathing suit as the stranger glanced at her body.

"I heard Mama screaming," Pablo said. "When I came in, he was on top of her on the floor, in there." He pointed to the back room. Then Pablo went into the back room and returned with her rice sack. He shook out the dust with a couple of sharp pops and handed it to her. She tied it around herself and squeezed Pablo's shoulders in gratefulness.

The American went behind the tree and began to untie the rope that restrained Domingo. "This man's a little whacko," he said, "but I don't believe he'd ever hurt anyone." Then he stood and glanced over his shoulder at Rico lying on the couch.

As soon as Domingo was freed, he bolted out of the room where he urinated forcefully right outside the doorway.

Once again the American glanced at Rico, who had not moved. He came to her again and offered his hand. "I'm John Patterson," he said. "Who are you and how is it you're here?"

"I'm Ciara Malloy. This is Pablo Rey. We lost our ketch in a sea storm," Ciara said. "We're stranded here." She motioned across the room. "Rico's hurt."

"Why were you holding the machete up in the air like that?" Patterson asked.

"The snake," Pablo said. "You saw the snake outside. Mama killed it. It climbed down that tree and down over Domingo. Mama didn't want it to bite him so she killed it."

"But you say he tried to rape you, Miss?"

"He was hurting her," Pablo said, adamant. "Mama was screaming. I heard her all the way down the beach."

"So how was this man hurt?" Patterson asked, motioning toward Rico. "How is it he was able to sleep through all that screaming you were supposed to have done?"

Ciara gasped. Why had Rico not moved? Had he heard, he'd have come to her rescue if he had to drag himself on his elbows. No matter how much he hurt, if she was in trouble, he would have come to her aid. "He must be unconscious again," Ciara said, rushing to kneel at Rico's side. "He has a bad head wound, a concussion, I think."

Patterson followed and bent down and examined the head wound. He grimaced, pursed his lips and drew air. Then he pressed two fingertips against the side of Rico's throat. He tried a different angle. Then he straightened and signaled something to the other man who had accompanied him.

"C'mon," the other man said to Pablo. "Let's go find Domingo."

After they left the room, Patterson went to his knees beside her. He leaned over to listen for Rico's breath.

"He's unconscious again, isn't he?" Ciara asked. "I tried to keep him awake. He's been awake and up walking for three days."

Patterson pulled back the soft old blanket. He watched Rico's chest. Then he placed a hand flat on the chest. Finally, he said, "Miss, I'm sorry."

"Sorry? Sorry about what?" Ciara asked. "You're here. Now we can get Rico the help he needs."

"I'm sorry," he said again. He wrapped an arm around her shoulder and sighed. "Miss, uh, Ciara, this man is dead."

The words echoed in Ciara's mind as if they had been spoken in another world and she had been privy to hear. She did not know quite how to respond. She could not move. Patterson tried to help her up but she was frozen to the spot. Finally, still on her knees, she leaned over Rico to see his face. He looked to be peacefully asleep. She tried to turn his face toward her. His bluish cast had cleared. When she cradled his chin and cheeks, he felt too cool to the touch. She gasped, slow and hard. "This can't be," she said. "He's just unconscious. We're going to be married."

"Miss," Patterson said, again taking hold of her arm. "Miss, he's gone, and has been for a while. His body's already cool."

She pulled her arm away and threw herself across Rico's lifeless chest. Her sobs came with uncontrollable breaths. All the dreams and all the plans they had made went out of her in the form of tears. Now they could never have that talk, never make their plans for a future. She stuck an arm under Rico's neck and halfway sat him up and cradled him and rocked herself with him and cried and cried until she felt hands trying to detach her from her betrothed. "This is my Rico," she said. "This is my husband."

Patterson brought her to her feet and held her gently. "I'm sorry," he kept saying. "I'm so sorry."

They heard voices outside. "Oh, no," she said, frightened. "Pablo. We'll have to tell Pablo."

Pablo burst into the room. "Mama," he said. "Domingo ran away. We can't find him." Then he saw her crying. "Mama," he said again. "What's the matter?"

Ciara rushed to hold Pablo. She cried again and clung to him. "Oh, Pablo," was all she could say.

"Why are you crying?" he asked. "We're saved. We can get help for Papi now."

Ciara could only shake her head. There was no time to gather her thoughts before breaking the news. No way to break the news softly and her throat felt closed. "Oh, Pablo, my wonderful son," she said. "Papi is…" She whimpered horribly.

"Mama, what is it?" he asked, looking toward his father.

Patterson remained silent and watched sympathetically. She took a deep breath.

"Pablo," she said as her voice wavered. "You're papi is gone."

"Gone?" Pablo asked.

She could only whisper. "He passed away."

"*Muerto?*" he asked defiantly. "*Mi papa esta muerto?*" He looked past her to his father who lay on the couch uncovered to the waist. When they had laid him back down, they accidentally allowed an arm to dangle to the floor. The sight of that limp arm must have driven the point home in Pablo's mind. His eyebrows pinched together. He did not say anything more. He tightened his lips and stood staring, barely breathing, with a horrible frightened glare emanating from his eyes. Ciara kept her arm around his shoulders. It was all she could do. Finally, Pablo pulled away and went over and picked up the arm and gently placed it across his father's midsection. When Pablo held his father's hand, strangely, Ciara noticed the fingernails were no longer blue. The nail beds were a pale whitish-gray. Pablo kneeled and pulled up the blanket, but only to Rico's shoulders, then continued quietly staring at his father's face.

"Miss," Patterson finally said. "Miss, I'm afraid I'm going to have to report what I've found here."

"What...?"

"My buddy and I are with the U. S. Navy on Vieques. On our days off, we come this way to bring Domingo and a few other remote islanders their supplies."

"The Navy?" Ciara asked. "I thought Marines...."

"Miss," he said, taking her by the shoulders. "We're with the Navy. We're going to have to report everything we've seen here."

"Report...?" Ciara asked. She barely heard what Patterson said and knew she was going to have to pull herself together. "Report what?" she asked.

"What we've seen here, okay? One man is dead of a nasty head wound and Domingo tied to a tree because you say he tried to rape you? And you with a wild look in your eye poised with that machete in the air above him? I'm sorry," he said again. "I have to report what I've seen."

"Find Domingo," Pablo said quietly. "Domingo knows."

Aboard Patterson's skiff as they maneuvered around coral outcroppings in the tide pool, Ciara vaguely remembered having traversed the area when it was dark. Then, they had been saved by Domingo and gratefully looked forward to being rescued and finally going home to Puerto Rico. Now it seemed that trip had been a lifetime ago. Racked with guilt, she wondered what more she could have done for Rico. Being saved had been a once in a lifetime miracle. Now, it had all been for naught.

In a short while they boarded Patterson's power cruiser anchored out in deep water. Ciara pulled the borrowed shirt close to her body. She hoped never to have to touch another rice sack. The drone of the old cruiser's engine was a little too loud. Patterson's old boat had been refurbished somewhat. Anyone who lived in the islands and loved the sea had a boat, even if it meant refurbishing someone else's cast-off. If it floated, it could be made seaworthy, just maybe not storm worthy.

She huddled inside the cabin and could not help looking back. Not so much as a whisper of a cloud hung in the sky. The sky was unblemished baby blue, the sea exceptionally flat and the sun brilliant. Patterson's powerful cruiser cut a wake so deep the horizon disappeared before the water smoothed again. Rico's life had ended somewhere back there. So had hers.

As they headed toward Fajardo, Ciara watched Pablo sitting at his father's side on one of the cushioned benches out in the sunlight. Pablo refused to allow anyone to pull the blanket up over his father's face. Occasionally the breeze would gust and Pablo would push back the hair off his father's forehead.

Patterson climbed down to the deck and stopped momentarily watching Pablo who seemed oblivious to the fact that Patterson stood nearby. When he joined her, Ciara asked, "Just how is it you happened to be taking supplies to Domingo?"

"Our usual routine, sort of," he said. "Some people found him over ten years ago after his boat went down in a similar kind of storm."

"Him, too?"

"Yes, and I have a theory about why he assaulted you, if he did, in fact, do what you claim."

"He did," she said flatly. All her enthusiasm seemed spent. "He was so strong, he would have torn my elastic bathing suit right off me," she said as she yanked the shirtfront tighter closed. "Pablo hit him hard with a stick. I know you don't believe me, but—"

"Okay, okay, but listen to this," he said. "That storm you folks were in. That storm knocked down with such a fury, well, two other families are still missing."

"Oh, no," Ciara said.

"So you're lucky to have washed up where you did," he said. He took a seat beside her.

"We're lucky you came to check on Domingo," she said. "But I wish you could have come sooner." Tears streamed down her face.

"We had no way of knowing anyone was there," Patterson said. "The Coast Guard's doing the search for those missing people. Actually, I just learned on the radio that a child, maybe a young boy, sent out a distress call a few days back."

"A young boy?"

"Yes, his message kept breaking up. Something about a sea storm," Patterson said. "When they tried to ascertain his location, all he knew was Culebra or east of Culebra. They lost contact before they could ask the child his name. Could that have been your Pablo who made that call?"

Once again, Ciara was astounded by Pablo's tenacity. "He must have tried to use the radio when he was down inside the cabin, while his father battled the fire that claimed the sails." She could only shake her head.

"Whoever sent that mayday helped the authorities zero in on the eye of the storm," he said. "One day we'll have more sophisticated equipment that will tell us in an instant." He gazed off in the distance, deep in thought. Then he added, "This is the first of three days off for me and my buddy. We figured we might as well bring Domingo more supplies while we're participating in the search."

"You make these supply runs out of the goodness of your heart?"

"On our days off, me and my buddy have a shuttle service to some folks out here," he said. "Mostly fishermen like Domingo used to be. Domingo's family pays for the service, like everyone else. But let me tell you this. Domingo lost his family, too, over ten years ago."

"In a storm just like us?"

"His wife and brother and sister-in-law all died. By the time the authorities found a very battered and infected Domingo, his brother's wife's body had already washed up and he had buried her back up off the beach. Once they finally located her, the sister-in-law's family came to claim her remains."

The picture was all too gruesome and too real. She tucked her legs up under herself on the cushion and huddled inside the large shirt. "And the others?" she asked.

Patterson shook his head. "Domingo was never mentally right after that. They had to fight him to bring him to San Juan to stitch him up. They said his wound was so infected." Patterson grimaced. "Afterwards, he went looking for that island again before he had healed. Must have ripped out his stitches himself. Over the years I've learned that he believes his wife will come back."

Ciara gasped. "So he thought I was his wife? And maybe Rico his brother?"

"Just since we've known him, we've watched his mental capacity deteriorate. That may be why he tried what he did with you. He might have thought you were his wife finally returned. Your accident brought it all back to him."

"So that's why he was so attentive in the beginning. He treated Rico with such care, thinking he was his brother?" The last three days' activities paraded through her mind.

"It fits. He thought you were his wife. You've seen that back room," he said. "The pieces of china and stuff?"

"How do you explain that?"

"All stuff from his wreckage that washed up. Plus a lot of other peoples' lost belongings, I'm sure."

"He must believe he can put his life back together again," Ciara said as she shook her head. Feeling sympathy for Domingo was relief from her personal grief.

"Poor man. His mind's all but gone. I'm sure he ran and hid because he thought we'd make him leave the island now that he'd found his wife."

"I feel sorry for him," she said. "He was a fisherman?" Surely that was how he was about to catch the fish that he did for their meals.

"As I understand it, he was the most sought-after fisherman who supplied most of the major San Juan hotels with daily catch. He had a booming business."

"Then his entire life changed when his boat went down," Ciara said. The storm had changed hers and Rico and Pablo's lives, and the lives of those still-missing families as well.

Patterson gestured toward Pablo, who had not moved from his father's side. "He seems to be taking it well," he said. "I heard him tell his dad in Spanish that he knew he was in heaven. He asked him to watch over you both."

"I'm worried about him now," she said. Pablo had never known his mother. That fact had been what triggered her to be the mother he never had, for him, for Rico and for her own surprisingly strong maternal instincts. "Losing his father hasn't sunk in yet."

"That young man has a lot going for him," Patterson said as he pointed to his temple. "Kids can be quite resilient, but take it one day at a time, at least for the kid's sake."

"You don't understand," Ciara said. "He's not really my son." Then she began to cry again. "But I love him."

"He's this man's son and you were to be married? That's why he calls you Mama?"

"Yes," she said. "But now there'll be no marriage and Pablo will go to other family. I'll never get to see him again."

"Miss, I hate to say this again," Patterson said. "But my job is with the U.S. Navy. I have to report what I saw back there. There'll be an investigation."

"It doesn't matter," Ciara said. "I've lost Rico and Pablo. I've lost everything."

Chapter Ten

Pablo unlocked the front door ahead of her. A stack of smooth new boards for the remodeling lay on the porch floor near the outer wall; a finished interior door ready to hang leaned against the far wall. Sawdust littered corner spaces.

Pablo was trying to come to grips with what had happened to his father. His mood had become somber and stayed that way, holding in his emotions. In time, Ciara might have to help him let go to let himself grieve. If they had that much time left together.

Each time she entered Rico's home without him, she felt a sense of having betrayed him. She needed to sleep in the house to be close to Pablo, but doing so promoted the same feelings of deception. Especially as she lay in Rico's bed, the only other one in the house. Although she felt close to him as she lay on the side of the bed where he had slept, it did not make sleep come any easier. It was all so confusing. She could no longer sleep in her cottage at the rear of the yard. How often she had waited there in the dark for Rico; waited and watched through the jalousies as he worked in his office into the night. Knowing he would never again steal across the yard meant she would sleep alone forever. So, if without him, she would rather sleep in his bed.

Just as she was about to step through the doorway, she heard the front gate squeak.

"*Hola*, Senorita Malloy," a roly-poly man said as he let himself into the screened porch behind her. He pulled at his collar and sidestepped gallons of paint stacked in waiting. Nearly every time he drew a breath, he quietly wheezed. He was definitely uncomfortable in the heat of the day. It had not rained to cool things down. Though it wasn't necessary, he handed her his business card. Juan Lazaro-Vidal had been Rico's business attorney and personal friend.

Pablo stuck his head out of the doorway. "*Buenos dias, Senor Lazaro,*" he said sadly.

"*Hola, Chico,*" Lazaro said.

"Please come in," Ciara said as she shook his hand. She led him into Rico's office in the spare bedroom at the back of the house. Pablo clung by her side. "I want to thank you, Lazaro," she said, "for handling the funeral home and getting them to hold up on proceedings till we look at Rico's will."

"Si, Senorita Malloy," he said. "But have you seen Rico's trust?"

"His what? You mean his will?"

"Si, si. But it's not really a will. It's a new document called a Trust. Have you seen it?"

"I've never seen any of Rico's papers," she said. "They're probably all in Spanish anyway. You'll have to translate for me." She only vaguely understood Lazaro through his heavy accent in spite of him being fluent in English. Knowing they had a lot of documents to review, she excused herself to make coffee while Lazaro spread out the contents of his briefcase across Rico's desktop.

After the revitalizing aroma filled the house, Pablo brought the coffee and demitasse cups and saucers into the office using a large serving platter for a tray. As he placed the tray on the edge of the desk, he said, "I know where Papi's papers are, Mami." He pointed to Lazaro's black folder with the title showing through a plastic window in the cover. "Papi's got one just like that. It's in the bottom drawer of this filing cabinet." He bent to pull open the drawer. "Those are the papers Papi said to look at first if anything happened to him." Then Pablo must have realized his father had been preparing him for his later demise, not knowing how quickly it would happen. Pablo looked as if he might cry. Then his lips tightened and he stared at the floor.

Ciara went to him. "You were right then, weren't you?" she asked, putting her arm around his shoulders. Pablo had been adamant about delaying funeral proceedings until Ciara had looked at his father's papers. She bent down and rummaged through the drawer of files till she came to the label with the title "Trust" written on it. The folder was much thicker than the half-inch black binder that Lazaro had produced. She pulled out the entire file and brought it to the desktop and sat down.

They began to compare each document for dates and other validation to assure each had a matching copy. Pablo hung against the side of her chair. He had never been more than a few feet from her in the day and a half since they returned safely to San Juan. He had even begun to call her *Mami*, just as he had called his father *Papi*, instead of Papa.

"Pablo," she said. "Can you give me some time alone with Mr. Lazaro, so we can find out exactly what Papi wanted us to do?"

"Can't I stay?" he said, pleading. "He's my papi."

Ciara's heart ached for this child. She was the only family he had at the moment and she did not know if Pablo realized he would be sent away as soon as relatives could be located. That might mean sending her son back to Cuba. Her stomach convulsed at the thought. Pablo clung to her. She did not have the courage to break the news of their impending separation. It would be better to learn where he would be sent before saying anything. She clung to the idea that she had had him as her son for a short but very fulfilling time. She would keep him as long as she could. She felt tears welling up. "Please give us some time to go through these papers, Son, please?" she asked.

Pablo remained stoic standing beside her. Then he began to whimper. He reached for her and his height made it difficult to hold him to comfort him. Finally, he eased himself into her lap and began to sob. That was what he needed to do.

She held him tightly against her shoulder and even encouraged him to cry. "That's my boy," she said. "Get it all out." She held him tightly and rubbed his back as he wept against her neck. "It's okay to cry," she said. "Crying heals us." Tears streamed down her cheeks as well.

Lazaro squeezed his round body out of the chair and stood, then paced. Then he quietly stared out the window and dabbed at his eyes with a handkerchief.

Pablo's storm raged until Ciara began to wonder if a child could have a nervous breakdown. Then, all at once, he took a deep breath and stopped crying. He wiped his eyes, squirmed in her lap to face her, then pressed his hands against her shoulders and looked her straight in the eyes. "That's all," he said. "That's all I'm going to cry."

"But it's okay to cry," she said. "Anytime you need to."

"No," he said. "Papi told me men don't cry much. So I'll never cry again." With that he wiped his eyes once more, regained his composure and eased himself off her lap. "I'll be in here if you need me," he said as he left the room.

Ciara sat quietly stunned while Lazaro blew his nose. Pablo's actions seemed too abrupt. She did not want him to stuff his emotions deep inside and later manifest in some psychologically harmful manner. Already he was trying to be the man of the family but he needed more time. "I'm going to lose Pablo, aren't I?" she asked.

"It's your decision," Lazaro said as he smiled strangely. He stuffed his hand-kerchief into his pocket, and squeezed himself into the chair again as his belly pushed against the desk., Then he found one particular packet of papers from among those he had brought. "This is a guardianship document," he said.

"Guardianship?"

"Let me explain. Rico covered all aspects of what was to happen to Pablo should he—Rico—not be around to take care of the boy." Lazaro began to unfold the document pages.

"He really loved him, didn't he?" Ciara asked.

Lazaro's serious glance hinted at more. "This document awards you guardianship over the boy should anything happen to Rico."

"Does that mean I get to keep him? Rico trusts me with his son?" Emotion and gratitude and love welled up again, as well as understanding of just how deep Rico's love for her extended. "Where do I sign?" she asked.

"You'd better wait," Lazaro said as he squeezed her hand briefly. "Let me ex-plain. The guardianship document places Pablo into your care. It says here...." He searched the paragraphs then pointed with his pen. "Pablo will be placed into your guardianship and you have sole custody, care and control for an in-definite period of time. It says that Rico does not wish his child returned to Cuba but that you are to use your own discretion and conscience and to search for Rico's sister and ex-wife." He looked straight into her eyes. "Pablito does have a mother, Senorita," he said.

"And if I don't find her, what about his Godparents? He was christened in Cuba, you know. One way or another, I will lose our son, won't I?"

"Forget the Godparents," Lazaro said with a wave of his hand.

"What?"

"Look here," he said as he pointed to another paragraph. "This document says the Godfather eventually became sympathetic with Fidel Castro and that Pablo is not to be returned to the Godparents unless it's the last resort."

"But can we override the baptis—"

"It goes on to say that Rico gives you a choice of accepting the conditions or you can refuse. I'm sure his only concern through this document is that Pablo receives the best care and direction the situation allows."

"What happens if I can't sign," she asked. "How can I accept temporary guardianship of this child, all the while having to locate family to send him away?" She lowered her voice to a whisper. "I'd have to find Pablo's mother. Lazaro, she abandoned him when he was an infant. How could I send him to that poor excuse for a woman?"

Again, Lazaro's glance had that strangeness in it and was beginning to un-nerve her. "If you don't sign," he said, "then custody of the boy goes to me. And I will have to find a home to put him in until I locate his mother."

Ciara swallowed hard. Allow Pablo to be placed into a foster home? Never. Back to Cuba? Never. But maybe back to his mother? She sighed heavily. Rico trusted her. But Rico wanted to raise his son in Puerto Rico. Somehow, regard-less what it took, she was going to see that Rico's wishes were carried through. "Where do I sign?" she asked.

Curiously, Lazaro pulled the document away. "There is much to learn," he said. "Let's examine all the papers before you sign anything, *esta bien*?"

Lazaro next explained that Rico had chosen to utilize a relatively new method of bequeathing his holdings to his heirs. That was what a Revocable Trust was all about. "A will can be contested," he said. "Rico had to know that what he wanted done could not be ripped apart in probate. A trust prevents that from happening."

"I've never heard of a-a Revocable Trust," she said.

"It's a new form of passing your estate to your heirs," he said. "Just now legally catching on."

Lazaro's words sounded suspiciously like a prelude of things to come. En-velopes pulled from Rico's file folder lay on the desktop; envelopes that had been mailed then returned by the Post Office unopened. Several of them were addressed to the same person at different addresses. There was also a list of names and addresses of people she did not recognize, each one checked off, many more than once. An insurance policy was still folded with a string bind-ing it. A stack of medical papers lay underneath it all.

Ciara's curiosity needed to be satisfied and fast. "I understand I'm to lose Pablo," she said. "Lazaro, give me the gist of Rico's trust information so I'll know what Rico wanted done. Let's get through these other papers."

Lazaro sipped his coffee but stared straight into her eyes, another prelude of things to come. "Well, first of all," he said, "you need to know about Rico's holdings, his properties."

"I already know," Ciara said. "He was remodeling this house and cottages. He had almost finished the house that I helped to design, you know, out in Valle Arriba Heights? I guess he was going to put it on the market when we returned from...."

Lazaro smiled sadly. His head hung to the side. He evidently knew more than he could explain in one breath. He opened his copy of the trust and began to explain. He told of half a dozen other properties in Santurce, Old San Juan, Rio Piedras and Caguas in which Rico maintained part ownership. Lazaro would now see to the selling of Rico's interests and the funds would be placed in trust for Pablo. Rico had numerous bank accounts and an investment account. "Those accounts are to be turned over to you," he said.

The lengthy list of Rico's holdings was staggering. "To me?" Ciara asked.

"To help support the boy," he said. "If you accept guardianship."

"Oh," she said. Certainly Rico would not have used money as an enticement for her to keep Pablo.

Lazaro smiled again, touched the side of the coffeepot and then refilled his demitasse. "*Ay, Chica!*" he said as he sat the pot down. "I don't know where to begin."

"You mean there's more?"

"Si, si," he said, shaking his head. "Many things you never knew. I can tell by what you say."

"What don't I know?" she asked. "I knew Rico better than anyone. Well, maybe you knew him better."

"What I'm saying is that he prepared for you and for Pablito."

"For Pablo," she said. "That's all I ask."

Lazaro smiled again. "Open it," he said. "*Por favor*, the insurance policy."

Ciara hesitated then timidly began to pull at the string around it. She opened out the thick document and handed it to Lazaro.

He flipped through the pages till he found what he wanted. "*Aqui esta*," he said. He leaned closer so she could see and pointed as he explained. "This is a one hundred thousand dollar double indemnity life insurance policy."

The amount was startling but that was all she understood. "Double indemnity?" she asked. "Doesn't that mean they pay double?"

"Providing death is accidental and not from suicide."

"Well, good," she said. "That's a lot more for Pablo's future."

"Not Pablo's," Lazaro said. He looked at her in that peculiar way again. "You are the beneficiary, Senorita."

"What?"

"Pablito is well taken care of," he said. "We'll get to that. This money is for you, free and clear of any obligations."

The tears came easily. "He did this for me?" She remembered having, at times, doubted his love when she couldn't pin him down to a wedding date. How foolish she now felt.

Lazaro briefly placed his hand on top of hers. "You were to be his wife. He loved you."

"I'll do something in his memory," she said. "I'll make sure the world never forgets him."

"I'm sure you will," Lazaro said, again with that hint of mystique. Then he said, "Senorita, that house in Valle Arriba Heights?"

"What about it?"

"It is yours," he said quietly.

Had she heard right? Is that what happened when a person died? The heirs got whatever the departed owned? "I'll sell it," she said, "put the funds in trust for Pablo."

Lazaro frowned and shook his head. "Senorita," he said again. "It was to be your marriage house."

"My... my... what?" she asked, stunned. Now Ciara knew why Rico had involved her in all aspects of the design of the house. She had been hoping to work in this manner alongside Rico when they were married. She had been offered a new creative outlet and loved designing that house. Rico had given free rein to her ideas, and all along, unbeknownst to her, he had involved her so that she would get a house that she loved. That must have been why working on that house always made him smile. That must have been what he had planned to tell her when they sailed. She covered her face with her hands and whimpered.

She needed to excuse herself from the tension and went to find out why Pablo was so quiet. She found him sitting on the floor in front of the TV. He had turned down the sound and his eyes stared blankly without seeing. When he heard her, he simply looked up and half-smiled, then pretended to watch TV again. She stooped beside him, hugged him and kissed the top of his head.

She wondered what further provision Rico had made for Pablo and how much time she might have left with him.

"Don't cry, Mami," Pablo said. "Papi said crying is unnecessary."

She nodded. "Okay," she said. Yet, she had a feeling this would not be the last time that she would shed some tears. After regaining her composure, she went back into the office.

If it were not for the fact that Ciara already knew Juan Lazaro-Vidal as a kind and patient man, somewhat methodical and slow, she might have already lost her temper with him more than once. The look in his eyes said there was much more to come and waiting to hear more, which may not be positive news, more than aggravated her. Ciara did not like having to follow through with Rico's last wishes. He was supposed to be alive and with her so they could live out their lives together. That was all she ever wanted. Now Rico was dead; Pablo would be sent back to a mother who did not want him, and she would be left to soothe over her loss with two hundred thousand dollars and an empty house. Were shattered promises to be her legacy of life in the tropics? No money or worldly possessions could compensate the losses. Lazaro could tell her nothing more that would make life right again, but from the look in his eyes, he had much more to disclose.

Chapter Eleven

Ciara needed to rummage through Rico's accumulation of old papers and find a way to locate any of Pablo's living relatives. Anticipation of having to deal with the tightening red tape strangling Cuba filled her with a sense of dread. Fewer and fewer people were being allowed to leave that island country, but what an irony. Now she would have to see that Pablo was returned. No one dared return to see family members left behind for fear of being prevented from leaving again, or thrown in jail for having left the first time. Someone actually returning to Cuba would be a first. Pablo's mother had left Cuba with her lover. Ciara found some solace in the thought that Pablo could be sent the United States instead.

Lazaro touched her hand gently and brought her out of her pathetic reverie. "There's more," he said. Then he sighed heavily.

"What more?" she asked. "I know what I have to do. Rico also had a sister he never talked about. Help me find her—"

"Senorita," Lazaro said. "There's a reason why he never spoke of her."

"You know about her?"

"Si, si. She had breast cancer," he said, motioning to both sides of his chest. "Her illness was too advanced so I don't know if she's living or dead. It was years ago and now Fidel Castro has cut all communication with Cuba." He waited a moment, and then said, "You see those medical papers there in front of you?"

Strange that she had always thought it was the United States that cut ties with Cuba. Rico had said once that any Cuban citizen who chose to leave would not be allowed contact with loved ones and could never return to Cuba without facing imprisonment. But she could not concern herself with that right now. "Yes?" she asked, looking at the documents.

"They're from the boy's surgery years ago."

"Oh yes, his stomach."

"You've never seen them before?"

"Lazaro, please. I've not seen any of Rico's personal papers. I know Pablo had an emergency appendectomy."

"That doctor butchered him."

"Anyone can tell that by looking at that damned scar."

"Did you know that Rico was able to get a big settlement from the doctor's malpractice insurance?"

Ciara was surprised. So that was why she had been listed as beneficiary on the life insurance policy instead of Pablo. Rico never mentioned any settlement, but then, it was something Rico would not talk about, at least not till they had a chance to discuss more details about their lives. Surely the money had been put aside in the trust he had established for Pablo. Rico had made solid plans every step of the way. He had such an ability to foresee all aspects of a situation.

Lazaro touched her hand again. Only this time, he stopped her from digging farther into the pile of papers. "Senorita," he said cautiously. "The rest, what you're about to learn, may come as a shock to you."

"What else could shock me, Lazaro?"

He only frowned and rubbed a hand thoughtfully across his brow. "I'm afraid...," he said.

"What could be worse than Rico's demise, Lazaro, and me losing Pablo? Let's get this over with."

"Si, Senorita," he said again. "If you'll allow me to explain and I'll show you on these papers as we go along."

"Okay."

"See, here are the papers of Pablo's surgery," he said as he pulled the pages from the pile. They looked like a doctor's medical records. "But look here. There is reference to Pablito almost dying when his appendix ruptured. He needed a transfusion."

"How did Rico get these? I thought medical records were always sealed."

"Not when there's a legal case. Both attorneys get copies. Anyone can get their own records," Lazaro said, flagging a hand as if to dismiss that bit of news as unimportant. "You just cannot get records that are not your own."

"I see," Ciara said. She sat quietly waiting. It was all she could do.

Lazaro pulled still more pages out of the pile. "These are the blood records," he said, pausing again. Then he said, "*Ay, this is muy dificil.*"

"Everything will be difficult for a while," she said. "Please, Lazaro, let's get through this."

Then it was his turn to gather his thoughts. Finally he began again. "Pablito had to have blood. They made tests before they could give the transfusion." Beads of perspiration broke out on his forehead. He took a deep breath, then said, "Pablito's blood didn't match his father's type."

"Well, his blood wouldn't be exactly like his father's," she said. "Don't you agree? He would have some of his father's and some of his—"

"Senorita, listen," Lazaro said.

Something in his eyes told her she might not wish to hear what he was about to say, but she had no choice. "Go ahead, Lazaro. What else could you possibly say to me?"

"The blood," he said again. This time he glanced toward the living room then lowered his voice. "Pablo's blood did not match his father's."

"I guess I don't understand what you're saying."

Lazaro stood. He paced. The waiting was nerve racking. Finally he came close to her and bent down placing the knuckles of both fists while leaning over the desktop. In a whisper, he said, "Pablito is not Rico's son."

Ciara nearly fell out of the chair. She clutched the edge of the desk. "How dare you!" she said. She rose, went to the door to the hallway and closed it. "How dare you!" she said again.

Perspiration ran off Lazaro's forehead. He picked up some medical pages. "Si, si, Senorita. I am sorry. It is true."

"The medical records are wrong!" she said through clenched teeth. "Rico raised Pablo by himself nearly from birth."

"Si, Senorita. He did that. And he loved the boy with all his heart."

"How dare you, Lazaro!"

But still, Lazaro picked up some of the unopened returned mail. He found the divorce documents. "Read here," he said, begging and pointing to the envelopes. Sweat fell in droplets onto the papers. "Here is the wife's name and the addresses where the mail was sent and returned from. *Mira, por favor, aqui esta.*"

Ciara looked and read, "Amalia Marcos-Flaminio." It was returned from Atlanta, Georgia and stamped with the single word "Refused." Another with the same notation was returned from Mobile, Alabama. Another from Florida with the notation "Forwarding Order Expired." Another returned from New York, that one stamped "Addressee Unknown." Her hands shook. "Why would he try to find his ex-wife?" she asked.

"See the divorce decree?" Lazaro asked. "See the date?"

She looked. "Yes," she said. "The date is about a year after the time Rico said they separated."

"And the date of the first returned letter from Georgia?"

"Almost two years after the divorce. What does that prove?"

"He was able to contact her as long as she wanted the divorce. She signed the divorce papers in Georgia." Lazaro quickly flipped to the notary information on the final page and made sure she read it. "Years later, when he tried to find her to tell her about Pablo, she eluded him."

"That's what these letters are? Him trying to find her to tell her about Pablo?"

"Si, si. In my *officina*, I have copies of the letters which are here, inside, un-opened."

Ciara looked again at some of the postmarks. "He was trying to find her even after we met," she said.

Lazaro paced again. "It is true," he said. "She is the mother of the boy, born when she and Rico were still together."

"She deserted Rico and Pablo—ran away with the neighbor. Rico told me all that."

"Yes, with the neighbor, with whom she had been having an affair for years. No one knew how long." He looked at the floor and shook his head. Finally, he looked up with tears in his eyes again and said, "The boy is from the mother with the other man." He picked up and waved the unopened letters in the air. "To this day, the mother does not know."

Ciara whimpered. Slowly, the entire scenario came into focus. Rico needed to get away to talk because he had so much to say. That was what he tried so many times to tell her. He wanted her to know everything before they married. Rico knew how much she loved Pablo and how much Pablo adored her. The truth had to be known. That would be the only way Rico could marry, because he and Pablo began their life together as father and son and he intended that they would finish it that way. By the time Rico found out that Pablo did not carry his blood, it was too late. Rico's love for Pablo, like his love for her, was irreversible. She smiled sadly, her vision blurred by tears. "Rico must have rejoiced at not having found his ex-wife and at being able to keep Pablo," she said. That would have been the greatest secret of all that he would have disclosed to her aboard the Mercy.

Rico had made an honest effort to find Pablo's mother. He must have endured unthinkable emotional pain. After his mail was returned, he had dropped the search, kept Pablo and allowed their love and respect for one another to deepen. What a man Rico had been. What a totally wondrous human being.

Numbed, Ciara went through the rest of the paper work with Lazaro translating. The final stipulation of the trust was that Rico wished to be cremated and his ashes held to eventually be scattered over his parent's graves once Cuba was opened for visitation. Lazaro's words again about Rico's sister probably having died filtered in. Then Lazaro was leaving. He took her by the shoulders and pressed his face to hers, first one side, then the other, kissing each cheek. He shook hands with Pablo and patted the top of his head. At the doorway, he said something about returning later in the day after the autopsy was completed.

That evening, Lazaro returned as promised. All his emotions showed on his face. He sat on the sofa. When Ciara asked Pablo to leave the room, Lazaro thought Pablo mature enough to hear the autopsy findings and asked that he stay.

"Okay," she said. "Rico's head wound was just too much, right? Without medical attention, his concussion got worse instead of better?"

"Didn't you tell me Rico was up walking around for three days?"

"He was."

"Well, he didn't die from a concussion," Lazaro said. "He had a mild concussion but, in fact, his head wound had been healing nicely."

"Then what took him from us?" Ciara asked. She did not remember Rico having any other wounds. He had no broken bones. During the three days he walked around, the only thing he suffered from seemed to be an inability to draw sufficient breath, and exhaustion. After what he had been through, he had the right to feel tired.

"He got water in his lungs, si?" Lazaro asked.

"Yes," she said. "But he didn't drown. For a while in the water, he was unconscious, and then revived."

"They found much salt in his lungs."

"Papi had his face in the water," Pablo said. "We blew our breath into his mouth and he revived."

"Si, si. Then seemed okay?"

"That's right," Ciara said. "But, Lazaro, that didn't kill him."

"I'm sorry, Senorita," he said. "It did, in a way. The doctor called it 'secondary drowning.'"

"Lazaro, I don't believe he drowned. He just got a lot of water in his lungs."

"Let me try to explain the way the doctor said it me." He scooted forward to the edge of the couch and used his hands to gesture. "Once a quantity of salt water gets into the lungs, the person can feel okay for a while, maybe a few days. Then they feel tired. They can't get their breath."

"That's what happened to Papi!"

"Si, si. They can't get their breath because the lungs are filling with body fluids. They cough. The breath is very labored. The body turns colors.

"Rico was bluish!" she said. "His nails too."

"Si, si. Then the body makes liquid in the lungs and tries to wash out the salt and the liquid makes it hard to get oxygen. As a result, the person drowns in their own fluids."

"You mean Rico's own body killed him?"

"In a way."

Ciara felt guilty. "Why didn't I know? I could have helped him?"

"Not much is known about secondary drowning, as it's called," Lazaro said. "But with more and more people spending time in the oceans, more research is being done."

"Research? I've never heard of secondary drowning."

"It's a relatively new term. Nothing is known at this time. The researchers are doing experimental therapies—respiratory therapies—to learn how to make a person—what you say—expel fluid from the lungs?"

"If we could have known that, we could have saved Rico."

"It's only in the experimental stages. Till now, many people die from this thing, this secondary drowning. There was nothing you might have done for Rico—"

"We could have tried," Ciara said. She stood and paced. "Why wasn't this research made public?" she asked angrily. "We could have tried."

"They are only now, in the 70's, doing research. Little is known yet."

She could not reason it out. Try as she might, she had to remain strong and face the facts. Nothing she could do would bring Rico back to her. Now she knew how families of terminally ill patients felt when loved ones die only a short time before a cure was announced.

Several hundred people, most of whom Ciara had never met, attended the wake for Rico. With Cubans still considered the outsiders and not wholly accepted by many Puerto Ricans, members of the tight-knit Cuban community always turned out in support of such serious affairs. Lazaro's wife miraculously organized the entire proceeding, all of which Ciara endured in a blur. She would not have known to whom to turn and was grateful. Pablo clung to her side.

Out of respect for the throngs of friends who needed to see Rico one final time, Ciara consented that he be placed in a coffin for viewing even though he was to be cremated. He lay in the elaborate masculine coffin with a multitude of floral arrangements and wreaths seeming to dwarf the area of the coffin. Ciara and Pablo sat near the head of the coffin. A large close-up photo of Rico, with his magnificent physique trimming the sails of the Mercy, stood on an easel near the foot of the coffin. The throng of friends paraded past to pay last respects. Some kissed their fingers then pressed them to Rico's cheek. Some wailed in Spanish and cried while others whispered condolences as they hugged Pablo and her.

Lazaro and a photographer stepped forward. Ciara and Pablo stepped aside so Lazaro's friend could photograph Rico in his coffin.

Pablo tugged at her hand and gestured with his eyes in the direction of the doorway. A pale middle age American man looking out of place entered the crowded church.

"Daddy!" Ciara said as she ran to him. She collapsed against his chest as Pablo came up behind and took her hand again. Feeling Pablo's grip was all that kept her from collapsing.

"My God, Ciara," her father said. "You've been through hell."

She swiped at her eyes. "Daddy," she said. "This is my son... uh, Rico's... uh, our son, Pablo."

"So this is Pablo." He offered his hand but then embraced Pablo as well. Then they walked forward to the coffin.

Her father whispered, "I'm sorry I haven't been more active in your life, Honey. But you up and moved so danged far away."

Ciara could only stare at Rico's face. "This is the last time I'll ever see him, Daddy," she said as her voice broke.

While Ciara's father spent time with Pablo, Ciara endured the next two days struggling to translate all the paper work to decipher what Rico needed her to do. Lazaro came again. She wondered if she could live up to what Rico expected of her, especially now that her life was falling irreparably apart. Not having had knowledge enough to save Rico's life threw her into near helplessness. Or perhaps the lack of focus came from the fact that today was the day Rico's body was to be cremated. No last look. That happened at the wake. The next time she would see him, he would be handed to her in a handsome, yet cold, lifeless urn. Eventually when Cuba opened to visitors, someone was to take the ashes to scatter over his parent's graves outside Havana. She determined it would be her and Pablo.

She had no choice but to face the fact that she must go on without Rico. Nothing could change that. She determined to remain strong. If she lost Pablo, too, then every last contact with what Rico stood for would be gone. She was the mother who had raised that boy for the last four years, the only mother Pablo knew, and the first child she truly loved. Was she to be stripped of everything in one damnable swoop of fate? She and Rico had doted upon Pablo and made plans for their future together. Did everything have to cease so abruptly? Could she not carry on in Rico's absence? "Of course I can," she said, feeling a surge of anger and rage, quickly tempered with determination. "Of course I can!"

"*Que es...?*" Lazaro asked, showing surprise at her excitement.

Ciara rose and went to the living room and stood in the doorway watching Pablo sharing one of his books with her dad. Pablo turned his head slowly when he realized she was nearby. She smiled for the first time in days. She was onto something as the memory of Lazaro's subtle remarks nudged at her conscience. His demeanor said he would support her regardless of her decision. Waves of excitement washed over her as her emotions careened up and down. Everything had been left to the dictates of her conscience.

Ciara went to Pablo and hugged him tightly. She could not explain to this child that she might become embroiled in a legal battle to keep him. She needed to help Pablo understand so that he would not live in fear of what was to come. She, herself, did not know what that might be, but they needed to enjoy their time together and, somehow, seal the bond they shared. Perhaps if she knew that Pablo would love her always, as she would him, it would make permanent separation bearable, if that was possible. Tears spilled out of her eyes. She could not help but feel the pain. Her father watched sympathetically. She had an idea that slowly made her smile again. Though her idea was astounding, she could not muster much enthusiasm about being separated from this child whom she so loved.

"They want to send me back to Cuba," Pablo said as tears filled his eyes. "Don't they?"

She pulled away and looked him in the eyes. "Not yet," she said. "But promise me something." He waited and stoically wiped a tear before it fell. "Promise me that if they take you from me, promise me that one day when you're old enough, you'll come back and look for me."

"Can't you come to Cuba too?"

"I cannot, Pablo. But promise me you'll come. I won't go anywhere. I'll stay right here in Papi's house and wait for you." The idea brought both sadness and joy that welled up together until she thought she could no longer breathe.

Pablo's chest heaved but he would not allow himself to cry. He looked straight into her eyes. "I promise, Mami," he said. "I'll come back. I promise."

The choice was totally hers. Pablo deserved to live the lifestyle to which he was accustomed; the one for which Rico strove so diligently to provide, at least, until she located Pablo's mother. However, Rico had worded the guardianship stipulations in a manner that left everything to Ciara's conscience. Only she had the discretion of searching for the unconscionable Amalia Marcos-Flaminio who had not in all the years contacted Rico, if only about the welfare of the child that she bore. Into what kind of a stunted life would she be sending this wonderful child, with a woman who cared not one iota about his well-being?

Had Rico intuited all possibilities so much as to include the one with which she was now faced? Had he left the wording open to interpretation because he hoped the woman in his life or the guardian would understand the callous nature of the child's mother and not return him to such a person, or to his Godparents-turned-Communists? Had he written in just enough so that if little or no effort were made to return the boy to his mother, some social services do-gooder group would not hold the guardian accountable? Could Rico have really thought that way? Had he inadvertently set up the ultimate challenge of proof of her love? Had he knowingly covered all bases that assuredly?

Ciara hurried back to Rico's office. Lazaro looked at her curiously. "I won't ever have children now," she said. The words stuck in her throat.

"*Que*, Senorita?"

"Where's the Guardianship document?"

"Senorita?"

"Where?" she asked again as she began to rummage through the papers. Lazaro pushed it across the table to her and she found the last page and signed her name and dated it.

Lazaro looked stunned, but also relieved. "I'll sign as witness," he said and did so. "You realize this will have to be finalized in the courts, Senorita?"

"Get it through, Lazaro," she said. "Please. It's what Rico wanted."

Two days later, Ciara's father returned to Colorado with a promise to visit as often as possible.

Pablo announced he was ready to go back to school.

"Are you sure you're ready?" Ciara asked. "It's going to be rough."

"Papi wanted me to study hard," he said. "I'm going to study hard. I want to grow up to be just like Papi."

The weekend before school was to commence they went for some private time on the mostly deserted Luquillo Beach out past the Isla Verde Airport on the way to Fajardo. Rico had appreciated the remote area frequented only by locals. He also knew that in the years to come, Luquillo Beach, as well as all of Puerto Rico, would feel the pains of growth and expansion. He had looked forward to playing an active role in sensible, controlled modernization.

Ciara's new bathing suit was a respectable one-piece, the kind Rico preferred instead of those pushup bra-type bikinis that were becoming skimpier and skimpier. The color was white with splashes of dark blue and magenta to match the colors the Mercy wore. She and Pablo sat and spoke only occasionally. It had not rained since the light nighttime showers passed.

Pablo wanted to walk by himself. For a while he kicked at sand drifts and picked up fallen coconuts and angrily heaved them off the beach and into the bushes. Ciara remembered how upset he had been at having his H-E-L-P sign obliterated when he intended for someone to see it from the air and come to their rescue. Surely he felt as helpless as she did.

Pablo angrily heaved coconuts into the brush and spoke vehemently saying things she could not make out from the distance. But it was not too long before he stopped abruptly. He loved to dig in the sand and always came up with beautiful conch shells with brilliant pink interiors that had washed up and been covered with sand by the tides.

Pablo found one, but he would not return until he had at least one in each hand. Those shells were discards from the sea and no longer alive, so he had no qualms about claiming them. Their backyard attested to that. Finally, he returned with two large ones and a third smaller one and placed them on the beach towel beside her.

"That one's you," he said. "The biggest one is Papi." He curled up his lip. "That small one is me, I guess." His usual elation was not there. He smiled sadly and then walked down the beach in the opposite direction.

Ciara drew up her knees and hugged her legs and stared out to sea. A deeper sadness crept over her. Somewhere out there a little to the southeast, Rico lost his life. She laid her head on her arms and her chest heaved with anguish, but tears would not come. She would not cry again unless her loss was total. Rico loved the ocean and she realized how being near the sea made her feel close to him. He had fished off the dark rocky abutment that jutted out into the water nearby. Many times, they fed their sandwiches to the birds when his fresh catch became their pan-fried lunch. Now she watched Pablo atop some rocks. So what if Pablo was not of Rico's blood? He was every bit Rico's son and she saw Rico in Pablo's mannerisms as he pretended to throw out a line like his father had when fishing. It made her heart thankful.

She studied the four-carat diamond engagement ring Rico had given her. Sunlight danced from its infinite depth. She had found the two-part matching wedding ring with its brilliant bevy of surrounding baguettes and now wore that too. In her mind and heart, she was forever committed to Rico. In her soul, they were married.

The memory of Rico's last words filtered in and she heard them as if he had just spoken. *Yo te amo, Ci-Ci*, he had said. *Tu eres mi vida... Pablito y tu.* "I love you too, Rico," she said, whispering the words toward the sea. "Yes, we are your life, and you will live through us, Pablito and me." This was her legacy of the tropics but life was not over yet.

They had stayed too long on the beach. Evening was upon them. The Coqui began to sing as shadows lengthened, and the plagued mosquitoes began to bite. She looked for Pablo and called him to her. They ran toward each other and when they met, she dropped to her knees and they hugged.

"I love it here," Pablo said. He dug his toes deeper into the sand. "It's the beach that Papi liked the most. Can we come here again?"

"Yes," Ciara said as understanding filtered into her mind. "We can come as much as time allows."

Ciara rose from the sand. New resolve filled her. She would see that Pablo always remembered his father. She wrapped her arm around his shoulders. His arm slipped around her waist, and side-by-side, they stood quietly gazing out over the sea.

Adrift

Chapter One

"People die at Keʻe Beach, Lillian," he said. "Why do you keep going back there?"

She forced herself to remain quiet a moment longer than usual to quell an urge to put Glen in his place. "Careless people," she said, enunciating each word, "die at all beaches." Then she remembered how many people had been having accidents and floating up dead at that particular beach.

Lillian Avery sometimes crossed her fingers and secretly prayed that life would remain peaceful for a while. Many close calls and a couple of unexpected near-death experiences in the past made her wary, though she would not let Glen know that. Those experiences had served to hone her senses. She simply saw them as markers along life's way, on her way to making her long-standing dreams come true.

For the past year, she had made her home in paradise and considered herself one of the fortunate few to reside on the lush garden island of Kauai in Hawaii. Her secluded acre in the Wailua Homesteads made an exemplary statement of the lifestyle she chose in which to complete her metamorphosis. She loved the constant mild temperatures, being surrounded by water and having views of the ocean from a distance on one side of her home, with mountains and waterfalls like ribbons for a backdrop on the other. Lilly felt secure falling asleep with windows open while listening to the tropical downpours that occurred at the thousand-foot elevation during the night.

On her newly acquired property, that included a rambling three-bedroom island house and guest cottage she teasingly called her villa, Lilly planted a variety of tropical fruit trees and flowers.

Much of the island's fresh organic produce was available from inland farmers in a different town each day. The local-style markets took place in parking lots.

Tubs and crates spilled over with tropical fruits, vegetables and flowers vended from the backs of pickups and vans and usually sold out in an hour.

Fresh fish could be had from local fishermen who sold their catches from ice chests along the roadsides. Once in a while she got lucky happening upon a hukilau at a beach. Anyone who helped haul in the net was always given a share of the catch. Although not an expected reward, this show of gratitude for the help was an everyday part of island life.

Lilly adjusted her needs to what she found around her. She cast off most of her frivolous desires and lived simply, having decided everything she needed was no farther away than a five or ten-minute drive. About the only reason she might leave the island would be to shop in Honolulu on neighboring Oahu for necessities not available locally. Sometimes she chose to simply go without.

For recreation, she hiked the trails that enabled her to explore remote regions of Kauai, like the *Valley of the Lost Tribe*. She had created the lifestyle she dreamed about for so long. But the security of repose could not dispel her adventurous nature. A lifelong fascination with sea life always led her to the ocean.

"What is it with you and water, Lil?" Glen asked. "I thought you were an all-around sort of person."

Her hair always bristled when he called her Lil. She had been Lillian or Lilly all her life and had not so much as implied permission to use a nickname. Glen's habit was to assume certain liberties until convinced he was overstepping bounds. At times it seemed to take forever for him to see the light, even when bluntly told, but she found no lure in becoming his mentor.

Glen was one of the first guys she met after settling on the island just over a year ago. He appeared attractive to her, but his appearance was deceitful and the relationship went nowhere. At least he turned his back on the Maui-wowie crowd and was not a gigolo like most of the men that had crossed her path over the years. Her friends said those men had all been attracted to her strength. Somewhere out there was a nice man for her who would respect and support her need for independence. Lilly was fairly certain that Glen was not that person.

At her insistence, he acquiesced to removing his shoes before entering her house, as was the custom in Hawaii, adopted from the Orientals. He probably had the iron-rich red dirt stains on his own carpet from wearing shoes indoors. Yet, the way he acted, heaven forbid he should see a speck of dust in his house.

Now he stood barefoot inside her living room, wearing designer shorts and a polo shirt, razor-cut wavy brown hair, manicured nails and presenting an image of perfection that took a lifetime to perfect. But that was all it was.

"I make my living in the ocean," she said. "This all-around person has the rest of her lifetime to experience this corner of heaven."

She really did not owe him an explanation and felt uneasy about why he questioned her passion. She never understood what was going through his mind and his life. He never talked about his hopes and dreams, as if he had a mysterious life going on that he kept secreted. One thing she knew is that he had never learned to share himself. She determined that this was one day his elusive nature would not throw a damper on things.

"You've gone swimming nearly every weekend since we met," he said. The tone he used with such simple words made them sound negative.

"I'll probably continue to do so till I've tired of every last beach on this island," she said. "That's *if* I tire....". She was letting him get to her in spite of her vow.

She wore her swim suit and was ready to go. She tied a blue batik print pareau over the suit with a decorative knot over her chest. The gathered folds fell loosely open to her knees. As she ran her fingers through her new short curly haircut, she noticed Glen scrutinizing her. He would have preferred she look more like an island girl and let her hair grow very long like dancers in a hula halau. Had she allowed her hair to lengthen, along with dark eyes, the tan and staying slender, she might have looked more local. But such coquettishness was best left to the young. The amount of time she spent in the water almost demanded short hair. What difference did it make? She had not yet allowed a man to dictate her image and she was not about to let it happen now.

"C'mon," she said, grabbing his hand, trying to coerce him into relaxing a bit. "I want to show you something."

"What now?" he asked.

Lilly dragged him down the hallway toward the back door. "Something I've just finished," she said.

"If we're going out back," he said, "you know it hurts my feet to walk barefoot outside. Let me get my sandals."

She sighed and waited till he retrieved the footwear from outside the front door and carried them through the house.

They stood on the patio under the reaching arms of a decades-old Royal Poinciana tree. In the summertime, the branches would be weighted to the ground with voluminous leaves and red-orange blooms. The detached garage was to the windward side of the acre with a covered breezeway between it and the main house. Lilly had turned the adjoining tiny one-bedroom cottage beyond the garage into her hobby studio. She thought again how she would paint the interior walls with underwater scenes, much like she had decorated the cottage where she lived in Puerto Rico.

It was curious how she once lived in a guest cottage on someone else's property in Puerto Rico. Now here she was on a different island, owning property with an adjacent guest cottage and herself living in the "big house." The thought made her smile.

On the opposite side of the lot, clumps of torch ginger, heliconia, pikake and yellow allamanda, planted by the home's previous owners, followed the rock wall around to the front yard. Lilly had the entire sloping back lot landscaped into knolls and swales for a decorative effect and proper drainage.

"Where are we going?" Glen asked.

"To the creek," she said, as she padded barefoot past her fruit trees, strategically planted to best catch needed sunlight. She paused at the banana grove. Spice smells drifted up from the nearby herb garden along the lava rock wall. The rosemary scented the air all year. Trees and varied species of plumeria and ginger growing wild on the adjacent land, combined with her newly planted blooms, turned the air into breathable ambrosia. She waited for Glen but he had not followed. "I thought you'd want to see the focal point of the back yard," she said, calling to him.

"You mean that bench and Japanese temple statue?" he asked, pointing toward the corner.

"Is that all you see?"

"You did some decorating out here too?"

"Come see the stream. Not everyone has a stream to play with on their property."

The stream meandered out of the forest on the adjacent undeveloped rear acreage. It cut across one back corner of the lot, disappearing across the next acre behind a severely weathered plantation house. All her fruit trees stood opposite the stream in the far corner. She could spend time by the stream in sunlight or shade, any time of day.

Glen stayed where he was but lifted up on tiptoes. "Oh, a footbridge," he said. "Do you really need a bridge to get across that shallow ditch?"

"I don't believe I'm hearing this," Lilly said. "I've installed a beautiful Japanese garden out here. Don't you feel the peacefulness of the setting?"

He looked at her as if he thought trying to sense a certain feeling was hokey. "A lot of people have these gardens," he said.

She rolled her eyes and looked up at the sky. How could he be so all wet without ever getting into water? The world was full of good men. Why had she not been able to attract one of them? "It is going to be a wonderful day," she said to herself.

As she walked back toward the house, Glen watched. His eyes flickering toward the sun then back to her body. "You're such a lovely shade of bronze," he said.

Of course, he would notice that. Though he frowned upon her pastime of swimming and snorkeling, catching sight of her bathing suit under the loose pareau excited him. Somehow his logic did not do a thing for her.

"Where's your bathing suit?" Lilly asked. She was only poking fun at him in a subtle way and knew he wouldn't answer because he would never wear one. She headed back toward the house.

"Your property's almost finished," he said. "You'll need another project."

"Got one," she said. "Come February, my vegetable garden will go in right about there." She pointed over near the wall beyond the herb garden where climbing Purple Passion bougainvillea honored the sun with a profusion of blooms. "I want to be as self-supporting as possible," she said.

"At least your projects keep you mostly at home. If you were a public person, I'd never get to see you."

"Wha-at?" Lilly asked. "How I spend my time has nothing to do with your schedule."

"Lilly, what I meant was," he said, pausing, evidently conjuring an excuse for his blunder. "The way you throw yourself into a project, if you had a job or something during the week, your hobbies would take up the weekends and I'd—"

"Not... on... your... life," she said. "I'll be swimming more than just weekends once I've got my land the way I want it. My time will be devoted to underwater photography. That's the work I do and I don't plan to retire as long as I find enjoyment in the sea. I also plan to take scuba lessons."

"Scuba? With your ear problems?"

"Never know until I try," she said.

"That'll be a first. You've already admitted to never having formal swimming lessons or ocean instruction." He shrugged. "You ought to get married." The mention of anything that personal always took her by surprise. "Let a nice guy support you," he said with a sheepish grin. "Pay someone else to do this work in the dirt."

Lilly never found much reason to become angry, but now ire was beginning to press its way out from deep inside. "Don't ever say that to me again," she said. "You're living in the past, Glen Mackey. Lillian Avery is a woman of the New Millennium. I've never been prey to the myth of shining knights on white horses. So don't even think of parking your rusting suit of armor in my closet."

He laughed. Did he think she was making a joke? The way he saw it, by the time a person was their age, they should be able to pay for a housekeeper and other help to perform laborious duties. Like he could now afford, so he would not have to strain himself.

Glen's effort at subterfuge had never been more evident, seeming about to erupt like a silent pernicious sore. The thought of him or anyone trying to cajole her into being more accommodating turned her stomach queasy.

She walked back into the house. His footsteps paused as he held the door open while removing his sandals and letting in a few flying pests. Would he never learn?

Resentments take up too much space in the heart, her mother had said. Just move on. Her mother had always been right. Lilly was not about to let this casual friend ruin her day.

Chapter Two

Glen threw the footwear outside the front door then came back and sat down. Out of the corner of her eye, Lilly watched him pull his toes apart and look at an area rubbed raw by the strap of his new rubber beach sandals. She was surprised at having convinced him they were better to wear in the sand than were expensive loafers, and they got him out of always wearing socks. She fumbled through a kitchen drawer and came up with a small Band-Aid and offered it to him.

"Whatever happened to hiking, local studies at the library and all your other interests?" he asked as he meticulously applied then reapplied the strip.

She bit her lip to ward off any influence of him being unable to see the positive side in anything. That remark was Glen's way of hinting he would like to do something other than sit on the beach and wait for her, but what would he offer to do? Sit on his patio and fall asleep? Sometimes he fell asleep on the sofa, never mind making it to the patio. Or he would suggest they sit under a gazebo with a cool drink at some resort, watching others swim in a chlorinated pool.

When they met, she told Glen that she was a swimmer and that was the main reason she moved to Hawaii. Surely if he had other interests he would have participated in them by now. In the six months they had known each other she had never discouraged his interest in other activities. They enjoyed the beginnings of a friendship, but no way was she going to allow him to attach to her like a shadow.

Lilly began to suspect that he tagged along to make sure she would not bond too closely with anyone else with her similar interests. That kind of possessiveness was not allowed as far as Lilly was concerned. What was he afraid of? He never openly addressed his fears and probably hoped being quiet meant never having to deal with them. Surely at times, he seethed inside. His inaction and superficial conversations were a dead giveaway. Lilly had not entered the friendship to provide shelter for his muddle of irrational apprehensions. They were going to have to address those issues, and soon.

"You don't like hiking," she said, reminding of something he had already made clear. "Or drawing or painting or photography. What activities do you enjoy now that you've retired?"

Seeking a mate was not the reason she moved to Kauai, though the wish for a loving companion did linger in the back of her mind. Something always felt lacking in her life. The type of men she met never eased the persistent inner prompting, perhaps only concealed it or kept her too busy to address her feelings.

"I'm retired," he said, smiling, "and not in a hurry to get involved in anything."

Certainly Glen, too naive to perceive her yearnings, could offer no appeasement to a need she, herself, had not fully identified. She had been aware of her repressed feelings a long time, but one thing she could never suppress was that she was happiest around water. Whatever her life's purpose, it had to have something to do with water.

"As a child," she said, "did you ever swim? Take lessons… whatever?" Santa Cruz, where Lilly grew up, had a great beach. But without a reef and something more exciting than waves, it had not been conducive to snorkeling, of which she, even as a child could not get enough.

"Water's not my thing," he said.

Well, it was hers. In the late 1960s, when the overflow of hippies from San Francisco's Haight-Ashbury district spilled down the coast and into Santa Cruz, the man she hoped to one day marry fell prey to the counterculture. When it seemed all her hopes and dreams dissipated into thin air with his marijuana smoke, she took that as her cue to leave. Living with free love and staying high was not a lifestyle she could embrace.

Seeking a better beach led her to the dazzling white sands of the Caribbean and the move changed her life. Lilly had been happy during the years she lived in Puerto Rico and enjoyed the warm Caribbean waters. She inadvertently discovered a sense of fulfillment having begun to photograph wonders beneath the sea, creating pictures that were very much in demand and which sold island wide, especially among the tourist trade.

With her pictures in tow, she visited children's wards in hospitals, convalescent homes and classrooms, even homes of the poor whose shanties along the rivers and streams had mud floors. She talked about life in the ocean, as much as a snorkeler and amateur photographer came to know. They enjoyed her storytelling and laughed with her as she learned to speak Spanish. To the poor and sick, she gifted spectacular blow-ups of her casual photos. It was her way of providing a firsthand glimpse to those who could not venture into the depths. Enjoying her exciting hobby of photographing wonders beneath the waves became a way to bring a lot of light into the lives of those less fortunate.

"Glen, why not try charity work?" she asked. "There's a lot of reward helping people not as well-off."

"I don't have anything to offer along those lines," he said.

Years later, after returning home to care for her aging mother, Lilly began vacationing in the Hawaiian Islands. The experience filled her with a similar sense of renewal that came over her when she lived in the Caribbean.

"What about hospice? You'd be helping others who have little hope."

"I don't think I could deal with people dying around me," he said, grimacing with a shudder.

After her mother passed away, Lilly began to get that gnawing feeling of something missing again. She needed to do something to make her life worthwhile. No longer having commitments of any kind, the Hawaiian Islands beckoned.

Now blissfully settled on Kauai, she finally felt at peace. A yearning to go some place new no longer existed. She had grown wise enough to realize whatever purpose or inner appeasement awaited would happen wherever she found herself near water, in spite of rude awakenings like a friendship dangling in limbo.

Glen had been fun when they were first introduced at a mutual friend's party. Now it seemed parties were all he looked forward to, activities where he could wear the fine clothes he had worked so hard to afford, and where his feet could be planted on terra firma and he could remain in control as he did his furtive little dance called "rubbing elbows."

"I do enjoy reading," he said.

"At least you're getting some fresh air when you read by the ocean," Lilly said, smiling politely. He always looked too neat for a day of letting one's hair down at the beach.

The more time she spent with Glen, the more his presence began to be deflating. With him, she felt adrift yet restrained, like a ship dragging an anchor with broken flukes. Yes, they would have to deal with their issues if they were to continue seeing one another.

Actually, she wished he would make an effort to get over his fear of water, get therapy and put an end to his claustrophobia and myriad other hang-ups. The better she got to know him, the more she realized they had little in common. He was a gentle soul though, but only because his life created many hesitations to protect him, he could hide no other way than to be nice. Both she and Glen were in their mid-fifties, too old to harbor hang-ups that drained vitality. Life was too short to settle for only the secondary gains of clinging to fears.

"I enjoy the picnic too," he said.

"You don't have to go," she said, smiling. "Surely you have something else you wish to do."

"We've discussed that," he said, waving a hand.

"It would be nice to have you in the water with me," she said testily. "I could teach you about the fish and—"

"You know I don't like water," he said stiffly. He always glossed things over, never explained himself so someone might be able to provide encouragement, maybe help him further understand himself.

"Listen, Glen," Lilly said, still encouraging. "Every kind of exotic fish and water creature known to the Islands can be found at Ke'e Beach reef. Moray eel, crab, coral."

"That's what you keep saying."

As she crammed things into her beach bag, she picked up a page-sized plastic card bearing pictures of all the species of colorful reef dwellers. "I've seen almost every one of these," she said. "Did you know that one third of the hundreds of fish species found around the Hawaiian Islands are found no place else on earth?"

He glanced around her living room and dining area. Enlarged copies of her photography of different sea life hung strategically placed to compliment her island style decor of hardwood floors, blond bamboo furniture and floral print fabrics copied from 1930's and 1940's designs. Framed smaller photos sitting on miniature easels complimented the collection of exquisite oriental vases. The smaller pieces all shared space inside a locked koa wood cabinet that also held her mother's green floral funeral urn.

"What will you photograph once you've seen them all?" he asked.

"That's just it," Lilly replied. "I'm not even close to photographing them all. It's easy to get sidetracked following just one fish and trying to find a good angle." As excited as she became with each new species she identified, it was easy to stay in the water too long. "If I don't get good shots at the moment," she said, "I'll may never find that perfect specimen again."

"Yeah," he said. "But once you stayed in so long, your hands completely shriveled."

"That's what lotion's for," Lilly said, again smiling, but noticing how deep Glen's fears had seeped. How could he look so together and yet be so full of hang-ups? If he thought she would stay in the water only a few minutes at a time in order to save her precious fingertips from shriveling, he had a lot to learn about dedication.

"Now you've found the Pacific Green Sea Turtles," he said in a tone that implied yet something else to keep her occupied.

"Oh, yes," she said. "The Honu." That same surge of excitement rolled through her as when she first saw those magnificent creatures.

"That ought to be good for a few weekends," he said, half-smiling.

"Listen, Glen," she said, "I've snorkeled for decades and made a living selling my photographs." She sat down beside him. "My first experience with fish was thirty years ago when I was in the Virgin Islands off Tortola. A flat round Rainbow fish hung in the water about twelve feet below, completely without fear of curious humans. It had to be fifteen inches in diameter!" She gestured with her hands, showing him its size. "That was quite a remote area during the sixties. That fish probably hadn't been harassed to make it apprehensive. It hung in the water and watched me as I swam down. It made no effort to dart away. When I got close enough, its skin was even more scintillating from the sun streaming through the crystal clear water."

"And from then on, you were hooked on fish," he said, showing little interest and failing to recognize his pun.

Lilly smiled anyway. "That fish was so beautiful," she said. "To think such wonders exist beneath the waves."

"You can have 'em," Glen said, waving her off. "The ocean's too rough, especially this time of year."

What on earth was he doing on an island? She would have to handle the situation tactfully, but she certainly would not allow someone else's shortcomings to hold her back. He chose a long time ago to deny his issues. She had nothing to do with his choices or their causes.

"I listen to the surf reports," she said, smiling, upbeat and reminding him of something he already knew. "At the very least, I know enough not to panic in the water." His fear of water prevented him from acknowledging her enthusiasm and capabilities. Then she remembered being busy in her garden and not having tuned in the surf reports since the prior weekend.

Quickly, she calculated from something she remembered having read. If high tides returned each day approximately fifty minutes past the previous day's high, since last Sunday—seven days—that would place the next high tide about five o'clock that afternoon.

"Remember that guy who washed up dead at Ke'e Beach a while back?" Glen asked, intruding into her concentration. "Tide was calm that day, too, but look what happened." He paused only a moment. "Listen, couldn't we go to another beach that's a little more sheltered?" he asked. "No offense, but you're not the strongest... well, accidents can happen to the best of swimmers out there in deep water."

Chapter Three

They stopped for breakfast in the heart of Old Kapaʻa Town at a cozy eatery owned by one of Lilly's many friends. Rose looked at her sadly as she walked in with Glen. That was the same expression Lilly received from everyone when they saw her with him. Had Glen already been on the island so long that everyone knew him and felt the same about him as she was beginning to feel?

Usually, Glen would not dine at quaint local restaurants. He preferred the sterile coffee shops and dining rooms of the luxury tourist hotels. He would really get dressed for an occasion like that. Never mind that the rest of the patrons were mostly tourists who wore shorts and tees.

While waiting for breakfasts of crepes and fresh tropical fruit, Lilly stared out the French doors that opened invitingly onto the narrow sun-washed street. Area business owners had painted their buildings in bright colors and trims. Occasionally, tourists or a local resident or two would amble along looking into the windows of shops.

Across the street at a tiny hole-in-the-wall java hut, customers sat on weathered wooden chairs and benches in the front garden, basking in sunlight. A couple of people read newspapers. Young surfer dudes hung out with their boards, waiting to hear where the waves were best. Silence was broken by an occasional passing car or two or by the pounding of the surf beyond Kapaʻa Beach Park at the end of the block. No one moved about quickly. Old Kapaʻa Town, especially on a sleepy Sunday morning, held a certain charm for Lilly. Kapaʻa was part of the perfect setting in which she wanted to live the rest of her life. Peacefully.

Once on the road again, sunlight became brighter and with it came humid heat. Lilly drove with the windows opened, no longer having long hair to become snarled in the frantic breeze as she cruised along. Occasionally, a dark rain cloud passed over. Glen would always raise his side window and turn on the air conditioning. He had just done that again, reached over and flipped the air on high because he expected rain. She felt a familiar irritation seep into her thoughts again.

They skirted Anahola and passed where the dairy used to be in the area of Moloaʻa before Kilauea. The pungent odor of cows that used to hang in the air had disappeared.

Many times, Lilly used the dairy as a marker to direct acquaintances and an occasional tourist to various locations on the North Shore. She had to smile. Islanders gave directions according to the proximity of the ocean or mountains or what building or roadside marker might be along the way. She found herself doing the same thing one day. She gave directions to Omao Road, saying it was the second left on the *makai* side, the ocean side of the road, just past the turn-off to Kalani's nursery. Never mind the nursery was on Punee Road. Everyone knew Kalani's nursery, so no need existed to identify the road by name.

"Keep your eyes open for papaya trees," Lilly said. "Guava too. I brought my picker." She nodded toward the collapsed back seat where she kept the long pole with a net basket on one end.

Glen's expression soured. "You're probably stealing someone's fruit," he said, complaining about yet something else. Actually, he detested picking wild fruit, especially along the roadway. He said it made them look poor to passers-by.

She knew he disliked the textures of mango and papaya and did not much care for the taste of guava, pink or yellow. Yet, he relished the puree she had made from YV, the yellow miniature guavas. He surprised her once, eating them right off the tree, just like she did. Maybe there was hope for him.

"Honestly, Glen," Lilly said with a smile. "All this wild fruit is available for anyone to pick just like the wild flowers. Why do you think they call this the Garden Island?"

"You'd think you have enough fruit trees in your yard," he said.

"My trees are too young to bear fruit," she said. "So until they do, when I see any kind of tropical delight, I'm stopping."

"One of these days, you'll find yourself in trouble on someone else's property."

"Give me a break, okay? The shoulders along public roads are county easements."

"What will you do when all your own trees fruit at once?" he asked.

They drove past Kilauea and in a few minutes arrived at the downgrade of Highway 56 just past Kahiliholo Road. The area was one of the special places that drove home the reason why Lilly loved Kauai. "Took this forest over five years to heal from Hurricane Iniki," she said.

Glen barely glanced up. "Yeah, yeah," he said. "Watch your driving."

His elbow rested against the window. He clung to the handgrip above the door and stared straight ahead at the pavement. He always claimed she drove too fast, but she thought that was because he moved too slowly. She always drove when they were together because she didn't want to crawl along at twenty miles per hour.

From out of the thicket of low-lying shrubs and Cajeput paper bark trees, the feathered, far reaching branches of Albesia trees nearly touched from both sides of the road, well over seventy feet above. The forest was such a lush deep green. Descending the grade, with the mist-shrouded mountains of the Halelea Forest Preserve looming ahead in the distance, was like dropping into the base of a secluded paradise all its own.

They headed downward past the observation lookout over Kalihiwai River and Valley. Mountain water run-off in a one hundred-foot waterfall, crashed onto large lava rock slabs near the road on the *mauka* side. The flow ran under the pavement and gushed over the lower cliffs on the makai side. From another spectacular downfall, it fed into the Kalihiwai River below and to the sea. The peacefulness of the area always made her draw in a long breath and let it out slow and smooth.

Most of the island's scenery had that affect on her. It did not matter if she was up on Crater Hill viewing the mile high Mt. Waialeale and entire north shore to Bali Hai or looking down into the bottom of Waimea Canyon from up near Koke'e State Park. She would hold her breath momentarily, and then let out a long sigh of satisfaction. No matter how many times she might see the same mountains and valleys, the same ocean views, she would always look forward to the next time she might set eyes upon them.

Soon, they were nearing Princeville. "Wanna stop at the lookout?" she asked.

"The taro fields in that valley have looked the same for several hundred years," he said. "We've already seen it."

"You've got that right," Lilly said, trying to stay upbeat. "Fortunately, most residents are conscious of preserving the island's character and qualities."

"Well, they exploit them to tourists who pump dollars into the flagging economy," he said, raising an eyebrow. He would know about the financial end of things. Glen kept track of the economy and all the political and social news around the island, but being retired and not frequently mixing in those circles, Lilly wondered why he needed that type of knowledge. He never so much as discussed anything he learned and would seem thoroughly irritated when she tried to elicit his opinion.

She, in any case, respected the temperament of the island haven. She read everything she could about the natural qualities of Kauai, including some information about the rip currents and tides in most of the local swimming areas and around the Pacific Ocean. Yet, all those statistics about longitude and latitude may as well have been a foreign language. Lilly did not have a good sense of calculating.

Raindrops splattered on the windshield. She turned on the wipers when it seemed the shower would last more than a few seconds.

"Hope the rain doesn't spoil your plans," Glen said.

She saw nothing but sunlight up ahead. "A little shower never stopped this swimmer."

At times since their meeting, conversation could be strained. At other times they might talk at length if they happened to hit on a topic both were in the mood to discuss, but never had they been completely at ease with one another. This was probably all she could expect of their friendship and she was not about to dwell on such things today.

Armed with a library copy of Ernest Hemingway's saga The Old Man and the Sea for company during rest periods, she planned to snorkel to her heart's content and photograph life beneath the surface of the sea on and around the colorful coral reef. Glen would spend the day reading and napping in the shade. That was a long time to be immobile. She wondered how he got enough exercise.

They made their usual stop at the first shop along the road in Hanalei advertising snorkeling equipment rentals.

"You're renting again?" the friendly young clerk asked. "You could have purchased new equipment by now."

Lilly needed to buy a new set of gear. Sometimes rented masks were not airtight and five or so miles of winding cliffside roadway were just too far to backtrack to get a replacement. More than once, she had to make do with the equipment she rented. "Guess I'd better stop putting off the necessities," she said. "After I learn to scuba, I'll invest in new photographic equipment too."

The clerk leaned close so her boss would not hear. "You should at least be renting where they credit your rental against the purchase price," she said, whispering.

"I've been too busy working around my house to shop," Lilly said. "When I'm working in my garden, it's all I care about. So I end up putting things off." She rolled her eyes. Lilly knew she had fallen into the habit of putting things off. Sort of like the procrastination that permeated the dispositions of most people needing to shed a hectic life.

"It's two to three today," the clerk said. "You still going out to the turtles?"

"Two or three foot waves never bothered me," Lilly said, smiling nicely. "Have you snorkeled Keʻe?"

"I've been on this island eight years," she said. "Every time I hear about another person drowning out at Keʻe…." She shook her head. "I'll swim at waveless Anini or maybe the tide pool at Lydgate Park, thank you."

"Go to Keʻe in the summer," Lilly said. "When the water's mostly flat. Tunnels Beach is good too. There's no reef or much sea life close enough at Anini."

The clerk shook her head slowly. "Labor Day's long past," she said, offering another gentle warning.

Tides usually changed after Labor Day. The surf got rougher and swells and surges were the norm. She remembered hearing that somewhere or maybe reading it in all the detail she studied about the ocean's ebbs and flows and the globe's tilt in relation to the pull of the moon. She had also located a great site on the Internet that published that type of information. Early September was the height of the hurricane and typhoon season happening through the end of November in the South Pacific and along the coast of Asia. That would continue to strongly affect currents along the Hawaiian archipelago. At those times, it was dangerous just being in the shallows.

Lilly offered her credit card to secure the rental and then someone came close behind her.

"I'm going too," Glen said.

Lilly jumped in surprise at hear his voice. When she turned to see what he meant, he stood holding up snorkeling gear he had chosen. "But you've never snorkeled," she said.

"C'mon, Lilly," he said. "I've vacationed in other resort areas."

The clerk glanced questioningly between her and Glen. "Okay," Lilly said. "But you take care of yourself. I'm going to do my work and won't be around a lot."

"I guess I should give this island a try," he said nonchalantly.

Something told her that he sensed they were drifting apart and sharing her activities would be a gesture to stave off the inevitable breakup.

"What about a swimsuit?" she asked. She never knew him to bring one and hoped he hadn't.

"Underneath," he said, pulling at the waistband of his shorts. "Even brought a tee shirt. It's in my book bag."

First Lilly frowned. Then she smiled secretly as she signed the rental slip. After all of Glen's complaints about getting into the water, he must have known all along that he would one day try. Perhaps he had always worn his swimsuit under his shorts. Maybe it just took him a long time to convince himself to do something. Anything.

Chapter Four

Lilly witnessed the effect of a Pacific typhoon on Kauai about two months earlier, before the last drowning victim floated up. In late August into September, Typhoon Bing passed over Guam and skirted Saipan. Quite unpredictably, it cut a sharp northeasterly turn, missed Japan and headed toward Alaska where it died out over cooler waters. During its course, the waters of the Pacific, all the way to Ke'e Beach and along the entire group of Hawaiian Islands, had been so churned no one could swim. In addition, the winds had been peculiar.

Lilly had not swum that day. She went into waist high water and was immediately washed down toward the reef's end. That was the closest she came to swimming in *Puka Ulua* channel, which swimmers were warned to avoid and where the strong undertow swept out to sea. She ended up nearly dashed against the lava rock wall bordering the channel. Strangely, instead of waves lapping to and from, the current ran parallel to the beach in a circular sweep; the very direction the typhoon had churned the water across the entire Pacific Ocean. Eight to ten footers pounded the breakwater. Parents wouldn't allow their children to play in the surf for fear they would be swept away. That had been a day Lilly knew better than to even try to cross the reef.

Little two-to-threes mentioned by the store clerk brought out surfers hoping for even higher waves. Or snorkelers, like herself, who did not mind that the water was not flat.

Without conversation, they had almost passed through the slow waking town of Hanalei, where all the streets are named after Hawaiian fishes. Then Glen reminded her that he wanted a latte and that they needed to buy lunches to store in the cooler. Lilly did the shopping while Glen jaywalked to a coffee shop.

The road narrowed through a hilly area then came down to water level again at Lumahai Beach, known as *Bali Hai*, where portions of the movie *South Pacific* were filmed. Farther along, they waited for oncoming traffic at the famous single-lane twin bridges crossing picturesque Wainiha River. Two horses grazed unhurriedly on grasses growing along the mud banks that extended out to the island between the two bridges.

"It's amazing no one honks in the Islands," Glen said.

"Heard 'em in Honolulu a time or two," Lilly said. "But it's almost *kapu* to do it at all."

Later, Glen looked toward the rolling sea. "Smart people stay in the shallows and don't venture out past the reef," he said. She did not respond. "More and more people will swim out to get a look at the turtles, though, once they learn about them."

"The same reason I go," she said. "That and all the rest that's out there."

He clung to the edge of the seat as they drove around a bend and felt the van sway over another dip in the road. She saw it coming. Even she flinched at having to drive over roadsides rimming cliffs that threatened collapse with the next heavy rain, or maybe with the next heavy vehicle.

All along the way, on the mauka side, patches of red dirt showed like chafed skin on the hilltops and slopes. Years earlier, Hurricane Iniki's wrath had uprooted much of the plant life leaving nothing to hold the loose red dirt in place. From afar, all those patches of earthen slippage made the island look like melting, pink guava ice cream. They would remain that way until shrubs and foliage crept in and reclaimed the soil.

The road wound around the cliffs. In some places, the two-lane road narrowed, the cliff side slowly giving way under the weight of traffic. Tall yellow markers with red tips warned drivers of soft spots. Another warning was the patched and already cracking asphalt, laid down to temporarily cover in the slippage till a better remedy could be found to shore up the drop-off.

At each turn, a magnificent view opened out beyond indigenous and introduced flora, trees and shrubs. Lilly could take her eyes away from driving for only a fraction of a second to peer through the branches at white water or a picturesque cliff side across a bay. "Don't you just love the views?" Lilly teased facetiously as Glen's eyes remained riveted straight ahead.

"What about sharks?" he asked. "I heard there are reef sharks out there."

"Probably," she said. Her agreement was meant to convey until he was brave enough to swim out and have a look, he should not try to scare her out of any enjoyment.

"I'll see the turtles when your pictures are developed, Lillian," he said stiffly. Evidently, he caught the inflection in her voice.

She could not help smiling to herself. "That's my mission for today," she said.

"You know that since about 1979, the Pacific Green Sea Turtles have been protected by the Endangered Species Act," he said as a sarcastic reminder.

"I'm aware of that," she said. "Humans are not allowed to harass the Honu in any way, including touching."

"Why people want to ride those gentle creatures, most certainly frightening them, is beyond me," he said. Glen was right, but why was he taking a stand for something he had never witnessed?

"Those people wouldn't try to ride another human being," Lilly said, agreeing. "I wonder why we can't simply coexist. The turtles aren't threatened by our presence until someone tries to capture them."

"How long before they swim away and never return?" Glen asked. "Wouldn't that deprive them of another natural feeding ground?"

He had a point, even if it sounded like a quote from a textbook, and he was using it trying to convince her to stay out of deep water. She felt fairly certain that he would stay in the shallows if he decided to swim. His conversation had always been tinged with warnings. If he thought she would buy into his fears.... "I'm not a threat to the turtles," she said. "I don't bother them. I'm sure if I did, they'd move away from me, but they don't."

"What about those two that kept nipping at you?"

She smiled, remembering the peculiarity of the unexpected behavior of the turtles. "I can't imagine why they did that. They just kept nipping, not at my skin but at my bathing suit, like they were playing with me."

"Did you touch them? Push them away?"

"Someone grabbed the large one while it was stationary and tried to ride it. I swam away."

"Have you seen them nipping at other people?"

"I wasn't watching for it," she said. But an idea flashed through her mind. "If I ever saw them doing that," she said, "it would make for a very interesting photo."

"Maybe they sense your good intentions," Glen said with a mocking smile.

She pretended not to notice. "I have no idea. It was like they were playing. A large male and a smaller female."

"You can tell the difference?" he asked.

"Males have longer tails," she said. "I've seen that female before. She had this huge triangular piece missing on the right side at the edge of her shell. A good two inches wide and two or three deep."

"A bite, you think?"

"The cut's too sharp, too angular and it's singular. Could have been the prop of a boat motor," she said. "The wound looked like it had healed and continued to grow open that way, but I'm no expert on turtle wounds."

As usual on Sundays, Ke'e Beach at the end of the road in Haena on the North Shore had been their destination. Having purposely arrived before ten in the morning, their favorite place under the canopy of trees was still available. Lilly grabbed her camera out of the kit, and left behind the strobe and related equipment, for which she had no need while photographing in ambient surface water. The strobe mount needed repair anyway.

She glanced out over the water and marveled at the intense beauty of shimmer of the tide pool in the morning sun. She was surprised to see waves breaking out beyond the reef that looked more like four-to-six than two-to-three. Super Typhoon Keith, far south of the Islands, was headed westerly toward Guam at that very moment, which could cause high waves in Hawaii.

The waves regularly broke in two locations many yards to the left and right of the small underwater canyon the turtles seemed to favor. The breakers to the south pounded the deep area where the lagoon emptied into the sea and where rip currents were known to occur. The northerly waves were farther away rolling easterly toward Ka'ilio Beach. The middle area was nearly flat, which meant that anyone snorkeling straight out to where the turtles lingered would not be pounded onto the coral by incoming white water.

Since Lilly swam alone, she usually went into deep water only when others ventured out that far. Where she snorkeled was also dependent upon how the current felt.

At their usual sitting spot, as brown leaves and seed pods crunched underfoot in the sand, they unfolded beach chaises and put the cooler in between. Behind them, the reaching branches of False Kamani trees, laden with flat round leaves, provided ample shade. A couple of wild roosters and a scruffy looking beach hen with a brood of newly hatched chicks wandered by. Doves and red crested cardinals landed in the sand, waiting for someone to throw a morsel.

On the other side of the access path, fronting a stand of ironwoods, were tangles of older ironwoods with exposed roots. Years of pounding sea swells and winter surf had washed away surface soil and worn the roots smooth. Children loved climbing the odd, gnarly shapes that were also great for holding slippers and towels left to dry.

Glen slathered a thick coating of #50 SPF onto her back and shoulders and she did the same for him, feeling a strange sense of intimacy in spite of not wanting to touch him. After applying the lotion, Glen wiped his hands on a towel he always brought specifically for him to do just that so he would not smudge his clothes and reading materials. For added protection, he put on his tee shirt.

As Lilly applied sun block to the rest of her body, Glen said, "The water's rough. If you can't get your photos today, there are other times." He actually sounded more concerned rather than sarcastic, until he shook his head slowly and mumbled, "Green turtles!"

"Did you know they're not really green?" she asked, unwilling to be deterred.

"Green sea turtles are not green?"

She had never expected him to read much about the turtles. Living vicariously seemed another of his annoying habits. "The carapace. That's the shell. It's shades of browns with flecks of gold and olive. The underside is kind of yellow-orange."

"So what part's green?"

"It's body fat," she said, unable to keep from smiling.

"It's what?"

"Body fat. You've heard of green turtle soup?" Lilly asked. She dabbed some lotion under her eyes, careful not to spread it in areas where it might make her facemask slip.

"Yeah, but—"

"It's made from calipee, the greenish tissue found inside the plastron, the stomach shell."

"I suppose you're going to tell me the nondescript coloring of these turtles protects them in the ocean?"

"Exactly," she said. "It's called counter shading. It's common to sea animals. You should see their shells though, Glen." Now she was excited again. "Some turtles look as if yellow paint had been splattered against their shells. Color bursts out in random patterns."

"Someone like you would see the beauty in that," he said, smiling politely.

She gathered her gear, leaving the portable radio inside the beach bag and shoving it under the chaise, sort of out of the rain should that happened. When she returned from her swim, she would listen to Hawaiian music on her favorite AM station. Something about the tonal quality of AM brought to mind a former time in the Islands when music was simpler and AM was all there was. She attached the lanyard around her wrist that would allow the fluorescent orange camera and casing to dangle freely in the water, and then headed toward the surf. Glen raced ahead to the water's edge because the hot sand burned his tender feet.

The sun disappeared as a low gray cloud drifted from over the mountains behind the beach. The smell of the air changed, announcing rain. Bringing a brief reprieve from the scorching sun, big drops splattered in the sand leaving smooth round circles in a random pattern. Lilly knew the sprinkle would last only a moment or two till the cloud passed out to sea, so she kept walking. When it rained, Glen usually made a dash for her van, where he would stay until the sun reappeared. She wondered how he would react when it rained while he was in the water, because it surely would.

Chapter Five

Lilly tugged on her swim fins while sitting in the lapping water at the edge of the rolling tide pool. Glen managed to get into his fins with ease. Maybe he did have some experience in snorkeling. That seemed encouraging. But he evidently did not know to walk backwards with the awkward flippers in shallow water. He fell quite ungraciously. Lilly did not know what to do to keep him from feeling embarrassed so she turned her back and began to make her way into deeper water, pretending she didn't see and inadvertently showing him how to do it.

Quite a few tourists were already in the water, a sign the beach would become crowded over the course of the day. When she and Glen stood in waist deep water, she turned to face the waves, which was common knowledge to do, to keep from being knocked down. He did the same.

Lilly fumbled with her mask and snorkel, adjusting till the tension was just right and no water leaked in. She stretched out and floated face down. The exceedingly warm water felt like a silken massage. She felt unrestrained in the ocean and preferred this freedom instead of being cooked in a confined hot tub. She swam over the coral in the shallows and into deeper water, getting the feel of the current with her body. Long ago, her snorkeling instructor said anyone could learn a lot about the tide by taking a few moments to perceive it kinesthetically.

Surprisingly, Glen swam right beside her. He seemed to want to get her attention by gesturing a lot with his eyes. She could not read his expressions through the mask and decided to avoid looking at him.

The tiny skirt on her bathing suit waved with the pushes and pulls of the current. She turned toward the west end of the lagoon, still gauging the feel of the tide and noticed that the sand on the sea floor was being slowly shaped into long rolling mini-dunes by the undercurrent. A lizardfish dived into a dune and buried itself except for its eyes and tip of its snout, and waited for unwary smaller fish to come within striking range.

The water at Ke'e Beach was usually clear unless too many swimmers kept the bottom stirred. Sand inside the lagoon was almost as white as in the Caribbean. Lilly had fond memories and lots of photographs from her experiences snorkeling the waters around the Virgin Islands.

Her attention was pulled back into the present as several enormous Blue-spine Unicorn Tangs passed below her. A blue and rust Ornate Wrasse also passed by. The reef dwellers in Hawaii were somewhat wary, having been teased by swimmers. In unison, all the fish darted away quickly, up and over the reef as someone's swim fin prodded their midst. When she looked, she saw that it was Glen poking at them.

Chasing a Unicorn Tang and not watching ahead, a snorkeler bumped against her legs. She stopped kicking and drew up her feet so she wouldn't slap him with her fins. She pulled away using her arms. Another snorkeler bumped headlong into her side. She grunted, stopped and came upright to see if he was okay. He, too, stopped and lifted his mask. "I'm sorry," he said. "Sorry. You okay?"

She removed the mouthpiece. "I'm okay," she said, frustrated.

He repositioned his mask and frog kicked over to friends who, in ignorance, stood on top of the coral! Most people did not know that coral is a living creature. She pitied those who swam barefoot. She remembered having swum across the reef in a very low tide. As the shallow surf washed out, it left her lying completely and hilariously exposed on top of the reef. Lilly had only smiled. Openly expressing simply could not be done while wearing a mask and snorkel, but she could appreciate a good inner laugh. She also felt thankful the tide had not set her down on one of those poisonous black and white banded sea spines.

The lagoon was becoming crowded with people who knew little about swimming etiquette and respect for life in the sea. Lilly did not want to be near these people. She glanced out across the reef and saw several snorkelers farther out in deeper water and others on their way.

Excited about photographing the turtles, she headed in that direction, meandering over the reef, taking time to view all the magnificent life supported by it.

She felt the incoming surge push her back toward the shallows, making her bathing suit skirt billow upwards as she floated backwards. The outgoing pull helped her make up the distance, as her bathing suit skirt imitated the pulsating bell of a jellyfish. Only three feet of water covered the top of the reef. She watched schools of colorful tropical fish in perfectly synchronized dances.

Several colorful *Humuhumu nukunuku apua'a*, the Hawai'i state fish, nibbled in coral crevasses nearby. This Picasso Triggerfish had diagonal black stripes and vibrant browns and whites. It had blue lips, a red spot at the base of its pectoral fins and golden triangle-shaped lines at the rear of its body; a much different pattern than found on most fish. Lilly had not been able to photograph the elusive species because they were very skittish and difficult to approach. As she hung motionless in the water, one just happened to turn sideways and she quickly snapped her first photo of the small fish with the long name. Then Glen swam up beside her and the fish sensed his movement. When she looked again, the Humuhumu were nowhere to be seen.

Glen brought his body upright and took a stance on the coral. She felt like smacking him.

A red and white-spotted Trapezia crab retreated down among coral heads as they passed. Long white tentacles of spaghetti worms fanned out from their hiding places, gathering a meal. Pink Ina, small rock boring urchins, filled thousands of holes. One bold, red-orange Slate Pencil Urchin caught her eye and she maneuvered around and photographed the perfect specimen from various angles. She already imagined the enlarged photo cropped, matted and framed.

Sea cucumbers lay everywhere, ready to evert their entire digestive tracts when threatened. All around, every kind of reef fish ducked and darted, some ejecting sand through their gills as they ate. Many bore brilliant color markings, near metallic blues, reds, greens and golds, pure and bright, as if to reflect sunlight into the depths, like swimming neons. So much to see, and each time was as if it was the first.

Several weeks before, in the murky water stirred up by people misusing the reef as a platform, Lilly watched a man hanging onto a turtle's shell, both heading right toward her. Once the man let go, the turtle came to a stop barely two feet in front of her as she hung in the water without moving. The turtle did not react, but simply looked at her with its huge black eyes. Her emotions had swelled in sympathy for the great creature. She felt so connected, as if they had just had a meeting of minds. Instead of darting away from her, the Honu ducked its head into a crevice, the rest of its body precariously floating, its tail end protruding up from between coral abutments as it tore off bites of delectable seaweed, known as *limu* or sea lettuce. That was one of the rare times she had not had her camera with her.

Glen still remained beside her. He seemed to be holding up well and she was thankful, though she also wished he would not follow. She wanted to work and the irritation she felt at his being alongside inhibited her. She wondered if he had always known how to snorkel, whatever might have caused his fear of getting into Hawaiian waters; and whatever caused him to overcome it so quickly? Since he was doing well, she decided he was on his own and she would go about what she had set out to do.

An underwater canyon opened out below her. Water distorted her view, so her best guess was that the light sandy bottom was at least thirty feet down. Coral jutted, craggy and sharp, not having been walked on like coral in the shallows. The fish were much larger. Several people snorkeled nearby. The deep water was clear until a large wave broke over the reef. The unexpected rush seemed to frighten Glen.

Lilly removed her snorkel. "Go back," she said. "If you're not used to strong waves, go back." He only shrugged. Frustrated, Lilly bit down on her snorkel and ducked her head back under the water.

Detecting a familiar sound, she noticed several sea turtles feeding, their hard underbellies grated against coral as the waves jostled them. Only ten feet to her left, a dozen Honu of varying sizes floated at the top of the water, scrutinized the edge of the reef, and ducked down often to grab a morsel with their short hard beaks. Occasionally they were momentarily motionless as they poked their snouts above the surface to breathe.

Other snorkelers crowded in, which startled the Honu. Lilly found it impossible to take pictures. She found the others' lack of caution in their approach incredulous and could not blame the Honu for becoming more and more evasive.

A man grabbed one of the turtles by the sides of its shell and swam away with it. In his effort to hang on to the turtle, the man was totally unaware that one of his fins slapped someone else in the face. As Lilly watched, the man struggled to hang on because the turtle was much stronger and tried to escape. The turtle headed for deeper water and the snorkeler released his grip. When the man rejoined his friends, he signaled with two thumbs up and churned the water with his fists like he still had some sort of statement to make. His ego and his treatment of the turtles infuriated her.

Lilly wondered if the turtles saw her as just another threat and if her intended gentle visit was as intrusive. She would never harass the turtles, and, had she been alone with them, would have maneuvered cautiously around for a good photo angle without placing herself in their natural paths.

She spotted two turtles coming in from deep water, heading easterly along the outer reef. Taking the opportunity to distance herself from the rowdy crowd who could as well drown one another with their careless antics, she followed the two Honu as they nibbled their way along the crags. She spotted a few more farther ahead in favored deeper water and leisurely made her way over to them hoping for a perfect photo.

As she moved closer, waiting for the right light and angle, the water darkened and turned cool. Without lifting her face to look around, she knew a cloud momentarily blocked the sun. She wondered if a sprinkling of rain would accompany the cloud, and at that, envisioned Glen running to seek shelter in the van. As if a manifestation of her thoughts, Glen appeared at her side.

Once the cloud passed and the water began to sparkle again, she kept her distance but followed the turtles along the reef. The sun's rays were like soft spotlights that illuminated the Honu. With dashes of bright colors from reef fish in the background, she knew her photos would be incredible.

After a while, she lifted her face out of the water to see where she was in relation to the shoreline. The area where she entered the water was always the best point of reference. She looked around and was astonished that the beach and tree line were unfamiliar. They must have swum completely around Ka'ilio Point. She felt unnerved about finding herself in unfamiliar waters and even more so now because Glen would chide her for being careless.

Chapter Six

The portion of the reef around Kaʻilio Point jutted farther out into the ocean than where she usually swam and the entire strip of beach followed the coast-line for miles. They could simply walk back along the sand if they tired of swimming.

The turtles were headed west again. She and Glen could follow them along the reef back to where they began. Since she had already taken some great photos, she would rest and read a while, about Ernest Hemingway's old man and his battle with a marlin too far out at sea.

She kept her eyes on the Honu and watched them sometimes dive to nibble limu growing on deeper edges of the reef. Carefully, she dove too, to learn how those oxygen breathers fared in deep water. She had another perfect setting and photographed a turtle feeding on a large clump of swaying purple cabbage. The colorful seaweed needed sunlight nearer the surface to thrive but seldom grew near the surface at Keʻe anymore, because of humans abusing the reef.

She watched the Honu and suddenly knew. Quickly, she rose to the surface for another breath of air. The way the long purple strands of limu billowed back and forth with the tide was the same movement of the skirt on her bathing suit while she swam. The turtles nipped at her because they associated the movement of the deep purple, red and pink bathing skirt as limu.

She dove again and took a couple of close-ups of a turtle's head stuck deep into a large clump of the seaweed. After another shot of one turtle nipping at the leaves, she rose to breathe again.

The next time she dove, she saw something out of the corner of her eye that shot a piercing warning signal through her nervous system. Fairly deep down under a ledge in the reef, a small gray reef shark glided slowly around near the sandy bottom. That was how they settled in for a snooze.

She quickly rose again and found Glen hanging motionless at the surface watching. She signaled him to move away quietly. But he didn't understand what she wanted him to do until she pointed to the reef shark and he saw it. He seemed instantly frightened, swimming off and splashing until she managed to catch his arm and grip it painfully to shock him into stopping. She held up a finger in front of her snorkel signaling that they remain quiet. Glen seemed near panic. He spit out his snorkel and kicked even harder and made gasping noises. Lilly caught up again and grabbed his arm and spun him around as best she could. She spit out her snorkel. "Quiet!" she said, mouthing the word instead of screaming it. She tipped her snorkel to let it drain before putting it back into her mouth. Glen watched her and calmed and then did the same while she held onto his arm with a tight grip.

They treaded while Glen caught his breath and regained his composure. She kept hold of his arm to guide him and they finally swam away underwater so they would not churn up bubbles and make noises on the surface.

This type of shark was small, less than three feet long, but known to attack. Sudden movement, open wounds, even women swimming while menstruating, could attract sharks. She wondered about the blister between Glen's toes and if it had bled. She looked back and kept the shark in sight. If it started toward them, she would have to fend it off with anything durable to probe its eyes, gills or nose. Sharkskin is rough. Using a fist to club it would only chafe her skin and cause bleeding, sending the shark into frenzy and attracting other sharks.

Maybe she could somehow get her swim fins into its mouth. She felt the camera dangling in the water against her arm. It was the only thing durable enough for such an assault. Bashing the shark in vulnerable places with the camera would be their only defense.

The shark showed no sign that it had been provoked by Glen's panic and had not followed. Still, for safety's sake, they continued to distance themselves from it. They came up for air, breaking the surface as quietly as possible and emptied the snorkels by allowing them to drain instead of making noise by blowing a gust of air forcefully through them to eject the water. Then they slid quietly beneath the surface again and followed the westward movement of the turtles. Feeling safer at a distance, Lilly began to regain her focus.

Surfacing to eject spent oxygen and to breathe, Lilly filled her lungs with fresh air and dove again. Glen silently mimicked her, probably his way of controlling his panic. But for some odd reason, now she could not go down very deep. She felt like she was being pulled sideways from the reef. She tried to swim against the horizontal pull but it was stronger. She caught a glimpse of Glen far behind her rising toward the surface. Then she knew. She was being pulled out by an undertow! She forced herself to relax into the drag, knowing she could hold her breath about ninety seconds, but she had already been down a while. She willed her strength to last. Then, quite quickly, the sea coughed her back to the surface. When her head came above water, she found she had been pulled far from the reef.

Glen had surfaced for air and stayed on top of the water, evidently not affected by the undertow. When he saw her, he began to swim toward her. She motioned frantically for him to stay where he was, but he didn't heed the warning and swam out anyway.

Adrenaline kicked in. Using powerful breast strokes, she began to swim toward the reef and hoped Glen would understand and do the same. She felt a strong pull in the opposite direction. The wind picked up as another dark cloud passed overhead from the direction of *Pali ʻEleʻele*. The strange sizzle of raindrops pelted the ocean's surface as the downpour overtook her. She kept swimming, feeling the sting of rain on her back. The cloud quickly passed out to sea and she felt the familiar heat of the sun again.

The outgoing tide retreated. When the current headed inward, she kicked and swam forcefully, to add power to the surge that would get them back to the reef. But the inbound surge was too mild. She stared at the ocean floor through the mask, wishing the ocean wasn't so deep there, a reminder of how serious their situation had quickly become.

Coral formations were different in deeper water. Nearer the beach, the thick compacted main body of the reef was worn smooth. On the ocean side of the reef, the corals had never been exposed above the tides. The way they formed looked as if the tides dragged at them as they dropped off deeper and deeper, toward the ocean floor. No long sun loving limu waved in the current at those depths.

Lilly visually followed the bottom till it dropped out of sight into threateningly dark water. A small flicker of light caught her attention and then disappeared. Hopefully it was only a reflection from the silver side of a fish.

With frantic splashing, Glen was beside her. "What are you doing way out here?" he asked innocently. He didn't wait for a reply. He ducked his head underwater and looked down.

She and Glen raised their heads at the same time. While she treaded, Lilly let her snorkel dangle. "I signaled you to stay back, Glen," she said irritably. He looked confused. "I got caught in an undertow."

"Okay, let's swim back," he said. He was not unaware that as they treaded, they were being pulled farther still away from the reef.

Every seventh wave would be a strong one. Or was it every ninth? Lilly felt a moment of confusion. Of all the information she had read, what might help her now? She had read so much, but now it was all jumbled. She had not been counting the waves but knew how to detect the difference in the current with her body and the tide was pulling them farther out to sea, faster than she realized.

With a sudden force, she tumbled her over and over and water filled her snorkel before she had time to take a breath. She was pulled out an even greater distance. The top of her strapless bathing suit coiled to her waist. She held her breath. When the drag eased, she blew hard clearing the snorkel. While she gasped through the tube, she thanked God for the snorkel and the non-leaking facemask.

Glen had been pulled just as far, but a distance away from her. Lilly removed the snorkel and yelled, "We're caught in a rip!"

Stop. Breathe. Think. Act. As a child she memorized the emergency plan. Her nerves tingled. She willed herself not to panic.

Surfers used the rips to take them out, but they had surfboards to take them back in.

Don't panic. Float. You don't need a surfboard. Body surf. Does Glen know how to body surf?

After a pause the surge went toward the reef again, but she was clearing her snorkel and it happened too quickly for her to catch much of the momentum. She bobbed on the surface like an unmoored buoy. The next inbound surge didn't contain enough of a push that would enable her to surf, but she flutter-kicked and pulled evenly with her arms anyway. A stronger surge would happen and push her to safety again. Glen seemed to follow her lead, but struggled too much and using up vital energy. She maneuvered her way over to him. She saw panic in his eyes through the mask.

"Don't fight the pull," she said. "Save your energy." Out that far, the roar of the sea almost drowned out her voice so she yelled the instructions again. Glen nodded.

By the time she again noticed the bottom of the ocean, she could barely make out the sand and sparse coral formations. The water was darker and murkier, having been stirred up by the stronger, deeper tide. Or was it dark and murky because it was simply too deep for any light to penetrate down there?

A school of large fish swam by and darted away when she turned to get a better look. A little farther away, a school of smaller fish twinkled like a suspended glittering mobile.

Lilly's mind flashed back thirty years when she was in the Caribbean. No one knew exactly how deep the bay was when the crew of the *Caribe* dropped anchor off Sandy Cay between the islands of Jost Van Dyke and St. John. The pure white sand and crystal clear water made the bottom look close. Shells and starfish were clearly visible from the seabed and had been so tempting that Lilly dived down to get a closer look. By the time she realized she had gone way past her limit, the pressure on her ears had become painful. When she decided to surface, she had already held her breath too long. By the time she made it to the surface, her lungs felt like they were on fire. Everyone on the ketch hung over the side, watching her and laughing. *You amateur!* one of them had screamed.

She was not an amateur now. She had learned much more since living in the Caribbean. Then again, maybe only amateurs got caught in rips. At least now she knew how to survive in deep water till help arrived. The first rule was never to panic. She needed to assure that Glen didn't either.

Lilly wondered how deep the water beneath her might really be. Unlike the magnificent white sandy bottoms in the Caribbean that reflected light, the darker sands of the Hawaiian shores got progressively darker farther from shore. Either extreme made it just as difficult to guess at depth.

The reef was nowhere in sight, nor were the turtles. She looked up again, spat out the mouthpiece and lifted her mask because she couldn't believe what she saw.

"This can't be," she said. "We must be more than a mile from the beach!"

Lilly remembered having been on the beach looking out toward the deep side of the reef. It never looked that far away. She also remembered being in the water on the deep side of the reef looking back toward the beach. From that vantage point, the same distance seemed more expansive. Maybe they weren't as far out as she thought.

"Hey-y!" she yelled at the top of her voice, knowing she had better make it loud and clear. "Help! Somebody-y-y!" she said, and then realized how feeble her voice sounded against the road of the ocean. "Out here!" How would she know if anyone heard or saw her? She waved her arms. The camera dangled on the lanyard, the orange rubber body looked bright against the dark water, which was why it was orange. She began to wave the camera high in the air as she yelled again and again.

Glen made a feeble attempt to yell. So much of his energy had been spent on panic. Mostly, he just waved. Lilly knew that in addition to whatever else he might be feeling, he was embarrassed. At least, for all the times he adamantly said he didn't like water and wouldn't get in, now he seemed able to keep himself from drowning.

She couldn't tell how much progress they made as they worked with the inbound surges. She had no choice but to keep trying to ride in with the current. Each time a set of larger, more forceful waves pushed toward shore, they increased their effort. When the push subsided, they had time to rest. Glen still followed her lead. The waves out that far were big enough for avid surfers, but why weren't any surfers out that far today? Perhaps one would come along and rescue them. She had never been on a surfboard.

Again and again, she body surfed inbound white water while Glen struggled a short distance away. She thought he would surely drown when the wave faces broke, but he always came up again.

The outbound pull always claimed them. Then she remembered. When caught in a rip, swim lengthwise with the waves. That technique had always worked closer to shore. When swimmers became caught in waves breaking at the beach and found they could not get into shallow water, if they swam lengthwise with the waves and away from the outbound pull, the current would eventually wash them in. That was the way they would get back to safety. She set her direction easterly across the current and Glen followed. Of course he would. Glen probably had no idea how to get them to safety. He kept his distance but followed her lead and that was good. If he got too close and panicked, he could take her down with him.

Then again, it happened. An outbound rip so strong it felt like her rubber fins would be torn from her feet. She tumbled over and over, swallowing seawater through her snorkel. She choked pathetically and then sneezed the salty brine into her mask.

God, help us!

When she stopped tumbling, she realized she still wore the fins, without which, she would have little strength in her kicks. She treaded water and ripped the snorkel out of her mouth and gasped for air. "No-o!" she said, screaming and hitting the water with her fist. "No-o-o!" Then she realized if she could scream that loud in anger, she ought to be spending the energy screaming for help. She waved for help and screamed and screamed till her voice broke. When she quieted, her eardrums continued to vibrate.

Too busy keeping himself afloat; Glen had drifted a distance away from her. He, too, had been tumbled, but she couldn't tell how he was faring. His screams were feeble, as was his arm waving.

She looked up toward the sun, avoiding looking directly at it. If she guessed correctly, it was close to noon. In a few hours the tide will have changed and the sea would rush to shore again. The two elements they had in their favor were time and tide. She put the snorkel back into her mouth and Glen did the same with his, just in case another surge might catch them unaware.

Chapter Seven

Conserve energy!

Lilly's arms were exhausted. She shook them to revive them. One of the easiest ways to rest was to go limp and float face down in the water with the help of the facemask and snorkel to breathe through. After all, that's exactly what snorkeling was all about, lying limp on top of the water, breathing through the snorkel and enjoying the sights. It didn't take much effort to stay afloat. Before she rested, she made her way to Glen and told him how to rest. She was sure he had no clue about what they might do next in this situation and he would use up precious energy fighting just to tread water. Yet, he would fight to stay alive. That was all that mattered. Hopefully, he would not panic again and drown.

Lilly was thankful that she always used sun block. She hoped it was as waterproof as the label claimed and wished she could re-apply it as the label directed. Every two hours.

As she floated, hanging limp in the waves, she visualized her strength being sustained. After some time, she noticed the skirt of her bathing suit as it billowed up and down, which told her the current was at last in their favor and pushing them toward the shore.

She lifted her head out of the water and found them both facing open ocean. They had been floating in the wrong direction! Treading, she swung herself about to get her bearings and found she could barely make out the dark strip of trees that grew along the beach. Somehow they had gotten turned around and were bobbing away from the island.

As hard as she tried to keep her wits, panic gripped her. Lilly did not know if it was again adrenaline that ripped through her body, but something set every nerve on edge. Adrenaline in this situation was a sign of stress and only good at times when it provided energy to swim from danger. Otherwise it could be debilitating.

Clearly, they had not attracted anyone's attention on the beach when they yelled earlier otherwise help would have arrived. How far might their voices carry from where they were now?

She spat out the mouthpiece, giving her lips a chance to find their normal posture again. She waved anyway and yelled fiercely. From that far at sea, trees and the upper portions of the mountains were barely discernible. No one on the beach could see her now.

The noontime glare off the water hurt her eyes. She had kept her face in the water so it wouldn't get sunburned. Yet, the sun was just right for flashing a signal toward shore. Why hadn't she thought about that before? She ripped off the mask and angled the glass to reflect the sun's rays. Glen seemed relieved to have something that provided renewed hope and did the same.

"Hey-y!" she yelled with all the power her lungs could muster. "He-y-y, out here! Someone, he-l-l-p!" Lilly had no way of knowing if the mask caught the sunlight just right to send a signal to anyone who might happen to be looking their way. "Keep flashing," she said. "Someone will see."

Their effort was short-lived. Another rain cloud approached from over Na Pali and passed slowly. Rain pelted down and stung the top of her head and shoulders. They hurriedly put their masks back on and held themselves low in the water. The air and surface water turned cool. A chill came over her. If only she had brought her strobe. If only it worked. It would have been the perfect beacon.

Treading water, feeling the surge, Lilly gauged the current as best she could. She rested, wanting to be ready to ride the next inbound flow. She ducked her head and waited. That was when she felt the pull and saw the skirt of her bathing suit billow up around her hips. They were being pulled out again.

She found herself making screaming noises to ease the panic out of the moment, as much as she could with teeth clenched around the mouthpiece.

She reminded herself that a forward thrust followed every backwards surge. When it came, she would kick her legs with all the strength she could muster. The strain would keep her warm. She waited, but the surge did not come and she went backwards again.

Swimmers were instructed to float with a rip instead of opposing it. Sooner or later, it will let go and the swimmer will wash up somewhere. Lilly looked up at the distant Na Pali coastline. Her strength was ebbing and she would welcome being washed up anywhere.

She swam over to Glen. He was using more effort than necessary to stay afloat. "One thing we won't do is panic," she said. "We'll hang in the water and wait for the tide to take us in." She explained how they should position themselves while they waited, but it was only diversion to squelch Glen's anxiety.

With the sun just past straight up and the surface shimmering like cut crystal, the place where she and Glen had sat on the beach would have lost some shade. Glen would have moved his chair into the parking area till the sun sank farther west and stretched the shadows.

Glen removed his mouthpiece. "We missed our lunchtime," he said.

That irritated Lilly. "Do you always have to eat your meals according to the clock?" she asked. She spit out a mouthful of water. "Why don't you try asking your stomach?"

"Where are those behemoth cruise liners that always hug the coast?" he asked.

Lilly suspected she and Glen had floated way out past the route where the cruise liners skirted the shoreline. Yet, a few of the passengers and crew had binoculars. Maybe they would not all be looking toward shore and admiring the island. Lilly could send some sort of signal and someone on board might see. Her hopes were dashed when she, again, realized what time of day it was. "They pass way before noon," Lilly said. "In order to circle the island and dock by four o'clock at Nawiliwili Harbor." Neither she nor Glen had seen any ship from the high vantage point of the road as they drove. Today would not be the day a liner might pass. "The tide was low this morning," she said. "Should turn anytime now." She put the mask on again and inserted the mouthpiece and counted the sea swells.

Six. She waited. Was it the seventh wave that was the stronger one?

Seven. The surge was not as spectacular as she had hoped. Perhaps every ninth wave was the biggest.

Eight. Now she was ready.

Nine. But no big surge pushed her. Had she fought so many waves that now she was unable to tell which one was which? Then another backward pull yanked at them.

She came upright and ripped off her mask as she lifted high. She was astounded to see that they were way out in the swells. Never mind the six to eight footers that broke in frothing white foam on the deep edge of the reef. They were out in the swells. Up they went and down again. She thanked God that from childhood she had always found motions like these to be fun and never got sick on rides like roller coasters. Up they went and down again. Each time a swell lifted, she tried to see the shoreline. In a way, she didn't want to see how far away they had been pulled. She didn't want to wonder if they would ever get back to safety. "Don't think like that!" she said, admonishing herself.

Glen kept his face in the water and hadn't heard.

Of course they would get back. Lilly felt the sea was readying for a big rush. She glanced at Glen to make sure he was ready. She replaced her mask and ducked her face into the water and waited. Finally it came. She swam stealthily and covered what seemed to be a great distance. She kept her kicks uniform and strong and arm pulls rhythmic and constant. More pushes like that and they would be home safe. Then the huge swell began to pull backwards and they probably went out farther than any distance they had made up. When she looked again, Glen had drawn closer.

We won't panic. All we have to do is relax and we'll stay afloat.

She felt like crying but the snorkel and mask made it impossible.

Don't be ridiculous. Crying takes energy. Relax and float. Let the trusty swim fins do the work.

Stop. Breathe. Think. Act.

Tour boats skirted the Na Pali coastline and usually passed Keʻe Beach. But a long-time dispute had caused many of the tour companies to move their boats, helicopters and businesses to Port Allen in ʼEleʼEle on the southwest shore. Any hope that a passenger-carrying craft might pass looked bleak.

No way existed to gauge how far out to sea they had drifted. She could no longer see the shoreline but just water and dark trees or mountain tops as she lifted high on swells and used the mask to continue sending signals.

Fatigue began to set in. "Why burn energy treading water?" she asked herself, already knowing the answer. She would get her bearings, position herself and wait for another big one. She put her mask on again and moved closer to Glen, knowing he still followed her lead.

Make sure we're headed toward shore… look up once in a while.

Floating took much less energy. With the help of the gear, they could simply lie on top of the water. She closed her eyes and concentrated on the feel of the current against her body. The tide pushed, pulled, and pushed again.

Lilly did not know how long they floated, working with the surges, relaxing during the pulls. She hoped they had made some headway, though she was unable to determine by the size of the trees on shore or any other landmarks she tried to establish. The outbound rip was not pulling as strongly, a sign the tide was turning. But what did it matter? Now they were out so far, a mile in either direction would make no difference.

Don't think that way either!

She treaded and removed the mask and snorkel just as a diversion. Treading submerged gave her back and shoulders reprieve from the scorching rays of the sun.

A large bird gracefully glided easterly overhead. "A Laysan Albatross," Lilly said. "Go to Kilauea Point. Go to safety in the refuge." Two more passed.

Lilly didn't know much about the habits of those large cliff dwellers.

"Birds coming ashore," Glen said, yelling above the sea roar, "almost always means bad weather out at sea." So now they might have a storm to deal with as well as the current.

"Is a storm approaching, bird?" she asked, watching the last one disappear in flight. "Will we experience rougher seas?"

She remembered a rumor that a person, once caught in the North Equatorial Current and swept out to deep sea a couple of miles, would never encounter land again.

Chapter Eight

Lilly was good at remembering geography. The flow of the North Equatorial Current came from the eastern Pacific, flowing west-northwesterly and up around the populated Hawaiian Islands. The overall current flowed all the way to the uninhabited northwesterly islands of the Hawaiian archipelago, like Nihoa, Necker and Tern Islands to the Gardner Pinnacles. As the current turned and headed southwesterly, it flowed between all the islands of the archipelago, all the way out to Midway Islands and Kure Atoll.

Something told Lilly that if they got caught in the southern flow of the North Equatorial Current, based on their current location, a small chance existed that they might wash up on the remote island of Niihau to the southwest of Kauai. But only if they remained close enough to the coast of Kauai and could sustain enough energy to keep them afloat. A little luck and a lot of prayer would help too.

"Don't even think it," she said aloud to herself. "You're going home." Glen had not heard. He was some distance away again. Lilly could not allow herself to believe anything less than getting home.

Her thoughts, forced in a more positive direction, settled on why she was in the water to begin with. The Honu females nested on the tiny islands of the French Frigate Shoals near Tern Island out in the archipelago. Between breeding, they regularly crossed the North Equatorial Current to return again and again to feed along the coast of the inhabited Hawaiian chain. They would cross that current again to return to their breeding grounds when in season.

For many years after birth, Honu hatchlings lived at sea till they grew large enough to come ashore to breed. The tiny turtles, beginning life no larger around than a silver dollar, lived for years at sea somewhere unknown within the North Equatorial Current without being swept deep into the Pacific. So how strong could that current be?

If caught in the current, Lilly expected that they would be torn away from all habitation, dragged by tides till they drowned. It had not happened yet and she was a survivor. True, the turtles had food to sustain them while they swam and they would have none. They could become the food for something larger. Her throat felt parched. Lilly looked at her fingertips. Shriveled.

She felt as if they had been caught in some sort of doldrums. "How is it we got caught in a rip anyway?" she asked, almost smiling at the irony. After a bit of reflection, she answered herself. "Because you, Lilly, are just one swimmer among millions, not much different from anyone else. This could happen to you as well as any other person in the water." Then she was consumed with guilt having prodded Glen to getting into the water and felt responsible for putting him in such a dire situation.

She realized they needed to make the most of what little they had. She looked up and watched as clouds drifted slowly toward her. In the distance, she saw a dark, rain-swollen mass and knew it would reach them in moments.

"Rain!" she said. She screamed and reached upwards. "Go ahead. Rain hard! Send us big wet sloppy drops!"

The cloud passed over. Rain fell. Lilly tipped her head back and said, "Thank you, you big dark water filled sack." She needed to shut up and keep her mouth open. If only a few drops fell in, a taste would be enough to quench her thirst momentarily. Other clouds would come. The thought renewed her hope.

Big sporadic drops splattered on her face, a couple on her tongue. She swallowed quickly and opened her mouth wide again. Another drop fell in, then another. She let the fresh rainwater seep around the inside of her mouth. She savored the moisture, the coolness and then swallowed.

She looked around and spotted Glen who had been watching her. "Drink!" she said, yelling it. "You need it!" He was either too far away to hear or too embarrassed to tip his gaping mouth upward.

The cloud broke apart and scattered across the sky. The rain was gone, but three scant mouthfuls had been enough to restore her wavering courage. She watched the feathery scraps of clouds meet together in the distance and swell again. Dark streaks of rain poured into the ocean. She was compelled to give thanks for the restorative moment, and again for her mask, snorkel and fins. She thanked herself for the ability to stay calm and positive for deliverance to shore.

She located Glen again and made her way over to him. He was trying to float on his back, which was nearly impossible to do while wearing snorkel gear. Before she could say anything, they went backwards again. She pressed the mask to her forehead to keep from losing it. The backward pull was not a forceful one, but it was long. "Thank you for being an easy pull," she said to the sea.

With that last pull into still deeper water, Lilly figured she should be thinking about how she had lived her life, and should give thanks for all the wonders she had seen. She wondered if she had ever given enough thanks. She adjusted her mask, bit into the snorkel, and began to silently express her gratitude as she floated face down.

Her body felt sluggish. Her limbs felt cool, even though the sun warmed the surface water. As she wondered what else she might be able to do to help them both, a swell lifted them and she was able to see only a dark remnant of the island. She corrected the direction she was headed and Glen made his adjustments. Another swell lifted and lowered them and something scraped the length of her lower legs and ripped the swim fins off her feet!

If it's a shark, let it be swift!

Her heart raced. She closed her eyes, floated motionless and prayed but remained calm, hoping not to again attract the predator's attention. Fear coursed through her. She couldn't feel her legs. When traumatized, body parts sometimes go numb. It was the body's built-in protective mechanism. She hoped that was all it was.

Nothing else happened. Lilly opened her eyes and looked around below the surface but saw no shark, no frightening creature from the deep. No blood-tinged water. She came to an upright position and treaded, groping for her legs, which now stung from the salty water. She reminded herself never to panic, even as panic threatened to engulf her.

Sharks can smell a single drop of blood in the water from miles away.

One at a time, she brought her legs up as best she could and examined them. She found no blood, just scrapes, but the wounds were turning red and swelling all the same. The scrapes stung like prickly needles. She sucked air through her teeth and breathed quickly, trying to stem the pain.

Worried about predators and blinded by reflected sun, she now had to keep looking underwater for anything that moved. Not that she would be able to do much to save them if another attack came. Glen continued treading water a few yards away, oblivious to the new peril. Nothing that might have claimed the fins moved in close proximity. She stretched out her body and felt the loss of strength in her legs and feet without the footwear. She felt weakened. Not until then did she realize how much the fins kept her buoyant.

Keeping watch, as she turned around in a circle, something coarse brushed her arm. She yelped and withdrew the limb quick as lightning and closed her eyes waiting. When she opened them again, she was almost slapped in the face by the webbing of a fisherman's net.

A drift net?

One of her fins was caught in the net. Trapped schools of confused fish swam in tangled circles; thousands more fish than she had ever seen together at one time. Predator bait.

First was the scrapes on her leg, and now a net full of captive fish. Both were main attractions making them perfect prey for large predators. She wanted to scream but could not. All she could do was breath hard through the snorkel.

She felt thankful, though, that it was only the net that had brushed down her legs and pulled off her fins. Lilly's first impulse was to go after the entangled fin, but she was afraid of becoming snared in the net.

Drift nets are illegal.

As it swept the sea, the net would be attached to intermittent surface buoys to keep it afloat. Buoys would hold them up. On second thought, to get close to a buoy attached to a net languishing back and forth in the current would almost certainly lead to becoming entangled in the webbing.

"Should we hang onto this thing?" Glen asked, yelling to be heard.

"You might get caught in it," she said, waving him away.

Without the fins, which were mainstays in the water, and with her legs feeling exhausted, she might be thrust again and again against the netting and become ensnared. She toyed with the idea that someone would come to draw in the catch and would rescue them, if this was not a rogue net lost to its owner.

Once Glen became fully aware of the danger, they worked with the tide taking them backwards away from the net and into still deeper water. Having nearly overtaken them, the net floated between them and the distant shoreline. Some drift nets were one to two miles long. Clinging to the hope of getting closer to shore was not important enough to succumb to the grip of some fisherman's folly.

The net drifted closer. They moved farther out. Buoys attached intermittently along the rim of the net bobbed. Lilly cautiously swam in for a closer look. The buoys were made of Styrofoam and cork. From where they were, they couldn't tell how big the net might be or how large a sweep it made. It moved slowly, seeming to take forever, as it drifted in a westerly direction, with them being pushed along with it.

A dark and hazy shadow appeared fairly deep down in the opaque water as the net languished. Terrified, Lilly fixed her gaze on the shadow. It didn't seem to move with any purpose and, in fact, seemed to loll about in the depths. As it floated with the pushes and pulls of the current, she realized it was a drowned sea turtle pitifully tangled in the webbing. It rolled to and fro and each time the current shifted, and more of the net caught around the Honu's lifeless extremities.

Lilly began to cry, letting all the noises escape through the snorkel. Anger replaced fear.

Damn you, net, and damn your owner!

She struggled to distance herself from the net. Each time the current shifted, the net moved perilously close. She kept her face in the water to keep watch. The turtle flopped and rolled first in one direction, then another. The turtle's long front flipper beckoned like Captain Ahab's arm when he was caught in the ropes and bound to the sides of the great white whale, Moby Dick. The weight of that dead thing riding it out below pulled at the net and released; pulled at the net and released. As she stared into the depths, something on the surface bumped the side of her head, one, two, three times. She froze all movement. The mask blocked peripheral vision.

She couldn't think rationally about anything but to remain still. Again, something nudged the side of her head. A scream lodged in her throat. She envisioned herself getting eaten by something or tangled in that net and never having a chance, just like that gentle Honu.

Something nudged again. Certain sharks employ a tactic called *bump and bite*. They first nudge their prey and then swoop in for the kill. In anger, the only response Lilly could muster was to prepare to face what was about to have her for lunch. She slowly reached for her camera, the only weapon available. She lifted it above her head and bit down on the snorkel as she forced herself to turn as she treaded water, poised for the fight of her life.

Chapter Nine

To her surprise, after scrutinizing the surface water around her, no menacing vertical dorsal fin of a predator circled in for the kill. Instead, she came face to face with the other swim fin floating on the surface.

She spat out the snorkel and screamed with relief. She had forgotten that some swim fins floated and simply rose to the surface when they came off. Lilly grabbed it and, with her face in the water, had difficulty getting her lifeless leg to bend in order to force her foot inside. Finally in place, the pressure of the rubber against the side of her foot made the chafed skin burn.

Get over it. Be greater than pain.

Glen came to her side and spat out his snorkel. "What was that all about?" he asked.

Lilly look at him and shook her head. "I thought we were being attacked."

"By what? Where?" He turned quickly in the water and looked around.

She didn't expect him to understand. "Never mind," she said. "I was wrong."

They made their way along the net hoping to again find her other fin. Once located, Lilly reached out and tried to wriggle it free. It only became more tangled. She gave it several hard yanks. "It's no use," she said. "Get away from this death trap."

"Wait," Glen said. "We could cut it loose."

"Cut?"

"I have a knife," he said.

"A what?"

"Here," he said, fumbling below the surface. "In my swim suit pocket."

"You just happened to have a knife?" Lilly could not believe the pomposity of his words and his grin. She gasped and had to spit out the mouthful of water she almost swallowed.

"For protection," he said.

Glen produced a little pocketknife and fumbled to open it. He had already opened it and, just as she reached him, offered it to her but with the blade coming at her. She quickly jerked her hand away but Glen had already let go. He grabbed for it then jerked his hand up fast, having nicked his finger on the blade. They watched the last glint of sunlight reflect off the blade as it sank.

When Lilly looked at Glen, he was looking at his bleeding finger, which he held stuck up in the air. She got up close to him just as he was about to wash the blood off in the water and forced him to stick his finger into his mouth. "Drink!" she said. "Drink your blood."

"Why?" he asked as he choked with her forcefully thrusting his finger deep in his mouth.

"Blood, you idiot, blood draws sharks."

Glen did not pull his finger from his mouth for quite a while. When he did, it had stopped bleeding. "That was close," he said.

"I don't care what it takes, Glen," she said. "You keep that finger out of the water, you hear? Way out of the water. Don't get us attacked because of your carelessness."

"Okay," he said.

His tone told Lilly he was feeling defeated. This was now a life and death situation. "I don't care how you stay afloat," she said, hearing rage in her own voice. "The moment you notice that cut turning red, you suck it again."

Glen began to distance himself from her, treading water and saying nothing.

With the help of one swim fin, Lilly felt stronger, more secure. She decided to make one last effort to retrieve the other fin from the net. She got up close. The help of the one fin on her foot provided just enough stability in the pushes and pulls of the water and she was able to make several passes at the net. Each time, she forcefully pulled at the tangled knot till finally it was free. She did not rest till the fin was back on her foot. Then she distanced herself from the net and floated face down, limp in the water hoping to restore her energy.

While floating, she watched the dead turtle flop to and fro as the net ambled in the current. The passing of the net was slowed by the weight of the turtle.

While Lilly felt relieved about her swim fins, she was still outraged about the dead turtle. She could have swum with that very turtle before. Something that did not deserve to die in a net now anchored it and the net would, more than likely, trap anything else that came near. She wondered whose net it might be or whether it had been abandoned or lost due to drifting.

She shivered and felt goose bumps rise on her arms and legs. Her joints began to stiffen. Her eyes burned from the glare off the water. It was difficult to think but she forced herself to do just that. She starting organizing her thoughts, in an effort to maintain some control, if only over her mind. She began with what she knew that very moment, that her body might be shutting down. Shivering was the body's reaction when trying to maintain its heat. When the body cooled too far and the shivering became too violent, it meant the internal organs were shutting down. If uncontrolled in time to heat up again, the person would never recover.

She wasn't a cold weather person. That was why she always chose warm weather climates. Her mother had always joked that she could get hypothermia standing too long in front of the opened refrigerator.

Lilly forced her legs to move. Her arms were okay, but her fingers were stiff and her upper lip was numb. Her next thought caused her to bolt slightly and pull off the face gear. "Where are all those noisy helicopters?" she asked, looking toward the sky. Why hadn't one flown over? From such a sweeping vantage point, a pilot could see her flashing a signal.

She guardedly watched the net buoys bob and drift. If only the net would pass. The tide had not taken them backwards for quite a while, just pushed them in the same direction as the net. The expansive net languished, swaying to and fro, like a barrier between them and safety.

In exhaustion, Lilly looked up to the heavens. "What lesson am I to learn from all this?" she asked softly of the sky. "Mom, you always said everything in life had a message."

She remembered her mother's strength. Her mother had been tough in a quiet way. Lilly never knew her dad that well, so she did not know how much of him she had inherited, but if she had only a little of her mother's courage, it would be enough. "What was it you used to say, Mom?" she asked. "Stay quiet, stay positive and conserve strength?" Her mother had won her battle with cancer and gone on for another great twenty-five years. Her mother did it. Her mother won.

"I need your strength and wisdom, Mom," Lilly said. "Help me be strong, so I can win, like you did."

She willed the visions of her mother to control her shivering. The memories warmed her.

She spoke to the water, trying to see her own reflection, wishing she could see her mother. She looked up again. "What do you make of this situation, Mom? Are you up there waiting for me?" she asked. "Is dad there too, or is he still on the road testing your patience?"

Lilly wondered why she was talking out loud to herself. Thinking her thoughts and vocalizing the words had become good company. So was the thought of knowing she was still alive and able to speak. She wondered how Glen was doing as he floated a short distance away.

Ancient memories of Lilly's life paraded through her mind. She had read that this happened in near-death experiences. The memories didn't speak for her life or show that she had made a difference in the world.

A thought came to her as if it had broken through some sort of barrier. If she did not survive and her body washed up somewhere, so would her waterproof camera. Except to exploit the color to try to gain attention, or use it as a weapon, she had neglected its purpose as it dangled beside her arm.

"Photos could tell part of what happened out here," she said, as the idea shot warmth through her veins.

Someone had to know about the plight of that turtle. She pulled on her mask and snorkel and forced her limbs to stretch and move, and then cautiously inched close to the net. She set the focus of the camera and photographed the edge of the net under the water with the buoy floating on top to disclose the type of rigging it had.

She waited for another buoy to arrive, hoping to find telltale markings. There were none but she photographed the buoy and how it was fastened into the net. Maybe how the parts were manufactured and fastened together could tell who made it or where it came from.

Then Lilly had the best idea yet. Warmth flooded her in new waves. People needed to see what she had seen and she knew how to make that possible.

Chapter Ten

From somewhere came bursts of new energy. Who ever found her camera would learn the truth. She wished she had her strobe. Who knew how photographs in the dark depths might turn out? Still, she had to try to capture what she could.

She swam to Glen to tell him what she was about to do.

"Save your energy," he said. He looked about to swim away, and then turned to her again. "We aren't doing each other any good staying together. You do what you have to do."

Glen moved away from her as if he thought she was the harbinger of doom. Well, she had a job to do. Conserving energy to prolong death seemed ludicrous and was not the most meaningful way to spend the end of her life.

Without hesitation, she took the deepest breath possible and dove. She watched the net move back and forth, set the focus for the distance between her and the dead Honu, and then swiftly kicked topside. She did not have enough strength to blow the snorkel clear but yanked it from her mouth to drain while she breathed and built resolve.

She dove again and, as best as she could, gauged the distance she had just measured between the dead turtle and where she was when she focused. She clicked off sequential shots and surfaced. She took several deep breaths then down she went again, for a few more shots from different angles.

Lilly rose to the surface and, along the way, expelled short forceful breaths to give her lungs relief. On the surface, she breathed deeply again and again, oxygenating her system but being careful not to hyperventilate. Although her energy was nearly depleted, she needed to make one last dive.

Surprisingly, floats marking the end of the net drifted by. Lilly put her face into the water and realized that by the way the turtle dragged along behind, the net had shifted directions. The weight of the dead turtle restraining the net meant the turtle would probably be the last thing to pass.

She decided to dive down behind the net and come in closer to the turtle to get a shot when its flipper rose and flopped back and forth. If the pictures were blurred because of the dark murky water, the raised flipper with its unique skin pattern, coloration and shape would set the identifying image.

She wanted to get close enough without running out of breath, and hoped she had enough energy left to get down that far and back to the surface without drowning. Yet, why did she doubt herself? She was going to do it anyway, even if it was her last gesture.

God, give me strength.

She dove forcefully with strong propelling kicks. The water temperature became colder as she went deeper into almost darkness. As the net pushed forward, dragging the lifeless Honu, Lilly focused then shot to the surface for another breath. It felt good to float and rest without fear of the net rolling back and ensnaring her. She dove again, hoping for the right moment. Just as she was about to surface, the net jerked and the Honu's flipper waved just like she saw it do earlier.

Stay calm. Stay in control.

Tiny bubbles rose quickly up and out of sight as she expelled a spurt of air to lessen pressure inside her lungs. Simultaneously, she squeezed off a few more sequential shots as she maneuvered in different directions.

The menacing net suddenly billowed backwards and drifted over her head. The natural tendency of having lungs filled with oxygen made her buoyant and she might float to the surface. If that happened how, she would be pushed right up into the net. She had to dive deeper. Now. She felt panic, but her worst enemy could be her own imagination and fright.

Stay calm. Conserve energy, she mentally repeated like a silent mantra.

She thought she had been near the bottom. What a laugh. She went way down this time, down and under the net, all the while reminding herself she had always been able to hold her breath longer than most people, but the pressure on her ears was suddenly unbearable. She expelled another short breath. The net pulled away. Lilly looked upward and saw the sparkling turquoise mixture of sunlight and frothy bubbles high up at the surface and found it encouraging.

She struggled to stay deep while swimming away from the vexatious sea reaper. The mesh trap came at her again as she struggled for distance. She expelled another small pocket of air.

By now her lungs ached. The arches of both feet began to cramp. She turned, looked back and watched the net billow away, then come at her again. When it came toward her, this time, it remained out of reach and she began to ascend while trying to prevent her lungs from expelling all the spent oxygen at once.

Lilly kept the sloshing aqua waves of the surface in sight and pulled demandingly with her arms. Her knotted feet felt useless, the cramp in the right arch extended up the calf. Up, up she swam, arms groping, pulling upward with powerful breaststrokes, lungs burning. She spat out a breath into the snorkel. By then her lungs were screaming and emptied in a forceful profusion of bubbles and pressure escaping around the mouthpiece.

Hold on. You're there. Hold on!

Suddenly, everything seemed to move in slow motion. She could not rise fast enough. Entering the region of turquoise near the surface, she ripped off the headgear prematurely and swallowed a slug of saltwater that flowed alternately down both her throat and windpipe as she gasped. Her nostrils and lungs were instantly inflamed.

As she broke the surface choking, she gagged, retched and then vomited up the salty brine. Gulping air, oxygen rushed in all the way to the bottom of her starved, painful lungs. She remembered that ingesting one cup of seawater all at once could kill some people. She shook, repulsed and exhausted, but thrust two fingers down her throat to induce vomiting again.

In a moment, she alternately pinched the sides of her nose and blew out the salt from her sinuses, then ducked under for a wash.

"Stupid!" she said, screaming. "You don't have to kill yourself!"

She again felt the pain of the foot cramp that had spread up her calf. Lilly doubled up and grabbed at her feet using the flippers for a better grip, remembering to bend her toes backwards to stretch out the arch. Afraid of losing the flippers to the tide, they would have to stay on. She pressed her toes backward from under the swim fin.

While trying to ease the severity of the cramps, she inadvertently rolled over backwards and swallowed more water and nearly lost her mask and snorkel in the roll.

"One leg at a time," she said once she righted herself. The cramps were tightening. She gave preferential treatment to her right foot and leg where the muscle contractions burned the worst. Holding the toe of the swim fin enabled her to pull her toes back while stretching out the leg against the pull. Next she grabbed the other fin and stretched both arches and legs but noticed how little energy she had left.

As she tended herself, she turned and watched the edge of the net and the buoys drag away across the top of the water and become indiscernible in the dark rolling swells. Glen was nowhere in sight.

She pressured her toes backward until she was sure the cramps would not return. She breathed deeply sending more oxygen into her body. She massaged the muscles that had cramped. When her breathing calmed, she pulled the mask down over her face again, drained the snorkel and put it back into her mouth and floated limp, resting, trying to regain strength, but a new menace had crept in. Dizziness overtook her.

With nothing stationary to grasp as an object of reference, she hugged herself and squeezed her shoulders as she dangled in the water shivering. She curled again into a ball with her face in the water, felt some warmth in her tucked position and stayed that way till long after the vertigo passed. Then she stretched out on the surface to absorb as much heat from the sun as possible. She tried to float with her torso bent backwards so her front side could soak up some warmth, but she had no strength. Floating face down would have to do. That position took the least effort. The direct heat of the sun and the warm tropical waters were her only hope of warding off hypothermia.

Lilly stared into the depths. Few fish passed by. When a school did happen along, they darted away as soon as they saw her. She could not identify all the types of fish. Many species seemed different in deep water. Seeing any life form eased the gnawing solitude she had begun to feel.

Deep down, something moved stealthily in the direction of deeper water, but too deep for her to see clearly. One movement was all, perhaps that of a loner. Some sharks were loners and the sighting was a little intimidating.

Barely moving, she floated, not only to conserve energy but because she remembered the reef shark and knew others lurked. Maybe by remaining as still as possible, she would not attract predators. Moments like these tested her bravado.

The sound and feel of water lapping at the sides of her head became tiring. Water plugged her ears and would not come out when she knocked the heels of her hands against her temples.

Stay calm. Conserve energy.

Her thoughts focused sporadically. From somewhere, she realized that if she lost the camera, no one would know who had died. Lilly mustered her energy and righted herself in the water. Her arms were weak, but she scraped the mask up and off her face and left it precariously perched on her forehead with the snorkel dangling. She brought up the camera and focused on a hand she held extended. Then she held the camera at arm's length, turning it to face herself, and squeezed off a couple of shots. The movements took all the energy she had left. She tipped her head back in the water and managed to reposition her headgear. As she floated, her thoughts drifted to what she might look like in the snapshot. What a time for vanity.

Then she remembered Glen and knew she should take a photo of him too. When she looked around, he really was nowhere in sight. He might have drowned and sunk. Lilly put her face in the water and cried, her salty tears blending with the salty drops of ocean inside her mask.

She might have slept, if that were possible. She did not know how long she drifted or to where. She looked around. The swells were no longer breaking into white water. No water had gotten in through the top of the snorkel. She had had air to breathe. She was still alive.

By the position of the sun, she guessed it was between two and three o'clock in the afternoon. Her stomach rumbled, a definite signal her energy needed replenishing, but she couldn't let that frighten her. She was not using a lot of energy just floating, so she felt she would be fine in that respect. She had gone for hours without food before and always had energy.

Rise above it. Be greater than hunger.

Lilly floated, staying limp. She forced herself to think of something other than the island, the place she knew as paradise.

Are you waiting for me, Mom? I was there to help you make your transition. Will you help me now?

She thought of her dad and how he had been out of town on one of his trips when he died. She and her mother had not been with him. She imagined her mom and dad, together now, watching and waiting for her. She couldn't think of anything that she needed to do, no regrets, and no one she needed to apologize to, except Glen, maybe.

Maybe she should have apologized to Glen for not being more understanding about his fears. Maybe as a friend, she could have encouraged him to talk about them. In the beginning she had, and he always denied them. She should not have nurtured a friendship with him. The friendship made her judgmental, wanting him to be what she thought he should be, and vain, thinking that he should change simply because she thought he should. That was an injustice to both of them.

Now that she saw her relationship with Glen more closely, she had no loose ends. Did most people have unfinished business? Had she been lethargic about life? Had she been reluctant to get involved and do her share to improve the world? Why was it she had not a care? Had all the lessons of her life been learned so that now it was time for her to go?

If this is the way I am to go, I can't think of a better place.

As much as Lilly detested clichés, at least she would have met her Maker doing her most favorite activity. Maybe there was some redeeming quality in that saying after all.

Chapter Eleven

Lilly floated with eyes closed. She was cold and exhausted. She could almost hear her mother's advice from a time they had camped and were snowed in by an unexpected blizzard. When you're too cold, she had said, stiffen your body.

Lilly felt the pushes and pulls of the tide. Vague memories of her mother and childhood home flickered and beckoned. She slipped in and out of consciousness and felt confused and did not know to which images she presently belonged. Stiffen and stiffen again, her mother said. Then relax and feel the heat rush in.

Slowly, Lilly extended her limp body on the surface, though she had no idea where she was. Using all the energy she could muster, she stiffened, then again. She stiffened a third time but it was a weak attempt and she went limp from exhaustion and began to sink. Still, the stiffening worked. Warmth rushed through her calves and thighs and up the front of her chest and settled around her neck and shoulders. She found energy to keep herself on the surface. She stiffened again and then relaxed. A discernible measure of warmth lingered, seeping strength into her body. Yes..., but her thoughts lacked enthusiasm. The lack of energy affected her mind like it did her body.

Stiffen and stiffen again, her mother's voice firmly instructed.

Feeling disoriented, she didn't know if those were her mother's commands she heard, or her own. She remembered lying in a snow-covered tent, shivering and freezing. Why did she now feel so adrift?

Knowing she and her mother survived, she drew strength from her mother's resolve. It helped keep her focused.

Images of the net swept through her mind and filled her with caution and fear. The pull of the tide was no longer grabbing at her. She stiffened again and noticed another measure of warmth slowly make its way up her body. Through a haze of jumbled thoughts, she realized that she still had the snorkel to breathe through and that she was floating in water and needed to keep herself buoyant. With the warmth urging her, she breathed deeply and held it and stiffened again and felt still warmer. Or could it be the water was warming?

Then there it was again, that quick pinch. She gasped through the snorkel. A charge of fear electrified her senses.

Another pinch that felt familiar. A bite on her buttock, then another. Lilly opened her eyes and weakly turned to ward off the attack, but to her utter surprise, right beside her swam a monstrous nipping green sea turtle.

She lifted her face out of the water, looked around and saw land in the distance and felt confused about why she was out so far.

Na Pali?

Reflection from the fading sun off the water came only in a trough from the horizon beyond Na Pali to the west. She sensed the time was late in the day and couldn't understand why she was that far out in the water at that hour and alone.

The aqua water became clearer, like the memory of what had happened to her. The closest shoreline was the uninhabited steep fluted cliffs of Na Pali. The tops of the flutes remained tipped in sunlight. Shadows filled the deep narrow valleys between them. She scrutinized the angular cliffs and remembered the fluctuating horizontal break in the forest thickets that would signify the location of the twelve-mile Kalalau Trail. She felt really alone. Floating had always been a natural thing for her to do, but a thought seeped into her mind that she may be in need of help. She looked again, remembering that occasionally, the trail dropped fairly close to the water. In delirium, she spat out the snorkel and screamed. "Help! In the water. Help!"

The Honu kept nipping.

Many beaches accessible only by water abounded at the foot of those ragged cliffs. If she could just make it to a beach, people in a helicopter would certainly spot her. Or she could somehow climb up through the forest, barefoot and all, to reach the Kalalau Trail and safety.

"Hel-lp!" she said. "In the water."

She wondered if her screaming would frighten away the turtle. She didn't want to do that. Just the Honu being near made her feel safer.

Another more realistic look around told her she was not that close to shore. She felt perilously low in energy, sluggish. She put the snorkel back into her mouth and gazed below at the Honu in wonder. Deeper, several more turtles swam under her and kept moving toward the shore. All the while, the big Honu kept nipping at her bathing suit. Another gigantic turtle cruised up along the other side. The small female with the scarred carapace swam up and also began nipping. The familiar sight of her was overwhelmingly reassuring. Lilly relaxed and blacked out again.

Another pinch on her hip brought her back to consciousness. The Honu were amazing creatures that deserved understanding and protection. Another surge of energy restored her hopes, even as her new measure of strength began to ebb again and she could not fight off the biting.

She stretched out and moved her limbs and that sent warmth and energy through her body. She noticed the camera again and remembered having taken photos and it made her gasp. The rush of oxygen had a clearing affect. Slowly, she reached for the camera and focused, then waited till the female was in a position so she could snap a couple of exacting photos of her triangular scar. Too, she could not resist photographing the other one stretching out the skirt of her bathing suit as he bit and pulled. Truly, a reason existed for everything.

She couldn't guess the quality of the photos she had just taken. The energy she used should best have been spent on keeping herself afloat.

She had always told people never to touch those magnificent creatures. Let them have peace in their natural habitat. Like the turtles that had just passed deeper down, they all seemed headed straight toward shore. She knew she needed to be there too, and now she was having trouble keeping herself from sinking. Her energy and will were nearly depleted.

That one big powerful turtle had stayed at her side. One Honu even turned its head to peer at her. The turtles had not veered away when she stirred. They hung protectively close. One swam across the front of her and disappeared behind as disappointment filled her. Another turtle arrived, right alongside as if waiting for her to hitch a ride.

Lilly did just that. She did not want to scare them but groped and clutched both sides of the biggest Honu's hard shell and hung on in desperation. Surprisingly, the carapace was slimy with algae and was a little difficult to hold onto. The turtle seemed to know it had a job to do. Lilly struggled to hold on as her hands slid. Then she remembered that these turtles could not pull their heads back into their shells. She was not likely to get her fingers caught if it decided to retract its head. She stretched, reached to the upper edge of the shell and found a better grip.

The Honu swam at the surface and gave no inclination of trying to submerge. Lilly was able to rest a bit letting the turtle do all the work. As she rested, she almost slipped off the turtle when she felt consciousness leaving again. She fought to stay alert.

The Honu moved in spurts as their powerful flippers reached out and pulled at the water again and again. The sea became clearer. The sandy floor drew up, with a coral formation here and there. The Honu continued to pull her into shallower water, now all sparkling aqua. Yet still, the Honu swam.

When Lilly raised her face out of the water to get her bearings, she saw that she and the turtles were headed easterly. By swimming lengthwise of the current, they allowed the tide to push them toward shore. One big turtle hauled her while, surprisingly, the little female swam on her left and a big male stayed on her right. She felt giddy, drunk. Her mind reeled. It felt like a game, but something told her never to let go.

A school of gigantic Blue Ulua overtook them. The presence of other creatures helped Lilly feel safer. She laughed inside the headgear and gave thanks for those magnificent creatures, to which humans give far too meager credit.

Childish delight bubbled up as she rode and felt the surge and pull of the tide and felt the monstrous turtle turn on the speed against the backward pull. With renewed vigor, her body warmed and her legs worked again. In an effort to help, she tried to kick her legs, only to find she could barely feel them.

After a while, Lilly lifted her head again and could not believe her eyes. The near high tide had been in their favor and she and the Honu were headed right into a little pristine cove.

Chapter Twelve

The Honu slowed. It was time to let go. Before she released her grip, the little female turned its head and looked straight at her with its big dark eyes. With the next surge, Lilly released her grip and the surf tumbled her into the shallows. Her hand dragged in sand. Each time she tried to stand a wave knocked her down. Each time a wave washed over her head, she thought she was at sea again. That had been sand she felt momentarily under her knees. Realizing this, she fought to stay on top of the waves and to let them wash her higher onto the beach.

As soon as she clutched fistfuls of sand in the shallows, adrenaline caused a kinetic rush the likes she had never known. Without the steadiness of the weight of that monstrous turtle and the protective ones alongside delivering her to the beach, she would eventually have been dashed against the jagged black lava rock outcroppings.

Struggling to stand while wearing the swim fins, her knees finally buckled and she collapsed in ankle deep water. She tore off the mask and snorkel and dragged her limp body far up onto the dry beach away from the slamming surf of high tide. Stinging hot sand grated against the length of her scraped legs but she didn't remember how her legs were scraped and cared little. Some sand found its way inside her bathing suit and burned her chest but still, she cared little. The parched sand stung her arms, elbows and knees. When far enough away from the water, with numbed withered fingers, she pulled off the swim fins and dragged them up beside her.

She rolled over and laid back onto the burning sand as if needing to feel something other than the coolness of a drowning death in waiting. Contact with the sand told her that her back and shoulders had been scorched.

Feelings of denial overtook her as she strove to remain conscious. She drifted in and out of consciousness as if trying not to go to sleep. Her head spun with delirium. Her front side had not felt the sun much in the water. Now she welcomed the direct heat and blacked out again.

Then a haunting noise made her come alert and raised goose bumps. Something dragged with slow ominous scraping sounds that drew closer and closer.

"What else?" she asked, feeling unable to withstand another threat. She remembered the turtles having brought her to shore, but that felt long ago.

The ominous noise dragged closer in slow rhythmic scrapes accompanied by no other sounds. She felt the sand move near her. Then all was quiet and still. Adrenaline surged again. Mentally, she psyched herself for yet another onslaught. Fearful, she opened an eye to see one huge Honu had dragged itself up beside her to bask in the sunlight. Its flipper stopped moving no more than an inch from her fingertips.

Lilly gasped. "Miracles do happen," she said, whispering. "Why aren't you afraid of me, Honu?"

She slowly moved her hand to gingerly touch the tip of the turtle's flipper. Her mind was foggy but her heart swelled with praise and admiration and thankfulness as she rubbed the leathery scaly skin with a sandy fingertip. The turtle did nothing, just lay there and took in the sun as several more turtles beached with the small female following.

"What would it take to make people understand?" Lilly asked.

Painfully moving her aching body, she set the focus again and, including some of her body in the frame, took a shot of how close the Honu rested so near and another shot of her fingertips touching the Honu's flipper. "That one's for my eyes only," she said. Then she snapped a few close-ups of each turtle's countenance in sunlight. After that, Lilly lay back down and said a million thanks to the powers that be for sending the Honu to deliver her safely into the cove.

As she became more coherent, she moved her head from side to side as she lay in the sand, studying each turtle close up out of water. "How gentle you are," she said softly. "How is it you didn't swim away?"

Those magnificent creatures needed protection. She already knew what needed to be done. She had planned it out in deep water. When she thought the only thing to survive would be her camera, she had taken all those telltale pictures hoping others would one day see that drift net wreaking havoc.

"I photographed the Honu that was caught in the net," she said softly. The thought made her sad. "I photographed you, little one," she said to the female, "with that cruel gouge in your side." Slowly, Lilly rose to her elbows again and squeezed off a few choice close-ups of the female's damaged carapace more clearly discernable in daylight.

The Honu beside her lifted its head. Turtles do not see as well on land as in water. Thick tears constantly washed across its eyes, cleaning them and at the same time getting rid of its body's build up of salts. She focused on the natural cleansing action of the eye and snapped a couple choice frames before it dropped its head to rest again.

"I've got it all," she said. "I'm going to tell it to the world the whole story. No harmless turtle should be killed or maimed for the benefit of selfish human motives. No harmless turtle should be so much as harassed."

The moment she realized she was safe again on land, she remembered Glen and the whole scenario of their plight played out in her mind. Glen had disappeared from sight out in the ocean. She sat up quickly. "Glen," she said. "Gotta get help for Glen." She needed to find out exactly where she beached, find someone with a cell phone. She struggled to stand but her legs gave out.

While adrift, she thought her life was about to end. She had mentally wrapped up loose ends. "Heavens, no," she said, feeling the urgency of the moment. "I was only taking stock in order to find a new place to begin." In the past she had let things slide, watched events go wrong in the world without taking a stand. "I've got to do something besides vote every two years."

Perhaps the many injustices of today's world had overwhelmed her. She had gotten into the habit of believing she could not affect change. Like with Glen, who had been dead weight. When she thought of Glen being lost at sea, she choked back tears. She did not have to single-handedly change the world, but she could start with the one in which she existed.

Having been handed back her life, she would do something about the issues that annoyed her; like launching a campaign to protect the Honu, like getting updated photography equipment. Setting right the sour state of affairs with Glen should have been a priority. "I have been asleep," she said. "Too quiet, too long, but now I'll even talk to myself aloud and not care whether doing so is right or wrong."

She struggled to right herself and fell again and again, like a newborn animal trying to stand for the first time. She had had no nourishment all day and her head spun. Finally, she stood with knees bent and feet apart to keep her balance, and looked around trying to identify the area. "This is how I'll do my part," she said, looking back at the turtles. "You wonderful creatures saved my life. What more could I do than help you have yours?"

The sun's position hung at about four o'clock in the afternoon. Without knowing what happened to Glen, she could wait no longer. It was time to begin finding her way back to Ke'e Beach, on land, regardless of the ragged cliffs, regardless of the venomous centipedes. Regardless of the prickly Neptunia grass known as *hila-hila* to the locals.

"Injustice," she said under her breath. She had read that the missionaries, in order to teach the Hawaiians to wear shoes, introduced Neptunia grass and ironwood trees to the Islands. "Pathetic," she said.

Lilly dropped to her knees to conserve energy and scrutinized the thickets around her. The Na Pali coastline contained some of the densest forests on Kauai. "If need be," she said, "I'll cut the excess shape from the flippers with a rock and wear what's left as rubber shoes." Anything was possible because nothing would ever be as arduous as what she had just endured.

She stood again and took a couple of steps and tested her legs, finding them weak and rubbery. She looked at the turtles basking in sunlight. Strangely, her presence and movements had not frightened them.

The pristine cove, one of many accessible only from the water, looked fairly secluded. "I wonder where we could be," she said.

Between each crashing wave of high tide, she heard the sound of running water. On the back of the cliff wall, a tall, thin and sparkling waterfall elegantly cascaded down black lava rock ledges into a cool-looking alcove. Tall False Kamani, pandanus, lauhala and many species of palm squeezed together in the forest above the fall. Maile, hau, pikake and the pernicious passionflower vine intertwined with myriad other species and comprised the thicket that used the trees as ladders to sunshine. "So many species, so much to learn," Lilly said, as she scrutinized the cliffside.

Suddenly, she heard voices. "Hikers," she said, as she tried to see them. "Hikers on the Kalalau."

"Hey, up there," she said, yelling as her voice cracked and failed her. Yelling seemed futile now that she was safe on land. The trail was close enough to hear people's voices. She would make her way up the cliffside without needing help. Then, in looking around for the best access upward, she realized exactly where she was.

A high plateau surrounded by trees and tangled thicket was on her left. "That's *Ke Au a Laka Halau Hula Heiau*," she said. Her mouth hung open. That meant the man-made basalt rock formation of *Ku Ulu a Paoa Heiau* lay adjacent on the other side of the plateau. The tiered layers of these heiaus were where portions of *The Thornbirds* had been filmed. A trail led from there a few hundred feet back to Ke'e Beach. As soon as she could climb out of the cove, she could get to her cell phone and call for help for Glen.

Years earlier, she learned heiaus were the remains of ancient temples when the Islands were inhabited only by Hawaiians. Even today, worship continued to be practiced among the many heiau ruins.

"I've been here," she said, taking a few more steps. "I know exactly where I am."

She looked up toward the plateau again. *Ke Au a Laka Halau Hula Heiau* bordered the cove. She remembered having stood atop the heiau plateau knowing access to the sheltered cove where she now stood could only be by way of the sea. Or, at very low tide, by climbing over the lava boulders comprising the retaining wall of Puka Ulua Channel opposite Ke'e Beach at the end of the road.

As she crossed the hot sandy beach, she focused on the gentle waterfall splashing down the black lava rock. From there, it found its way in a trickle along the edge of the sand at the cliffside to the sea.

"I thought I recognized this waterfall," she said. Amazingly, the Honu had delivered her no more than a five minute walk from where she began her sojourn on Ke'e Beach. "I should have known when I saw the fat Ulua swim by. They gather to feed at Puka Ulua."

She felt giddy. The only way out of the cove would be to climb up the black lava rocks to reach the top of the plateau. She thought about going back to Ke'e Beach by climbing among the boulders bordering the channel, but something about the relentless surf and the insistent rising tide swallowing the border of rocks told her she had had enough for one day.

"You haven't scared me away," she said to the sea. "You could have taken me but it wasn't my time."

She reached the shaded area at the back of the cove. "These feet of mine," she said, taking stock of herself, "toughened from walking on hot sand, will have no problem gripping wet lava rocks."

The wet rocks were slippery and Lilly had to climb cautiously, in spite of needing to hurry. She let the water run over her head and resisted taking time to run her fingernails through her hair to remove sand from her scalp. Each new moment restored her and gave her strength to keep going. She remembered the open wounds on her leg and worried about infection. The natural water run-off on the island, beginning at the Alaka'i Swamp atop Mt. Waialeale, could be loaded with the potentially life-threatening Leptospira that could invade through any skin opening or if ingested. The infectious genus of thin, spiral and hook-ended spirochetes could cause hemorrhagic spirochetal jaundice. Yet, if she contracted a leptospirosis, she would just have to get medication and set her mind to get through it. As it was, she needed to check in with a doctor as soon as possible about having breathed seawater into her lungs, which now ached between her shoulder blades. If too much salt had gotten into her lungs, the lungs would make copious amounts of fluid to try to wash out the salt. Her own secretions could drown her.

The silky waterfall poured over her shoulders but the skin on her shoulders tingled painfully and had already blistered. "White vinegar always takes care of sunburn," she said. The scraped wounds on her legs and feet had risen in welts. In time, her skin would heal. More important was that she was alive.

She tediously picked her way up the incline to the widest part of the water-fall where it splashed out in all directions. People are warned against standing under the larger waterfalls because of rocks being dislodged by the force of the downfall, but surely this gentle trickle could move no boulders.

Chapter Thirteen

Relentless surf thunderously collided in explosive white belches that sprayed high up the black lava rock cliffs below her. Yet, the picturesque cove, with its smoothed white sand surrounded by lush foliage remained serene. The beach really was not accessible from the heiau because of tangled underbrush. Lilly had accessed that heiau several times from the Ke'e Beach trail, but no real entrance to the small cove existed from atop the plateau. An occasional person trying to climb down the waterfall soon learned how steep and slippery the rocks were.

Lilly climbed slowly upward, keeping her body close to the rocks in order to avoid falling backwards. Climbing was difficult having to hold onto the snorkeling gear. She leaned a shoulder against the rocks and put the mask securely on again and propped it on her forehead leaving the snorkel dangling loose. That left only the fins to be dealt with. Certainly, she could not wear them while climbing and she needed her hands to grip. "Of course," she said, thoroughly pleased. No one else was about. She stretched open the front of her elastic bathing suit and shoved the fins heels-first down inside. "An added benefit should I slip," she said. "The fins would take the impact."

Everything was working in her favor. She began slowly and found that due to the irregular placement of the rocks forming ledges, she could scale the side of the cliff, until her energy wavered and she had to perch on a rock till her legs strengthened again. She climbed intermittently until she arrived near the top of the waterfall where something hung right above her swaying in the tropical breeze of late afternoon.

"Maile," she said. Maile was considered a fortunate omen and was available for the picking and said by Ancient Hawaiians to have mana or special powers.

Lilly stretched upwards, being careful to avoid reaching into a prickly flowering thicket of lantana weed. "Scratchier than hila-hila," she said. She tentatively clasped a clump of thick grasses for support and then stepped up to another rock. She reached farther but the vine was still beyond her fingertips. She climbed to yet another level, by then having precariously draped herself across the top of the trickling waterfall like a giant spider.

The vine was in her grip. Gently, she tugged to see where it traveled. From an overhanging tree, it dangled like a rope down the opposite side of the waterfall. That one trailing creeper of Maile had to be nearly eight feet long. Just as she was about to yank it loose, she changed her mind. True, the Maile might be a good omen, but did that mean she had to pick it? She had seen it. That was enough of a message. She turned it loose and, instead, plucked off only a couple of leaves. What she wanted to do did not take killing the entire plant.

Lilly held the plucked leaves gently between her teeth. When she got herself back to a safer ledge, she broke the end of one of the leaves and sniffed. The heady fragrance that emitted brought home the meaning of what it meant to live on Kauai. She thought about how people always had to get as close as possible to a thing till they entered its domain and overpowered it. "Well, this beauty can live on," she said, but she knew she could not be too critical of others. After all, she had broken a few rules herself today.

She arrived at the tentative trail set down by the curious who had tried to get close to the waterfall. She placed both bare feet onto the worn earth and relished the feel of packed red dirt beneath them. A surge of triumph came over her and she felt vertigo again.

The turtles began dragging themselves toward the water. The sound of their underbellies scraping along floated up from the beach. Lilly watched and choked back the urge to cry. The Hawaiians believed in personal deities they called their 'aumakuas. The spirit of a deceased ancestor would appear in animal form to warn of danger and to give strength and guidance. Was one of those turtles acting as her *'aumakua*? Who had the ancestor been? Had her mother truly been with her? As she strove to become acclimated to the Hawaiian culture had the mythology manifested in her life? "My 'aumakua," she said softly.

She was enduring like her mother after all. Yet, more than that, she had discovered a new sense of herself. She pulled the fins out of her bathing suit. Momentarily, she could only stand and look over the cliffside down into the cove where she had been coughed upon the sand. The relentless rising surf had already claimed the curious markings left by the Honu. Another tall wave washed in and thunderously crashed against the far cliffside spraying a magnificent pillar of white froth. "Wow," Lilly said. "I'm lucky I didn't wash in on that."

She needed to get back to the spot under the Kamanis and to her cell phone. The thought of Glen made her realize something else about herself. Glen's fears mirrored her reluctance to take a stand in anything. All she harbored were opinions. Now she would set herself on a right course.

She quickly made her way along the back wall of the heiau plateau that connected with the back of the cove and the waterfall. Remains of an ancient kitchen were still evident. Above that and to the right were clefts in the rocks where offerings were left. On other ledges hung dried and decaying grass skirts and flower leis, which were offerings left by hula dancers from a ceremony held weeks earlier.

Lilly did not know if what she was about to do would be a proper offering but could not allow herself time to wonder. Since Maile was revered by the ancient practitioners of hula and used in hula ceremonies, she placed the maile leaves onto the ledge beside a withered ti leaf hula skirt and turned to face the ocean with arms uplifted. "I give thanks for having been given back my life," she said. Suddenly she felt as if she had been too melodramatic and looked around to see if any tourists clamored about and had watched, but she found herself alone.

The sun hung low in the west. Lilly made her way down through the various levels of the heiau trying to rush when she knew she shouldn't. Suddenly, dizziness set in again and she began to shake all over and her legs gave out. She slipped and ended up on her rear end on a boulder and was stunned. She could now be suffering from heat exhaustion and could be headed into a heat stroke. She pushed the thought out of her mind. It was all she could do to keep from blacking out. She broke out in a sweat. She concentrated on seeing things around her and finally laid her face against the flat side of a rock and welcomed its coolness. She turned to the other side. She pressed her back against another rock for a time. Feeling something other than the baking heat of the sun helped her remain conscious. She remained seated until the pain in her buttock eased and she got her bearings again. "Don't kill yourself," she said in frustration. Exhaustion threatened to overwhelm her.

She felt everything closing in so she concentrated on looking out to sea. Someone had said from land to the horizon represented about a four-mile distance. She actually wished to know how far she had drifted and could only know if she went out that far again. She vowed to get into a boat one day soon to find out. "It wasn't my time," Lilly said to the ocean. "You can't keep me away. I've some important matters to attend."

It felt good to be alive. She marveled in it, but salvation was bittersweet. She thought of Glen again. Maybe he had not drowned. Maybe he was still adrift. Why was she dallying on the path?

She wasn't sure she was ready to try to walk again but had to. A crude stone pathway wound through the thickets and separated the two heiaus. She navigated these more cautiously, noticing that her energy had not been restored. Her legs felt numbed and wobbly. Her hands shook as she grabbed at rocks, bushes and shrubs to keep her balance. The surf incessantly battered the dark rocks that kept the ocean from washing away the embankment. Again rain pelted. In giddiness, she wished to sit and let the water pour over her. Her better judgment told her to get help for Glen. "I'm alive," she said as her emotions first soared, then plummeted. "I'm starting over, with a new purpose." Fate had been kind. She made it to the wide shady trail bordering the channel above the rock wall and headed toward Keʻe Beach. Rain trickled through the trees and splashed over her like a blessing. She was reminded how parched she had become. Her stomach rumbled. She had a sandwich waiting in the cooler and would eat it after calling 911.

Finally, she cut across the corner of the end of the paved road and back onto Keʻe Beach. Many of the beachgoers stared. A few feet farther, she came upon two familiar chairs and a red cooler with its lid left opened. Someone had eaten both sandwiches and drunk the juices. All the ice had melted. Her bottle of juice, now only half full, floated in the water, reminding how she had bobbed for hours. The cool drink for which she thirsted was certainly now tepid. It had just sprinkled again, and her pareau, lying neatly folded on the chaise was soaked.

Hawaiians would never take others' lunches. Even tourists did not do that. Strangely, she remembered she had left her pareau loosely draped over the back of the chaise. Glen had always folded her pareau. She always threw it haphazardly over the back of the beach chair. After all, it was just a casual bathing suit cover-up, but the fact the breeze kept it waving always seemed to unnerve Glen and he would always fold it.

Lilly dropped the camera and snorkeling gear onto the chaise and opened out her pareau and dunked it into the water in the cooler. She brought the sopping cloth up to her face and drizzled water all over her painful shoulders. The water was still cool enough to counteract heat threatening to cause her to have a stroke and collapse in the sand. She eased herself onto the chaise and doused herself again and stuck the end of the cloth into her mouth while others on the beach nearby watched curiously. She remembered that she could not drink the juice bobbing in the bottle because too much liquid while suffering any degree of heat prostration could cause her to pass out. Finally feeling somewhat restored, she pulled a towel from the beach bag under the chaise and stood to head for her van and cell phone.

"Where have you been?" a voice approaching from the thicket of nearby trees asked emphatically. His tone was no surprise.

In shock, Lilly whirled around. "Glen?"

"What took you so long?" He held her cell phone to his ear. Into it, he said, "She's back. She's okay, I guess." He clicked out of the call and approached.

"Glen?" was all she could ask. She gripped the backrest of the chaise to help her stand. "You made it back?"

"Once the net passed," he said, shrugging. "The tide changed. That helped."

"You left me? Just left me out there by myself?"

"Well, I wasn't going to get myself killed because you wanted to take more pictures."

"I almost drowned!"

"I just called 911," he said, holding up her cell phone. He had a couple of large Band-aids wrapped around the finger he had sliced. He dropped the phone into her beach bag. He had even taken the time to change into dry clothes.

"You made it back in time to eat a leisurely lunch first? Then you just now got worried enough to call 911?" She nearly screamed. "When did it dawn on you that I might be in trouble?"

"Well, I made it back. I didn't see why you couldn't."

This was absolutely the last she would tolerate Glen's irrational logic. She had to force herself to keep from losing her temper. Her stomach rumbled. She needed nourishment. "Where's my sandwich?" she asked.

He quickly glanced at his watch. "It's nearly dinner time," he said. "I had to eat. We can get you something on the way back."

"You ate my sandwich?"

"Where have you been?" he asked. "Don't you know what time it is?" As long as she had known him, his conversation was always laced with fearful questions.

"Swimming," Lilly said, bending down to pat the towel over her legs and feeling the sting of the scrapes. Bending over also reminded her of her burning lungs and exaggerated the pain between her shoulder blades. "We've got to leave right away," she said. Yet the ride home with Glen would feel worse, having to listen to him air his fears.

"Look at that sunburn," he said. "Your shoulders are one big blister."

"Just help me pack up, okay?"

He did not move but craned his neck one way or the other checking her condition. "Why did you stay out so long? Why didn't you just come in after the net passed?"

Lilly continued to dry her hair and remove sand from her limbs. She noticed that where the Honu had plucked at her bathing suit skirt, it had pulled loose at the seams. People nearby continued to watch. "Pack up, Glen," Lilly said.

Glen made no effort to help and continued to ogle her wounds. "How'd you tear your suit? And just look at your legs. You'll be scarred for life. How the—"

"Glen," Lilly said, interrupting in a tone that demanded his attention. He looked up expectantly. "Glen," she said again. "Shut... up!"

Reunion

Chapter One

"Hurricane season's almost over," Ciara said, though rain pelted down outside the window. "Most likely that storm south of us will die out, don't you think?"

"All the others have this year," Lilly said. "But every storm is different."

"Can't wait to remodel," Ciara said as she glanced at the walls of her living room. "Berkley's looking at my blueprints right now."

"Looking at your prints?" Lilly asked. She took a sip of tea. "Even though he doesn't do remodeling?

"He just wanted to check them," Ciara said. "I thought that was nice of him. Didn't he help you on your house?"

"No, he refuses to do remodeling, likes to build a house from the ground up," she said. "He has no patience for the problems encountered with restoration, especially with houses like ours where the floors are mounted above ground on concrete blocks."

Lillian Avery had watched an attraction flare between her friend Berkley Mead and Ciara Malloy when she first introduced them. The way Berkley took to Ciara cast a dubious shadow indeed. However, Berkley's attitude was the least important in a string of events that bordered on pandemonium since Ciara's arrival four months earlier. The reunion kept Lilly on a perpetual high ever since Ciara moved to Kauai and they finally got to know each other through more than just a passing glance, like when they were neighbors in Puerto Rico. It had been over thirty years since they lived next door to one another then.

From the moment Lilly met Ciara at the Lihue airport, they bonded like two schoolgirls and soon learned their interests and life's work could complement one another. Recently, Lilly acted as Ciara's power of attorney through the closing of escrow. She helped Ciara purchase the acre and old plantation house next to her property. Ciara, grandson in tow, alternately made two trips to the Mainland and Puerto Rico, gathering belongings and seeing Pablo off to Central America. Ciara's massive storage container was delivered and sat in her front yard. With so much rain, weeds had grown up around the base and the old metal hulk already looked as if it had been sitting there for ages. For two people whose lives had almost touched decades earlier, living next door to one another again seemed like a gift of the new century.

With her friend and neighbor settling in, Lilly would have to tactfully address the situation with Berkley to keep it from ruining her relationship with him or Ciara or both of them. Even though she cherished Berkley's friendship, Lilly could not remember a time when she actually needed Berkley in her life. She cared for him and enjoyed his company but the relationship had stalled, like all her relationships had. Then the way his eyes lit up when meeting Ciara made Lilly feel insignificant. So maybe she had not made him feel wanted. Maybe now was much too late to try.

"How long have you two known each other?" Ciara asked.

The question took her by surprise. "About a year," she said.

"Berkley's a refreshing upbeat sort of guy," Ciara said.

"But a little too carefree and unencumbered," Lilly said. She did not know from where that perception of him originated but that had not been necessary to pin down in the type of relationship they shared. After having known one man with myriad hesitations and phobias, she was pleased to know Berkley; not that she needed to compare the two. She was not dependent upon Berkley for anything but he sure knew how to put all his knowledge to use. He specialized in building custom homes on Kauai and sometimes on the other Hawaiian Islands. Then along came Ciara, with her home needing remodeling. When he and Ciara met and began to talk about home construction, Lilly felt him slipping away. It showed in his demeanor and in the longer periods of time he spent with Ciara. Not until that time did Lilly realize how much she cared for this man, the first person in a long time with whom she hoped to take a relationship beyond where all of her others had failed. Now he would help Ciara, who really did not need any.

Ciara knew about building and remodeling. It was what she did in the Caribbean after her husband passed away. Just took over the business and kept it going. She said she had not had nor wanted a serious relationship since her husband died. What could Berkley possibly see in her? Certainly, it could not be the fact that Ciara was raising her grandson while Pablo was away in the Navy. Berkley had taken to the child too. Lilly felt sad, hoping he was not using the boy to get to Ciara. Perhaps she was seeing a side of Berkley she had not had a chance to know. What she suspected was something she wanted to resolve and put behind her as soon as possible.

"Most of my belongings will have to stay in that behemoth metal crate," Ciara said. "I'm not dragging anything more into the house only to have to remove it again when construction begins."

"You won't have long to wait," Lilly said.

"I'll just bite my tongue," she said with a wry smile, "every time I have to go rummage for something."

Lilly had helped her assemble only those items immediately needed for day to day living and that would benefit from the protection of being inside the house, which was less humid. Ciara had a lot of precious memories connected to everything she brought with her, like her photo albums. It took a long time before she finally offered to share her photo albums as Lilly had hers.

Ciara had always seemed hesitant about disclosing much of her past. She was more careful than secretive about how she said things; as if there was a lot she avoided saying. Sometimes the way Ciara told things sounded glossed-over. A peek into the photo albums would tell Lilly more about this energetic widow with sad hazel eyes who had, perhaps quite innocently, captured the attention of the illusive Berkley Mead. So, oblivious to the continual rain and an island-wide flash flood watch, they sat side-by-side on the futon sofa in Ciara's small front room ready to take a walk through a pictorial history.

Just then, the winds gusted and palm trees bent. A light sprinkle of rain penetrated through the fine screen and half-opened jalousies covering the windows behind where they sat. The draft rippled the edges of the doily on the end table across the room beside an easy chair. A masculine blue and green funeral urn sat boldly in the middle of the doily. A framed photo of a very young Pablo and his father stood beside it.

"My house must be a little more dilapidated than yours was when you bought," Ciara said.

"But picturesque of an all but forgotten Hawaiian era," Lilly said. The fact that her house had better withstood the elements all those years was one reason Lilly chose to buy the one she did. That and the view and the way her house was situated on the lot. The before and after photos of her property had encouraged Ciara to buy the parcel and old house next door, even though it needed much more work. Lilly knew she would miss looking out of her lanai windows and seeing the weathered and picturesque shack on the hillside on the next acre, but who better to renovate it than Ciara?

Ciara was adamant. Buying the decaying structure was a trade-off, she had said. She wanted to live next door. Besides restoring, she would expand a bit. She would try to retain as much of the ambiance as possible. Remodeling was, after all, nothing new to her.

Little Rico, Ciara's three-year-old grandson, came to lean against her leg and she instinctively put an arm around him and drew him up onto her lap. Ciara exhibited strong and natural motherly instincts that Lilly had great difficulty identifying in herself.

"Wait till you see some of the houses I designed," Ciara said. "Seems home-building or remodeling's always been part of my life."

Lilly sat her tea mug on the end table, put on her reading glasses, and wondered why Ciara would allude to the houses instead of the people in her albums. But then, her own albums contained mostly photos of fishes and a few more recent ones of a friend, Keoki, among the sea life.

Ciara spoke of her work a lot, including the children's books that she wrote and which continued to earn her a small fortune. In the late sixties in Puerto Rico, Lilly had hoped to meet Ciara and perhaps collaborate on a child's book or two. They might have combined her underwater photography and Ciara's cute stories. Then Lilly's mother had written about having cancer and Lilly quickly moved back to Santa Cruz.

"Back then, I had told Rico," Ciara said, "that I also wished to meet the "California woman" to collaborate. The next thing I knew, the interesting neighbor that Pablo frequently spoke of had moved away." Both she and Ciara had been well intentioned, but never got to meet. They both stared at one another, remembering, and then shaking their heads.

Ciara searched through the stack of albums till she found one in particular. It was the record of the houses she had designed and built. The many interior and exterior photos showed different stages of construction. The houses seemed a bit old fashioned and all were designed in concrete block for island living. A person had to think back to that particular era and realize that in those times, what Ciara designed were custom homes of the day. The styles were many and varied and spoke volumes about the range of creativity of this energetic woman.

The first page of the next album lay opened. Ciara quieted. She touched the lips in the photo of a dashing Latino man. "This is Rico. You remember him at all?" she asked as she slipped into a reverie. Her hands trembled when she finally turned the page. On and on the photos went capturing her, Rico, Pablo and occasional friends, mostly around the Calle Delbrey house or on board the Mercy in happier days.

"Secondary drowning," Lilly said as she remembered Ciara's explanation. She remembered what it felt like having once sucked salt water into her lungs. "I'm so sorry. With what we know about respiratory therapy today…"

Ciara breathed heavily and signed long. "A lot of research a little too late for us," she said. "Now they know how to make people expel fluid from their lungs. They even poke holes in people's sides and into the lungs to drain them." She shook her head and sighed. "It took a lot more deaths to bring the problem to light."

"I'm so sorry," Lilly said again. She reached to squeeze Ciara's hand and found it trembling still.

Compared to the early photos, Ciara had put on some weight with age. Yet, she retained a little-girl quality and could stylishly wear a crop top tee and pair of shorts that made other women envious. Lilly's swimming lifestyle kept the weight off her. Like her black hair, Ciara's once-glistening brown curls now contained a few early strands of gray.

The next album continued with more photos of her, Rico and Pablo together. Too soon Ciara turned the page and said, "This is where life changed."

Lilly knew well what was coming. "That's all you have?" she asked. "Not even two albums with your husband?"

"That's all," she said as she twisted the prominent wedding rings on her finger. "But I'll carry him in my mind and heart to my grave."

All the diamonds in Ciara's wedding ring set were so large Lloyd's of London could well have insured them. Yet, the size of the stones was not what attracted Lilly, but the brilliance. All those years, as good diamonds do, they continued to flash their unending message of love and commitment. Lilly could not imagine what it might feel like to receive such a token of one man's promise. She could not imagine what it might be like to return that commitment. She wondered how, through all the years, the need for love, marriage and family had eluded her. She wondered why she never felt motivated to seek out a lasting partner. She began to think about examples in her past, her friends' great marriages and her own parents' estranged but enduring relationship, and how alone she felt as a child.

While staring at Ciara's symbolic sparklers, in a new way she felt lonely and incomplete. Once in a while through the years, the sparkle of a piece of jewelry would bring to mind a fleeting memory of old wishes and dreams that might have been. A singer's exquisite evening gown would remind that she liked to dance and had not done so for decades, and longed to, but for the want of a dance partner. A singer's certain voice, even the lyrics, brought fleeting moments of hopes that might have been. Suppressed dreams would surface momentarily to keep her in touch with her former self; dreams that reminded of misplaced intention and unexpressed yearnings as she caught a mental glimpse of them and remembered. She shook her head to clear her mind.

Yet, where were Ciara's wedding photos? For someone who lived a life in remembrance of her late husband, surely she would show those as well. Perhaps she kept them as cherished memories only unto herself. "Oh, look," Lilly said, pointing to the next page. "Pablo's growing up."

"Look here," Ciara said as she turned more pages. "Here's Pablo in his Ensign's uniform when he first joined the Navy." She smiled broadly. "Being Cuban citizens, he was naturalized when his father got his American citizenship. Pablo was accepted into Annapolis after high school."

"Dad-dy," Little Rico said as he pressed a dimpled finger onto the photo.

"I remember Pablo as a tall boy," Lilly said. She marveled at the remarkable changes, having only months earlier met the grown-up Pablo. "I'm happy to see him in these pictures at different ages. I always wondered how that brilliant young man fared. But he doesn't look a thing like his dad."

Ciara took too sharp a breath but it sounded like she meant to keep it subdued. "He looked more like his mother," she said. She glanced at the other albums on the floor at her feet then bent around Rico and chose one. "Pablo's amazed that you went on to learn Spanish after you left Puerto Rico," she said. Again, it sounded like diversion from something she did not wish to discuss.

Rico watched them both and listened quietly as they spoke. He looked as if he understood every word.

"Is his father that intense?" Lilly asked as she watched Rico's gaze jumped from her to his grandmother and back again as each spoke in turn.

"Rico, why don't you go in the bedroom and watch TV," Ciara said as she eased him off her knee. "Go ahead. Lilly and I want to talk some, okay?"

"TV," Rico said. "TV." He left by himself but would have no trouble using the remote. He was too smart for that. Additionally, he had already achieved the computer and electronics level of literacy of a five or six-year-old.

"Let me show you something," Ciara said as she flipped through pages. Finally she pointed to a particular photo of Pablo with two people. "That was taken in New York," she said. "When Pablo was old enough, I had to encourage him to find his mother." She choked up again. "That was the second hardest thing I've had to do in all my life."

Again Ciara seemed too over-wrought for the telling of something as simple as helping Pablo locate his mother. The way Ciara had told it, Pablo knew from childhood that his mother had gone away. All that remained was for him to find her so that he might re-start the relationship of have some sort of closure. Logically, that's what should have been done, but then, Ciara seemed by nature more emotional about things.

Lilly studied the two people who had posed with Pablo in quite a few photos during what seemed a very congenial time. She must have been a beautiful woman when younger and all the signs said she strove to at least keep her face in good condition. "Pablo's mother never stayed in touch?" she asked.

"Her name's Amalia," Ciara said. "No, never once in all the years did she try to contact Pablo." In one photo, Amalia stood between her husband and Pablo who wore his Navy uniform. "Pablo was in his early twenties there." Amalia looked well dressed and pampered but the years showed in her matronly figure. What she and Pablo had most in common in those years was hair color and waviness.

"That man is Amalia's husband?"

"His name's Tito," Ciara said. She tapped a fingertip on the photo of a tall self-assured looking man with a full head of white hair.

Pablo's facial features definitely were his mother's. She must have had strong genes that overpowered Rico's. Pablo so looked like her. He was quite tall, as tall as his mother's husband. Thinking back to when she lived in Puerto Rico, Lilly tried to remember how tall Rico might have been. Ciara had tensed again as Lilly studied the photos. "This is the man Amalia left Cuba with?" Lilly asked.

"It took a while to find her but we succeeded. It was my husband's wish."

Once again, there was that sense of avoidance in how she replied. "That must have been a satisfying closure for Pablo," Lilly said. "Does he stay in touch with them?"

Ciara took a moment to regain her composure as relief showed in her expression. She turned the page. "No," she said. "Since Pablo's mother left when he was a baby and Pablo didn't find her until he was in his twenties, she and Tito were only cool toward him. His mother and her husband made good in the New York garment industry. Amalia's a fashion designer." Ciara took a breath then continued as if still trying to rationalize the whole scenario. "They accused Pablo of being someone else who assumed her son's identity in order to benefit from their money."

"No!"

"Pablo's mother never wanted him and her husband evidently never wanted children. Pablo tried to prove his relationship with a whole slug of documents we had. When Tito wanted to research to see if they were legal, Amalia claimed they were forged and said she never wanted to see Pablo again."

"His own mother?" Lilly asked, shaking her head in disbelief. "Was she ever told about Little Rico…her grandson?"

"Pablo sent his mother a letter about having a grandson after Little Rico was born," Ciara said. "It came back marked 'Refused'." Then she mumbled, "History repeats itself."

What was that supposed to mean? "So they don't know about Little Rico?"

"They'd never come to the phone either. They have a maid or a secretary or someone."

Lilly tried to assimilate the facts. Ciara's life seemed complicated, but a whole lot more intriguing than her own had been. Still, something in Ciara's telling of the details said she was disclosing only enough to appease the moment. Lilly had not lived so long that she was unable to tell when someone wished to keep a secret. Something in Pablo's documents must have threatened Amalia's security with her husband. The more Lilly got to know Ciara, the more she realized Ciara had a lot of tragic history that should probably remain her secret and hers alone. Ciara was her friend. If and when she wished to talk, Lilly would be there for her. That's all that mattered. "Will Pablo live on Kauai when he retires?" she asked.

"Maybe. He's not sure where the Navy Seals will take him," Ciara said. "The rest of his duty will be along the West Coast of the Americas, though, and he'll make Commander before he retires."

"That's not long now, is it?"

"Not long. Anyway, he insists I'm his real mom and wherever Little Rico and I are, that's where he calls home."

"So that's why you moved to Kauai? Because Pablo's on the West Coast?"

"And because I love the tropics," she said. "And because I learned you were here. When I saw your biography and your photographs of the Honu in that Hawaii magazine, I just had to look you up."

Ciara flipped ahead a few more pages. Rain continued to pour in a steady rhythm outside their sheltered conversation. Pictures of Pablo and his wife, Dolores Diego, appeared next. "He was thirty four there," she said. He looked the same when Lilly met him a couple months earlier at age thirty-eight. Pablo's hair showed reverse coloring. All his hair had prematurely grayed with only small dark areas remaining at his temples and around the front of his ears. His wife, Dolores Diego, looked absolutely adorable. "They met in Panama," Ciara said, "the first time Pablo was stationed down there." The next few photos were family pictures of Pablo and Dolores with their new doll-faced baby, named after his grandfather.

"So this is Little Rico's mom," Lilly said.

"Was."

"I guess so," Lilly said. "Since she's gone."

"Too bad she couldn't have walked a mile in someone else's shoes," Ciara said. "Some of us face times when we don't want to live either. Pablo and I would have stuck by her through anything."

"When did she commit...?" Lilly couldn't finish her question.

"Dolores had just gotten sentenced. She didn't wait to see if she could appeal or get off with good behavior. Nothing. She just left that note about not wanting to have her son grow up knowing his mother was locked up. Then she stripped off and hung herself with her prison jumpsuit. Some logic, huh?"

"Surely she was remorseful about the hit and run too," Lilly said, "when she was sober and they told her what she did?"

"Lillian," Ciara said, touching her hand. "They say that post-partum blues stuff can make some women crazy. She was told not to drink with those anti-depressant pills they gave her."

"Couldn't that have gotten her sentence reduced? Gotten her into therapy?"

"More than that," Ciara said. "How could she have gotten so deep into alcoholism to begin with? She was from a poor family and Pablo waited so long to marry. When he thought she was the right one, he lavished her with everything. He has money, Lilly. He had the military to support him, so his inheritance only grew over the years. Dolores could have had it all. Pablo even hired a hot-shot attorney who was positive he could get her case appealed and get her the help she needed."

"It sounds like she might have had more on her mind than just her child," Lilly said.

"You mean she couldn't live with running down and killing a mother and her two kids?"

"Yes," Lilly said. "Maybe she was remorseful, if only about her alcoholism and saw no way out."

"She could have had it all," Ciara said. "She had no inner strength."

"Having it all doesn't necessarily give you strength either."

"No," Ciara said, shaking her head. "That comes from within."

The last picture of Dolores was of her coffin at the funeral home and Ciara flipped quickly past. "Death is something you never get used to," she said.

The next photo was of an elderly man and Ciara hugging side by side in brilliant sunlight in the driveway of a beautiful home with tall palm trees in an upscale neighborhood. "That's the last photo of Daddy," she said, "in front of the house Rico and I built. That was during Daddy's last trip to Puerto Rico."

"Did you sell the Valle Arriba Heights house?"

"Oh, no," Ciara said. "I'm keeping that house forever. Couldn't bring myself to move in though. Rico and I built it, but he never lived in it."

"So you stayed in the house on Calle Delbrey?"

"Yes, because that's where I felt closest to Rico. I finished his remodeling, even added an upper floor," Ciara said. "But I'll never sell those two. I want to move back to Calle Delbrey before I die."

Lilly said nothing. Losing one's spouse so prematurely could never be easily healed. Losing a loved one in a horrific boating accident was a trauma bound to scar a memory for all time. Losing yet another family member the way Dolores took her life might have tipped any normal person over the edge.

"What about that beach property, where you first lived?"

"Oh, I kept that too. Anything that Rico and I shared, I kept. I built a house there. It's leased as a B&B."

As Ciara quietly flipped through pages of the album, her expression showed will and determination to carry on.

Her strength was just like she had noticed in Pablo a couple of months earlier. He, too, expressed a lot of determination as he spoke of his dearly departed wife and the future he hoped for his son. The way Ciara described her husband's strength, Pablo must have inherited a backbone from Rico then emulated Ciara's courage.

Ciara flipped back to a section showing her husband. One enlarged photo covered the page. It was of Ciara as she sat on a sleek wooden chair in front of two tall bookcases with an old picture of Rico hanging in between. She had that same stoic expression on her face and held a very masculine blue and green funeral urn on her lap. "That is that urn, isn't it?" Lilly asked as she motioned across the room to the end table.

Ciara grimaced. "That's Rico," she said. "I've been waiting all these years for Cuba to open up. When tensions with Cuba began to ease in '98, I again applied to go there and scatter Rico's ashes on his mother's grave like he wanted." She shrugged. "I was still denied."

"Ever try again?"

"Every year since."

"How about that Cuban baseball coach who defected?" Lilly asked. "Why would there be such a big to-do over sending that guy's six year old boy back with his father?"

"Yeah," Ciara said. "That tells me things aren't quite on the up-and-up in Cuba like they'd have us believe."

"Yeah, right. If life is so great there, why are people still trying to get out?"

Lilly studied the photo. She was not necessarily thinking about Ciara having kept Rico's ashes all those years. What she understood for the first time in knowing that Rico's ashes had a final destination was that her mother's ashes did not. Her mother's ashes sat in the green floral urn locked in the koa wood cabinet with expensive Japanese vases and figurines as if it was another decorative work of art. Suddenly the act of saving her mother's ashes seemed ludicrous or at least selfish. She needed to set her mother free, spread her ashes somewhere special and let her go, just as Ciara needed to get to Cuba and experience closure of her obligation. Surely that was one reason Ciara seemed so indentured to Rico's memory.

As Lilly's mind wandered, she experienced a jolting revelation that the perfect place for her mother's ashes to be scattered would be at Ke'e Beach on Kauai's North Shore. The memory of her mother, and hearing her mother's advice, was what saved her from panic and drowning herself when she was caught in that rip current. Her mother had been with her out there in the swells as surely as if she had been swimming along side. Lilly need not return to Santa Cruz to find the proper place that her mother may have liked her ashes to be spread. Her mother had not been happy in California, living alone while her husband was always on the road for business reasons. That alone was what kept Lilly from returning to California with the urn. Her mother had been lonely there. Lilly still intended to go out on a boat to see just how far out she might have been pulled in that rip current. She would make plans to do that now, and to include the spreading of her mother's ashes at the same time. A huge wave of relief washed over her.

Ciara nudged her and then turned the page. A photo of an expansive park with playground equipment and a commercial building filled the next album page, followed by a photo of a plaque. Lilly pushed her glasses higher on her nose and read the title out loud: "*The Pablo Frederico Rey Children's Park and Swimming Pool.*"

Ciara was all smiles. "This is so special to Pablo and me," she said.

Lilly studied the photo again. "They named the facility after your Rico."

"I did," Ciara said. "I wanted to do something so Rico wouldn't have died in vain."

"I'm sure he didn't," Lilly said.

"You don't understand. When he died I wanted to do something so the world, or at least the people of that island, wouldn't forget him. He left us well off, Lilly. I used some of the money to buy five acres way out near Luquillo. That was Rico's favorite beach. He knew the area would get built up sooner or later and it did. The land I bought was near the sea and I deeded it back to the Commonwealth." Ciara looked away, and then looked at her again as if to get her undivided attention. "Rico loved his son more than anyone will ever know," she said succinctly. Her eyes pleaded. "They both loved the ocean. That's how I wanted him remembered. When I deeded the property back, it was with a stipulation that what they built focused on children and swimming."

Lilly felt humbled by the deed. She felt new respect for this widow whose commitment ran far deeper than mirrored on the surface. "I'm beginning to like you," she said, teasing as she squeezed Ciara's hand again.

Just then, Rico ran into the room. "*Abuela*," he said. "Hur'cane." Then he stretched out his arms and turned circles in the middle of the rug.

"Where did you hear that?" Ciara asked.

He made noises like the churning wind as he kept turning. "TV," he said.

Lilly and Ciara stared at one another. The realization that he had heard someone speaking of a hurricane on TV said the tropical depression moving westerly from the northern coast of South American must have been upgraded. The last Lilly had heard was that it was directly below the Hawaiian chain. What had been a tropical depression could not have been upgraded to hurricane status so quickly. Usually a tropical depression increased in intensity until it became a tropical storm, which then, may or may not become a hurricane.

Ciara smiled nervously and pushed the album aside on the sofa. "Bad things always happened to Rico when it rained."

"You're not superstitious, are you?" Lilly asked, noticing an increase in the rain outside the window.

"Not me," she said. "But my shack on the Isla Verde Beach in Puerto Rico did blow away in a hurricane."

"But because of that, you met Rico. Isn't that what you said?"

"Well, yes," she said, smiling as if it had happened only yesterday.

"This storm is well below the Big Island," Lilly said. "Doppler radar on Kwajalean in the Marshall Islands is gearing up for the possible hit should the storm continue building." Something in Lilly's recently learned attitude of always being prepared would not allow her to shrug off an upgraded weather condition. She had learned all about Hurricanes Iwa in 1982 and Iniki in 1992. Everyone was saying Kauai was due for another. About every ten years, people said. That meant they were way overdue. During remodeling of her home, Lilly installed all the required hurricane clips and straps and bolted her house down to the concrete underpinnings. She wondered if she had made her seventy-year-old plantation home strong enough to withstand nature's wrath. She did not care to have another hurricane prove it. "Still," she said, "let's find more news and get an update."

Chapter Two

Rain that had blanketed all the islands for days was due to atmospheric instability in the peripheral areas around the weather condition to the south. Tropical Storm Lilo was traveling at about ten miles per hour over the ocean's surface roughly eight hundred miles directly south of The Big Island, also known as Hawaii. The newscaster said that placed Lilo approximately five hundred sixty miles east northeast of the U.S. territory of Palmyra near Kingman Reef down toward the Equator. Residents there had already hunkered down or evacuated. Lilo was not expected to drop southward due to predictable wind currents. So those islands would not endure the full wrath of the storm. Still, related conditions had already begun to cause widespread flooding and wind damage. The storm had already developed a gigantic outer periphery.

A wall of rain greeted them when Lilly tapped the automatic garage door opener and the door began to lift. There would be no driving with opened windows. She closed them and turned on the air conditioner.

"Oh, phew, mildew!" Ciara said, covering her nose and mouth. "When's the last time you used that thing?"

"Oh, phew!" Rico said, mimicking and laughing from his car seat behind Ciara.

A flatbed jalopy pickup rattled by on the road below. The driver honked twice. Ciara strained to see.

"Toot, toot," Rico said, imitating the sound as he stretched to take a look.

"That's Kenji and Masako Nakamura," Lilly said, noticing a load of supplies covered by a tarp over the back.

"Oh, that old farmer with his paralyzed wife."

"They bought that last acre on the other side," Lilly said.

"I've noticed no one honks on Kauai. Is that old man just boisterous?"

Lilly laughed. "We sort of keep tabs on one another," she said. "One toot when they go out; two when they return."

"Do you toot?"

"No. They don't have anything to do but sit and watch the grass grow. They know every time I come and go."

"Not too private, 'eh?"

"Ah, they're sweet people and I like to know they're okay. Did I tell you that they were thrown into relocation camps during World War II?"

"Oh, that's disgusting!"

"The way they tell it, they were both very young, had just gotten married and came to Hawaii for a better life."

"Then they got taken to the camps?" Ciara asked, grimacing.

"That's where Masako contracted polio," Lilly said. Ciara quieted, looked pensive. "They're really sweet people, and great neighbors. It's just our three houses up here on the hill. That farmer over the gully behind us only recently cleared the rest of the hillside and valley for his cattle and horses."

"I wonder what all this land looked like with several hundred years' growth on it," Ciara said.

Lilly smiled. "You've only to look farther back beyond the cleared acreage," she said. "Toward the Makaleha Mountain Range and those stunning water-falls."

Sumo, Lilly's wild orange tabby that had adopted her and taken over her house, darted across the driveway in front of them. Lilly wondered where Sumo had disappeared and why he was out in the rain now. Normally, he would be in the crawl space under the house or inside if she could catch him to wipe his feet first. He was soaked, but even with his coat slicked down he was one very large cat.

They drove slowly down the red dirt road that divided their properties and, between swipes of the wiper blades, looked across the valley toward the back of Sleeping Giant Mountain. At times, rain swirled, driven by the wind. They paused at the paved road and watched an immense dark cloud pass over the distant fields. Wall after wall of downpour traipsed across Queen's Acres and drenched the cows still in the fields as it continued toward the Wailua River to the south. Many of the cows turned their rear ends toward the onslaught, but kept nibbling at the rain-soaked grasses. High water overflowed the meandering stream that crossed the pasture under a thick stand of tall hau trees. More cows jostled together under the haus which seemed their favorite refuge from the sun, now nearly crowded out by rising water.

"I hope that storm dies out at sea," Ciara said. "I need time to hurricane-proof my house."

"It's weathered at least two hurricanes already," Lilly said. "Who knows how many more before they started keeping track?"

"But it sat under the shelter of trees and thicket," she said. "Now all but the indigenous trees have been cleared."

Lilly had watched the farmer clearing the lot in preparation for the sale. Two Monkeypods, an avocado and a mango tree were the only ones left in the back and a stand of plumeria remained in front.

They made their way along back roads to Kamalu Road, then onto Kuamo'o Road as red mud from the iron-rich soil oozed out of ditches and made roads slippery. A newscaster reported that Tropical Storm Lilo was gaining intensity and that the far-reaching cloud cover and rains over the Pacific Ocean and lower half of the Hawaiian Archipelago were expected to continue. Small craft warnings had been in effect for days.

"Reminds me of Puerto Rico," Ciara said.

"In Puerto Rico, when Hurricane Ana blew the roof off the backyard cottage I rented on Calle Delbrey," Lilly said, "I had to move in with a neighbor till the cottage was restored."

"That hurricane really was what brought Rico and me together," Ciara said. "I should tell you about that some day."

"I'd love to hear about your relationship," Lilly said.

"The hurricane's why I moved into one of Rico's cottages, next door to where you lived. That's when I learned of the neighbor who took underwater photographs, taught children about life in the sea, and who had been dislodged temporarily."

"Ah, the island life," Lilly said.

"Didn't someone send you a cooler full of Puerto Rican delights?" Ciara asked.

Lilly thought a moment then could not help smiling as she remembered. "Umm…*pasteles, arroz con pollo, guisados.* What memories."

"Pablo brought it to you?"

Lilly gasped. "It was from you? It was you who prepared that delicious food that Pablo and another boy carried over."

Ciara smiled. "We never got to know each other. Don't you think that's weird?"

"Yes," she said. "But I remember that food. The lady I stayed with—her house was old and ratty and the roof leaked and everything was wet. She knew better than to use the electric range for fear it would cause an electrical fire." Lilly was amazed at the memories that flooded into her mind. "Another neighbor loaned us a gas cook top till the old range could be replaced."

"But did you like the food?" Ciara asked with a teasing smile.

"That cooler fed two of us for days," she said. "The lady I stayed with went to thank Pablo and, I guess, his mom. Again we didn't get to meet."

"No biggie," Ciara said.

"Is that your life's calling, Ciara? To care for people?"

"Seems to be what I'm handed."

"You just manage what comes and make the most of it. That's what got you through the tragedy with Rico and raising Pablo?"

"Well, the way I see it is that if I couldn't be the mother Rico thought I would be for his son—the person I wanted him to know I was—how do you think that would affect the way Pablo turned out? He'd already been abandoned once."

"You've made such sacrifices."

"Not really. I considered him my son too," she said. "We have a choice in what we do with our lives. I saw my choices. I could have walked away, but for what? To wreak final havoc in the life of an innocent kid—whom I happened to love? No way."

"You didn't want your freedom? Get away from it all and start over?"

"Lilly, this is my life—Rico and his memory and his son. Now Little Rico. This is my life and I hope I'm doing it well."

The more she and Ciara talked, the more they seemed destined to share a portion of their lives. Their friendship was totally spontaneous, at least from Lilly's point of view. She could learn something from this courageous woman who bravely met all challenges head on. Lilly had walked away from anything that bothered her. Life was too short for hassles, but maybe she had missed something after all.

They passed *Opaeka'a Falls* and began descent. On the downgrade, traffic was halted by flagmen. A line of vehicles had formed. As usual in heavy rain, rocks had become dislodged and fallen onto the road from the steep hillside just below *Holoholo Ku Heiau* up on the plateau. More red-brown water ran in torrents across the road and spilled over the shoulder to the valley and wetlands below.

"Look at that," Lilly said. "One whole lane is blocked."

"Look at those two huge boulders over there," Ciara said. "Those guys are going to sweat trying to get them out of the way."

That previous night, the flash flood watch had been upgraded to a flash flood warning and was in effect for all low-lying areas across the entire island. The watch was to help people be aware. The warning was to say that flooding in some areas was imminent. Since Lilo was passing close below the Hawaiian chain, it would be wise for people to check supplies and hurricane kits for necessities. The warning was not intended to create a panic situation but to keep islanders informed. Though Hurricane Iniki occurred back in 1992, being unprepared at that time was still fresh in everyone's minds.

"If a storm of this magnitude intensifies," Ciara said, "combined with low pressure, the winds can elevate the ocean's surface by up to forty feet."

"We have a full moon coming," Lilly said. "You know what the full moon does to the tides." She turned the windshield wipers up as fast as they would go.

When they reached the beach area where Kuamo'o intersected with Kuhio Highway, Ciara strained forward to see through the windshield. "Would you look at that," she said. "How often do you see waves that big on Wailua Beach?"

"Never," Lilly said.

"Geez, those must be twelve footers."

"If we have a hurricane, after the wind and rain will come the storm surge," Lilly said. "Waves might reach twenty-five feet or more, a real pipeline."

Rico squirmed in his seat, stretching to see everything, as if he understood their conversations.

"Isn't Kauai known for big waves?" Ciara asked.

"On the North Shore," Lilly said. "But here, in this low spot? The road could be flooded."

Already, too many people and vehicles had converged beginning in the Waipouli area all the way north. Any block of shops that contained even the smallest food store was glutted with cars.

"Everyone on the island waited till the last minute to stock up," Ciara said.

"Not to mention us," Lilly said, rolling her eyes.

Highway 56, the only road through the beach area was a traffic nightmare. Fronds on the orchards of tall old palms bordering the road, from the Coconut Marketplace northward, strained uniformly in the direction of the wind. Numerous trees had already fallen, luckily having missed roadside power lines. Small shrubs and other green debris were being blown about. Fallen coconuts flopped around like footballs. Young children, used to not wearing rain clothes in the warm humid temperatures, ran and tried to slide on their feet in the water in grassy areas.

"Abuela, boo-boo." Rico said as he strained upright and pointed. A shrub had blown across the highway and wrapped around the base of a coconut palm.

"Look out!" Ciara said as a car in the next lane dangerously hydroplaned over water. Puddles filled low spots with no place to run off that weren't already filled to capacity.

Police, wearing hoods and rain ponchos whipped by the wind, directed traffic everywhere. Lilly dropped Ciara and Rico at the front entrance to the supermarket then went to find a place to park. The lot was full. Never before had she seen traffic being guided inside the private parking area as well. She was directed to a parking spot being vacated and finally made a dash for the store as rain pelted.

She and Ciara walked the aisles and carefully selected only items that could be stored should power outages occur. Rico, sitting in the cart, needed to examine everything being placed inside. He liked being told the names of each item so he could pronounce it. He had great curiosity and could well end up a linguist.

"You're not buying much," Ciara said as they tried to keep their items separated in the cart.

Ciara chose meatless items that could be eaten cold and from the container if necessary.

"Don't buy much in cans if you plan to store them," Lilly said. "Cans rust too fast. You knew that about the tropics, didn't you?"

"Did you learn that here or from your short stint in Puerto Rico?" Ciara asked as she threw a sideways smile.

People pushed past and others were in such a hurry that items were being knocked from shelves and kicked aside on the floor.

"I've canned a lot of homegrown stuff," Lilly said. "We'll share it. But you're not buying a lot either. You vegetarians ever eat?"

"Vegetarian, thanks to you."

"Me?"

"It was Pablo's idea," Ciara said. "When he was young and took your classes to learn about life in the sea, you taught him fish and other creatures had to live too. Somewhere along the way, he decided he wouldn't kill another living creature in order to eat."

"Oh, sure," Lilly said with a smile. "Pablo's a Navy Seal and a vegetarian?

"I know," Ciara said. "He told me their indoctrination involved learning to live off the land. For weeks, they were forced to eat rats, skunks, cockroaches, beetles, anything that moved." She grimaced. "But he's still a vegetarian when he can be."

Lilly was fascinated by the details of Ciara's life. The way she lived came so natural and made everything else seem superficial. Ciara and Pablo's lives continued to amaze her. Surely there was much she could learn from them. She wanted to know all about them and what made them the people they were. More and more, she found herself wanting to know all of Ciara's secrets and what made her so committed to the hand she was dealt. She was drawn to Ciara as if having found a long lost sister. Feeling attached to someone warmed her. "I've never seen the store this crowded," Lilly said.

As each new arrival braved the downpour, water was carried into the store on clothes and shoes. The floors became wet and slippery with red mud. As panic buyers emptied shelves, stock persons tried to replenish with cardboard boxes glutting the aisles. Maneuvering shopping carts became difficult. Finally, the store manager announced over the PA system that traffic in all aisles would move from the direction of the produce department on one side toward the meat and dairy on the opposite side of the store. This would eliminate people tangling shopping carts against the flow of traffic. Too, establishing a little order would eliminate chaos and temper flare-ups every time someone's ankle was clipped.

"Guess if you miss something in the tour," Ciara said, "you have to make your way back to the produce section and start over."

"If anything's left by the time you get back to it," Lilly said.

Someone came up from behind and wrapped an arm around her shoulder. "Hello, Lilly," he said. "Remember us?"

How could she not know that deep resonant voice? "Keoki," she said. She had met him in the spring of 1999 when a ninety-five foot fishing trawler sank on coral off Kapaʻa Beach. Twelve-foot waves battered the boat to smithereens and spilled sixty-five thousand gallons of diesel fuel. She had tried to learn if reef fishes and other sea life were harmed. Keoki, a marine biologist, had been sent in for that very purpose.

"Fancy meeting you at a time like this," he said.

He stood a little too close, but with crowded aisles, everyone seemed a little too intimate. Strange, too, since they met, was how Keoki turned up at the most unexpected of times and places. She looked around to find Berkley fighting his way through the glut of people and making jokes farther back in the aisle.

Rugged Berkley stood out in a crowd. He was not quite six feet and working in construction kept his body fit. Sunlight kept his floppy longish hair bleached. He had slanted eyes that could flash a gorgeous smile or look meaner than wild Sumo when he was cornered. Berkley's looks always reminded Lilly of lyrics in an old country-western song that said, "The best cowboys have Chinese eyes." Then, of course, his face had mellowed with age.

"Keoki, what are you doing back on Kauai?" Lilly asked.

"I moved here," he said, "to my favorite island. With all the island hopping I do, my job isn't affected by where I live."

"How long—"

"Didn't Berkley tell you?"

"Tell me what?"

"I've been staying with him for the last two months while he upgrades the house I bought near Kalihiwai Ridge. He never tol—"

"Never mentioned it," she said. Lilly guessed Keoki's friendship meant more to Berkley than hers if he was remodeling Keoki's house. Maybe it was a newer home that needed little work, unlike her old house. Too, it seemed strange that Berkley would not mention Keoki having moved to Kauai, even though she had seen little of him. The last four months had been a virtual whirlwind since Ciara arrived.

She introduced Ciara and Rico saying, "This is Keoki Nikolao. He's the person who introduced Berkley and me."

Keoki raised an eyebrow and glanced away momentarily. "So, are you ladies preparing for the next big one?" he asked as someone bumped him and he brushed close again.

Berkley finally joined them and seemed curious at how close she and Keoki stood. He had nothing in his basket but two small boxes of biscotti. He chucked Rico's chin and made him laugh.

After snatches of conversation and being forced along by shoppers trying to remain polite, Keoki and Berkley said their goodbyes and headed for the checkout counter. Lilly wondered why Berkley had not shown more concern for her well being, especially if a hurricane should hit. She felt bewildered. He must have really lost interest.

"Wow," Ciara said. "What a gorgeous Hawaiian man."

"Keoki? He's hapa," Lilly said. "His mother is Japanese-Hawaiian. His father was American-born Greek."

"What a combination. They gave him a Hawaiian name?"

Lilly rolled her eyes. "Actually, his name's George Nicholas," she said. She could not help but smile. Having been on the island a few years and being accepted as a long timer *Kama'aina*, the locals began to call her Liliana or Lilia, the Hawaiian translations of her name. The Hawaiians believed that when a name is given to someone or something, it begins a life of its own. She wondered how Ciara's name might translate.

As they neared the front of the store, Ciara lifted up on tiptoes, looked ahead of the crowd, and stared when she spotted Keoki again. "Delicious," she said.

"Ciara, are you attracted to him?"

"What a gorgeous face. He's tall and lean...."

"He's a scuba diver, and looking to meet someone," Lilly said. "Makes it rough for other guys. As the saying goes, 'on this island, there are ten men to every woman.'"

"I'll bet they don't all look as good as Keoki," Ciara said, still craning her neck. "I can appreciate a Japanese-Greek god." She came down off tiptoes and then went back up. "Oh, let me have just one last glimpse."

"He's our age, Ciara, super intelligent and has a most beautiful soul. Are you sure—"

"Lillian Avery."

"But Ciara," Lilly said. "Haven't you ever wanted to meet—?"

"No," she said.

"Well, you certainly have feelings."

"Yep."

"It would be wholesome to express them."

"I do," Ciara said.

"You do?"

"Yes, I think of Rico."

"That's not what I meant," Lilly said. She had to be careful. This was none of her business. She, herself, had never had intimate long-lasting relationships. They were just never a priority. With what she knew of Ciara's devotional abilities to one person, she wished Ciara might find happiness. "You could love again."

Ciara glanced at the floor and bit her lip. Then she looked up and said, "If you only knew what Rico and I had, Lilly. If you only knew how complete our relationship was, from a simple look, eye-to-eye, to a night of lust." She shook her head. "There'll never be anyone else."

"You don't know that."

"I can tell from the moment I meet someone."

"You just went gah-gah over Keoki," Lilly said as she chuckled. "He's a wonderful person, and available."

"He doesn't have eyes for me," Ciara said. Her eyes twinkled. "Not for me."

Suddenly the voice blared over the PA system again. Tropical Storm Lilo had just been upgraded to hurricane status. Wind speed had jumped to nearly eighty miles per hour. Lilo's direction had not changed and if it stayed on course and managed to miss the Marshall Islands, it would probably burn itself out at sea in a couple of weeks. A sudden cheer went up from all the shoppers. The store manager continued to announce that if Lilo stayed on course and gained momentum instead, it could strike Guam or Saipan in the Mariana Islands across the Pacific. No one cheered about that. With devastating regularity, Guam had a record of being hit every few years by hurricanes with greater intensity, known in the Far East as typhoons. Many people from Kauai had joined other workers in the Federal Emergency Management Agency and rushed to Guam after Super Typhoon Paka decimated that island in December 1997.

When the voice on the PA system ceased, utter silence filled the store. Then chaos broke loose again and the noise level rose as shoppers scrambled. Yet, panic was not necessary. She and Ciara needed to get out of the store and away from these people who were letting their imaginations run away with the idea of another Iniki. After all, it was still only a slight possibility and could not happen unless atmospheric wind currents forced the hurricane to change course, like it did with Iniki.

If the hurricane did not change course, a lot of people would be stuck with a lot of food and grocery bills because the shelves had been laid bare in quick order.

"I know a little something about the Marianas," Ciara said.

"What's that?" Lilly asked as she glanced toward the checkouts hoping to catch a glimpse of Berkley.

"The ocean bottoms have trenches," she said. "Did you know that?"

"Uh-h-h, no."

"Rico and I have sailed near the Puerto Rico Trench. That's the Atlantic's deepest point at minus almost twenty eight thousand feet."

"Really," Lilly said, still looking about.

"The Marianas are near the world's greatest ocean depth, at minus over thirty six thousand feet," she said. "Hey, ocean swimmer, are you listening? Did you like my little oceanography lesson?"

Lilly smiled. "Yes," she said. "We're gonna write great books together." Then she caught sight of Berkley as he exited the store ahead of Keoki without looking back. She felt bewildered, as if she did not exist. At a checkout counter, she spotted Moki and Lynne, one couple of whom she was very fond and who were so intimately close to one another they were known among friends as being one person living in two bodies. They teased and haggled over a product to buy, then ended up laughing and, seeming unsure, put the package back on the shelf. Their delightful actions could be easily read. Lilly wondered what it would be like to be that close to someone. Suddenly it was evident she would never have anything that special with Berkley. The thought was sobering, her feelings of longing, new.

Ciara touched her hand again. She always did that to make a point. "Lilly," she said. "I have a feeling you're a person I can trust."

"I am," Lilly said.

"I feel like we've known each other all our lives."

"I've felt the same."

"Promise me something, about our books?"

"If I can," Lilly said as she chose several jars of ready-made soup mixes. "Where are you going with this?"

"Well, you know about Rico and how dedicated I am to his memory," Ciara said. "Now you know about Pablo and his mother. Well, there's still more to our history."

"That's all it is," Lilly said. "History. Life makes us who we are today, but we keep going forward. Don't you agree?"

"Yes, forward," Ciara said. "That's why I've done something special for Pablo's future, and for Little Rico's."

Lilly was curious. Ciara's entire life was centered on the memory of her late husband and his son and grandson. She had even planned into the future for that son and his child. Lilly did not know where her own future might take her but she was not worried about it. Ciara had evidently been concerned enough to make plans. Her life revolved around three people and could only be what that future was built upon. "What have you done?" Lilly asked.

"Well, like I said, there's more to our lives, Lilly. Rico and I had something few people ever know." She paused then said, "I've written memoirs. I hope someday to publish them. They'd be one of the greatest love stories ever told."

Many people felt their lives comprised the greatest love story ever told. Simply put, it merely represented how deeply they felt things. Ciara was really wrapped up in her life. Some of the hunches Lilly had as she intuited between the snippets of Ciara's conversations said there could be more, much more, and very intriguing. "So why don't you publish now?" Lilly asked.

"Well, it's like we talked about. You and I will publish a few children's books together," Ciara said as she smiled. "Soon, I hope."

Lilly smiled and nodded and was pleased an idea generated decades earlier could finally be carried out. "Your royalties are for the future you plan for Little Rico?"

"Yes, but that's not what I meant to say," Ciara said as she grabbed the last two small cans of Sterno off the shelf. She pointed to the section on pet supplies and Lilly grabbed an armload of cat food. Then Ciara blurted it all. "Could you promise that if anything happens to me before I publish those memoirs, that you'll take them and do it for me?"

"Ciara," Lilly said. "Be serious. Nothing's going to happen to you. Besides, the publisher of your children's books could probably refer you to people who publish memoirs. What's stopping you now?"

"I can't do it yet," she said. "The final chapter hasn't happened. I need to get to Cuba with Rico's ashes first."

Chapter Three

"Hawaii is the most remote land mass on earth," Lilly said. "The radio stations are all we can count on to stay informed."

"I'll bet stranded tourists appreciate that," Ciara said.

Between playing music and commercials, the disc jockeys aired calls for help with swollen streams overflowing and other storm-related problems. The small beach town of Anahola to the north had already sounded its flood-warning siren. Evacuation of homes along the swollen Anahola River all the way down to the beach had begun. Reminders being aired told people to get out of low-lying houses and to higher ground as copious amounts of water poured off the Makaleha Mountains.

Before they reached the Kuamoʻo turnoff, sirens blared and vehicles on both sides jostled to the shoulders of the road. Fire Department rescue vehicles screeched past. The smaller, more maneuverable truck in the lead carried a couple of red-orange surfboards and a body board strapped on top.

"That particular truck careening down the road with sirens blaring," Lilly said, "means the big waves generated by this weather pattern has lured a few ardent surfers."

"And someone's gotten into trouble."

The newscaster made another announcement. The rancher who grazed cattle above the wetlands between the Wailua Houselots plateau and Kuamoʻo Road needed help getting his cattle to higher ground before they drowned.

Opaekaʻa Stream crossed under a low stone bridge on Kuamoʻo Road and washed into the Wailua River. The state's only navigable freshwater river was now muddied with red dirt. Much of the embankment shrubbery was under-water.

The uphill flow of traffic was at a standstill on Kuamoʻo as Lilly and Ciara thankfully made their way home. The downward flow of cars passed through the only open lane. Like other drivers, Lilly could do nothing but throw the transmission in park and shut the engine down if the wait threatened to use up too much fuel. She had three quarters of a tank of gas but it seemed ludicrous to wait in a long line to top off at the pumps. Besides, she had a full five-gallon can in the garage that she kept for the riding mower.

"Look at that," Ciara said as she opened the passenger window and stuck her arm out and pointed in the rain. "There's that farmer."

The man stood chest deep in water from the overflowing Opaekaʻa Stream that had flooded the wetlands and his crop fields. He groped his way along by pulling at shrubs and small trees mostly underwater now. Two other men struggled along farther down. They waved sticks and yelled to prod the frightened cattle to move. The animals' heads were barely all that stuck up out of the floodwater that had evidently overtaken them and their owner unaware.

"Look across the valley," Lilly said. "Under your seat, Ciara. Binoculars."

Several pickups with men riding in the open backs came down out of the Wailua Houselots subdivision. Clad in tee shirts and shorts, they jumped out and ran to help herd the cattle toward higher ground across the wetlands.

"It will be slow going for those guys," Ciara said.

"For sure," Lilly said as she leaned across to peer out the window. "They'll have to lead the cattle along trails no longer visible in order to avoid having the animals walk into ditches that border some of the fields."

"Oh look, Lilly," Ciara said. "Traffic's moving again."

Reaching the top of the hill, Opaekaʻa Falls, where a former Hawaiian queen had long ago bathed, gushed, obliterating the dark rock wall that normally protruded decoratively between ribbons of frothy white. Shrubs that grew in crevices on the wall between the ribbons had been washed away. The usually white water was now tinged a dirty red as torrents poured, picking up iron rich soil along the way. "The weather's worsening," Lilly said. "I can feel it."

"You, too?"

Later, after having put away her groceries, Lilly drove across the lawns to Ciara's place. The lawns were only mowed island weeds anyway. Normally, she would run over, but not in that wind and rain. She knocked, called out as she kicked off her rubber sandals, then walked in and let her eyes adjust to the dim interior. Ciara was preparing cucumber sandwiches with Brie. Rico was already happily eating a pickle wedge and laughing at the way it crunched.

"Want one?" Ciara asked, motioning to the sandwich board.

"I am hungry," she said. "Yeah, maybe I should."

Rain drummed on the tin roof. Something about that sound was typical of the Islands. Lilly listened and marveled as the wind blew. The runoff created accompaniment as it dripped from all sides of the roof and pattered onto leaves of shrubs and the rocks outside the windows. A few MacArthur palms, which had not been removed in the clearing of the lot, had grown prolifically over the years and brushed against the screens and jalousies as they rustled in the wind.

Ciara had laid down braided rugs to cover floorboards worn by decades of foot traffic. She had the ability of throwing her belongings here and there and everything looked like it was all part of her decorating scheme. A small blanket draped here, a couple cushions thrown there. Yet, the modern additions only enhanced the texture of the wooden floors and single sided walls with their exposed 2x4s that spoke of a younger Hawaii long gone. Lilly wondered how much change Ciara would bring to the house. She had changed her own quite drastically in creating double walls and finally putting on a shake roof. However, it still retained an island plantation home ambiance.

A gecko traipsed across the ceiling, probably looking for a place to sleep. Geckos are nocturnal, but Ciara's ceiling was open to the roof and it was dark up in the peak. Lilly had always caught the cute little lizards and taken them outside to her garden. Ciara had just seen the gecko and made no effort to catch it. "I don't remember having geckos in Puerto Rico," Lilly said.

"Tons of 'em," Ciara said. "Especially if you had plants around your house. They mostly stayed outdoors."

"Have you already gotten used to them being indoors?"

"Nope," Ciara said. "But until I can find all the holes where they come in, I can't keep them out." She raised her eyebrows and smiled and seemed not the least bit put off by having to live with them for a while. "They eat the spiders," she said. Then she turned from the counter and asked. "Have you noticed something suspicious about the birds?"

"Suspicious?"

"Yeah, you know," Ciara said. "In Puerto Rico we had those tiny little frogs that went 'ko-kee… ko-kee'—"

"Yeah, the coquis."

"What I've noticed here on Kauai are the doves. Every morning I hear them calling—"

"The birds," Lilly said. "I haven't heard many birds lately." She rose and went to the screen door to look out.

"Maybe not yesterday either?"

"We always hear the doves and meadowlarks and those danged mynahs," Lilly said. "They go off all day long."

"Not to mention the new generation of island chickens," Ciara added with a smile.

Lilly had already told her about how Hurricane Iniki had freed all the island's illegal fighting cocks to breed with all the domesticated chickens that had been blown helter-skelter. That was what had given birth to the new generation of wild chickens, and to roosters that crowed as if they had sand in their throats. "I can't remember the last time I heard one of those gravelly crooners," she said.

"So where are they?" Ciara asked.

Lilly remembered something she had read. "Some birds fly out to sea when bad weather's about to hit land," she said. "The Albatross at Kilauea Point glide out to sea somewhere. The white *Koaʻe Kea* tropicbirds with those long graceful tails find places to hide and don't fly at all."

"They must know something we don't."

They stared at one another momentarily. Finally, Ciara brought the plates to the table. "C'mon," she said. "Let's have lunch."

After a couple of bites, Lilly cautiously asked, "Are you sure you wouldn't like to weather this storm in my house?"

"Positive."

"You'll be staying in my cottage behind the garage once you begin renovations. You should have moved in there from the beginning."

"We'll be all right," Ciara said. "I got the roof leak fixed in the corner just in time. It should hold until I get this fixer-upper fixed." She smiled and was surely eager to begin renovations.

"Ciara," Lilly said. "Should Kauai be in line for a hurricane, you'd better consider waiting it out with me."

"Lilly, I've weathered a few hurricanes. I'm from Puerto Rico, remember?" Ciara asked, smiling as she reiterated her point. "Besides, I want to be near Rico." She gestured toward the urn.

"So bring him," Lilly said, again realizing Ciara's attachment. "We'll lock him in the koa cabinet with my mom's ashes. He'll be safe. You'll all be safe."

"We'll see," Ciara said. "I really want to stay close to my things though. I mean, I've got belongings in the container that Rico and I owned. Antiques and stuff." Then her eyes lit up. "I know," she said. "If a hurricane hits, I could wait it out in the container. It weighs tons. No big wind is going to carry away that steel box."

Being attached to belongings no matter what the sentimental value seemed too unrealistic. Ciara would be very safe inside the container, however ludicrous the idea. Lilly was not about to argue with a woman whose very life depended upon how much of her past she cared to save. Besides, she too, still clung to some of her mother's old relics, particularly to that old 1930s bamboo rocker and punee couch. Lilly had placed those out on the enclosed lanai where she spent most of her time when relaxing.

The rain stopped and started all afternoon. A few times the sun broke through giving false hope. Lilly could not help herself and stayed busy preparing her house and property for the worst. The computer in her bedroom could not provide up-to-the-minute news so the TV stayed on. Occasionally she checked for posts on the Internet from the Central Pacific Hurricane Center in Honolulu. After a power surge that could ruin even a surge protector, she unplugged the computer.

Each time she passed the koa cabinet and saw her mother's urn, she thought about finally disbursing her ashes. Many people placed the urns of loved ones in a columbarium where they paid perpetual rent for the space. Such was not for her. The reality of it was that her mother was gone and neither she nor anyone should have to pay for the departed to maintain an earthly presence.

She wondered about Ciara with Rico's ashes. Once Ciara would be able to scatter Rico's ashes on his mother's grave in Cuba, how might that change her life? Every last trace of Rico would be gone forever. Or would it? After all, she still had his son and grandson with her. If Lilly were right, then her guess would be that Ciara was tough enough to adjust.

Over night the rain worsened. Lilly woke several times and listened. Later during mid-morning, under a darkened sky, lightning flashed and took her by surprise. A few seconds later thunder rolled. The newscaster was saying there had been no change in the course of the hurricane but its speed had increased to ninety miles per hour. The Big Island was receiving torrential rain and island-wide flooding. Many people had already secured their homes and evacuated to shelters.

She tried calling Berkley to learn how he was but only heard the answering machine. Of course, he would be okay. Being a general contractor, he had made his house in the Wainiha Valley beyond Hanalei secure as a fortress. Lilly tried several times to reach him and got no answer, which meant he was probably helping others secure their properties.

She went to finish taking inventory of emergency supplies stored in the enlarged closet. That protected room was the center of the house and would be shelter should disaster strike. Having prepared for emergencies, about the only thing she had left to do was make sure adequate food and water was available for ready consumption should she become trapped in there for a long period of time. Many people had to remain protectively secluded in their hideouts for more than six hours while enduring Hurricane Iniki. Some people remained closeted overnight.

Lilly looked toward the Nakamura's house and saw elderly yet spry Kenji already boarding up his windows. No longer having many protective trees close by, the wind-driven rain pelted the fronts of their houses. The Red Wax palms Lilly planted among the tall older Manila and MacArthur palms in her front yard provided a barrier for her house from the weather. Kenji had not had a chance to remodel his home or do any planting and Lilly wondered if he ever would.

Later, Lilly again drove the short distance to Ciara's house across the lawn. The shipping container had been positioned close to the front of the house for ease in unloading. Now it protected the front porch and the house from the elements. It might also offer some protection should strong wind send anything airborne in that direction. She jockeyed into position close to the front steps so she could make a dash for the porch. Ciara had removed all the boxes and other items previously stacked outside against the wall near the front door. Lilly remembered how most islanders stored belongings in plastic tubs and cardboard boxes in their open carports. If those people in particular did not prepare themselves in time, all those possessions would be lost to the wind.

She found Ciara and Rico napping on the opened futon sofa in the living room. Ciara roused quietly when Lilly entered. The rain came hard again and lightning flashed.

"I see you've got your supplies together," Lilly said quietly so she would not wake the boy. "Which room will you stay in?"

"My bedroom closet," she said. She swiped at her face to wake up. "Here, help me carry these in there."

To Lilly's surprise, Ciara had already removed the mattress from her bed and leaned it against the closet doors. Candles, children's games, pillows and other necessities filled the closet and left little room for sitting. The top shelf had been emptied to keep things from falling on them. They placed the few food supplies inside the closet. "I'm glad you're taking this seriously," Lilly said.

Ciara only looked at her as if to wonder why she worried. "I'm not really superstitious about the rain," she said. "Not the way Rico was. I know how to be prepared now."

"Is that going to be enough room for the two of you?" Lilly asked. "Rico's a pretty active little guy."

Ciara put her hands on her hips and curled up the side of her mouth in a wry smile. "Did you come to invite me to your house again?"

"Well, yes, sort of."

"I'm staying put," Ciara said. "I've made up my mind."

That was the end of the conversation. Lilly had asked too many times. Still, as she let herself out, she whispered, "My door's always open."

"Wait," Ciara said softly as Rico stirred. "I've got an idea. If I don't do something to put your mind at ease, you'll worry yourself sick."

"Would I do that?" Lilly asked, smiling.

Ciara shook her head. "You know the honking signals the Nakamuras do?"

"Yeah?"

"We'll use lights, okay?"

"Flashlights?"

"Yep. We have a direct view between my living room and your lanai," Ciara said. "One steady beam says we need help. A series of quick flashes say we're okay. Okay?"

"I can deal with that," Lilly said.

At home again, Lilly closed down jalousies against the driven rain and changed out of her wet clothes. Passing the doorway of the smaller bedroom, which she used as an office, she noticed the red light flashing on her house phone. She had kept the land line, using her cell phone for close friends and business only. Just as she pressed the playback button and began to hear Keoki's voice ask about her welfare, lightning struck somewhere close and everything crackled as the electrical power fizzled out.

Chapter Four

The power company managed to get the electrical outage repaired. Most important at a critical time as this was that people were kept informed of the hurricane's course. Historically, many people remained unprepared for disasters. Not everyone had battery-operated radios.

Most likely, Keoki had called to check on her safety. She knew he was involved in bringing people from homes already damaged by wind into shelters. She hoped to hear from him again but most of the phone lines would soon be confiscated for emergency use should the threat of disaster become imminent. How thoughtful it was of Keoki to take the time to check on her.

The ominous sound of wind and rain worsened. Her decorations of dried bamboo stalks and silk leaves and flowers rustled. Loose papers flew and her mother's old handmade doilies blew off the backrests of the rattan rocker and punee. The new trees out front offered both a wind and rain break but the force of the winds still forced some rain to sprinkle through. The lanai had been built on the leeward side of the house and caught the trades as they wafted past.

Lilly hurried to close the shutters over the lanai screens. To think a couple of people thought her idea of shutters too impractical, too expensive for a simple screened-in lanai. How better would she protect openings covered only by mesh screen? She unlatched the shutters from their stationery places against the main house wall and pulled them open like an accordion. When extended over all three walls of the lanai, she pressed them flat against the windowsills and frames and locked them into place. The shutters were her invention, on which she had applied for a patent. Made to her specifications for maximum durability, they would withstand beatings from any airborne missiles.

The year had presented an unusually wet and rainy hurricane season. Just prior to Ciara's arrival, Lilly had completed additional reconstruction on her plantation style home. The greatest renovations included the smallest of the three bedrooms being divided in half with one half made into a walk-in clothes closet. The other half became a storage pantry behind the kitchen. The living room was extended and included the old-fashioned screened-in lanai where she sometimes slept instead of the bedroom.

Indoors, much of the framed art decorating the walls were photographs she had taken of the green sea turtles and the Honu, who had helped to save her from drowning off Ke'e Beach a few years earlier. The tiny one-bedroom cottage behind the garage was still her work studio but could also house extra guests when needed. Through the present circumstances, it became home to patio furniture and statues from the Japanese garden by the creek.

She listened to the newscast a moment longer. Hurricane Lilo still crept but had gained momentum to fifteen miles per hour with winds slightly more than eighty miles per hour. It seemed like it had stalled for a time when in fact it was changing directions. It veered from its course slightly westward then continued northward again, heading toward the curve of the archipelago. Perhaps now was none too soon to go outside and install boards over the rest of her windows. Wise old Kenji was a good act to follow. She looked to Kenji's house and saw that he had finished sealing everything.

The wind howled but the temperature remained warm. With all the rain, humidity was thick. It was a toss-up whether to wear shorts, which kept her body cooled, or to wear jeans, which kept the rain off her but eventually soaked through and stuck. She opted to stay in shorts. Wearing a rain poncho, cap and rubber boots, she dragged the cut sheets of plywood out of the garage and stood them near the windows for which they had been marked. She retrieved her battery-operated screwdriver from the garage toolbox and began removing all the screens. When she looked down from her perch on the ladder, old Kenji, wearing army camouflage rain gear and fishing galoshes, stood holding the ladder and watching.

"Kenji-san," she said. "You startled me." He must have walked over but should have driven. Still, he seemed pretty durable and, when Lilly glanced toward his house, it looked like his old truck was hunkered down in the carport to stay a while. He waved his own screwdriver and offered to help. Lilly remembered that in her younger years a man's offer of help implied she was a woman and weak, but Lilly had never believed such myths. Times had changed anyway, with many men's and women's jobs became interchangeable. This was Hawaii where neighbor helped neighbor, man or woman, and she would no longer be frowned upon as a woman wielding a masculine tool and doing a man's work. Besides, it was a matter of survival at which Hawaiians excelled.

When Kenji realized she knew what she was doing, he yelled above the storm, "You one smart Kama'aina." He waved the screwdriver in the air and gestured toward his house. "You build my house, yah?" he asked. "You make my house?"

By the time they finished boarding up, Kenji was tired but smiled and bowed a lot. Lilly wanted to drive him back to his house. It was the decent thing to do. His trousers had soaked through and both his and her boots were covered with red mud. Still, she mumbled, "Oh, what the heck." They washed off the mud with the garden hose and climbed into her van. After all, there was not a car on the island that did not have water stains, sand or red dirt in it.

"You come say 'Hi, Masako,'" Kenji said.

The Nakamura's single walled house was still in its rundown condition. It, too, had a tin roof. Like all houses built of wood, it had aged, but the worn old linoleum shined as if new. She kicked out of the boots but could not help bringing in water dripping from her poncho. Masako was all right. She had a sharp mind. Some of her body was what did not work properly. She sat in a wheel chair with atrophied legs and feet turned inward, one more than the other. They were brave people. Their nearest relatives lived on Maui to the south and were probably experiencing weather-related difficulties much more severe.

A multitude of colorful paper birds and other magnificent origami hung everywhere and danced on strings as fresh air wafted through the rooms. Masako's unique paper art could be found for sale in many shops across Kauai and on Maui. Her craft was how they supplemented their small pension.

"Where is your protected area to wait out the storm?" Lilly asked. Kenji motioned into one of the bedrooms and Lilly took a peek. She recognized a Zen Buddhist altar and other religious adornments. The room, as well as the rest of the house, was impeccably clean, undoubtedly the result of Kenji's energetic devotion not only to his wife but also to life. "But this is unprotected," she said. "You'll need to get into the closet."

Kenji only pressed his hands together prayerfully and nodded. "Yah," he said. "Yah, no kine problem."

By the time she went home, Ciara was outside struggling with her window boards. Lilly drove from the Nakamura's lot, directly across her front lawn and onto Ciara's. "I'll give you a hand," she called out above the storm.

"I think this won't be the only time I've felt lucky to have moved next door to you," Ciara said.

"Hey, what are friends for?" Lilly asked.

Later, at home again, she finished removing all the interior glass jalousie slats from the windows and stowed them inside the food pantry. Everything boarded up made the inside air stuffy. She propped open both the front and back doors. Finally, Lilly carefully began to take down her framed photographs and to stuff breakable belongings into cabinets and cubbyholes. Having decided nature best grew plants, she had cultivated nothing in pots that might become airborne missiles in a hurricane. She rolled up the large living room rug she herself had designed and hand hooked. It was a colorful collage of underwater life with tropical fish and those exceptional turtles. The rug, too, was stowed in the food pantry.

Lilly's house was hurricane-proofed with clips and brackets and she was not really worried or attached to her belongings but the activity kept her mind occupied. It was a strange situation in which she found herself, stuck inside a house with no sunlight pouring through the windows or trade winds wafting through to chase off the humidity. The only thing to do was wait it out. She kept the TV on and later read for diversion, but she could not keep herself from worrying about the others. She thought about Ke'e Beach and the tides and currents where she had almost lost her life and the Honu that had given it back. Like many birds in the Kilauea Point refuge flying out to sea, the Honu would swim far away from the bad weather.

Another news release brought her back to the present and told of another change in course for Hurricane Lilo. She looked at the pile of reading material accumulated on the floor beside her chair. All the books she planned to read now seemed uninteresting. TV bored her and music jangled her nerves. Yet, she found herself again enjoying the adorable stories in a set of children's books that Ciara had long ago written and recently given her as a token of their friendship. One thing was certain. When it came to children, Ciara definitely knew what she was doing.

After napping fitfully on the sofa, Lilly turned up the volume on the TV. Shocking news greeted her. Hurricane Lilo had performed a trick that meteorologists called a recurrence. It had unexpectedly and drastically changed courses, gathered momentum and was headed up the west side of the Hawaiian Island chain.

Adrenalin kicked in. The hour was late but Lilly called Ciara and found she had already heard the news. Then Lilly stepped outside the front door long enough to detect light coming from the Nakamura house. When she called, she learned Kenji had also been watching TV. The only thing to do now was wait it out.

By morning, Hurricane Lilo had wobbled east to west and back again. Had it not been buffeted by heavy winds and forced into a zigzag pattern, it would have already reached The Islands. Presently, it snaked northwesterly, following the curvature of the Hawaiian Archipelago but still to the south. By now, rain was so thick, so driven on Kauai, and certainly all the islands, that it would be ludicrous for anyone to be outdoors. The announcer warned about the potential for a sea swell and rising tides. Whole towns, like low-lying Hanalei on the North Shore and Waimea and Kekaha on the west, and portions of Poipu on the South Shore, would have been evacuated for fear of tidal surges. Lilly knew many people had waited till the last minute to seek shelter. Traffic on the one main road around the island must have become a gnarled mess with roads resembling an ant farm in a flood as people evacuated the beach areas.

She looked around her newly remodeled home. Humidity was so thick, even cardboard boxes seemed wilted. If the storm were to rip through her house, she stood a chance of losing everything. But if she was around to realize she had lost everything that meant she would be around to rebuild.

As dawn approached, all was quiet except for the wind and rain. It was strange not to hear cows lowing, a horse or two whiny and dogs bark. Pheasants, meadowlarks and doves always called to their mates and the common mynahs were never quiet. Every morning the gully beyond the back of her lot would come alive with the true symphony of nature. She would lie still listening. Curiously, what always came to mind was why all those birds had to call out to mates who responded from way across the valley. What had they been doing apart from one another during the night? Yet, this morning was different. All the creatures of nature must have found safe havens. Only occasional sounds could be heard from the distant hills.

Lilo's path had veered northward, straight up. Hope that Lilo would not reach the Islands had dimmed. The shifting wind currents could, hopefully, push the hurricane northwesterly again, away from ever touching land, where it could dissipate in cooler waters pushed down from Alaska. If they were lucky.

After three more hours of snakelike deception, the announcer said that Hurricane Lilo was again on a course that could push it close to the Big Island where it might then veer away from Maui, Oahu and Kauai. If it followed the current erratic pattern, the next time it swung back, it might then cut over deserted Nihoa and Necker Island in the northern archipelago. Like a snake, no one knew what it would do as it slithered along in zigzag fashion. Like a snake, no one could guess if it would strike and wreak havoc or simply meander. Too, Hawaiian meteorologists had renamed Hurricane Lilo. Due to its zigzag path, the new name assigned was Hurricane *Naheka*, which in Hawaiian meant snake.

Lilly wanted to be one step ahead of the storm. She would have her shower now, then disinfect the tubs and sinks in the house and in the cottage and fill them with water for drinking. Her large garbage cans sat full of water in the corner of the kitchen and in the bathrooms. That water would be used to flush toilets should the hurricane hit and cut off power and plumbing and other utilities.

Another news update said Hurricane Naheka had picked up speed. Its nearly unpredictable pattern seemed more erratic as it veered away from The Islands to the west. The newscaster provided a lot of technical information about the hurricane to keep listeners informed. He went on to say, "Storm busters were quite excited at having gotten exceptional pictures of the center of the storm, taken from their C-130 cargo plane." They would be the only ones to get excited about a hurricane. On the subject of hurricanes and typhoons, the newscaster continued to remind that this hurricane was already labeled as being much larger and more forceful than Super Typhoon Paka that previously hit Guam. He went on to describe some details about Paka as it had passed within range of the DWSR-93S Doppler Radar on Kwajalein Atoll in the Marshall Islands in 1997.

"The eye of the typhoon was clearly visible on long-range surveillance scans," the newscaster said. "A detailed study of the eye structure was made as Typhoon Paka passed within 150 km of the radar site."

"They keep saying this hurricane is bigger," Lilly said aloud.

The newscaster continued, droning on to fill the hours because the storm was the only big news of the moment. "Typhoon Paka had a double eyewall structure along with several mesoscale vortices rotating around both the inner and outer eyewalls. The double eyewall correlated with the decreased wind velocity surrounding the storm. When the older, inner eyewall collapsed—forming a single 40 km diameter eye—radar picked up the increasing wind speed that tightened around the eye. This is all great information, folks," he said. "I don't mean to scare anyone, but it's best to be informed. Fact is, however, that because of its present zigzag pattern and present location, Naheka will pass no place close to Kwajalein for us to get this kind of information. Just remember, our present storm is huge, with a potential to be much stronger than Iniki or Typhoon Paka."

Remembering having heard the eye of the approaching storm to be estimated at 45 km, Lilly rushed for her desk and calculator. She looked up the equation. One kilometer was 0.62137 mile. She multiplied. That meant the eye of Naheka was nearly twenty-eight miles in diameter. "Oh, no!" she said. "That's almost as big as this island." She calculated once more. "No!" she said again. "Paka's eye wasn't even twenty five miles." With a heightened sense of urgency, she stood and looked around at what else needed to be done.

Plastic sheeting covered everything and only that around those appliances still in use was not secured. She fastened the plastic over her computer and desktop and managed to lift the corners of the desk and slip the edges of the sheeting underneath the legs. Then she remembered her insurance and other important documents and had to undo the plastic at the corner of the desk to retrieve the papers from a drawer and place them in the closet. She was forgetting things. Was she really prepared for what was to come?

Back when she had been caught in a rip current and nearly drowned, she had been unable to do much for herself. A shark could have attacked, but none did. She could have been snared in that drift net but had not been. Still, having some gear with which to send signals could not have prevented her from being caught in a rip. Now she would always be prepared for another wild current. She was not about to give up her lifelong activity of swimming and photographing. Yet, not having experienced a hurricane of this magnitude, how prepared could she be should the main body of the storm reach Kauai?

She had to calm down and rethink all the steps of preparation. She hurried to her closet to recheck the emergency supplies. Good thing she did. She had forgotten her sneakers out on the stoop leading into the garage. They needed to be brought into the closet in case any glass broke and she would have to walk over the shards when finally able to leave the shelter of the closet.

Chapter Five

Adrenaline kept Lilly sleepless most of the night. She dozed intermittently through the morning and jolted upright when the Emergency Alert System went off, a steady sound lasting five seconds each numerous blast. The large yellow horns atop a tower were only half a clear mile away at Wailua Homesteads Park and the sound was deafening. She covered her ears. The warning meant people were to tune to any station for civil service and emergency instructions. The TV was dead, nothing but snow, so she clicked on the portable radio. When a hurricane warning sounded, it meant dangerous conditions were expected within twenty-four hours. The hour was already past noon. Lilly had long before turned off the gas line from the outdoor propane tank. Now she hurried to unplug all electrical appliances and turn off all the switches on the electrical panel. With the Kauai utility possibly having to exercise planned power interruptions, this could affect electrical flow to her home. The power surges could decimate any appliance or equipment still connected. Once again, she threw on her poncho and boots and made her way outdoors to the main breaker switch located near the water meter down at the road.

She glanced over to Ciara's property and found her doing the same thing. "Hey, Ciara!" she said, have to yell it. The wind and rain drowned out all sound. As she turned to go back indoors, Ciara glanced over. Both waved. How strange it was that they should be attending the same tasks but doing them alone when they might find much comfort in being together.

Inside again, Lilly lit a couple of thick candles and turned up the radio. Already, each station had ceased regular broadcasting and only aired updates about the hurricane. Absence of regular broadcasting also meant most phone lines had been confiscated for emergency use.

Time passed, evening arrived. She was bored. Then, quite suddenly, the wind velocity increased so that her house shook. Lilly peeped out the door frequently. She listened intently to every creak and groan. Still, she would not go into the closet until the last moment. She was both excited and frightened. It was too late to have planned to be with other people. Her attention was called to the fact that she had spent most of the crucial times of her life alone. That fact had never been important to her in the past. Now the message seemed driven into her brain, reminding that she had thought about loneliness many times through the years but paid no further attention. Right now, she thought about how nice it would be to have someone with whom to snuggle in the closet.

She listened to updates well into the night, too hyperactive to sleep. About eleven o'clock the newscaster was cut off mid-sentence. That station's broadcast tower had probably blown down. She tuned to another station and in a few moments learned the sketchy broadcast was being transmitted from Honolulu on the closest neighboring island of Oahu, almost a hundred miles away. She strained to hear through the static.

"As... of Kauai remain seques... shelters... homes, Hurricane Nahek... veer straight northward... slam into the island.... Wind velocity... jumped... one hundred fif... rising.... Category 5... getting our share... storm is wide.... Folks, pray... this snake... hurricane... is pushed westward."

As the wind intensified, it came in rustling or whistling sounds about every ten to fifteen seconds, the most curious rhythm she had ever heard. Perhaps now was the time to take cover.

Inside the candle-lit closet, she huddled in the corner with knees drawn up to her chest. Every time something hit the house, she ducked her head. The closet, the redesigned inner half of one bedroom, was a walk-in type in the center of the house and could not be bombarded with airborne objects. It was quite safe even though she continued to hear the pelting. Certainly nothing could hit the walls of the closet and her roof and trusses had been hurricane-proofed. This was her safe haven, the center of her universe, and at the moment, its only occupants were Sumo and herself. She looked at Sumo, drugged and caged for his safety. She smelled his familiar cat smell and listened to the peculiar scratchy noises his breath made while sleeping and found having another living creature near to be quite comforting.

No reason to remain huddled in fright existed. Slowly, she stretched out her legs and finally lay back onto a pillow. After a while, she ventured to look at pictures in a few magazines for diversion, but reading by candlelight was out of the question. She was bored again. Placing the candle out of the way, she began to rummage through some old boxes of records and keepsakes and felt warmed each time she connected to an old memory to again cherish. Then, contained in a shoebox, was a yellowed newspaper article with a photo showing Keoki on a body board dragging debris to shore from that fishing trawler that sank off Kapa'a Beach. It was a dramatic photo with jagged remnants of the vessel protruding above water and being battered by those twelve-foot waves. Keoki, the only one who knew how to handle that tide, or daring enough, dragged much debris to shore instead of leaving it to tangle on the reef.

She strained to reread the entire article and stared at the picture. The local newspaper had, about that time, begun publishing in color, which enhanced his glorious tanned and muscular swimmer's physique. He seemed at home in the waves. Strange how he was always showing up at the most unlikely places and times. Even in photo form.

The hurricane droned on sounding more like the rumbling of an endless freight train passing through. Whistling sounds came from the breezeway as the wind was forced through the narrow passage. Lilly dug out a box of cotton and wadded up pieces and stuck them into her ears. Finally, she dozed but was later awakened by a barrage of bumps and thumps of airborne objects. "A bombing by coconuts," she said, unable to keep from smiling. The next crash caused the sound of splintering wood and made her duck her head again, but she had accepted that no matter what happened, there was nothing to do but wait it out.

She watched Sumo. Perhaps now was a good time to get him used to being brushed. Somehow she had to control his shedding onto her rugs. She undid the latch and reached in and scratched his belly. Without opening his eyes, Sumo rolled onto his back, spread his legs in four directions and purred. His huge stomach felt like a firm bowl of jelly. "How ever did we get together?" she asked. "I saw you stalking me, you wild thing. You prowled my house until your curiosity got the best of you." She wondered how many of his nine lives he might have already used. She scratched again and Sumo purred loudly. She tried to remember where she had placed the brush she bought for him, and then realized it was probably out in the laundry room off the garage.

Frustration overtook her. One could never be totally prepared. Finally, realizing she was going to be sequestered for hours, she said, "Oh, whatever." She resigned herself to laying back and listening to the noises of the wind and of unknown objects colliding into her home as boredom really set in. Then, with her house being built on concrete blocks and above ground like many of the older homes in the tropics, she felt the floor beneath her shudder! It bowed upward lifting her and finally relaxed. She bolted upright into a stance meant to keep her balance. Her heart raced, but nothing else happened. She breathed a sigh of relief. Some low gust of wind had found its way beneath her house. During Iniki, whole houses had been ripped off their concrete blocks and catapulted through the air when a strong gust of wind caught them underneath.

Lilly could not help but poke her head out of the closet every now and then. She did not dare go completely out. If the wind were to tear off her roof, she could be sucked into the rush and hurled through the air along with her new shake shingles. Still, she poked her head out and listened, feeling rushes of excitement tempered with great caution. She wished to see. Just as she decided to creep to the lanai and peep through the cracks of the window coverings, she heard a new sound that made her hair bristle. She removed cotton from one ear, trying to better determine from which direction the noise originated. It was a high-pitched pulling sound, accompanied by metal rubbing metal that seemed to rise and fall with the pulse of the wind. Then a wretched rending sound came between the wails of the wind, an awful splintering of wood and the final squeals of pulling loose. She had seen videos of Iniki showing people's whole roofs being pulled loose and carried away with the wind, as easily as if they had been made of paper being blown away by a simple breath.

She thought of Kenji and Masako in their unsheltered bedroom and Ciara and Rico huddled in their tiny closet. "Please," she said. "Let them be safe," She pulled back into her closet, slid the door in place and sat down and prayed some more.

After more than three hours, the wind became exceedingly intense for a time with airborne objects fiercely striking the house. Then, rather quickly, the wind died down. An eerie silence pervaded. The build-up of intensity then sudden quiet could only mean one thing. The front of the eyewall, one of the strongest points of a hurricane structure, had passed over. The island or portions of it was, at that very moment, inside the eye of Naheka.

Ignoring warnings not to venture out in the calm when the eye passed over, Lilly grabbed her flashlight and rushed to the lanai to peep out. She unlatched and threw open one of the shutters. The full moon hung above and drenched the land in surrealistic reflections of glistening white. Already many of her palms had been stripped of their branches. Other branches and whole trees hung over nearly uprooted or broken. At the moment, there was no wind or rain.

A light flickered through the slats of the mismatched boards on Ciara's windows. Lilly flashed intermittently. Then Ciara's intermittent signal flashed. She and Rico were okay. So from where had that rending sound originated? She locked the shutter in place again and rushed to her front door and dared open it. She stepped out onto the front steps and peered toward the Nakamura's and was shocked. It was their tin roof that had been carried away, along with all the roof trusses. The top of their house had been completely ripped off. Then there was old Kenji trying to ease his paralyzed wife down the kitchen steps into the carport in her wheelchair. They were probably trying to make it to their truck to have a roof over their heads. Both looked soaked to the bone. Near the bottom of the steps, Kenji seemed to collapse and he, Masako and the wheelchair tumbled down the remaining steps to the concrete carport floor.

Lilly ran back to her closet. In a few seconds she had her sneakers on and raced out the front door and was inside the Nakamura's carport. Even the roof over the carport was gone.

Kenji looked as if he might break out in laughter. "Free fall!" he said.

"That was some ride, Kenji," Masako said, having dragged herself up against the carport wall.

Sitting in their old truck would not be the best thing to do. In past hurricanes, cars and trucks had been blown away by strong gusts and sent rolling like toys.

Lilly parted Masako's lifeless legs and stooped in front of her and reached for an arm. "Help me, Kenji-san," she said. "Get her up onto my back."

Kenji opened the passenger door to the truck. "Ya, safe here," he said.

"No!" Lilly said. "Not there. Help me, hurry!"

"Inside, hurry," Kenji said. "Inside, yah?"

"No," Lilly said, yelling as Kenji helped lift Masako. "My house. Come now!" Lilly jostled Masako's tiny light frame higher and gave thanks that she had always swam and stayed strong and fit. "C'mon, Kenji!" she said. Lilly hunched over and grabbed Masako's dangling legs while Masako clung around her neck. Lilly made her way swiftly across the yard toward her house as Masako laughed gleefully, enjoying the ride. Then Lilly noticed a few of her new expensive shake shingles nearby on the ground. The sight of those things lying there hit her as if a part of her had been torn away. A lump rose in her throat and she had to remind herself to stay focused. Life was the only thing of value at the moment.

Masako began to squirm. "Kenji," she said, trying to twist around to find him.

Lilly stopped and turned. Kenji was nowhere to be seen. Indoors again, Lilly deposited Masako on the sofa and ran back to find Kenji in front of the truck, having retrieved his toolbox. Then he attempted to lift Masako's folded wheelchair above his head to carry it. Lilly grabbed hold of the wheels while he held onto the handles and together they scurried across the yards.

Surprisingly, Ciara met them at the front door. She carried Rico on her hip. "Can I help?" she asked.

"They lost their roof," Lilly said. "They'll be fine here. How are you holding up?"

"We're doing okay," she said. "Not much shakin' in that old house. Pretty keen, huh?"

"You sure you're safe?" Lilly asked.

"Yep. You stay safe too," she said and headed back to her house.

Kenji toweled off Masako and Lilly retrieved some of her own dry clothing and left them alone while Kenji helped his wife change. Masako asked to lie down, so Lilly went to make room inside the closet. Then Kenji wheeled her in. One wheel on her chair wobbled. Next, it was Kenji's turn. Before he changed clothes, Lilly had an idea.

Knowing the eye of the storm would take a while to pass over, Lilly grabbed up a pile of kitchen towels and many packages of plastic sheeting she found for virtually pennies in garage sales and store closeouts. All those plastic sheets might prove to be the best purchases ever made. She and Kenji, with armfuls of the packages, headed back to his house where they wiped down the furnishings as best they could, covered them with the plastic and tucked the edges of sheeting under the legs of the heavy furniture to keep it in place. Kenji tried to salvage a dry change of clothes, but with the entire roof missing, water had already gotten inside closets and dresser drawers. It was anybody's guess if the plastic sheeting could prevent further damage, but they had to try.

Kenji grabbed up the few small altar statues he found laying in a corner among a bunch of dead Kauai snakes, the harmless four-inch red-brown cousins of the worm family. The fact that they saw so many dead snakes in his house meant the wood of the home was probably infested with termites and other miniscule creatures, which was the diet of those sightless snakes. Who knew?

The hurricane might be a blessing in disguise. Now that old house could be restored with new wood and kept treated for pests and he and Masako would have the palace they so richly deserved.

Back at Lilly's again, while she turned her back, Kenji slipped into a pair of her jeans and a shirt. He was small enough and she tall enough. He laughed boisterously as he rolled the cuffs of the pants and sleeves. Then they stood at the living room door watching the glow of night across the valley. If the eye was twenty-eight miles wide and traveling at fifteen or more miles per hour, that meant after the half hour they spent at Kenji's house it would take roughly another one and one-half hours to pass over.

Later, while nibbling on dehydrated mango and papaya wedges and sipping water, the winds came up suddenly and began to howl again. Wind whipped through the breezeway and made an eerie sound. They ducked back into the closet and secured the mattress in front of the door. All the while, Sumo purred.

Chapter Six

The noise and rumbling came fast as the backside of the eye wall overtook them. Kenji grabbed up some towels and put one over Masako's head to cover her ears. He did the same for himself until Lilly offered the cotton.

A barrage of objects began hitting the opposite side of the house. Kenji listened intently. Then he gestured and yelled, "The wind reverses."

Lilly pulled cotton from an ear. "Reverses?" she asked.

"Yah, first hurricane hits—lotsa' noise. Then eye passes. Everything quiet. Then other side of hurricane hits. Wind travels backwards."

"I remember reading that," Lilly said. "In the opposite direction."

"Yah," he said. "Dat's the way."

Masako pulled the cotton from an ear to listen. "Any trees that were loosened in the ground," she said, straining her voice, "will now be ripped out by the roots. Many more projectiles in the second half as the wind reverses." She spoke infrequently but when she did, she was always right and she spoke perfect English.

Kenji saw the picture of Keoki, squinted and leaned close. "You love Japanese man?" he asked, having to nearly scream it.

His question took her by surprise. "Keoki's just a friend," she said, hoping to be heard over the storm.

"You keep picture of just friend?" His eyes teased.

"He likes the fishes too."

"Lots of people like fishes," Kenji said loudly. "You keep picture of them?" He rummaged through his pocket until he found a small box of matches.

"Now, Kenji," Lilly said. "Don't go making assumptions." She could not help staring at Keoki's photo. It did not matter that she didn't see him much. When she did, he was a true friend. She had backed away from the friendship when she learned she would not be able to scuba dive because of her ear problems. In fact, she was severely disappointed when she learned that scuba was forever out of the question for her because of her ears. Still, maybe she should have tried to be a better friend. After all, no two people were exactly alike.

Kenji continued to stare at the photo, all the while preparing to light another candle, which he positioned on top of some boxes. He knelt, faced the candle. He scraped the match head with his thumbnail. His thumb moved slowly away from the match even as the head hissed and erupted into flame. His deliberate, almost ceremonial movements invited contemplation, the shifting down of mental gears, even if all he wanted to do was read that darned article. He looked up and smiled deviously then held the candle above the clipping so he could better see.

As time passed, they tried to sleep or read whenever the urge struck. They could go no place else. They nibbled food, sipped water. Masako wished for some sheets of paper and Lilly crept out to retrieve some from her desk drawer. With everything happening outside, the interior of her home was actually quite peaceful.

She retrieved the paper and secured the desk and turned to head for the closet when she heard a distinct sound through the cotton in her ears. That squeaky nail-pulling sound repeated. Only this time it was real close. She dropped to all fours and removed a wad from an ear and waited to hear the sound again so she might determine from which direction it emitted. The sound repeated, from the living room, perhaps. She crept hunched over and stayed close to the floor. The squeal came again, maybe from the area of the living room where the lanai had been attached to the corner of the house. It came again. She stuck the cotton back into her ear and crept toward the corner then flashed her light and was shocked at what she saw and had to sit down on the spot. The thick coat of wall paint showed damage. Flakes lay on the floor. The next time the creaking came, the corner wall near the ceiling pulled in one direction. It actually bent out of its straight up position. The corner of her house was pulling loose!

Lilly hurried back to the closet and handed the papers to Masako and fell to the floor in a stupor. Their very lives were being threatened and nothing could be done except to wait and see what happened.

"Are you okay?" Masako asked.

"The wall," she said, yelling. "In the living room. It's pulling loose!"

"Which wall?" Kenji asked.

"The far corner at the front. It's knocking paint down and it leaned. It just leaned, as if it were made of rubber."

Nothing more could be said. Masako proceeded to amuse herself with origami. Kenji tinkered with straightening an axle on the wheelchair. Sumo shifted to his side and stretched out.

Then a sound yet more wretched filled the air as they covered their ears and huddled together. The floor rose and fell again and walls shook. The slow ripping and shrill squealing of boards and nails pulling loose filled the air. Kenji threw himself across Masako. Lilly huddled into a knot beside Sumo's cage and protected her head. After a few moments, the walls stopped moving and all was calm as if the storm did not exist, even as the storm raged on. The draft that sucked air in and out of the louvered closet doors sent in cooler air. Something had happened to her home. She felt very alone but wanted to scream to be left alone, but nothing had happened to the closet in which they huddled and she was thankful.

Sometime later, she woke to only the sound of rain. Her body ached. She uncurled and realized she must have slept in that protective knot the remainder of the night, too scared to move. Too scared, or was it just about getting older with life becoming more cherished? At times, she had bumbled along through the years wondering what it was all about. More than once, at critical times, life became precious and forced her to fight to stay alive.

She had moved but had not yet opened her eyes, yet Sumo began to whine pitifully for release. He began to thrash around in the cage, as if he had been watching for an opportune moment to make his needs known.

She opened her eyes and stared into Kenji's face, whose eyes were also open. He half sat, half laid against pillows propped against the wall cradling Masako's head in his lap. "Did you sleep, Kenji?" Lilly asked, now able to whisper.

Masako stirred and Kenji's attention went to her immediately.

Lilly reached behind the mattress and pushed the closet door open a crack. The wind was calmer but the incessant rain continued to dribble out its rhythm. When she undid the latch on Sumo's cage, he took a few shaky steps and then made a beeline for parts unknown.

Both candles had burned down; all but the nubs remained. She had to make her limbs move. At that moment, they felt like they belonged to someone else. A crick in her neck made her moan.

Her watch said nearly seven o'clock in the morning but it was still dark, sunlight evidently blocked by clouds. Lilly slid the closet door fully open and the rush of fresher air made her thankful she had days earlier moved most all her clothing to the closet in the spare bedroom.

Kenji began to laugh after smelling his shirtsleeve. "Smoked cat," he said, laughing again.

Lilly hurriedly stepped into her sneakers. The morning air was chilly. She grabbed a sweater out of a box. "Grab something, keep warm," she said to Masako and Kenji.

The draft in the hallway and belongings lying askew on the floor foretold of a gaping hole somewhere in her walls. Remembering the weakening living room corner, she rushed to see. What greeted her made her yelp. Two large holes had been ripped through the living room wall.

She peered through the largest one. "My new lanai," she said. "It's all gone!" Nothing was left of the structure except the corners, which had been bolted to the concrete footings. The secured 2x4 framing in the corners remained but the roof was gone along with the rest of the walls. So was the wooden floor. Everything that had been inside the decorative porch had blown away; her mother's 1930s rocker and punee couch and the bookcases and end tables from the pre-WWII era. At first, she could not believe what she was seeing. Or not seeing. "So much for inventing window shutters," Lilly said. "They're only as good as the wall is strong."

Kenji wheeled Masako into the living room. The bent wheel of her chair squeaked out an intermittent rhythm. Kenji peeped out one of the gaping holes. "Hurricane stronger than new construction lanai," he said.

Lilly flashed her light around the living room. Furniture was overturned with pieces piled in tangled heaps. The tall gaping holes at each end where the lanai had been connected resembled two grotesque and haunting eyes.

"I'm so sorry," Masako said. She had completely lost her own home and possessions and here she was, concerned for this house.

Lilly flashed the light outside and strained to see through semi-darkness. "Look out there," she said as Kenji peered out beside her.

"Your shingles," he said. "All everywhere."

Black clouds hugged the earth. Humidity hung heavy. Occasionally daylight showed through.

"Just look at that debris," Lilly said. "The whole valley is littered."

Kenji flashed his light and sheltered his face from the rain blowing in. "Look," he said. "Palm tree all bend."

The small front grove of once majestic Red Wax, MacArthur and Manila palms, partially uprooted and leaning with broken fronds, could do nothing more to prevent wind from blowing rain into the house. In fact, rain ran in sheets off the torn roof and splashed down at the edge of the living room floor where one hole had ripped all the way down.

Finally Kenji stepped back. He looked tired. "Masako need sleep," he said, gesturing toward his house. "Too much excitement."

"You can't go home now," Lilly said. "Take my bedroom. It's surely dry in there."

Kenji pointed to the floor. "You have da kine sleeping bag?" he asked.

"No sleeping bags," Lilly said. "You two take my bed. I'll take the spare room."

Lilly peered out again, this time, straining to see toward Ciara's house. "Oh, no, no, no!" she said. Sticking out of Ciara's roof was the huge root ball of a palm tree with its clinging red dirt mass being soaked and dripping down inside the house. It looked to have been dropped in the area of the bedrooms. The entire roof had caved in. Some of the corrugated tin roof sheets dangled or lay strewn on the ground. The front of the house bowed inward.

Lilly raced outside and across the yards. A truck tire, a small kitchen table, seemingly unbroken, and a toilet bowl lay among other rubble. Down the hill lay a white clothes washer. The door of Ciara's steel container had evidently opened then closed again. The upper corner had bent back on itself. She almost stumbled over Rico's funeral urn stuck in the mud. "Oh, no!" she said again, afraid to imagine what else she might find. "Oh, no!"

She ran into the house and came face to face with that tree. It had come down in the hallway and knocked down the wall to the closet where Ciara and Rico had surely huddled. The floor was caved in. Palm fronds lay everywhere like monstrous arms claiming anything within reach. Mud, rain and roof runoff poured through the collapsed ceiling. "Ciara!" Lilly said, screaming. "Ciara! Rico! Where are you?" She climbed over the fronds and around the tree and searched the bedrooms and bath. The two were not to be found. A gruesome mental picture began to form. "No!" she said vehemently. "No!"

If Ciara had to evacuate, she would have gone into that container. That was where she said she should have planned to wait out the storm. Lilly raced outside reaching the container but could not open the door. It was stuck tight. She stood as tall as possible trying to see beyond the bent edge. "Ciara!" she said, nearly panicking. "Rico!" She tried to climb up the doorway but her sneakers only slid.

She rushed back to her garage to retrieve her ladder. Kenji must have had the insight of a psychic. He was already in the garage unfastening the ladder where she had secured it to the wall. "Kenji help," he said.

Together they raced across the lot, each carrying opposite ends of the ladder, and threw it up against the bent door. The heavy thud must have echoed inside. A tiny startled voice from inside the farthest corner began to squeak, "Abuela! Abuela!"

Lilly scampered up the ladder noticing jagged metal edges where the door had ripped apart. There was only one thing she could do. "Sorry, Kenji-san," she said. She stripped off her sweater and shirt and used them as padding so she could climb over the ragged edges. Worldly-wise Kenji showed no emotion at seeing her in her bra. He simply continued to hold the ladder steady.

Inside the container, the air was foul with the odor of urine and excrement. They both climbed over boxes and furniture to reach one another and Little Rico fell into her arms shivering and sobbing. He was soaked through and stunk.

"Your grandmother, Rico?" Lilly asked. "*Donde esta su abuela?*"

"She foo," he said as his little chest jerked with emotion.

"She foo? Rico, where's Ciara?"

"Foo!" he said. Then he waved his hands and arms in the air and said again, "She foo-o-o-o."

"She flew?" Lilly asked. "The wind carried her away?" She did not want Rico to see her panic. She pulled his head against her chest and choked back sobs, but this was no time for tears.

"The twee," Rico said. "The twee came down...." He made a whooshing noise like what the crashing tree must have sounded like to him. "We ran," he said. "Abuela went to get Grandpa and... and she foo." He continued to whimper.

Kenji peered inside from high up on the ladder. "I take baby," he said, holding out his arms.

Lilly climbed over furniture and boxes to where Kenji waited. "Careful," she said. "He's dirtied his pants."

"Aw, never mind," Kenji said, clutching Rico tightly to his chest with one arm as he eased his way down.

Lilly tried to retrieve her shirt from the jagged edges and found it had shredded and would not come loose. She left the clothes behind. She was more concerned about Ciara. When she glanced back, she saw Kenji dancing happily in the rain, most likely to calm Little Rico. "Hurricane finish," he said, turning circles and flailing his arms in the wind and rain. "Hurricane finish." When next she looked, Kenji had stripped the clothes off Rico and stood him in a bucket of water in the garage to wash him down. Lilly ran on, looking for where Ciara might be found. Nearly blinded by the still driven rainfall, she ran down the lane, circled around Ciara's house, cut back across her own yard, and around the Nakamura's house, which was in pitiful shape. The old boards just could not stand that additional strain once all the trees and shrubs had been cleared away.

She doubled back around to her lot. The shrubs at the back had been stripped bare and could hide nothing. She was hit and scraped when more of her roof shingles fell out of trees. Her fruit trees had also been stripped of leaves and smaller branches. More roof shingles dangled precariously and would come down with the next gust of wind. She ducked out of her orchard. All this and yet surprisingly, her cottage behind the garage had remained unscathed. The walls contained no marks of having been bombarded. The main house was pockmarked.

As she stood scanning her back yard, a shiver ran through her. Could Ciara have been dropped into that swollen creek? She ran to the top of a small knoll and realized that was where she recently planted her prized loquat tree. Nothing was left but the hole filled with red-tinged water where it had been forcefully yanked out.

Normally the creek was shallow, not much more than a decorative trickle. Now the water lapped over the banks and had turned the swales into pools that drained into one another before running down the side yard to the front of the property. Fine time to see her landscaping functioning as was intended.

Lilly strained to see in either direction of the creek but red dirt washing off the mountains had dyed the water opaque rust. A black and white soccer ball floated on the current. Other items were being dragged. Yet, the creek was barely deep enough that a body might be completely covered. Something would have to show, but nothing did. Lilly climbed over the fence and made her way beyond the back of her property and followed the creek as best she could. Ciara was not there. She backtracked and followed the creek down through the edge of Ciara's property and on a bit, but found no trace of Ciara. Lilly breathed a sigh of relief that at least Ciara had not drowned.

She might have been perspiring but the cool rain on her bare skin gave her energy to go on. She ran again down to the main road, which was littered with debris of everything imaginable. Then she saw them. Power poles along the main road had fallen, snapped like mere twigs. Wires lay strewn. Other poles leaned, threatening collapse. She would take no chances. She ran down the shoulder until she passed the downed wires and came to where the poles looked fairly stable and crossed the road. Then, there it was, just what she had hoped for. A whole length of fencing along the pasture was gone, simply gone. Mounds of red earth were all that remained where the fence posts had been yanked out leaving red mud oozing in the rain. Without knowing if a power line had come to rest on the wire fence somewhere, had no break in the fence been made, she could have been electrocuted had she touched the metal. Then she remembered that stepping into water that contained a live wire could have the same effect. She shivered from fright, but those thoughts were fleeting. She had to find Ciara.

Crossing the pasture, she was sent flying when she stumbled on hidden rocks. Dazed and bleeding, but undeterred, she ran toward the trees down by the creek in the pasture. Water overflowed the low areas bordering the swollen waterway making it difficult to get underneath the bare branches of the hau thickets. The tree-lined area would be the last place that could hide a person since all the land had been cleared. Yet all the trees were now skeletons of their former selves and Ciara was nowhere to be found. Then Lilly spotted something else. Her mother's rocker swung from a long branch of a nearly naked Cajeput tree farther down along the bank. Its tangled pieces clickity-clacked together sounding like a wind chime ringing out in mockery.

Lilly stomped her foot in defiance. "No!" she said. As she made her way closer and stared at the chair, she realized the damage was irreparable. Yet another memento of her mother's life had to be relegated to memory.

Chapter Seven

Masako slept with her arm thrown over Rico who snuggled in the curve her body made after Kenji rolled her onto her side and drew up her legs. Delicate origami birds, animals and boxes lay on the bed nearby. Lilly never knew if Kenji and Masako had children. It was strange how much of life could pass by without being noticed, how much was taken for granted.

"A job well done," Lilly said, as Kenji helped her drape black plastic sheeting over the gaping holes. Boards previously stored in the garage were the only mainstays now to hold that plastic in place, as the wind snapped it back and forth.

"Rain no come in now," he said.

Lilly had to smile. "I'll bet Sumo's found a new paradise," she said. The flooding would bring out any surviving hordes of ants, cockroaches, mice, geckoes and other creepy-crawly predator food, including the centipedes. "I hope that hungry chicken population survived too." They had been greatly responsible for keeping the centipede population in check.

Soupy drizzle came down persistently but had lost most of its urgency. The wind still toyed with anything movable. Lilly grabbed her binoculars and slipped into her rain gear and went out to salvage what she could. She thought she heard someone behind her and turned, hoping it was Ciara who had crawled out of her safe place, but it was Kenji dogging her heels.

"Kenji help," he said. He had not slept most of the night. Either he had boundless energy or he was a somnambulist.

Water and red mud oozed everywhere. The condition of the landscape had worsened since after the second half of the storm. A multitude of articles lay strewn, no longer belonging to anyone. Splintered boards and torn window screens littered. Patches here and there twinkled in momentary sunlight, telling of glass that had shattered when it was dashed against the ground.

"Look at our trees," Lilly said. Soggy limp clothing and other materials hung from every conceivable appendage and flapped in the breeze.

"One natural clothes line," Kenji said. "After rain, solar dryer."

"We'll all be using solar drying for a while."

"Aha," Kenji said, looking across the road. "The pasture is now dump yard."

Lilly sheltered the binoculars with her hat and peered through them to the broken homes along the road on the far side of the pasture. "Just look at all the damage," she said, handing the binoculars to Kenji.

Erosion had already claimed the side of her yard, fed by the stream at the rear, which ran down through her side yard toward the main road. Nothing could be done for her property just then. Too, anything that had been deposited by the wind would stay where it was, to be later retrieved by the County trucks and taken to makeshift dumps. Lilly wanted to get into her van and look for Ciara. She turned to head for the garage. "I've got to find her," she said. "Wanna come?"

"Wait," Kenji said, pointing toward the road. "Hot wire."

She remembered the fallen power poles and wondered if the wires were still live. They went down to take a look. The wet lines crackled and popped. That only said one thing. "More wires," she said, directing Kenji to look farther down the road. More poles leaned precariously and wires snapped back and forth.

"No drive now," Kenji said. "You hit wire, you get fry!"

He was right. Since the power had not been knocked out—at least not in their area—the power company needed to shut it off. They might not do that till they learned of the severity of the damage. Otherwise power was needed, as much now as just before the storm.

Lilly paced, soaked through and dripping wet in spite of wearing rain gear. "We've got to find her," she said. Ciara having been carried away by the wind was a gruesome thought. Carried by such a force, little hope existed that the wind would deposit her gently somewhere. Lilly remembered the many advantages that she had available to save herself when she had been caught in a rip current. What could Ciara have had at her disposal to help her while being hurled at breakneck speed through the air?

Lilly shook her head, not wanting to dwell on negative thoughts. She needed to retrieve Rico's funeral urn. That would have been the most important material item to Ciara among all her relics. Retrieving that urn and keeping it safe might be the only thing she could do for her now.

Her next steps sunk into mud half a foot deep that kept a sneaker when she pulled her foot free. Water washed over something white nearby that was nearly covered by red ooze. She kicked at it. The item was a large book safely protected by a plastic cover, a waterproof plastic cover. Both she and Kenji bent down and jiggled it out of the ooze and let the rain wash it off.

"Safe inside," Kenji said.

Then, through the plastic, Lilly saw the title of the volume and read, "For Love of a Child: Memoirs of Ciara Malloy-Rey." She held the volume to her bosom and began to whimper.

"No cry," Kenji said, taking hold of her arm gently. "Please, no cry."

Lilly remembered the conversation she and Ciara had in the supermarket before the storm. Had Ciara's request been a cloaked premonition? The re-membrance of what Ciara asked her to do made her heart pound. Yes, in time, she would publish these memoirs for Ciara, for Pablo and for Little Rico.

Lilly retrieved her shoe from the mud. Before Kenji went to rest, he also helped gather whatever lay loose in Ciara's demolished house. Some of Ciara's items they brought out were the photo albums and keepsakes and the framed photo that had stood beside Rico's urn. She found it lying on the floor with its glass shattered, but was able to salvage the picture, which had soaked through around the edges. They also grabbed up dry clothes for Rico they found in the dresser. They had intended to fasten a plastic sheet across the opening of the container but the meaning of doing so seemed lost now that the hurricane had passed. Plus, they could find no way to secure the sheet and everything inside the container had for hours already sat unprotected facing headlong toward the oncoming rain. All that remained was to see what might be salvageable later.

"It's Ciara's husband's ashes," Lilly said to Masako as she watched. Lilly cleaned and wiped down Rico's funeral urn. When she went to unlock the koa cabinet to place it safely inside, she found the piece of furniture had been moved! That heavy koa wood cabinet that had taken four stout Hawaiian men with a hand truck to put in place had been moved by the wind eight inches from its usual spot. Strangely, nothing inside had been jarred or damaged. Dis-covering that cabinet out of place unnerved her, as if she had just realized that vandals had intruded.

Lilly puttered to keep her mind occupied. She and Kenji had managed to get the furniture at least upright so it was usable. Masako had been awake for a couple of hours. She kept Rico entertained by reading to him from Ciara's books. He knew the stories well and read along. Occasionally, Masako would speak a word in Japanese and point to a picture and Rico would pronounce the Japanese word too. For a while, she even had him folding simple origami.

The thought that Lilly could not do anything for Ciara filled her with guilt. "This is driving me nuts," she said as she paced again. "I wish they'd do something about those live wires." The last time she checked they continued to sizzle and pop. Her patience was surely being tried. "The rain wouldn't bother me if I could drive to look for Ciara."

"I'm afraid the rain's only gotten heavier," Masako said.

In fact, it had intensified, which was not unusual for a post-hurricane clime.

The sole radio broadcast from Honolulu still crackled. Visible and thermal data would be made available by official storm watchers on the Internet and would include spectacular satellite images looking down on Naheka as it slammed ashore on Kauai. Like Iniki, unofficial reports put wind gusts at well over 200 miles per hour. The announcer went on to report that Oahu was the hardest hit of the remaining islands, sustaining horrendous island-wide wind damage and massive flooding and mudslides pouring down from the Koolau Mountain Range.

"Makes me wonder how our island fared," Lilly said. No one would know the extent of damage to Kauai until Kauai's own communication systems were restored.

All the lower islands of Maui, Molokai, the Big Island, and even Lanai and Kahoʻolawe, sustained the same onslaught but in lesser degrees. No word had been received from the Forbidden Island of Niʻihau seventeen miles west of Kauai, next closest in the twisted path of Naheka. By choice, residents there lived in huts emulating lifestyles much like the ancient Hawaiians. One TV and one radio were known to be in use on the island. It could only be hoped that these people had known in time to prepare themselves. That was the way they chose to live, not wanting outside interference.

Finally the announcer said that Naheka had slammed onto Kauai from a south westerly angle, had stalled while the eye sat on top of the island as it changed directions and moved off to the north west again. Its energy decayed rapidly as it hovered over land, but surprisingly, had picked up once it was out over the warm Pacific Ocean again. Due to its irregular path, Naheka would be watched closely until it finally lost strength.

"They've aired the same news for hours," Masako said.

"Probably haven't been able to get any updates from here," Lilly said.

"Why don't you turn it off?"

Lilly did and silence from the lack of static and the garbled radio voice was soothing. As usual after a hurricane, nothing could be done but wait and she was not good at passing idle time. Had it not been for the incessant rain, she would have already taken down the boards covering the windows and put up her screens and jalousies again. Fresh air in the house would have helped settle her nerves.

She began to think about how she might be able to carry out some of Ciara's wishes. Certainly, once Cuba opened, Pablo should be the one to take his father's ashes to be spread there. Maybe she would go with him and Little Rico. She had never seen Cuba and the duty and opportunity would be a most propitious one. She shuddered at the thought that it might be both Ciara's and Rico's ashes they would take together. "They'll find her," she said. "Somehow... somewhere."

"They will find her," Masako said reassuringly.

"Who?" Rico asked. Then he asked, "Where's my abuela?"

Masako distracted him and tried to keep him occupied.

Perhaps by the time Cuba opened, Lilly would have completed publication of those memoirs. She glanced at the white volume lying on the end table and went to hold it. She sat down and found a strange determination occupying her thoughts. "Ciara asked me to publish these memoirs if anything ever happened to her," Lilly said.

Masako cast a dubious glance at the book. "Have you already read them?"

Rico watched attentively as Masako continued to deftly fold origami creations, her fingers nimble and rhythmical. He tried to fold with her. "Ori-gami," he said.

"No, I haven't," Lilly said. She rubbed her fingertips along the edges of the cover and felt a knot form in her throat. Eventually, she was going to have to read those memoirs. She would learn everything that ever puzzled her about this dedicated but secretive woman. She would learn all her secrets and Lilly was sure there was plenty. She stared at the name on the cover. "Ciara Malloy-Rey," she said, reading aloud.

"That is her name?" Masako asked.

"Yes, that is her name," Lilly said, smiling at Masako, whose simple statement told her not to give up, not to dwell on the worst scenario. Lilly realized how much she loved Kenji and Masako. They expressed so much through their actions of caring, with a look in the eye and a few choice words. Kenji had not slept long. He must have used his salvaged figurines to set up a makeshift altar in the bedroom, from which they heard him begin to chant as Rico listened attentively.

Lilly's thoughts had stayed on Ciara's name. That was another glaring inconsistency. This was one of the few times she saw the use of Rico's last name with Ciara's name. On the escrow documents, which she had handled in Ciara's absence, the only name used was Malloy. She always used Malloy. Even her driver's license was printed with Malloy by itself.

During the time when Ciara and Rico would have been married, it was still the norm for the woman to take the man's name. Lilly thought about that more than once. She remembered that women had not begun retaining their maiden names till the early '80s. The question of name was intriguing and one of the mysteries that was Ciara.

Lilly leaned her head back as thoughts swirled about Ciara and her family. Lilly never meddled in anyone's affairs but felt irresistibly drawn into the mysteries held tightly secreted by this friend she quickly loved. The images of Pablo with his mother, Amalia, and her white-haired husband, Tito, floated in. The old photos of Rico, during the period just before his death, came to mind. He had been a glorious Latino if there ever was one. Lilly visualized the Pablo she had recently met, with his hair turning white, and wondered why he resembled his mother but looked nothing at all like Rico, his dad.

Something was amiss, something that would not gel. She opened the cover of the book on her lap and fanned the pages. Everywhere throughout, handwritten or typed notes were stuck into the spine. Snapshots of Rico, Pablo and Ciara were included. Most of the attached pages were typed. The paper in the earliest sections had yellowed, the photos faded.

Curiosity prodded her onward even as she began to feel that she was invading Ciara's privacy. Perhaps she should not delay. Perhaps it was time to read the memoirs. She would certainly have to do this in order to take the next step toward publication. When would be the right time to read? Nothing much could be done presently because perhaps tomorrow or the next day cleanup and rebuilding would begin. Perhaps it was better to wait till her house was back together. There was no rush now. No evidence existed to prove Ciara's demise, and not until she knew for sure did she have a right to invade Ciara's secret world. Ciara had entrusted her past, a trust that Lilly found she could not breach. With that decision, she felt a great burden lifted from her.

Just as she closed the book, pages slipped out from inside the back cover and fell to the floor. Lilly strained and bent forward over the massive book to retrieve them. On the top page, in bold letters, were the words, *Last Will and Testament of Ciara Lona Malloy.*

Lilly couldn't help herself. She flipped the first page and scanned, then the second, which was all there was. The last paragraph read:

My body is to be cremated. If, by that time, I have not succeeded in scattering Rico's ashes over his parent's graves in Havana, Cuba, then my ashes are to be co-mingled with Rico's and placed into a new urn large enough to accommodate our ashes together. Then he and I will remain together forever.

Tears welled up and Lilly's hands shook as she shoved the pages back into the book. It served her right. She did not need to be reading anything about Ciara's demise. She glanced at Masako, who had evidently watched, and quickly looked away. Lilly closed the cover and placed both hands on top of it. "For now," she said. "These memoirs will remain Ciara's secret."

Masako smiled. Then she asked, "How do you say Ciara in Hawaiian?"

"I was wondering that too," Lilly said, drying her eyes. She rose and went into the pantry, where she had stowed all her books, rummaging till she came up with a couple of Hawaiian language dictionaries. Back in the living room, she browsed and then said, "You'd have to imagine how the Hawaiians did it. They didn't have all our consonants, so they tried to pronounce a name as best they could."

Masako looked thoughtful. "Maybe pronounced something like *Kikaha*," she said.

"Then eventually the middle "k" would be replaced with an *okina*, that backwards apostrophe, right?" Lilly asked, gesturing in the air with a fingertip.

"So it would sound like "*Ki'aha*," Masako said.

The sound of the name was musical. "Oh! Say that again," Lilly said.

"Instead of Ci-ar-a, say Ki'a-ha."

"Ki'a-ha, ori-gami," Rico said and laughed at the bird that he and Masako had just made. He took the bird and noisily exaggerated its flight around the room.

Lilly was surprised to find that Kikaha was a real Hawaiian word. "Kikaha means to soar, glide, poise," she said. "Do you know how much that fits her if she was carried away by the wind?"

"Maybe she won't want to be reminded of her flight," Masako said.

"Let's save it," Lilly said. "Let her decide."

Chapter Eight

Lightning and thunder rolled the likes of which she had not heard since before the hurricane. Rain came again in torrents. Clouds obliterated what little sunlight had tried to break through. In a few moments, thunder rolled again, but this time it was punctuated by the sound of a car horn. Headlights flashed through the open front door. How could anyone drive with live wires laying everywhere? Surely someone came to tell her that Ciara had been found. That was the only reason anyone would brave the conditions to drive at a time like this.

A car door slammed. Before she could move the bulky memoir album aside, someone jumped onto her front porch and rapped sharply on the screen door.

"Lilly!" a deep resonant voice called out. "Lilly!"

Lilly knew that voice. In the beam of the headlights, she saw the figure of the man kick out of his boots and quickly shed his rain poncho and drop it to the porch floor. The screen door opened and he let himself in just as Sumo wailed and skittered between his feet, angry and in discomfort. The cat skidded to a stop, twitched his ears sharply to flick off the water, and then irritably shook water from its paws.

Lilly rushed to the doorway. "Keoki," she said. "How…?" She must have stood with her mouth agape, surprised at the presence of both Keoki and the cat. Keoki's expression was one of utter relief. He looked ready to cry. Suddenly he stepped toward her and scooped her into his arms and held her so close she had to push him away to catch her breath. He smelled like fresh rain.

"Lilly," he said. "I was so worried."

"You knew we'd be okay, didn't you, Keoki?"

Keoki looked at the black plastic and rolled his eyes.

"Come, Rico," Masako said. Lilly heard her wobbly wheelchair roll into the bedroom and Rico's little footsteps patter along.

"Ori-gami," Rico said.

"I-I had to know if you were safe," Keoki said. He seemed confused. "For sure, all of you, you're okay?" For some reason, he sounded as if he expected that something might have happened to her. "I was so worried."

Keoki had taken a chance to get to her. Her emotions went out to him. It was strange how he showed up at the most unimaginable times. "The live wires," she said. "How did you—?"

"The power was finally cut," he said. "Island-wide. The sea swell decimated the South Shore, too much flooding. The damage is incredible." He paused, stood straighter and threw his shoulders back, then smiled teasingly. "But me and my all-terrain braved the back gullies and muddy haul cane roads to get through." They both laughed, and then he held her again seeming as if he could not stop himself. He sighed what surely was a sigh of relief. She thought she heard him choke back emotion. "You're okay after all."

Lilly felt a little uncomfortable at being in this man's arms, this man who cared to come and see that she had weathered the most horrendous aspect of island life. She pulled away from him although he still held her at arm's length. She had to ask. "Berkley," she said, unsure she should even mention the name. "I thought Berkley would come."

"Forget Berkley," he said, seeming a little annoyed. "Berkley left the island just after we saw you in the supermarket."

Lilly was stunned. Berkley had left her to fend for herself and had not so much as bothered to call to say he was leaving. "How could he?"

"Forget him," Keoki said. "He only thinks of himself. You know that."

She was embarrassed to realize she did not know that, or had not faced the truth about Berkley. "But you called," she said. "Thank you, Keoki. Knowing someone was thinking of us meant so much."

Keoki simply stood looking at her with that compassionate, expectant stare. He wanted to say something. She just knew it, but he was not about to and that irritated her when people held back and expected her to be some sort of mind reader. Still, something in his quiet nature said he was not about to open his mouth and ruin the moment. He was expecting her to realize something. His patience and support was his way of letting her see something on her own; to see him for the person he was. He was waiting for her to acknowledge him.

That was what his showing up at the most opportune times meant. He had always been there for her. He did not want to take liberties and, with seeming egoism, gush all over her. He had given her the option of taking the next step. In his quiet hopeful way, the way he expectantly looked into her eyes now, he had always given her that option. Overwhelmed, she stood on tiptoes and threw her arms around his neck.

"I'm so glad you're not hurt," he said.

"Thank you, Keoki," she said, whispering, "You've always been there for me."

"It's me who cares for you," he said. "Always has been."

She pulled away to arm's length. "I didn't know you felt that way."

"Life's too short, Lilly, too ephemeral," he said. "I'm not keeping it a secret anymore."

Their eyes locked in an intense stare full of respect, admiration and expectation. "I didn't know," Lilly said again.

"Have always cared," he said softly. "This is the last time I'll see Berkley take you for granted."

At that moment, Lilly understood so much. She had become sidetracked with Berkley. Keoki had not introduced them with the intention of bringing her together with his friend. Like the few other men in her life, the relationship with Berkley had not been consummated. Surely Keoki knew and that was why he kept coming around and making known his presence. Here was a man she had always admired and wished to get to know better. How blind she had been.

"Can you forgive me?" she asked. The words slipped out before she had time to censure them. She had never begged a man for favors of any kind, but here was attentive Keoki and her comment had sprung forth in total naïveté and naturalness. She tried to smile and felt the corners of her mouth twitch. Now she understood Keoki and that ever-present look in his eyes and it made her heart pound. They simply stood looking at one another. It was both maddening and heightening for Lilly. She simply did not know what to do next.

He pulled her close again and she watched him watching her every reaction. Then she was in his arms and wanted to be there. All her anxiety and repressed loneliness was shattered at that very moment. He held her tightly. His arms were strong and sure, yet gentle. "I couldn't bear the thought of you being hurt," he said softly.

She resisted melting against him, but the desire to do so was nearly unbearable. "I… care… about you, Keoki," she said softly. "I… really do." It was difficult to admit such feelings, difficult as with anything she felt a first time.

He touched her chin and tipped her face back. She thought he would kiss her and she was not ready and felt panic. Instead, he kissed her cheek, slowly, gently, and with much meaning. Then he pressed his cheek to hers. His hands moved slowly over her back and the back of her head. He knotted up a fistful of her hair. "Mmmm…!" he said, using restraint as he pulled away.

This was something she had forgotten about a man, his need to be a man, a need she just might, in time, want to encourage in this one. She felt conspicuous in her desire, like he was reading it on her face and on her breath. He stared that stare again then suddenly looked beyond her and pulled away completely. She heard Masako's wheelchair.

Then Kenji was beside her with his hands pressed together looking at Keoki. It was amazing how Kenji's eyes always teased. "*Hajimemashite, Keoki-san,*" he said eagerly, then bowed.

"This is Kenji Nakamura," Lilly said and then turned. "This is Masako, and you've met Rico."

Keoki beamed. "*Hajimemashite, Kenji-san,*" he said with a proper bow. "*Masako-san.*" He bowed again to her.

Hearing Keoki speak Japanese was yet another aspect of the man to marvel. Of course he would speak Japanese, and maybe Greek. He was definitely fascinating and one man she knew she would get to know.

Before Keoki could acknowledge him, Rico blurted, "Did you bring my abuela?" His sad begging voice shocked Lilly back to reality.

"His what?" Keoki asked.

"His grandmother," Lilly said. "That's Spanish for grandmother."

He tensed, seemed startled. "What's happened to his grandmother?"

"She's missing, Keoki. Ciara's missing. Rico said he saw his grandmother picked up by the wind and carried away."

"No!" he said as his eyes widened. He knew something.

"What is it, Keoki?"

"Carried away by the wind?"

"Yes. It must have happened as Rico said. We can't find a trace of her. I'm afraid she's—"

"At the hospital," he said, barely whispering as if he didn't want Rico to know. "At the hospital." His words tumbled out in a rush. "They don't know who the woman is. I had to come and make sure it wasn't you in that hospital bed."

He spoke quickly. Lilly hoped Rico had not understood. "Who's at the hospital?" she asked quietly. Her heart raced.

"Quick, put the boy in the bedroom," Keoki said in low tones. She didn't have time to ask why. He said, "Please, quickly."

"Come, Rico," Masako said again as she wheeled her chair around. "Come, come."

"Want my abuela!" Rico said, beginning to cry.

When they were out of earshot, Lilly asked, "How did you hear she was at the hospital?"

"I don't know that it's her," he said. "No one knows who the woman is. I came to make sure it wasn't you, Lilly. I was so worried for all of you up here on this hill with no protection around you."

"Ciara's missing, Keoki. Rico said she flew."

The look in Keoki's eyes was wild. He looked ready to run. He spoke fast. "Some woman was slammed through the wall of a house that had already sustained severe damage," He said. "Two doors up the road." He pointed.

"Ciara?"

"They don't know," he said. "The man in the house said that first his roof and side wall were blown away. Hours later, he heard a woman crying for help and he crept out of his closet to take a look. She seemed too mangled to move and all he could do was cover her with a tarp to keep the rain off her. He took a great risk and drove all the way down to the fire station while the hurricane was still raging. The paramedics came and got the woman and sped her to the hospital."

"Oh, thank goodness," Lilly said. "She's safe."

"Not yet," Keoki said. "I'm sorry, Lilly. Most major bones are broken. She's got a concussion... in a coma—"

"How did you hear?"

Keoki patted the mobile radio on his hip. "I'm in volunteer rescue, remember?"

Kenji had been quiet but understood it all. "Go to friend," he said.

"We must," Lilly said, moving toward the door.

"Wait, Lilly," Keoki said, catching her by a shoulder. "She's not expected to live. She could already be—"

Lilly stiffened. "If that woman is indeed Ciara, she will live. Get me there, Keoki."

Keoki put his hand on her shoulder, making her pause. "There's something more," he said. "She mumbles a name—what is it? Another language—"

"Rico! Does she say Rico or Frederico?"

"That's it, Lilly! Could it be her?"

"Right now, let's go."

"I'll get you there, but you prepare for the worst." He paused, again preventing her from leaving. Then he added, "Lilly, there's still more."

"Tell me now," Lilly said. Whatever she had to hear she wanted it all at once. Then she would know how to handle the situation afterwards.

"I only heard this from another guy, people talking, you know." He gestured to the radio again.

"What is it?"

"Her face is gone. She must have blown around some mud and rocks too. Her skin, here and there over her body, was ripped, especially her knees, like she tried to crawl. They think her legs were broken... her face... when she was slammed against the boards in that broken wall."

Lilly felt tears spill over and wiped them away quickly, as if she didn't have time for them. "How will we know her?"

"Just talk to her, I guess," he said. Then he added, "Hey, does Ciara wear diamonds? That woman wears these rings with huge—"

"That's her!"

"They can't get her to open her fist."

"That's her," Lilly said again. "If she has strength enough to keep that fist tightened around those rings, she has the will to live." Then she remembered something. "Wait," she said and she ran to her bedroom and ripped the plastic covering from around the desk. She rummaged through a drawer and found copies of Ciara's legal documents which she had needed when acting as her Power-of-Attorney." She hurried back to the living room and grabbed for her rain poncho and found Kenji offering it to her.

Keoki started for the doorway. "She won't know you, okay?"

"She will when I talk about Rico," Lilly said. Then she hesitated. "Wait, Keoki," she said, touching his arm. "If there's one person who can get through to her, it's Little Rico. She'll come around when she hears his voice. I know she will.

And Pablo—Rico's dad—he's in the Navy Seals. The military will let him come, just because he's got family here."

"Army Reserve choppers are due from Oahu, Lilly," Keoki said.

"He'll be on one of them," she said. "Ciara will pull through this."

"Don't get your hopes up, okay? She's almost gone." His eyes were trying to prepare her for the worst. "Let's go," he said.

"Believe me, Keoki, she's a fighter," Lilly said as she slipped into her poncho. "She would even know if little Rico was in the room without hearing his voice."

"Then let's grab the little guy and make a run for it," he said.

As they rushed out the door with Keoki carrying Rico, the rain stopped and the sun broke through. A plump gray dove landed on a drooping palm frond nearby and warbled for its mate.

Chapter Nine

Even if Keoki had heard that all electrical power was cut, he decided to play it safe and not drive over any wires lying across the pavements.

"We're not taking the main road down at the beach," he said. "If the storm surge comes in, there'll be massive flooding where the highway dips down to beach level." He glanced over at her. "Hang on."

The route through eroded gullies and muddy haul cane roads took nearly an hour for them to travel the normally eight or nine miles to the hospital by regular route. Everything, manmade or natural, lay in a state of devastation. The entire island seemed covered with debris. Keoki's expression was tense and he never spoke as he navigated the treacherous hillsides. Brittle Albesia branches lay everywhere. Trees were felled. At times his arms flew around the steering wheel, maneuvering to avoid sinking into red dirt bogs and ditches, as the vehicle slipped and spun. He was a man on a mission and never eased up on control of the vehicle till they emerged on Kuhio Highway in Kapaia and raced for the hospital at the top of the hill.

In spite of the rough ride, Rico had fallen asleep on Lilly's lap under the seat belts and inside her rain poncho with his little face sticking out. She kept her arms securely around him and realized for the first time how much she loved this child. A fleeting idea came to her that if anything were to happen to Ciara, she would want to care for precocious Little Rico at least until Pablo retired from the Navy. She gritted her teeth and shook her head and quickly dismissed the idea of Ciara's demise.

When they finally pulled into the hospital parking lot, a security guard stuck his head inside the vehicle and asked if they were hurt. After that, they were directed away from the emergency entrance around to the front parking lot.

Few cars were parked, probably only those belonging to medical personnel who waited out the storm all night in the facility. Family would have left most hospital workers at the facility and driven home so cars would not glut the area. Sometime during the ride to the hospital, the rain has all but ceased. They hastily threw their ponchos back into the vehicle and headed to the front door.

The hospital and grounds was a hive of activity, with workers removing protective coverings from the glass doors and windows.

A Hawaiian woman at the front desk did not have to check the records to know the location of the injured woman. "Penthouse, third floor," she said, sharing an in-house colloquialism. "Check at the nurses' station first."

The normally fast elevators took forever. When they stepped onto the third floor, a lot of people in hospital garb were coming and going. It seemed just another day at the hospital, with the exception of the window workers. Keoki picked up Rico and carried him. Rico's gaze darted around as if questioning, looking at everything as he began to be more fully awake.

They stopped at the registration desk. "Ciara," Lilly said in a hurry. "Where is Ciara?"

"Who?" the clerk asked.

"The unidentified woman," Keoki said.

The clerk smiled. "Our only patient from the storm so far."

A passing nurse heard the conversation and leaned close. "She was in surgery most of the night," she said. She glanced at her wristwatch. "Been out a while though. Being sent to ICU just about now."

Lilly started to walk away. "Where, please?"

The nurse stepped in front of them. "Are you family? Do you know who she is?"

"She's my neighbor," Lilly said. She motioned toward Rico. "This is her grandson."

"She won't know any of you." She gestured toward Rico. "I wouldn't take him in. She's in a coma."

Lilly could not believe how old fashioned some things stubbornly remained. Having loving family around could be the best thing that could happen for a patient. "She'll know Little Rico," she said. "She'll come out of her coma."

The nurse's reaction was one of sympathy. "Ma'am, if you folks will step over here and give me a little information—"

"Can't we see her first?"

The nurse already had the chart in her hand, intent on doing her job. "Her name?"

Lilly produced the packet of Ciara's information. "Her name's Ciara Malloy. Here's her information. Please, can't we get in there with Rico?"

The nurse accepted the packet and sighed, surely having been up most of the night. "Sure, go ahead," she said.

The hallway was glutted with boards being removed from the observation room windows at the far end of the hallway. Workers came with a dolly to haul them away. Lilly and Keoki picked their way through the boards leaning against the walls and Lilly stepped into ICU first.

Ciara's bed was backed up against the wall next to the doorway, as if the patient could look across the room and see outside when the bed was raised. Who, recovering in ICU would be aware such things? A doctor was just leaving. First, he looked as if he was about to ask them to leave. Then he opened both hands and said, "I guess it's okay. She won't know you're here though." He hesitated, then said, "Poor woman, the only thing fortunate in this is that she was our only casualty. We had time to work on her all night."

"Her face...?" Lilly asked.

"She's had some plastic surgery—"

"Already?"

The doctor paused by the doorway. "As you know, Kauai has no resident plastic surgeon, but Honolulu has many. So Dr. Yardley and his assistant flew from Oahu to stay with us before the storm hit. In case we had a patient, just like this."

"She's already had her face operated on?" Keoki asked.

"Yes, we had no choice. She'll need more." The doctor shook his head in pity. "You folks understand, don't you? We had to operate. Without knowing who she was... in her condition... a team of us doctors decided—"

"We're so grateful," Lilly said, grabbing his hand. He seemed tired but nodded his thanks. She watched the doctor's shoulders droop as he left.

Both of Ciara's legs were in casts and elevated on pillows. So was her right arm and shoulder, looking as if her collarbone had been broken. She wore a neck brace. Her face was totally bandaged with patches over both eyes. Her nose was covered with a splint. Only her lips protruded. Ciara's left arm had been placed across her midriff where her fist was clenched as Keoki had heard.

Her diamonds flashed when the jewels caught the light as Lilly walked around the bed to the other side.

Keoki stood Rico beside the bed and all Rico did was stare. He was too young to understand. He kept looking up at Keoki who held his hand. Then Rico saw his grandmother's hand with the diamonds and tried to reach up and touch them with tiny fingers showing dimples on his knuckles. Something inside his little mind clicked into place. "Abuela!" he said, with so much disbelief coming from one so young. "Abuela?" Then he frantically tried to climb up the side of the bed using the bedrails.

"Easy, little guy," Keoki said, grabbing hold of him.

"Want my abuela!" he said, kicking and fighting his way to get to the top.

Keoki sat Rico beside Ciara who had not stirred. "Be careful. Don't hurt her," he said.

Instinctively, Rico snuggled down into the hollow at the side of her waist and lay there on his side facing out with eyes wide open and staring at nothing. Finally, he squirmed his way up so that his head lay on Ciara's upper arm near the bend in the elbow and he faced her. Her arm lay across his neck; the fist still clenched.

Lilly felt like she was going to pieces. She walked away and looked out the window and swiped at tears. Soon, Keoki's arm came around her shoulder and she turned into him and he held her. Neither spoke.

They stood looking out the dark blue tinted windows, across the flattened, decimated sugar cane fields toward the sea.

"What's that?" Lilly asked. "In the clouds."

"Look at that!" Keoki said, moving them both closer to the window.

Twin-bladed Army Reserve CH-47 Chinook helicopters dropped down out of the clouds and hung in the air waiting to put down at the Lihue Airport. Like big birds bringing sustenance to the nest, one by one they dropped slowly to the ground and out of sight from their view at the window.

Lilly heard a rustling on Ciara's bed and turned. Little Rico stood on his knees facing Ciara. Her arm slipped lifelessly, out to the side. Rico stared at the face he could not see. Soon he pulled himself up on tiptoes and bent over her with his little bottom sticking up in the air and placed his hands on both sides of her head. Like Lilly had seen him do so many times before, he sweetly kissed his grandmother's lips. Then he sat back on his legs beside her.

Tears poured out of Lilly's eyes till she could barely see. Then something else had moved. Ciara's fist slowly relaxed, the hand fell open and went limp as if all life had gone out of her. Her head relaxed sideways. Nothing else moved. It seemed she had died.

Trying to stay calm for Rico's sake was nearly impossible. "Keoki," Lilly said, keeping her voice in a whisper. "This can't be."

"Abuela," Rico kept saying. "Abuela." When he got no reaction, he crept up again and planted another kiss.

After what seemed like an eternity of denying her demise, Lilly caught a glimpse of Ciara's finger's twitching. She struggled to raise her arm but couldn't. She was still alive!

Rico reached for his grandmother's arm and shook it gently. Somehow, he must have understood and lay back down beside Ciara. She was too weak to respond.

Now Lilly heard something new, the sounds of helicopters close by; too loud to be heard across the distance from the airport. She looked out the window and saw two choppers speeding toward the hospital. They headed out of sight and then men were scurrying on the ground three floors below, signaling upwards.

"Medical supplies," Keoki said. "They would bring medical supplies directly here." That was why no cars were left standing in the rear parking lot.

The whop-whop-whop sound of helicopter blades filled her ears. She looked in all directions out the window but could not see the craft. Then, all of a sudden, one Army-green camouflaged Chinook slowly dropped right in front of them in the parking lot. It was so close and real and so big that Lilly had to take a step backwards as she gasped in amazement. It came down on its two rear wheels and paused long enough before settling the front end for Lilly to see a couple of the uniformed men inside, already preparing to disembark. The other chopper was directed to put down farther away at the back end of the lot. Underneath the helmets they all wore to stay in touch with the flight crew, it looked as though one or more of them had white hair. Then all the men scrambled as the crews exited their craft.

Lilly leaned forward and pressed against the windowpane, trying to see white hair again. Finally, she tugged at Keoki's arm and whispered, not wanting to cause Little Rico to have false hopes. "Pablo's here! Keoki, he's down there!"

"Did you see him?" he asked, whispering. "Where?"

"I saw him. I know I did. He's methodical. It's his training. He'd come here first to make sure his family was not hurt. Then he'd go to the house."

Just then, one man with white hair exited the far chopper, putting on his uniform hat. "That's him, Keoki," she said, low so Rico could not hear. "In his uniform. I knew it." The man seemed to be asking directions of one of the ground crew.

"What's his name Lilly?" Keoki was already headed for the door. "His last name?"

"Rey. R-e-y."

From her high vantage point, Lilly was still not sure the man was Pablo because his back was to her. Soon Keoki appeared on the ground running across the lot to him. She tried to imagine how Keoki might address him. Pablo Rey? He might ask. Are you Pablo Rey? She heard it all in her mind as she watched Keoki grab the man's arm and then the white haired man looked up. Keoki would have prepared Pablo, told him about his mother's condition. The white haired man grabbed up his small duffel bag and, together, he and Keoki raced back toward the building.

A small duffel bag. Lilly knew the devotion this family held for one another. Pablo had not bothered to change out of his uniform for the trip. He had probably been approved for emergency leave and gone to the base airport in Panama as soon as he heard the hurricane was expected to slam into Kauai. He probably bought that small duffel bag and toiletries right there on the base while waiting for the flight out. He would have bought a simple change of clothes at a layover airport as he zigzagged his way up the coast from Panama to California, then on to Honolulu. Knowing how this family stood by one another, Lilly guessed there would be no reason for him to go back to his living quarters just to change into civvies and methodically pack a bag. Not him. Not Ciara's son, a Navy Seal, who knew how to live on the fly. He would arrive by any means possible wearing whatever he had on his back.

Lilly sensed the depth of Ciara's family's commitment to one another. A commitment she could only dream of for herself.

Moments later, Keoki and Pablo burst into the room looking as if they had run up the stairs instead of waiting for the elevator. Pablo fumbled nervously with his hat in his hands as his gaze darted around the room and found Ciara. He looked stunningly handsome in his uniform.

"Papi!" Little Rico said, standing with arms outreached and nearly falling over the guard rail of the bed.

Pablo dropped his duffel bag where he stood and threw his hat into the chair and went right to his mother as Rico leaped off the bed and into his arms. The hat glided across the chair seat and dropped onto the floor. Keoki bent to retrieve the hat and laid it on top of the duffel bag that he pulled over near a wall.

Keoki came to stand beside her. Lilly swallowed hard and could not look away. She could only watch and hope that with both Pablo and Rico present, Ciara would regain consciousness.

Pablo sat Rico on the bed and then bent down and kissed his mother's lips, just as little Rico had done. He took her hand. "Mama," he said softly. "Mama, come back to us."

Lilly's heart wrenched. She sobbed into Keoki's chest. Then she heard the muffled whimpers from somewhere inside all the bandages. Like a person crying who could not move her face because her jaws were wired closed. Like a person crying with desperate spurts of joy.

"Abuela!"

"*Gracias a Dios!*" Pablo said, crossing himself.

"Come," Keoki said.

Lilly allowed Keoki to lead her out of the room because she could not dry her eyes fast enough to see where to walk. They went to the glass-walled observation area next to the ICU. It was at the end of the wing and looked out over the grounds and provided a broader view of the activities going on below as supplies were being unloaded. Lilly looked out toward the airport where the last of the string of helicopters was just putting down.

Keoki took her into his arms. "Life's too short," he said. His arms were firm around her and felt reassuring. Keoki's caring seemed to pour from him. She needed his strength because at that moment she had none. She melted against him and did not shy away when he began to kiss the top of her head and rub her back. She wrapped her arms around his neck and found comfort in his attentiveness. Keoki kissed her, though gently, because it seemed he could no longer hold back his feelings. In the past, she had left him no choice but to retreat into the background of her life, but he had only a couple hours ago declared his feelings and intention. He would no longer hold back. The rest was up to her.

Now she wanted him to care. She wanted to learn to care for someone special and have that love and devotion returned. She pushed it away all her life and now came face to face with the reality of it. She already loved Ciara and Pablo and Rico and realized she had love in her heart to give. Could she give that certain kind of love that a man needed, something she had never done, and doubted she was capable of?

She pulled back and looked up into Keoki's eyes. If she was to receive the kind of love she yearned for, she was going to have to give it too. "It's going to be a rough road from here," she said.

"You worried about Ciara or yourself as well?"

"About you."

He smiled briefly. "Oh, you don't worry about me. I intend to see this through." He paused, like he was not sure he should say what he might be about to. He began slowly. "Can we get to know each other, Lilly?" His slanted eyes were clear and full of sincerity.

At that moment, all she knew was that Keoki had not deserted her. Not during the hurricane and not during the entire time she knew him. She was the one who had gotten sidetracked and was left wondering why people came and went her entire life, leaving her with a numbness that had become commonplace.

Lilly realized she had perpetuated her own myth; that good men did not exist, that the few good men would remain as elusive as her father had been. She had always chosen men who kept their distance, like her father, the only example of a man she clung to. That was not what she wanted and had never been.

She tightened her arms around Keoki's neck. His arms went immediately around her waist and he pulled her body close to his. He moaned as if she had just opened the floodgates of his feelings.

She pulled away so she could see him. "Keoki," she said, whispering softly as she gazed into his eyes. Then she slowly brought her lips to his because she needed to take the initiative. He did not hesitate and returned her kiss and pulled her body even tighter to his. She opened her mouth slightly and Keoki seemed to understand full well what that meant, that she was opening herself to him, being vulnerable, because she trusted him. Keoki could not remain pressed against her for long. He pulled away and said, "I'm here for you, Lilly. Do you understand?"

"I-I know that now," she said.

"Lilly," he said. She could only listen and stared intently into his eyes. "I want to understand everything about you. I don't think you need much of a shoulder to lean on. You're not that kind of person." He touched her cheek. "I just want to be the guy who stands tall beside you."

She kissed him again. This time he took liberties and she welcomed his tongue against her lips. Her tongue met his in a slow and sensual dance until she felt weak and ready to collapse. Keoki pulled away and pressed her face to his shoulder. She felt his erratic breathing and heard him stifle a moan deep down inside his throat. All these natural things about a man, what a man felt and how he expressed himself had eluded her. Yet, here she was, standing with this wonderful gift of friendship and love being lavished on her from a person she deeply respected, and all she wanted to do was keep the momentum going. She almost felt like a young girl again, most certainly fresh and new with sensuous feelings coursing through her. She wanted to kiss him again but Keoki touched a fingertip to her lips and would not allow the moment to sweep them away, not in public. Somehow she knew he would wait till the right moment and it would be right for her as well. One thing was certain; she wanted this considerate and gentle man and would let nothing stop her now. She would devote herself to a relationship with his kind and spiritual soul. She wanted to reward him for his patience and felt a rush she, yet, had to suppress momentarily. The time would come and she would not hold back.

They stood without speaking, locked together in an embrace. He held her snug against him, as if she were a precious gift he had just received. Gone for the moment was the tragedy in ICU. Gone were the rescue and replenishing efforts of the chopper crews below. The entire world melted away in one pure moment of love; one intrinsic moment that was untarnished by neither fear nor hope and was the beginning of life anew.

The sound of a powerful motor started and the distinct pulse of chopper blades began again. Keoki swung her around so that she could see the gigantic Chinook dramatically lift in front of them right outside the window as Lilly stared and held her breath. Then it took off, flying low over the cane fields, in the direction of the airport.

The hospital PA system pealed a routine message.

Then Pablo entered the room behind them and asked, "Can you come, please? Talk to Mom. It would do her good to know you're here."

* * *

About the Author

Writing has been an interest since I was a child. Many of the scribbles and bits of profound thoughts that I committed to paper when younger remain on paper. Some of the ink has bled out into the page making many of the words nearly illegible. Nothing may be done with these notes except to affirm that writing has always been an interest.

In the late 1960s while I lived in San Juan, Puerto Rico, I thought I would write a few short stories. Then I thought I'd like to write a novel. One such novel was started but remains unfinished. I had to rush home to San Francisco due to an illness in the family. It was a permanent relocation for me. With the new life came new responsibilities and, unintentionally, writing was put aside. Now, among all the other stories I'm writing, I am revisiting that novel. That would be a huge undertaking. That story sits on the back burner with many other projects. Yet now, decades later, my muse has begun kicking out scenes and lines of dialogue that can only fit that story.

In the 1970s I wrote for and helped publish a monthly newsletter. From that time on, writing began to come to the fore, little by little. In the 1980s, after much experience, I published my own monthly newsletter and began writing poetry and short stories.

Not until being rear-ended in a car accident in 1990 did I begin to seriously think about publishing anything. Physical therapy lasted nearly three years and left me with nothing to do but think. I decided if my body didn't work well, my mind still cooked. From shortly after the accident, sitting still at my computer didn't cause my body to ache; it only hurt when I moved about. I sat. I conjured stories. I wrote.

My first novel was a whopping 134,000 words and immensely cathartic, not to mention being great experience at finishing such a monumental task. That book has not been published. In fact, I used some of the detail to include in

River Bones, my third published novel. However, now, twenty-seven years later and much writing since, I am rewriting that first story. It could use a lot more cutting to bring the word count to saleable size, but at least I have a lot of material from which to choose.

So far, my published novels have been:

The Tropics: Child of a Storm - Caught in a Rip - Hurricane Secret, an adventure / suspense trilogy of novellas patterned after my own near-death escapades at sea. The setting begins in the Caribbean and then moves to the Hawaiian Islands. In her review, an editor at our local newspaper said: "*Stories that shatter the myths of stereotypical islands of paradise.*"

"…a strong core of emotional conflict that is never far from the surface and haunts every line."
~ **Valerie Storey, author of *Better than Perfect* and six other books, fiction and nonfiction.**

Note: *The Tropics* is out of publication. This eBook, ***Legacy of the Tropics***, is the rewritten and expanded version.

* * *

My first screenplay was created from the first novella in this book and titled ***Sea Storm***. It made the Semi-Finals in a *Moondance International Film Festival* competition.

* * *

My second novel published was ***The Ka***, a paranormal Egyptian suspense, taking place in Valley of the Queens, Egypt. It is slipstream fantasy-suspense with many scenes taking place in Ancient Egypt. *When archaeologists attempt to decipher hieroglyphs in a newly discovered tomb, unbeknownst to them, the glyphs are coded with spells and magic that throws them back into Tutankhamon's 18th Dynasty and reveals a secret that will change history.*

"Page after page, a long cast of complex characters come to life creating worlds both real and fanciful. Mary Deal seamlessly meshes these two universes in order to transport the reader back and forth from present to past."
~ **Elizabeth Sullivan, Ph.D., Clinical Psychologist, Somerset, CA**

"…the historical accuracy, detail, and story line, which kept me riveted… I was captivated as if living the story with the characters."
~ **Nadia Giordana, publisher of** *Mississippi Crow Magazine*; **award winning author of** *Thinking Skinny.*

* * *

Next was my award winning thriller, **River Bones**, which I set in my childhood hometown area. *A serial killer terrorizes residents among the lush orchards and croplands of California's Sacramento River Delta.*
River Bones, a mystery thriller, and the original Sara mason story, was a winner in the *Eric Hoffer Book Awards* competition, and people seem enamored with its characters.

"Mary Deal can take her place alongside Tami Hoag as an Alpha Tier One mystery writer with an occasional flair of Hitchcock."
~ **Ken Farmer, Award-winning Author and Actor**

"…a story of old wounds and the power of healing through friendships and love, while uncovering the truth about these crimes of passion at the riveting end."
~ **Barbara Deming of the** *US Review of Books*

* * *

My fourth novel, also a thriller, is **Down to the Needle**. A woman's long search for her abducted child leads to an inmate on death row mere months away from lethal injection for a crime she didn't commit.

"…the tension becomes almost unbearable…"
~ **Brian L. Porter, award winning author,** *A Study in Red - The Secret Journal of Jack the Ripper*

"With driving action and intense plotlines, *Down To the Needle* is a standout mystery thriller from a solid literary talent. Highly recommended.
~ **Renee Washburn,** *Apex Reviews*

* * *

One of my short stories, **The Last Thing I Do**, published in the Anthology, From Freckles to Wrinkles, by Silver Boomer Books, was nominated for the coveted *Pushcart Prize.*

* * *

I previously wrote a column for *The Garden Island,* Kauai, Hawaii's local newspaper. My eBook, aptly titled after my column, **Write It Right – Tips for Authors – The Big Book**, is a compilation of my articles on writing. The column was published sporadically. Comments from readers wanting more articles faster than the paper published them led to the formation of that volume of writer's references.

"What I enjoy most about Mary's articles is how straightforward she is in presenting information. She doesn't mince words, a tip in and of itself. Rather, she delivers short-cropped, to-the-point guidance."
~ **Mike Angley, Special Agent (USAF, ret), Colonel (USAF, ret), award-winning author of the** *Child Finder Trilogy.*

* * *

Off Center in The Attic, Over the Top Stories, is the first collection I have created. *Humor and nonsense, flights of fantasy into other realms, fright, disgust and disappointment, silliness and wonderment, and the sadness of reality and heartache. It's all here and more in stories that may leave you a little* Off Center in the Attic, *conjured through a mind that may be a little* Off Center in the Attic.

Mary Deal is a master at flash fiction. Each story is a new world in just a few words. Her characters are well-drawn and the situations she puts them in range from the fantastical to everyday things that we all deal with.
~ **Kim McDougall, Author**

* * *

The Howling Cliffs, A Sara Mason Mystery, is the first sequel to River Bones. The story opens deep in the Vietnam jungle where Sara and love interest, Huxley Keane, and a team of veterans search for MIA remains. Then Sara gets involved in a missing child cold case on the island of Kauai in Hawaii and Sara begins to wonder if the investigation will cost her life.

The research and thought that the author has put into this book is astounding.
~ Mrs. B, Amazon Top 1000 Reviewer

Find Her Online

Her Web site: http://www.writeanygenre.com/
Linked In: http://www.linkedin.com/in/marydeal
FaceBook: http://www.facebook.com/mdeal
Twitter: http://twitter.com/Mary_Deal
Google+: http://tinyurl.com/pee5lxz
Goodreads: http://www.goodreads.com/
Cold Coffee Cafe: http://coldcoffeecafe.com/profile/MaryDeal
BookTown: http://www.booktown.ning.com/
Authorsdb: http://tinyurl.com/nnbk7lo

Her Art Galleries
Mary Deal Fine Art: http://www.marydealfineart.com/
Island Image Gallery: http://www.islandimagegallery.com/
M Deal Art: https://www.facebook.com/MDealArt
Pinterest: https://www.pinterest.com/1deal/

Lightning Source UK Ltd.
Milton Keynes UK
UKHW030400141020
371533UK00006B/49